T0194078

THIRD EDITION

A Family's American Odyssey
# CONFLUENCE

## Don McComber

Order this book online at www.trafford.com
or email orders@trafford.com

Most Trafford titles are also available at major online book retailers.

Print information available on the last page.

ISBN: 978-1-6987-0051-9 (sc)
ISBN: 978-1-6987-0050-2 (e)

*Trafford rev. 04/07/2020*

 www.trafford.com

North America & international
toll-free: 1 888 232 4444 (USA & Canada)
fax: 812 355 4082

# CONTENTS

# THE FAMILY LINE

## MAIN CHARACTERS

Sarah - William Augustus
Son: Macum, Giles, McCumber, b.1746
    Cousins: Adie (Adolphus), Doig
Son: Harmon McCumber, b.1800 m. Lydia,
    Friend: Harmon
    Brothers: Kanti, Donnal, Joseph
Son: Giles (Mack) McComber, b.1850, m. Fanny, b.1878
    Brothers: Adolphus, William
Son: Robert Giles McComber, b.1913, m. Fern
    Brothers in law: Myron & Francis Bateman
Son: Bill McComber, b.1944
    Siblings: Ray, Bill, Betty

# PREFACE

This saga takes place during the time period of 1746 through 2011, and shows where these intrepid family members fit into the history of adolescent America. The vast majority of the people, places and dates are authentic, and while most of the associated stories are basically true, many have been embellished. So there is no misunderstanding, except for well known or historical people, the subscripts $_r$ and $_f$ are used at the first mention of a person's name to signify whether they are real or fictional. In those days the word bastard was a non-pejorative term commonly used to indicate a child whose father was unknown. The spellings of some geographic locations and people's names have evolved with time. Invernefs has become Inverness and Shanendoh has become Shanendoah. There are many other colorful branches of the family tree that go unmentioned that could be the subjects for further stories on down the trail.

# PROLOGUE

Numerous clans and families have their origins in old Scotland, and one of those that survived intense adventures, name evolution, and twists and turns for several centuries is the line of McComber. There were several variations of the name used down through the generations starting with Macomber, meaning son of the valley, to the Gaelic MeicCumberland, meaning son of Cumberland; it was disguised to Macum for secrecy, became McCumberland, then shortened for convenience to McCumber and finally misspelled into McComber. In the early 1600's, three Macomber brothers immigrated from Invernefs to Bristol England, then to America about 1640, becoming some of the first Plymouth area settlers. Just over a hundred years later an exceptionally bright great granddaughter Sarah$_r$ went back to England for a formal education then unavailable in America. Then, while visiting a descendant of her great, great aunt in Scotland, she was caught up in the aftermath of the battle of Culloden with the English, involuntarily had a child, married, stayed there most of her life, and finally returned to America as a Grandmother. Even though the names Macomber and McComber are similar in spelling, they are totally independent genealogically as the only blood connection between the two is the woman Sarah. The bastard child she mothered, however, started a line of ancestors that continued to grow for the next two and a half centuries in the turbulence of the new America. This is the story of the adventures the stalwart members of that line encountered along the way.

The Katherine$_r$ was a small three mast merchant ship that had carried several dozen passengers to Philadelphia in November 1745. Then in the spring to begin her return voyage, she stopped in Boston to completely fill her hold and pick up several passengers, one of which was young Sarah Macomber. On the bright, early spring morning, there was a beehive of activity trying to get all the freight into the holds arranged in such a way that the heaviest was on the bottom and the lighter plus the provisions for the voyage on the top. Sarah was one of 12 passengers that had signed up for the return trip. She was apprehensive about leaving her friends and family, while at the same time excited about the adventure of visiting her relatives in Scotland. As a teenager, and a member of a respected family near Plymouth, she also knew she was vulnerable to approaches from unscrupulous adults. Her mother had spoken to her incessantly about always conducting herself to the highest degree of morality and being on guard to adult fraudulent advances. Finally, though she found herself standing at the stern rail and watching everything she knew in her beloved America slowly disappear below the western horizon. It was mid morning, the sun was warm, and the winds cool out of the west. The Katherine flew with the wind at full sail for days and the trip started smoothly. It wasn't long before the passengers and crew found that Sarah had a wonderful singing voice and sang all the old folksongs in both English and Gaelic. Every evening after supper, she entertained the passengers and officers with the old songs she learned from her Grandfather, who learned them from his Grandfather. Her voice was so striking, that she received instant attention from all that heard. Tears ran down the cheeks of the older folks; while others closed their eyes in complete silence as if they were in total rapture.

About a week out they encountered rough weather with high seas and heavy winds. The overcast sky was so heavy they couldn't see the difference between sky and sea. It added to the tension all the passengers and most of the crew felt as they seemed to be traveling with the storm and would have to make a radical turn to evade it. The crew rolled up most of the sails and turned to the north. This caused the ship to heel over sharply and alarmed everyone. The little ship shuddered and water rushed over the deck and spilled into every opening it could find. In no time, everyone and everything was wet and cold. People were getting sick and vomit was sloshing around on the floors with the stinking salt water. Sarah had bumped her head so hard she was light headed and had trouble standing up. The rough ride continued for another day, then another, and another. Folks started praying for the ship to sink and put them out of their misery. On the fourth day, the Katherine ran out of it; the wind ceased and the sun came out. Everyone cheered when the first of the sun's rays struck the stricken little ship. Bucket brigades were formed to get the slop and water out of all the compartments. People took off their clothes and washed their bodies with soap and salt water. Sarah sat and cried with thanks while the acerbic captain made fun of the passengers for being so soft. He bragged and boasted about all the rough times he and most of the crew had seen on the high seas and assured the passengers that the storm they had just been through was but a tiny and insignificant one. Sarah couldn't wait to get off the boat and vowed it would be a "long damn time" before she got on another. And it was. When the ship reached Bristol, she insisted on traveling overland to the north. Before she was to start her official schooling in the fall, she wanted to visit her ancestral aunt Ursilla McGillavry in Invernefs; she had no idea how this brief visit would completely change her life.

# MACUM, THE ORIGIN

$S$arah's Uncle Alexander McGillivray was commander of the Clan Chattan Regiment and well respected in the community. They were part of the Drummond Division for the Jacobites who lost the battle of Culloden, Scotland. Uncle Alexander was taken prisoner and later executed by the English lead by the Duke of Cumberland; it was April 1746. Blue eyed Sarah was a skinny but attractive young woman who could sing like a nightingale. Visiting in Invernefs, the closest village to the actual battle was a mistake because the soldiers of the Duke brought their wagons in and swept up all the young women and girls of child bearing age for the entertainment of the officers and commanders of the Duke's army. Sarah, her cousins and her Aunt were all taken and obliged to submit to whomever so desired. Her Aunt instructed her not to fight or resist as their goal was simply to survive, without serious injury, and return to their village. Sarah, however, could not convince the Duke's officers that she was an American stuck in the middle of their conflict with the Scots as her English was spoken with a definite Scottish lilt. This was normal conduct on the part of a winning army, and in the case of the English, it was their way of miscegenation of their opponent's society and they kept the females for nearly a month to be sure that most were successfully impregnated. It was Sarah's singing, though, that enchanted her captors. As she sang all the old songs handed down through generations, in both Gaelic and English, she touched the hearts of the older and won the hearts of the younger officers; it was for this reason, she was saved for the Duke himself.

Months later Sarah realized she was pregnant, and that her child would be the offspring of Prince William Augustus, the Duke of Cumberland. She decided to forego her education and stay in Invernefs and raise her son. In spite of their poverty, she had come to love the simple agrarian life and eventually married one of the local widowers. Her Aunt warned her not to reveal the father's name as the child would certainly be taken away by the English who controlled all of Scotland. Finally, in early 1747, a boy was born and given the name, McCumberland. It could have been spelled MeicCumberland in Gaelic, or MacCumberland or even MCumberland, all meaning the son of Cumberland, but was shortened immediately to hide the origin. Her Aunt thought she should name the baby McWilliam or Maugustus, but Sarah declined, and shortened the original name to Macum. Many people of the time, had both given names and surnames, but those that respected the old ways simply had a single name and "Macum" (pronounced Mack' um) was to be used by her child for several decades and numerous adventures.

After Culloden, a distinctive era in Scotland came to an end and another began. It put an end to the clans and the claims of the Stuarts. The importance in history is that it was the last of the clan structure and European feudalism and an entirely new system of leadership and law were put into place which shook Scotland to its very roots. The dispersal of the Scottish clans became the number one objective of the English. All the leaders of the clans and those that could read and write were either hanged or shipped off to America. It came to be, that poverty stricken northern Scotland was to remain that way for many subsequent generations. This drove legions of Scots to seek the promise of America. So a system of servitude or soft slavery was set up in which Scottish men, women and children were sent to America to become indentured (5 years) servants of rich Scots or

Englishmen in return for the cost of their transportation. It was this system that enabled three of the village bastards, Macum and his cousins Doig$_f$ and Adie$_f$ to reach the shores of the new world and then to be scattered and lost in the chaos that ensued in the new America. Adie and Doig were the children of Sarah's two older "cousins" and were Macum's inseparable comrades. Since they knew not the identity of their fathers, they took given names and added the surname of their grandfather McGillivary. Macum's true father and full name were never revealed even to him until on the eve of the beginning of his voyage to the new world, Macum's Mother told him his full name. In the din of the departing crowd in Brackloch, he understood her to say his true name was "McCummberrnn." It was May 1763.

During the majority of their early years together, the three boys helped support their families by stealing from the English. They were so good at it that some of the villagers paid them to steal specific and highly desired items like cooking pots and utensils. They were secretly schooled by their mothers in reading and simple numbers, for if they were so discovered they risked imprisonment or worse. It was Macum that negotiated their deals, counted their money and devised the plans they used to steal everything from food, to wine, to shoes, horses and even weapons. They ranged from Brackloch at the head of Loch Carron on the west down to Fort William on the south and Dalwhinnie on the east, most within the shire of Inverness They liked the English forts the best, Auguftus, William and George, for there the rewards and the risks were greatest. They ranged dozens of miles mostly to the south and west and ran most of the way on foot. There was a system of back trails through the countryside, suited only to foot travel that avoided the main roads and allowed them to travel unseen and unheard. They seldom had to carry their booty far as the three knew where to sell it in dozens of places, mostly in the towns from Unach, Garvanmore, Pittman, Arvmore and Raalachian on the west. They were welcome at most farms and homes in the towns as their primary targets were the English or English sympathizers which were hated by the general population. On occasion, they stole from the more well-to-do Scots, but it was usually food, either animals or vegetables and never money or personal belongings. They were likeable and sociable and regularly regaled their hosts with long stories of their escapades and songs of times past.

The times were difficult as the English controlled and abused without mercy. They helped themselves to anything of value they saw and insisted on tribute from the merchants and farmers alike. The English occupation bred ill feelings that would last for centuries. It was within this era that the three boys thrived and they did it through cunning and stealth not force and destruction. So clever were they, that they took the necklaces from the very necks of sleeping women without detection. Much of the year the weather was wet and cold; and they devised a way to keep their feet dry and warm on their long runs between towns. The foot deformities they inherited from their mothers didn't noticeably slow them. They wore crude woolen shirts and breeches and would pull on oiled leather ponchos to keep them dry in the persistent rains that lasted intermittently from early fall through late spring. They carried small books on all sorts of subjects to read while waiting for openings to strike. Books were one of the objects they stole and carried back to their mothers for study. Books were in short supply and being caught with them was a serious offense. Macum's mother was particularly interested in the soft vegetables like onions and cucumbers so, when the season was right, the boys brought the vegetables back to Invernefs with them. She used a special recipe passed down in her family for pickling them that created a sweet but spicy delicacy that everyone loved. Because they were so young, they avoided physical confrontation and when faced with harm would simply out run their assailants. They were so quick and agile and smart that none of the typical thieves along the roadways even tried to catch them. With their special footwear, they could run at a fast pace for miles and miles.

Finally in 1762, the English, through abuse and intimidation, were able to determine exactly who the boys were and began searching the countryside for them in earnest. They were wanted and hunted and could not return to their homes. The boys began to hear and then think about going to the new land called America and were entranced by the stories of the unlimited land and riches. Starting in April each year large boats would take hopeful immigrants from the small port of Brachloch at the head of Loch Carron to Port Glasgow, where they could try to sign up for indentured service in return for the long voyage to America. Ships also left Invernefs taking hopeful immigrants to Edinburgh, but the English soldiers were watching the crowds carefully, so this route was too dangerous. It was about 60 miles from Invernefs to Brackloch. The mothers of Adie and Doig, in their early 30's, were able to make their ways to Brackloch by early May 1763 to see their sons one last time. The boys were carrying with them fairly large sums of money, for the time anyway, and intended on giving most of it to their mothers. Macum, Doig and Adie had to flee Inverness Shire any way they could as it was simply a matter time before they were caught and hanged. The price on their heads would certainly lead to betrayal by someone, and there were fewer and fewer places of refuge available. Whether they could finally get to America was no guarantee, but they knew they must leave their beloved mothers and extended families forever. So, it was off to Brackloch for the final goodbye to all they knew and hello to an adventure beyond their dreams.

Sarah and her cousins had made several sets of clothing for their sons that they could take on the adventure. She had painstakingly stitched the pickle recipe, which she knew Macum loved, on a small piece of cloth the size of a kerchief and rolled it up with the clothes. The final meeting and farewell were short and sweet. Clothing and money were exchanged, and then the final embraces of mothers and sons, which would never see each other again, were followed by tears. Sarah whispered her son's true name and that of his father in his ear; he gave her an astonished look, then smiled at her one last time, and was suddenly off running up the gangplank and waving wildly his face filled with joy and anticipation of the grand adventure that lay ahead. Sarah cried openly with sadness and joy. Sadness for never seeing her beloved 16 year old again and joy for the promise of the full and happy life she knew he would have. She had always hoped that her unwanted, bastard son would live to father a line of descendents that would last for a dozen centuries. Little did she know that before her passing, she would once again gaze into his piercing blue eyes?

The ship, if you could call it that, was not a sea going vessel. It had one sail and rows of long oars protruding from oarlocks along each side on the lower deck. The adult passengers were expected to row. Just before they pulled up the gang plank, the captain and several of his crew went around and extorted more money from each of the passengers. When some refused, they were removed from the boat. Macum was not bothered as he knew he would have it all back, and more, before they reached the Port of Glasgow. As he handed over the additional cash, he smiled at Doig and Adie knowingly. They smiled in return. With some yelling from the crew and captain and some pushes from the folks at the pier, the boat was off. They would take a route that kept them protected from the open Atlantic down the inner sound several hundred miles to Port Glasgow. It was anything but a straight shot and they were constantly turning one way or the other so much they had to row regularly. Past the sound of Sleat, the Isle of Mull and around the point near Campbell Town, past the Isle of Arran, and up into the Firth of Clyde they went. It was a fairly smooth trip, but enough swells were encountered to affect some of the passengers and it was common to see folks hanging over the side evacuating their stomachs. All three of the boys were affected enough that they lost their appetites. After two days of intermittent rowing everyone was glad to hear one of the crew shout that the Port was in sight. As they drew closer, all aboard were astonished at the size of the ocean going ships. None could comprehend that as large as they were, they were mere matchsticks out on the open ocean.

When the captain took their money, Macum noticed he put it into a leather bag and some minutes later securely tied it to his belt with the leather drawstrings. A little diversion was all that was needed and he would position himself so the captain had to brush by him to see what was happening, only to be relieved of the bag with a swift slice of his knife. So, once the ship was tied to the pier and the gang plank attached, Doig and Adie provoked a fight between a middle aged woman and her husband. The captain responded and so did Macum, who then grabbed his traveling bag and dashed down the plank onto the pier. Doig and Adie were right behind him as they disappeared into the crowd. The captain didn't even know he'd been robbed until he attempted to pay for ale at one of the local establishments several hours later.

In 1763 the Port of Glasgow was a dozen or so miles from the city of Glasgow connected by the top end of the Clyde, which at that time was only a large ditch. Small boats ferried people from one to the other. The actual port at Glasgow wasn't dredged and built until a decade or so later, so moving immigrants and goods from one to the other was a slow and painstaking process. The Ship Diligence$_r$ was due to leave the port in mid-summer and planned to arrive in Boston in the fall. Three merchants were signing up immigrants for indentured service in America and consigning manufactured goods for sale there. Notices were posted at the Port explaining where to go and who to see in Glasgow about signing up for the voyage. Fortunately, Macum and his cousins could all read; and they set out on a dead run, packs and all, for Glasgow. They were much faster than the wagons on the road and small boats in the Clyde, and they ran all the way to Glasgow where they promptly got lost. It was by far the largest city around and the streets and alleys ran helter-skelter in all directions, without pattern or logic. Without any sun, they had no sense of direction. After asking directions many times, they accidently stumbled upon the small office they were seeking. Stevenson$_r$, Turner$_r$, and Burton$_r$, were the three merchants handling the affairs of the Ship Diligence, and standing just inside the door were a pair of English soldiers demanding to know the identity of all who entered.

Several dozen people were lined up outside the door to the shipping office, so Macum and his cousins had time to come up with new names they would use for the voyage. They didn't know who the English soldiers were seeking so they intentionally used the names of sympathizers of the English they had known from Inverness. As they approached the door, Doig noticed that one of the soldiers seemed to be looking them over with more interest than the other folks in the line. Most of the people around them were families, and three young men together aroused suspicion. So Doig, being the most sociable of the three, struck up a conversation with the family behind him. The children took to him right away when he bribed them with several small pieces of candy. The two year old even climbed into his arms for several minutes, while Doig told him a short fairy tale; it was an association the soldier noted with a wry smile. When it was their turn to identify themselves, they told the soldiers their aliases without a twitch or blink and were allowed to pass. Once inside, they signed the shipping agreement using the aliases. It looked to have several hundred names on it and they wondered how any ship could hold that many people. They were each given an indenture agreement document that had the name of their benefactor and location in America on it. To their mutual chagrin, each had the same benefactor but different locations. They were to be split up. The document had the details of their indentured service and what they were to receive once it was complete. Their benefactors would have a representative at the dock in Boston to receive them. So, all was set and they were to simply wait a month or so for the ship to sail. Their main concern was their eventual separation.

When the line outside the Merchants' office was gone, Macum went back in and negotiated a deal for the three to act as freight laborers in return for a simple room and one meal a day. During the month of June, 1763, they made countless trips by wagon hauling barrels, and boxes from Glasgow to the Port, and people back. They were so reliable, smart and hard working, Robert Stevenson suggested to his partners they make the three their agents for the term of the voyage. This would give them accounting control over the ship's stores that were needed to feed and care for the comfort of the passengers. They would also maintain control over the manufactured freight Stevenson, Turner and Burton were shipping to America and see that an accurate inventory was received and signed for once in Boston. Three small cots with pads and blankets were moved into their room and small payments in cash were made by the Merchants to each of the cousins every week. One additional benefit to being the Merchants' agents was when they reached Boston; they would be allowed to stay together. In return for the good will and treatment of the Merchants, the cousins nearly doubled the rate at which freight was moved from Glasgow to the Port. Their ingenuity and discipline were noted by Stevenson who personally vowed he would keep track of the boys in America. Reliable and trustworthy representatives were always needed by European merchants shipping goods to the New World. Of course, he didn't know the boys had used aliases. So, in spite of being thieves in Inverness, their Mothers had instilled in them the concepts of hard work, honesty, and responsibility that would help them all achieve success in America. Their skills as pick pockets and sneak thieves would also become handy from time to time; and, their physical ability to run long distances would save their lives. But eventually, it was those borrowed names that would get them into trouble. Finally, about mid-summer, they began to load the ship. The heaviest crates were put in the bottom followed by lighter and lighter and then food, and small boxes of clothing and blankets in the top of the hold where they could be readily accessed. Barrels and casks were put into special frames that prevented them from moving in rough weather. Some has small aisles between them for access during the voyage. It seems as if they were never going to be ready. Then, the day arrived when Captain Charles Robinson<sub>r</sub> passionately proclaimed, "We shall sail on the morrow."

# VOYAGE TO AMERICA

At first, the channel was quite narrow for such a large ship. Before they knew it, they were out in the wide part of the Firth of Clyde; then catching the wind, they blew past the isle of Arran, Campbell Town and out into the Atlantic. As land disappeared from sight, the three cousins stood at the stern rail with silent tears running down their cheeks. It was then; they realized what they had done. It was then; they realized that their lives would change forever and that the cool green of Inverness was gone. But, most of all, it was then; they realized they would never again see those who loved them most. So, they began to sing the old songs their mothers had taught them. Their voices were so full and clear and perfect of pitch, and their vibrato and harmony so deft that everyone turned toward them and listened. Then folks came up from the lower decks and crowded around them. Tears flowed from man and woman alike as the reality of what and whom they were leaving suddenly overwhelmed them as well. Everyone cheered and clapped between songs and they wouldn't let the boys stop for over an hour. Finally, when they went silent, everyone sat or stood for some minutes as if they were in a daze savoring the songs and the memories they dredged up. Slowly, the crowd broke up and went below or took to their assigned tasks. The wind was out of the northwest and the ship tacked hard to the southwest. So, the voyage began.

As the days passed, the excitement subsided and the boredom of the long trip took hold of everyone on board. The wind shifted coming directly out of the west, so the ship had to tack back and forth across it and headway was slow. There was so much water spray blowing across the deck, Captain Robinson had to restrict the passengers to cabins below. It was crowded and noisy and privacy rare. Taking care of your own personal needs of toilet and wash were very difficult. To make matters worse many were sea sick and the vomit buckets had to be emptied constantly. Some began to dehydrate and the captain and crew practically had to force them to take fluids. The stores of food seemed adequate and there was no worry for water, beer and wine. The first weeks were progressing nicely and even though it was difficult to sleep and crowded and becoming smelly, the passengers tried mightily to get along. Doig, Adie and Macum put on singing shows regularly which everyone enjoyed immensely, and the Captain had taken to paying them a small sum for each performance as it soothed the passengers for a time and helped them forget their strife. Some of the married women had taken to the boys and had become suggestive in their looks and subtle actions, but with the help of the Captain they resisted becoming involved. Among the passengers, there was a magician and several men with violins and one with a flute. It was common to hear music of one kind or the other coming from the passenger hold. When the decks were calm enough the Captain allowed musical presentations on the main deck. Their favorite time was just before sunset and it then the cousins liked to sing their saddest songs just as the sun was passing below the waves in the west. When they stopped, everyone would sit in silence for a half hour or so and watch the clouds in the west pick up the red hues of the sunset then slowly fade to shades of navy and black. If the Captain allowed, some would sit on deck and watch the stars and several of the crew would point out the different constellations. On moonless nights, it seemed as if the sky was completely full of stars. But, it was the clear nights of the full moon that were the best.

You could see clouds flitting across the sky and the moonlight shining off the waves and singing and music went on for hours.

Then late one night, one of the crew noticed a light flashing in the distance off the stern. Occasionally during the day, the lookout in his seat on the mainmast could see the tops of the sails of a ship behind them. It was unsettling to the Captain that another ship would be on the same exact route at the same time as they. The Diligence had two small deck cannons near the bow and two more near the stern, but that was not nearly enough to repel a determined and armed warship or pirate. They did carry a valuable cargo and to some, unarmed passengers were valuable when sold as slaves. It was unusual for pirates or slavers to take over a major ship like the Diligence, but it did happen several times each year. The Captain decided to change routes during the night in an attempt to lose the intruder, but the next day the lookout could clearly see the ship coming fast. The Diligence was low in the water because of the full load and wasn't able to make fast runs on either tack, so the Captain decreased the distance between turns in hope that the intruder would make a mistake and flounder momentarily directly into the wind. He was right and the Diligence was able to get over the horizon and out of sight just at nightfall. They turned hard northwest and ran all night on a long tack with the wind coming out of the west and by morning had lost the follower. The tension among the crew and passengers alike relaxed and things returned to normal.

The Captain gave the "come about" order and the ship turned back to the southwest to get back on course. About noon a ship broke over the horizon coming on fast on their port side headed directly on an interception course. The French ship blasted a cannon ball about 200 feet off the bow and the Captain of the Diligence pulled up the sails and went dead in the water. The French ship coasted to a stop adjacent to the Diligence and a party made ready to board her. Everyone aboard the Diligence was apprehensive and Captain Robinson told them not to worry that there was no animosity between the Scots and the French, and that the Diligence was built in Philadelphia and that was its home port. They were probably looking for English or English spies or sympathizers. When the cousins heard that, their hearts sank. They didn't know what to do. Their first instinct was to hide, but where? They only had a few minutes to do something, but what. If they had used their correct names on the ship's log, they wouldn't be in this situation. It was too late; the French boarding party was coming over the rail. Captain Robinson was there to greet them and had the ship's passenger log in hand. The French captain had a long list of Scots that were English sympathizers. Sure enough, the three names the cousins had borrowed from Inverness were on the list and they were taken off the Diligence and back to the Sagittaire, a double decked, 50 gun warship launched in 1761. They were told that they would be taken to Nova Scotia and imprisoned, then sold as slaves. They were allowed to take their clothing rolls and as they crawled over the Diligence's rail half the women watching were weeping. Everyone on the Diligence was upset as the cousins had kept them happy and entertained during the doldrums of the voyage. The children were waving and saying goodbye. The French Captain noticed this deep regard for the cousins and wondered just how three sympathizers could have fostered this kind of good passionate feeling with the other Scots. Surely the word would have gotten around throughout the real Scotsmen on the Diligence that the three were English sympathizers and they would have been hated and pointed out as such. His previous experience with these searches was that English sympathizers were quickly identified by the Scottish or Irish passengers, then, pointed out to him or his crew. Macum had tried to explain that the names on the passenger log were aliases and they too hated the English, but the French Captain would have none of it. The meaning of what Macum was trying to explain must have been clouded during the translation. Doubt had been planted in the hearts of the boarding party and they looked at each other in doubt. But, they proceeded over to the warship raised the longboat and the anchor, unfurled the sails and set off to the Northwest. In just a half hour the ships were out of sight of each other and the three prisoners were taken into the hold and pushed into a small room, the door slammed and bolted.

The only light in the room came from the cracks over and under the door. There were four other prisoners in the room and the stench from the waste bucket was overwhelming. It seemed like they were in there for days before the door opened. There was barely enough room for all seven of them to lie down on the floor without lying on top of each other. Water and bread was passed through a hole in the door. When they emerged, they were taken to the main deck and washed off with buckets of salt water, clothing and all. Their hands were tied before them and they were taken to see the Captain. The cousins looked like drowned rats as they were pushed into the room in which three of the French crew sat around a table. The young aid to the Captain spoke English pretty well and was able to translate about ¾ of what the boys said. He was not able to detect the accent of Inverness. The captain wanted to get information about their contacts in America. Of course they had none. All they had was the piece of paper with their indenture agreement and contact on it. The paper had been soaked and the printing was very difficult to read. The Captain took all three indenture agreements, looked them over and put them on a shelf to dry out.

Macum looked directly into the Captain's eyes and spoke slowly and paused after each phrase so the aid could translate. He told the Captain that he was the bastard son of William Augustus, Duke of Cumberland and that his name was McCumberland, which was shortened to McCumber and then to Macum. He told the Captain how he and his cousins made their living stealing from the English, how they did it and which Forts were their favorites. The Captain and his crew sat transfixed at the tale Macum told, and how articulate and well organized the story was. One of the crew was interested in exactly how the cousins could steal his money bag he had tied to his belt. So Doig and Adie went over to the porthole and looked out, then called the man over for a demonstration.

The room was dimly lit and the light streaming in the porthole partially blinded anyone looking that direction. When attention was on Doig and Adie, Macum positioned himself so the man had to squeeze between him and the table on the way to the port hole. Then when the man got over to the port hole, the two were going to show them the old thief ploy of distraction by one and theft by the other. Adie jostled him to distract and Doig brushed him gently feigning a heist. The man reached for his money bag only to find it was gone. He immediately thought Doig had taken it, and searched him. But Doig did not have it. He searched Adie and he didn't have it either. Then, Macum dropped it on the table and held up his untied hands; and everyone laughed uproariously. When they first sat down, Macum had taken a small blade from his shoe and cut the ropes holding his wrists and had held the rope around his wrists as if they were still tied. Then, when the crew member slid by, Macum sliced the leather tie strings and had the bag in his pocket before anyone knew what was happening. So impressed was the Captain with the intellect and slight-of-hand of the boys that he let the three move out of the dark and dank little prison room and bunk in the crew quarters. Within days, the cousins had earned the trust and admiration of the crew and sang to them in Gaelic and English which none could understand, but still enjoyed. They took up jobs others didn't like. They helped the cook and delivered meals to the crew that were on station during meal time. They especially liked to climb the rigging and take food to the lookout near the top of the mast. It was exhilarating. Of course all you could see was ocean in every direction, but the view was still great. The swaying of the boat moved the top of the mast back and forth 20 feet or more. They cleaned the pots and plates, cleaned the decks, oiled the wood, hauled the waste buckets and sang to the crew during meals. They became fast friends with the big and strong Jean Robert$_r$ (pronounced zjohn rowbear) the aid to the Captain, and they taught English to and learned French from everyone with a moment to spare.

The Sagittaire was weeks away from Nova Scotia and the Captain assigned more lookouts to the masts, day and night. He was concerned about suddenly coming upon a British war ship and being unprepared for battle. Then as they approached the North American coast, gunners were posted from first light until dark. Being relatively small, the Sagittaire would be able to use her speed and agility with good effect against larger and more heavily armed ships and could avoid a battle when out gunned. The French and Indian war had ended earlier in the year, but the animosity between the British and French was so intense that it was still common for one ship to send a few cannon balls into the side of the other. The Sagittaire's destination was Halifax on the southeast coast of Nova Scotia (meaning new Scotland). The garrison of French soldiers was moving out and the Sagittaire was to take several hundred of them down the east coast and around to New Orleans. The Captain asked Macum and his cousins to stay on the ship with them and help the cook. Adding several hundred hungry men to the ship severely overloaded their ability to feed and house everyone with reasonable comfort. Cooking and cleaning pots and dishes would proceed 16 hours a day and the crew and soldiers would have to sleep in shifts. It would be a time of controlled chaos.

Wine was the common drink of choice, and it was also common to have a considerable amount of it spoil; that is, wine that is left open and has turned to vinegar and slime. Macum knew the kerchief his Mother had given him, described how to separate the vinegar from the residue and use it in making pickled vegetables. And, he knew that many of the vegetables on board were starting to go bad. So he showed *the recipe* to the Cook and they set out to pickle the good vegetables that remained in their stores. The result was the highlight of every meal they served. The crew insisted on the pickled goodies with their salted meat and beans or potatoes. It was settled, the cousins would stay with the Sagittaire.

Even though the ship was on high alert, the only other ships sighted were merchants. Halifax was reached without incident and before they knew it they were docked. A message came on board that the Sagittaire was to stay in Halifax until September of the year 1764, and then move the garrison to New Orleans. This gave the crew and local shipwrights the chance to make the repairs the ship had accumulated in their recent encounters with the British, and left the cousins without a means of support. The Captain was loyal to the cousins and used his influence to find them positions as assistants to a surveyor, Joseph Des Barres$_r$, who had the job of accurately mapping the coasts and harbors of Nova Scotia and surrounding islands. Commodore Richard Spry$_r$ had commissioned Des Barres some months before to do the job. Everything had gone well until the winter started bearing down, and half his crew quit to head south. DesBarres had completed the preliminary survey in which the basic shape and size of Nova Scotia was laid down on paper. The shape was to be greatly refined with more accurate measurements of every detail on the perimeter of the peninsula.

This was to be the job of the cousins, but the water was so rough and the weather so unpredictable, they were limited to a few traveling days each week. There were long days holing up in the small hamlets around the edge of the peninsula, and the boys killed time reading every book they could lay hands on. During this time it was typical that they would spend days trying to get a single distance and direction from one shore point to another. Every bar, harbor, bay and shoal was to be mapped in detail. It turned out that Adie had a gift for freehand drawing the shape, to scale, of the inlets, bays and harbors. Des Barres was also very good at drawing maps, but he had to use the information provided by his assistants. Much of the winter was wasted because of weather and when the spring finally broke, Des Barres sent out four crews to different parts of the peninsula for detailed measurements. It wasn't until about mid-summer that Macum found out that his father, the Duke of Cumberland, had sponsored Des Barres' education. It was a strange coincidence but didn't create any problem and Macum never told Des Barres of his connection to the Duke. The knowledge the cousins gained in using the instruments to determine location, direction and distance would be of great value in their future. During the summer, the Captain of the Sagittaire contacted the cousins and returned their agreements to them he had put on his shelves during their first interrogation. He also offered them jobs on the southern trip to begin in the fall and he reluctantly agreed to drop them off at Boston Harbor, so they could honor their agreements. He admired their loyalty and dedication so much; he agreed to do this for them. Here they were free of the 5 year indenture periods, and yet they implored him to help find their benefactor so they could repay their debt. The Captain wrote them a letter, put it in a waxed envelope and sealed it with wax and his stamp, to be presented to their benefactor when they found him.

During their time in Halifax, they were in frequent contact with Jean Robert. As you might expect, the three cousins had started attending some of the drinking houses in the vicinity of the harbor. There were frequently scuffles and sometimes outright fights in these places and it was Jean Robert that always won. He was a quiet, stick-to-your-own-business kind of person, but when provoked or even attacked, used both his feet and fists in such an impressive way that most people stopped fighting just to watch him. It seemed he could beat three or four opponents at the same time. It wasn't long before he began fighting in the contests for money. The word went around Halifax and the surrounding towns that he could whip anyone in two minutes, and if you thought you were tough, look him up. The cousins even had handbills printed making the challenge, and they were spread over the whole of Nova Scotia. It became quite a money maker. One of Robert's favorite tricks was to allow his opponent the first five fist swings or kicks at him. Then, if they hadn't hit him, he would hit them. Many of his opponents gave up after four knowing that if they couldn't even hit him after four free swings, the fight was lost. But some would not give up and Robert would knock them to the ground, with bloodied faces and broken ribs, in a minute or less. In their spare time, Robert taught the cousins the basic skills needed to be good fighters. How to keep from being hit and when and how to hit back, were the keys. They were quick learners. The time for their departure from Nova Scotia was approaching quickly and their work with Des Barres was coming to an end. On their last day Des Barres paid the boys and added a generous bonus, then hugged them to him in a true display of friendship. He was a passionate man when it came to perfection of work and he greatly appreciated their skills and dedication to the same. That night they went to bed early for at first light, the Sagitairre was to sail.

# CHESAPEAKE

The wind was from the north and the Sagitairre flew before it. In mere moments Nova Scotia dropped out of sight below the horizon; the next stop was Boston. The entire eastern seaboard was now controlled by the British and even though a peace treaty had been signed in early 1763, they had to be vigilant as they still flew the flag of France. The ship was crowded and organization of who did what and when was the order of the day. The Captain made no bones about the fact that he was in charge that all the soldiers from the Halifax garrison were to do as told, period. To keep everyone entertained, contests of all kinds broke out. Who could raise the sails faster, who could climb a rope faster, who could run from one end of the ship to the other and back faster, and who could shoot a floating bottle better, were some of them. The three cousins were by far the fastest of everyone on board in the bow to stern run. Jean Robert was the champion in raising the sail. The boys sang to the group and many friendships were started. But, the wind started up out of the west and it blew them far off course out to sea and by the time they were able to tack back toward shore, the ship was way to the south of Boston. Rather than tack back to the northwest, the Captain decided he would have to take the cousins to somewhere around the Chesapeake Bay. Jean Robert asked the Captain for permission to leave the ship with Macum, Adie and Doig. His service agreement had expired earlier in1764 and he wanted to go with the cousins and pursue his own American dream. This saved his life, for on the trip south and around Florida, the Sagitairre was looted, burned and sunk.

So it was that the four friends were to be taken ashore on the north side of the entrance to the Chesapeake Bay, and left on their own, away from any known settlement. They were allowed to purchase food, tools and arms and take other items necessary for survival. At that time the entire area was covered with deciduous forests. The peninsula that runs between the actual bay and the ocean was a combination of tidal flats, marsh and low forest. On the west side a number of creeks emptied into the bay, while on the east, marshes and tidal flats went for miles. They reasoned it would be easier to get back up to Boston by following this route than trying to negotiate the western bank of the bay. They had no idea that Boston was some 500 miles away and that the Chesapeake Peninsula was several hundred miles long and up to 70 miles wide. They knew their first destination was Philadelphia, but knew not the hardships they would encounter even getting that far. West of the bay that land is frequently interrupted by rivers and creeks and dotted by tobacco and cotton farms. Even though there were more people, the route was much more difficult. The Powhatan Indians originally called this area home, but by 1750, most had been driven out, were killed or enslaved. A few small bands of the more belligerent lived on the Chesapeake Peninsula where they lived on clams, fish and a few deer. It wouldn't be long before our small band of explorers and the Indians crossed paths.

It was September 1764, a year of unusually severe fall and winter storms and gales. When the long boat slid ashore and the four friends jumped onto the beach, the crew threw their bundles of clothing and provisions to them, pushed the boat back into deeper water, turned and rowed back to the Sagitairre. In an hour the ship was sinking over the horizon to the southeast and as the four looked at each other, apprehension overtook them. The weather gave them no quarter and a strong northeast wind and rain began within the hour. It was nearly dark as they headed for higher ground, trees and hopefully some shelter. But, they settled under some trees and sat on their heels, snugly under their oiled ponchos until the rain finally stopped and the first signs of light came from the east. Dawn broke to an overcast and breezy day. A few rays of direct sun occasionally broke through and warmed them greatly. Macum checked his compass, and they set out to the north at a brisk trot. After several hours, they took a break beside a small stream and pulled out something to eat. The sun was much warmer by then and they were nearly dry, and as they relaxed they fell asleep. Adie woke with a start as something was crawling on his cheek. An Indian boy, not more than five or six, was bending over him and had touched his face. The boy jumped back and yelled something. Immediately, everyone was awake and looking up into several dozen brown faces that surrounded them. The young boy was saying something like mawmawnaw……….. over and over. The four travelers stood up slowly and looked around to see Indian men and women all looking them over carefully. No weapons were brandished and no threatening movements were made toward them. No one spoke except the boy repeating mawmaw………… The travelers picked up their packs and weapons and started to resume their trip, and this time the men formed an informal barrier blocking their path.

By this time, the group had grown to three or four dozen and a distinguished looking man with much lighter skin made his way through them and spoke to them in broken English. He called himself, Mamanatowick, Chief of the Powhatanes. Apparently one of his parents was English, because of his coloring and speech. He told them that his people were concerned because slavers from the mainland and sometimes from ships raided their tribe several times a year and made off with anyone they could catch out alone. The boys emphasized that they were only interested in going north up the length of the peninsula and had no interest or tolerance for slavers.

Mamanatowick offered to send several of his young men along with them to show them the best route north if they would give him an axe. He also asked them to stay with the tribe for several days and tell him of what was happening in the outside world. He told them the tribe did not like either the English or the French and that some of his people traveled to the mainland in the fall to help the farmers harvest their crops. It was a dangerous situation to do that because a few of the farmers were known to enslave any Indians they caught. But, most of the time they were able to trade their labor for metal items like pots, utensils, knives and axes or cloth and blankets. The travelers decided to stay a few days and see what they could learn about the country and who was there, where it was safe to go and where it was not. They had a general idea of the geography of eastern America and the major cities, but had no feel at all for the great distances involved. In Scotland or France a trip of 50 miles was considered major, but in America, 50 was just the start. They thought Philadelphia was no more than a day's walk and Boston just beyond that. Mamanatowick painstakingly described to them his understanding of their part of the region. He had traveled several hundred miles in all directions during his life and talked for hours and hours about the towns and people and other Indians. The outside world was frightening to them. Many of them had never been off the peninsula, their existence depended to a certain extent on their anonymity, and he asked the four not to tell anyone that he and his small band were there.

When the time came to begin their trek north, Mamanatowick picked out several strong looking young men to take them up to a bay, that later was called Delaware, where the peninsula joined the mainland. They set out at a brisk pace once again, and after several hours, the four travelers had to push the Indians to maintain a good pace. They were going up the very middle of the peninsula. Several times the first day, they took sharp turns to avoid an upcoming obstacle. It was almost uncanny how the Indians were able to choose a route that minimized energy. During the afternoon, they slowed down but the push continued until almost dark. The sun had set in the west and they were operating on twilight when they stopped in a well protected spot. During the day they had seen several sets of tracks of men that were wearing boots. This was very upsetting to the Indian guides and they wanted to turn back. Then they heard gunshots that seemed to be just yards away. There were more gunshots and screams and yelling. The group carefully moved up a small rise until they could see over the top. About 50 yards away, there were what looked to be about two dozen men fighting and shooting at each other. After about 15 minutes, one group broke away and ran off to the north, leaving the other bunch exhausted and binding up their wounds. About half the men looked dead and the other half wounded or dazed.

Just after the French and Indian War ended, the animosity of most colonists turned directly toward the British. As the years progressed up to the Declaration of Independence in 1776, British tyranny and colonist antagonism both steadily increased. Skirmishes between colonists and British were common as were fights between colonists that were loyal to the Crown and those that were not. The cousins were not privy to the general political situation they were facing and were unprepared for what was coming.

Our little group of travelers decided that they would send Jean Robert over the hill to find out who the men were and who they had just fought. Speaking both French and English should have given Robert a communication advantage. Physically, he could whip any group of three or four. At the same time, the cousins would keep the barrels of their loaded muskets pointed at the outsiders. They had only fired a musket several times and were totally unable to hit anything at a range of 50 yards. Robert stood and shouted in English that he was coming in to see if he could help. Three of the outsiders raised their guns and pointed them at Robert. He put up his hands to signal he was unarmed and meant no harm, and continued walking straight into their group. As he approached, he counted eight that looked dead, another four wounded and three seemed unharmed. He pointed back toward the cousins so the outsiders would know they were under the threat of loaded muskets. They spoke English. The three immediately dropped their guns, put up their hands and surrendered. But, Robert wasn't seeking any surrender and explained to them that he and his friends were just passing through on their way to Boston. They had no loyalty or sympathy for either side. They didn't even know what the fight was about and just wanted to avoid trouble. It was dark by now, and Robert withdrew back to his friends leaving the three to tend the wounds of the other four that were now moaning and crying loudly. Surely they would die during the night.

The Indians swiftly but quietly found a route around the intruders and continued on in the dark for several hours, before they came to a spot protected from the northeast wind. By the time they had something to eat and had settled in for the night, it was raining heavily. Robert told his friends that the outsiders were chasing a band of road thieves that had been harassing the countryside about 20 miles north. Five of the dead were from the band of thieves and the other two had gotten away. It would be a long night. Morning light was met with more rain, and the little band slowly prepared to continue on to the north and east, searching for the coast line. They figured to have traveled well over a hundred miles by now and were becoming bewildered about how much further it would be. After a cold breakfast of dried meat and pickled vegetables, they set off into the rain. Macum checked his compass to see for sure that the Indians knew which direction to go, and they did. It was amazing to the cousins that their Indian guides were able to maintain a sense of direction. With overcast skies and darkness and avoiding trouble, the Indian men still maintained the correct direction. They ran steadily through the rain and mud and slippery ground avoiding the low spots where the water was beginning to puddle up. Their feet were dry thanks to the unique footwear the cousins had devised years earlier in Inverness. That day passed, then another wet and cold night and finally after nearly another day of rain and wind, the sky started to clear in the west and the sun broke through. The little band stopped and laid their belongings around on the bushes to dry while they started a fire and warmed water for tea and boiled meat. The two Indians indicated to them that the Bay of Delaware was just over the hill to their northeast and that they would be leaving at first light the next morning. They could not communicate verbally, but through sign language and drawings in the dirt, were able to tell the travelers to follow the shore to the northwest and when it turned to the northeast keep following the river clear to Philadelphia. There would be many smaller rivers and creeks to cross but they were to stay on the east side of the big river.

First light brought with it a clear blue and cloudless day. The air was so clean and fresh smelling, everyone sat back and breathed deeply. The Indians had left several hours before and were surprised when the boys gave them firm hugs of farewell. The trust, friendliness and charisma of the cousins were irresistible even for the skeptical Indians. Friendships based on shared hardships were created. The drier ground made for faster travel and the cousins followed the big river around to the northeast with daylight to spare. In the distance they could see a road with wagons and horses and people and they could smell the smoke of wood fires somewhere to the west. They were back to some kind of civilization.

Philadelphia in 1764 seemed to the cousins to be as confusing as Glasgow. Streets and roads crisscrossed helter-skelter in every direction. They had plenty of money and found a place to stay the night, a hot bath and a good hot meal. They didn't realize it, but they had distinct Scottish and French accents. The American version of English seemed bland. They had covered nearly 60 miles that day and were tired. The road had been well traveled and was smooth and fast. There were bridges across the many creeks and small rivers, so they covered the miles rapidly. As they sat around the table that evening they reflected on their good fortune, and on how much they missed their mothers. It had been quite a journey so far; they had avoided physical harm, had learned simple navigation and surveying, and had made many friends, some of which they would see again and some that would remain but a memory. They had been able to avoid the groups of British soldiers that seemed bent on being as obnoxious as possible and openly harassed Americans. The British moved into homes and helped themselves to shelter and food and sometimes more. The situation was intolerable and would come to a violent end in a dozen or so years. The cousins and their friend found themselves in a thriving and aggressive but also dangerous place. They went to the first constable they could find, and inquired about where they could go to find a merchant, Stevenson, Turner and Burton. He told them to go to the town hall. But, they were unsuccessful and went ahead with a plan to travel on to Boston. There were roads all the way, but they were poorly marked and they frequently got off on a dead end and had to back track. The British had numerous road blocks usually on bridges and to avoid them the travelers had to go many extra miles. They continued on foot because they couldn't trust a rented wagon or carrier and may have needed to run at the drop of a hat. They were told it was over 300 miles to Boston and they would have to go through New York along the way. But, the main roads were loaded with British and they believed they must avoid them. They knew not the exact reason, but their intuition was correct. The British automatically suspected any group of young men, especially armed ones of heading for assembly in the American army. If they were caught, they would have been relieved of all their belongings and money and thrown into a stockade.

They decided they must head to the west, because as they continued toward New York, the British became thicker and thicker and they were in constant danger. So, west it was on the first road that went that way. Then their plan was to circle around and come into Boston from the northwest, where, they were told, the British were few. They moved quickly, much faster than the wagons going the same direction. It was Jean Robert that couldn't keep up with them and as the British road blocks became fewer they went faster, and this created a problem. Jean Robert's shoes were causing him foot pain because they were wearing out and had holes in the bottoms. Even when they stopped and made him better footwear, he couldn't keep up with the thinner cousins. They had gone west farther than they had planned because there was no road going any other direction. There were a few small clusters of dwellings along the way and they were warned they were going into Iroquois country. Days went by and the road finally changed to a single trail then a foot path and then nothing. They had gone steadily up hill and were in an area that would later become northern Pennsylvania and south central New York. The hills were steeper and the forest thicker. They were impressed with the size of the mountains for they had never seen hills so steep or tall. With the help of Macum's compass, they turned north and the going was no longer fast, but slow and painful. The only paths were occasional game trails. On their northward trek, because of the terrain they had to veer to the west, which they knew was taking them farther from their destination. They finally ran completely out of food and had taken to shooting an occasional animal. They had money, but no place to spend it. Winter was closing in and one morning they woke up to snow, about a foot of it. They realized they were in trouble. What they did not know was that they would soon have to run for their very lives.

# ONEIDA IROQUOIS

Now they were struggling. The footing was treacherous, the hills steep and the snow deeper. Jean Robert thought they should go back the way they came, but was willing to yield to the will of the three. They could only travel for a few hours at a time then stop and rest. The weather was clear, but cold. More days slipped by and they were finally able to turn back toward the northeast. As they lost altitude, the snow thinned, and then went away but the ground was still wet and slippery. Several times that last few days they crossed the tracks of other humans. From the number of tracks, it looked to be groups of a dozen or more. Then they started seeing fleeting glimpses of others through the trees. They were being shadowed. Several times they stopped and called out a greeting to the followers, and received no response. When they stopped for the night, they could hear movement all around them. Then in the morning, they could see the footprints. The footprints were not the boots common to white Americans at the time. They were soft soled prints similar to those left by the four travelers. The next day, they were lucky and shot a small deer. So they cut it up into quarters and carried the pieces with them until evening. They roasted one of the quarters over a big fire and when the aroma of the cooking meat was wafting through the trees, they invited their followers to join them in a feast. They stood and motioned to those hiding in the trees to come in to the fire and join them in eating. Slowly out of the darkness several fur-clad Indians came into the fire. Then several more, and finally there were nine visitors. The Indians were fierce looking men, and all of good size, yet lean and hard. They carried bows, metal hatchets and metal knives. Several had clubs with roundish fist sized rocks tied on the end of wooden handles. They each had a bag of corn that had been ground and mixed with fat and bits of dried meat, and they pulled these out an offered them to the cousins. Our four travelers sat down and encouraged their guests to do the same. Jean Robert slowly cut pieces of meat from the cooking deer and handed them to each of the guests. The boys spoke to them in both English and French and there was no response. Several guests turned and looked at one of their brothers and finally he began to speak very broken English. The group ate all the first deer quarter and much of another. The Indians were indeed Iroquois of the Oneida Nation out on a hunting and scouting trip. They wanted to be sure there were no English about and were fearful of any groups of men. The English had treated them poorly and could not be trusted. The boys emphasized over and over that they were enemies of the English also. But the Indians looked skeptical and eyed the boy's weapons.

By morning, the weather turned sharply colder and the sky was overcast. A brisk breeze was blowing in from the northeast and the Indians were having a sharp discussion our travelers could not follow. Several of the Indians motioned menacingly at our travelers and to the west. Finally the interpreter notified the cousins that they were to follow the Indians back to their camp for the winter. That to proceed to the east would only get them caught by the British. It would take the entire group nearly a week to get back to the main Indian camp. The cousins tried to explain that they had to go to Boston in the east. It was late November and winter was nearly upon them and traveling would be impossible. After several hours of discussion, our travelers decided to go with the Iroquois, but at the first sign of spring, they would head east. Their route to the west led them around the edge of Seneca land and at that time the Iroquois and the Seneca were enemies. The Seneca had yielded to British bribery and allied with them in return for regular deliveries of metal utensils and blankets. In the coming years, the British would try to ally with all the Indian tribes against the Americans. Our group of 13, fit and able men, were a formidable fighting force and they felt they could repel nearly any scouting party of Seneca they would encounter. The interpreter tried to explain to the cousins where they were going and drew maps in the dirt that showed ridges of mountains and rivers and lakes. He told them if they had to split up, to go west and showed them the best route to the main camp where they would be welcome. It was the strategy of the Oneida Iroquois, that if hopelessly outmanned by an opponent, to split up and run in all directions eventually to meet at the main camp many miles to the west. It was kind of an every-man-for-himself strategy. Some would be caught and killed, but most would survive to live on. It was in the best interest of the group. Our four travelers made a pact to try to stay together. If necessary each of them would go a different direction all generally west, and within a day try to find the same track straight west. Because of the rough terrain, this was easier said than done.

The Iroquois proved to be good travelers and could run at a good pace for many hours. They were amazed that their new friends could keep up so easily and were impressed with the oiled leather ponchos and the footwear the cousins had. Every man carried his own gear and weapons. They traded off carrying the deer quarters. After several days of steady travel, the meat was gone. They had been in ankle deep snow most of the time and had cut the trail of a sizeable party of Seneca that was headed south. The Seneca were one of the six nations of the Iroquois. When the British took control of the colonies in 1763, they tried their best to convince the Iroquois Nation to support them; but the Oneida and the Tuscarora supported the patriots while the Seneca, Mohawk, Onondaga, Cayuga supported the

British. The Seneca trail was only hours old and seemed to be
of great concern to the Iroquois. Several times in the next hour,
the Iroquois stopped and stood motionless for 10 minutes or so,
totally quiet and listening. A few flakes of snow were falling and
there was no wind; it was deathly quiet. There was a muffled
rustling sound from up the hill to their west. They continued
to stand motionless. The cousins very slowly loaded their guns
and the Indians prepared their arrows. The leader sent several
Indians off to the left and several more off to the right. They
moved off very slowly circling up the hill. The leader motioned
for the group to get down low to the ground. Suddenly over
their heads, they could hear the pfffft, pffft of several arrows.
They remained in a crouch, waiting. Again it was deathly quiet.
The cousins could hear their own heartbeats hammering in their
ears. This would be their first real fight to the death. Suddenly
the Seneca came running and screaming down the hill straight at
the cousins. Jean Robert was yelling to hold their fire until the
Seneca got close enough to hit. As they came into view, some of
the Seneca were falling from the arrows being launched by the
Iroquois on the flanks. The cousins took aim, Robert shouted,
"fire'" and all four pulled their triggers. An immense blast
dropped four of the Seneca, but the rest continued to charge.
The cousins raised their pistols and waited until the Seneca were
mere yards away and fired again. More Seneca fell. Arrows were
flying in all directions and one struck Doig in the flesh on his
shoulder. The Iroquois on the flanks were killing Seneca at will.
Then the cousins and their Iroquois comrades were overrun
with Seneca and each was fighting for his life. Several more
Seneca were killed in hand combat and the remainder turned
and ran back up the hill. For a minute the Iroquois and cousins
thought the battle was over. But before they could reload their
weapons another large band of Seneca came screaming out of
the trees. Now it was every man-for-himself, and the Oneida
scattered. Some ran to the north and others went south. It was
a headlong flight at top speed and the cousins had no trouble
outrunning both the Oneida and the pursuing Seneca. Doig

had pushed the arrow in his shoulder through the flesh and out the other side and was bleeding but this never slowed him down. Macum and Doig had run to the south hard for several hours and could not hear anyone following or any yelling from conflict behind them. They knew not the fate of Adie or Jean Robert. As agreed when the terrain allowed, they turned back to the west and continued on until dark.

Robert and Adie had gone off to the north along with several Iroquois. Again, they were much faster than either the Iroquois or the Seneca and could hear screaming and fighting behind them. After an hour or so, they paused to listen and rest. Slowly, out of the trees came several Iroquois that were wounded and had obviously had to fight for their lives. The boys loaded their weapons and waited along the track for any following Seneca, but none came. It was snowing harder now and their tracks would be covered in a few hours, but they kept moving and before evening had to almost carry their Iroquois friends. After dark, they found shelter under a low hanging fir tree and started a small fire with dry squaw wood and warmed some water to wash out their friends' wounds. Several of the cuts were deep but all were in either arms or legs and would heal well. One had a big knot on his head from one of the stone clubs. With the breeze out of the south, they felt safe that the Seneca would not be able to follow the aroma of the fire. They did not remember that the main concentration of Seneca was to their north. Some miles to the north, several of the Seneca in their main camp caught the faint smell of wood smoke coming from the south. But, they ignored it.

After a tense night during which Macum and Doig thought they heard gunshots echoing in the distance several times, it was still overcast and snowing lightly. Unless there were Indians with muskets in the area, which was very unlikely, it had to be the British. What were they shooting at? How far away were they? Which direction? Macum thought if they continued along the ridge for another hour then turned downhill and headed west they should be going on the right track for the main Iroquois

Village. That is, if he remembered the crude map the Indian had drawn in the dirt. When they were about to turn west, they stopped and were listening to a rustling sound coming from the east. They squatted, loaded their weapons, and listened as someone was coming from the east and moving fast. They were pretty well hidden by some low growing bushes, and could actually hear the rapid breathing of the people coming almost straight at them. They peeked through the bushes as the people came into view, but couldn't see enough to identify anyone. The three runners ran right past them as if someone was on their heels. They were their Iroquois friends and went over the ridge and straight down the slope into the river valley to the west. Macum and Doig didn't know what to do, so they stayed put. Having come up from the south, someone approaching on a track following their Iroquois friends would not see their tracks. After about 10 minutes three Seneca braves came on moving fast and following the Iroquois tracks in the snow. When they were a mere 15 feet away, the boys shot two of them. The other one charged straight at them and Doig shot him with his pistol. The sound of their guns would travel for miles and would certainly be heard by more Seneca or perhaps the owners of the gunshots they had heard earlier. The impact of the large balls of lead they shot was so great it would completely stop a charging opponent and throw him on his back. They picked up the weapons of the dead Seneca and set out at a fast run to the west. It wasn't more than 30 minutes when they caught up with their Iroquois friends and the group continued on all day without incident.

Adie and Robert fed their meager fire all night to keep their Iroquois friends warm and let it die out in the morning. The snow fell and completely covered their tracks and the branches of the low hanging fir. It was banked up around the base of the tree and formed relatively warm and cozy shelter. The main body of about 15 Seneca was following nearly the same track to the north that Adie and Robert had taken. Their path would take them within a hundred feet of our friend's hideout. The two wounded Iroquois were in no shape to travel and it would be at least another day before they could. Adie could not leave their little hide out because he would leave tracks in the snow and he knew the Seneca would be looking for them. So, he climbed up the trunk of the big fir tree until he could just see and would not be seen. Sure enough, about mid-day, here they came. The remaining Seneca were dragging some of their wounded or dead on travois and were not paying much attention to anything but getting back to their main village. They were talking in low tones among themselves as they trudged by. Adie sat motionless fearing that if he moved they would see him. Slowly the sound of the defeated Seneca faded away to silence. Adie and Robert sat quietly the remainder of the day and at nightfall, started the fire again. The big fir dispersed the smoke well and the banked snow against the low hanging boughs held in the warmth. The aroma of the burning wood could travel for miles up the valley floor to the north on the slight breeze. They cleaned and bound the wounds of their friends and fed them some of the remaining food they carried, for in the morning it would be off over the steep ridge to their west and then the next and the next. In spite of the language difference the four became life-long friends.

Macum, Doig and their three Iroquois friends found a place about midway down an east facing hill and made camp. They had learned to position their camps so the rising sun in the morning would warm them. They were only one day or so from the main Iroquois village. They had been losing altitude gradually and were just out of the snow. Several times during the last days they thought they heard booms from the west. There was no doubt it was the boom of guns or perhaps cannon, but the direction could not be determined with much accuracy. The Iroquois brave that could speak English was not with them and they didn't know the status of the others. Macum and Doig were concerned about Adie and Robert just as the Iroquois were about their comrades. But, the sounds coming from the west concerned them more.

The British had traveled by log barge to the southeastern shore of the Lake Erie and unloaded a sizeable force of infantry

including three cannons. Their mission was to obliterate the
Oneida Nation whose main village was some 50 miles to the
south. The Oneida had resisted their bribes and coercion and
had sworn allegiance to the Patriots, and the British had to show
them the punishment for their mistake. It was very difficult
to move a force of any size across country without notice, so
the British commanders did it by barge. They felt if they could
launch a surprise attack that would seriously injure the Oneida
late in the fall; the hardship of winter would about finish them
off. But the Oneida village wasn't just one big one; it was a series
of a dozen smaller ones loosely spread out over 15 miles along a
small river that eventually flowed into Allegheny. Within hours
from the first boom of the cannons and the attack of the infantry
on the northern-most village, the British were under relentless
hit and run arrow attacks from the Oneida. Sporadically, from
first light until dark, arrows rained down on them, and so many
Brits were killed a withdrawal was ordered. The British simply
were not fast enough to get a clear shot on the warriors who
would shoot and move, shoot and move. They couldn't even
build fires to warm themselves. The Oneida harassed them until
they were back on their ships and away from the beach.

By the time Macum and group arrived at the southern-
most village, the battle was over, and the British were in full
retreat. Everyone was preparing for winter. Food was smoked or
dried and stored; dwellings were sealed with mud. Fur clothing
and boots were pieced together and stitched. In several days,
Adie and Jean Robert showed up half carrying their wounded
partners. Four more never returned. Everyone settled in for the
winter. This was an area on the lee side of Lake Erie where
deep snow was common. The short days of winter were spent
either, hunting, foraging for wood, or chatting around a warm
fire. The four travelers would look back on this as one of the
good times. Jean Robert taught many of the men how to fight
hand-to-hand effectively. And occasionally, he would have to
beat a particularly belligerent Indian badly in order to prove that
his methods worked or meet a challenge of a particularly tough

man. But, the highlight of the winter was the songs the cousins sang. Of course, nobody could tell what they were saying, but the Indians screamed with pleasure during and after their sing fests. They sat breathlessly listening in total quiet until the boys finished the last note, then, they would erupt with laughter and applause. They would continue the noise until the boys would begin another song. The boys were the highlight of the winter and they loved it. The Oneida chief was Shenandoh$_r$, later respelled Shenandoah, and when the cousins met him he was 54 years old. He had been converted to Christianity and was a friend of the Patriots until he died in 1816 at age 110. He loved the cousins and spoke English quite well, so they had long talks about the outside world. They told him all about the voyage on the big ship and the ship with cannons. Later during the American Revolution, when most of the other nations of the Iroquois sided with the British, he refused. It was the influence of the cousins that helped cement his loyalty. The division of the Iroquois had already started with several skirmishes between the Oneida, Seneca and Mohawk. The very first time the Seneca had attacked the Oneida was the time that included Macum, Doig, Adie and Robert. The animosity between Nations became more intense for the next 40 years and ended with the dissolution of the tribes about the time Shenandoh passed away.

During the years the boys lived with the Oneida, they learned that the Iroquois Nation had actually included the five and later six major Indian tribes. Until the British interfered, the six had agreed not to make war on each other and every year there would be a council held to iron out their differences. Representatives to that council were appointed, by vote, of the women of each tribe. The Iroquois had agreed on a constitution, unwritten, and a bill of rights of sorts that was somewhat similar to the American constitution that was to follow in several decades. The cousins' wool clothing finally wore completely out and they cut them up to make stockings. They taught the Oneida how to make their unique footwear that alternated hard and soft leather with animal fat for water proofing, and allowed faster travel over sharp ground and kept their feet dry and protected. The boys wore the full leathers, fur side in, in the winter and shaved leather breechcloths in the summer. Even though they tanned in the summer sun, their skin was still much lighter than the Indians. They fought beside their Oneida brothers and when they had powder and ball used them effectively. Most of the time, they used the bow and arrow. They each fathered several children, both boys and girls whose names were largely lost to history. That is probably why, in later generations of Oneida descendents, blue eyes and Morton's toe both randomly occurred. The boys traveled much of the middle-west of colonial America ranging from the Ohio River on the south, the Mississippi on the west and north into what is now the state of Michigan. They kept their indenture agreements and the letters of recommendation from the Captain of the Sagittaire safe and dry all those years, and the piece of cloth with the stitched recipe was always in Macum's provision bundle. He unrolled it occasionally and held it to his chest, closed his eyes and remembered his Mother and the difficult days of Inverness. They had not forgotten their indenture agreements and felt drawn to the growing conflict of the Revolution in the east. So, one spring, they sang their last songs and amid strong hugs and tears and shouts of farewell and friendship, they tied their provision bundles on their backs, picked up their weapons and headed east. It was 1774.

# BOSTON

Their route to Boston took them northeast along Lake Erie then straight east parallel to Lake Ontario just north of present day Interstate 90. They were able to miss most of the rugged mountains as well as most of Seneca territory. Macum still had his compass. The farther east they got, the more roads they had to choose from. They tried to stay off the main roads, and wound back and forth through the small villages. The Americans welcomed them and at the first opportunity, they purchased woven and sewn clothing with the money they had kept all the years. Many of the American men were leaving their homes and joining Washington or their local militias in preparation for war with the British. Many more thought all the talk of independence was hog-wash and would have no part of it. But the cousins were determined to follow their obligation of service to Stevenson, Turner and Burton. Then if released, they would join with Washington. They traveled intermittently with some of the American men, who were on their way east to join the Army. The locations of the British were commonly known, so it was relatively easy to avoid them. Several times our young travelers had to run for several hours to elude the British, but their trip was largely without incident. After several weeks of hard travel and several hundred miles, they crested a hill and gazed down on the city of Boston.

The four travelers had to go slow and be aware that groups of men were British targets and ambushes were common. But after a day of looking, they finally found the store front with the names of the three merchants and went in. Mr. Stevenson himself was there. He had aged quite a bit and had gray hair, but recognized the cousins and welcomed them shaking their hands briskly. They each pulled out their indenture agreements and their personal recommendation from the Captain of the Sagittaire and handed them to Stevenson. As they all sat around a small table, Macum summarized where they had been the last 10 years as Stevenson studied all the documents and took a deep breath. Macum's story continued for nearly an hour. Tears formed in Stevenson's eyes and he tore up the indenture documents and threw them in the fire. He was overcome that three penniless young boys, could be forcibly taken off his ship, imprisoned by the French, then become friends with them, learned surveying, traveled hundreds of miles west, stayed with the Oneida for 10 years, then found their way back to Boston to fulfill their indenture promise. He removed his spectacles and dabbed at his eyes, and told them that he had a need for men of high principle and offered all four jobs working in his shipping business in America. They would be in charge of maintaining accurate inventories in his various warehouses and seeing that goods were shipped and payment received. Each of them would be assigned to different distribution centers, but all within several hundred miles of Boston. They asked for a day to make up their minds, headed back to the boarding house for a final evening meal together. The house had been taken over by the British.

The Quartering Act of 1765 allowed the British free quartering in any American house or hotel they desired. It was one of a dozen acts that heaped tyranny on Americans and created support for the coming War of Independence. Their clothing bundles had been retrieved by the owner and were hidden in a corner of the barn. As the four approached the boarding house, they became aware of their personal danger.

The owner met them on the street; warned them that they had been displaced and told them where their bundles were located. To protect them from British arrest, Stevenson had given each of them a letter stating they were in his employ and were not members of either American militia or army. They weren't confident this would work, however. So, Macum left the other three and proceeded to the barn to collect their bundles and was quickly confronted. He pulled out the letter, which was grabbed and taken to the commander. He was roughly treated and his hands tied behind him. The commander made him stand for several hours while he took his time reading the letter as he ate. Several loaded guns were pointed at Macum and periodically they would jab him roughly with them. Macum was defiant during this time. He was big and lean and strong and the British soldiers were glad, he was tied and took advantage of this. Reluctantly, the commander finally gave the order to release him and when Macum gave him a stinging glare with those blue eyes, the Brit knew he'd made a mistake. Somewhere down the line, the arrogant treatment would be avenged.

Robert was assigned Montreal because of his fluent French. Adie, Doig and Macum were to go to Charleston, Baltimore, and New York respectively. Each of these cities had a good harbor and a good network of roads servicing the adjacent country. Burton in Glasgow and Turner in London purchased manufactured goods from the economic centers in Europe, and shipped them to Boston, and then the goods would be further distributed and sold from there. At first, each of our four travelers would act as laborers but as they learned the business would be promoted gradually into more responsible positions. The cousins, because they could read and perform simple arithmetic, would be promoted into record keeping jobs. Before he knew it Macum was alone on a small ship headed for New York. The ship was loaded to the gunnels with goods for sale. He was feeling alone for the first time, uncertain of his future and genuinely worried about the fates of his three comrades. These were turbulent times in America and war was brewing; everyone knew it. He modified his name to Giles McCumberland, taking the first name of Jean Robert's greatly admired father (who spelled his name Gilles, which meant shield) and to better fit into the conventional dual name custom of his new country. So, with a new name and a new life in front of him, he once again stood at the aft rail and watched another port slowly recede below the waves.

One of the strategies of both the British and the Americans was to deprive the other of military supplies. So, merchant ships were constantly stopped by both and searched for anything that would help the military. The very next morning, Giles heard people shouting and running and the ship was turning violently. He dashed up on deck just in time to see a British Sloop unleash a nine gun barrage at the sails and masts above him. In a flash everything was a mess, the broken rigging and masts were everywhere. His ship had no means of defense and the Captain had the mate wave a white flag on the end of a pole. In no time the British were searching for anything that would help their cause. Food, muskets, powder, lead and tents were at the head of the list and his ship had none. Just as quickly as they came, the British left. Now the ship was dead in the water with one part of one sail serviceable. The crew worked all day and into the night moving broken masts and clearing up the rigging and by the next morning, they were ready to limp on into New York. The shoot first and investigate later attitude of the British galled Giles, but there was nothing he could do, but stand by and watch and keep his mouth shut.

The Stevenson and Burton building was several hundred feet from the dock and it took nearly another day to unload the merchandise from the ship, and store it safely in the warehouse. Stevenson's man in charge there was old Sean McDermitt, a hard drinking, hard bitten sort with gray hair, grim lips and eye glasses on his nose. He intermittently looked at Giles and frowned as he read the letter from Stevenson. It seemed to Giles that the old man must have been in his 70's and before he knew it he had a cup of some kind of foul smelling alcoholic drink in his hand and the old man was proposing a toast. Giles was only able to drink a tiny sip and that took his breath away, to the absolute joy of old McDermitt. When old McDermitt downed his drink, his voice went up an octave for a few moments. Giles was immediately put to work loading and delivering goods to neighboring stores in New York and the adjacent area. After a few months and with autumn approaching, he was moved into the position in the office of inventory clerk. More months went by and spring was approaching, when one day, Adie and Doig appeared in his office. The word had gone out that the Americans needed everyone to come join the army and Stevenson had released them from their jobs to do just that. That day Giles notified old McDermitt that he was to leave the next morning. He sat down and wrote a lengthy letter to Stevenson detailing what he had learned on the job and ways he had found to keep the freight moving faster and more accurately. He wrote another letter, which he also gave to Stevenson for transit to Glasgow, then to his Mother and told her of his adventure. The cousins had heard that the American Army was forming up in Massachusetts and were off to join.

# WAR

More Intolerable Acts were forced on the Americans by the British in 1774 and in October the Battle of Point Pleasant Virginia had added to the chaos and may have been the actual start of the war. West of Boston, the cousins asked around as to where they could join the army and were told to find a John Parker<sub>r</sub>. He was the Captain of the local militia and was eager to sign them up. He especially liked the fact that they carried four weapons, a hatchet, a musket, a pistol and the most impressive, a bow. They would need them all. He had them shoot for him and it turned out that they were just as accurate with the bow as with the musket at about 30 yards. Those soldiers that were not local citizens formed a little camp just outside Lexington, while the rest went back to their homes each evening. They had meetings and drills each day that showed them the basics of battle and some of the tactics. The word came in that the British were going to move out of Boston and come west to Concord to confiscate the American weapon's cache there. They would have to come right through Lexington, and Parker's militia was to slow them down without engaging them in battle. The British troops under Pitcairn arrived at Lexington at dawn to find Parker and his militia spread out in a double rank across the village green. Up to this point the British army had never actually fired upon a militia and Parker had hopes that policy would continue. But, it was not to be. Unrelenting the British lines approached led by a group of about 30 marines with bayonets drawn. The militia started to withdraw, and the leader of the marines shouted, "Damn them, we shall have them." Another cry came from the British lines, "Lay down your arms you damned rebels." Adie, Doig and Giles were positioned behind a stone wall just behind and to the right of the militia's lines. They were instructed to use their bows only if ordered, so they stood still, arrows notched in the string and bows half drawn. As Parker and his militia started to bolt and run back to the safety of the wall, someone bumped Adie and released his arrow directly into the shoulder of an oncoming mounted British officer, who flinched and accidently fired his pistol. It was the, "shot heard round the world." Uncontrolled firing broke out from the British lines with Major Pitcairn shouting "cease fire" with no effect. The firing continued into Parker's militia until the British drummer was able to be heard and the one sided attack broke off. Several of Parker's men had fired, but most had not. The British left for Concord with eight Americans dead and nine wounded. Adie McGillivray took a British ball in the middle of his chest and was dead on his 28th birthday, April 19, 1775. This skirmish lasted just a few minutes but was destined to change the world. Once in Concord, the British were unable to find the significant stores of powder, lead and cannon hidden there and after a significant skirmish in which a number of both British and Americans were killed, they left. Ambushes by Parker's men and others, further diminished the British numbers, particularly the officers. Several dozen were found to have died from arrow wounds; this fueled the belief by the British that the Indians were helping the Americans. Under the protection of the oncoming help of Earl Percy's Brigade, the remaining British returned to Boston. So, the American Revolutionary War had begun, and Doig and Giles found themselves smack in the middle. Captain Parker had tuberculosis and was to pass away shortly so his militia, including the cousins, was disbanded. Washington was made Commander in Chief of the patriot army, and Doig and Giles were off to join him at Cambridge. They stayed with Washington through Trenton, Valley Forge, Monmouth and finally Yorktown in October 1781. Both had been wounded several times and had advanced in rank, and after six or so years, the war was won, they were both released and went back to Stevenson to continue their lives. Neither would ever fully recover from the horrible memories of men screaming in pain, and they would never forget the suddenness of Adie's death. One moment he was alive and one breath later he was dead, blood oozing from the corner of his mouth and staring up at them with unblinking eyes. Giles saw Adie's dead face often when he slept those first years, but with time, the memories and horrors faded and the good memories of his years with Adie returned.

# NEW YORK

When the two cousins were released in late 1783, they first went to Boston to visit with Mr. Stevenson and arrange passage back to New York and Baltimore. Stevenson was glad to see them and embraced each with a stout squeeze and tears. When he heard of Adie's death, he sobbed openly, for he thought of the three as his sons. They had been exceptionally loyal and forthright and he intended to reciprocate. He had a letter from Adie's Mother that he had received via one of his ships several years before. She was the oldest of the three sisters and when (Macum's) Giles' letter reached them they were eager to reply, so Adie's Mother was the one to do the writing, with assistance from the other two. It explained that each of them had married to good and loyal Scottish men and had several children. The English had kept up their total dominance of the country and had taken most of the young boys for indoctrination and service in the Royal Army. Few ever returned. After the cousins had left from Brackloch, the English followed the mothers for several months hoping to find the boys. The word got around that Macum was actually the son of the Duke of Cumberland and a search for him was conducted for months and months before it finally petered out, unsuccessfully. Giles' Mother had put his letter inside a waxed envelope and stored it safely in the town bank. She would regularly go down and read the whole thing, for it was many pages, and have a good cry. These were not tears of sadness; they were tears of pride and joy, for her little bastard son's survival of the incredible chain of events and for his development into a responsible, caring and independent man. The Mothers were all in good health and they looked forward to the day when the boys would return, and that was it.

That evening, Giles sat down and penned another letter to his Mother, telling her of Adie's death and of he and Doig's escapades in the war. He was proud that he was part of the independence of his new country and that he personally knew George Washington. Giles described the surprised look of recognition, on the face of a particular British Commander that had assaulted him in Boston before the war, as the man gazed into his eyes, then blinked and died. That was the only dead Brit for which he did not feel sorry, as he knew that most of them were forced to be there and fight a war with which they did not agree. Many of them were Scotsmen. He told her that she was a Grandmother because he had fathered several Indian children in his stay with the Iroquois and they were under the care of his friend Shenandoh, the chief. He looked forward to seeing them again someday. He reassured her that Shenandoh was a literate and Christian man and not to worry about her grandchildren's upbringing. He described the Stevenson business and that Stevenson himself thought of him as a son and vice versa. He told her that he was to work in New York and in another year, would be going to Fort Pitt. It was some hundreds of miles to the west, near where he lived with the Iroquois, and he would represent Stevenson's interest in selling provisions to pioneers going down the Ohio and on west. Since a road had been built across the mountains and on to the west, Stevenson would be able to ship his imported manufactured goods by wagon to Fort Pitt. And, he told her that he had taken the name Giles McCumberland.

# FORT PITT

The year for Giles was uneventful, and the country grew with ship loads of immigrants that arrived almost daily. Most were to head west where the land was nearly free; all it would cost was their lives. The country basked in the absence of the British and newly found freedom; even though times were turbulent, and people could not agree on the makeup of their new country, everything was positive and hopes and dreams were prevalent. The goods in Stevenson's warehouses grew in anticipation of the westward push. Doig had married a French woman in Baltimore and built a house. Jean Robert was now the manager of the Montreal facility and he too had married. The time finally arrived for the three of them to part again, forever this time. Giles was again headed west, this time on the back of a wagon drawn by six fine horses. He had a letter from Stevenson, several weapons, his clothing roll and the recipe. Several well paid and heavily armed guards were on horseback, one in front and the other behind. As he crested the last hill visible from New York, he looked back and the faces of his three companions flashed in his mind, then were gone. With tears in his eyes, he set his sights westward. It was good to be riding instead of running. The sun was low in the sky and had turned the few clouds to an iridescent gold; appropriate for the promise of the American west and the adventures ahead.

Fort Pitt was located between the Monongahela and
Allegheny Rivers where they joined to form the mighty Ohio.
The main industry was the building of flat bottom boats for the
float down the Ohio. A boat a day was built and provisioned
and sent on its way loaded with hopeful pioneers dreaming of
a good life in the west. Giles and his helper, an Englishman by
the name of Harmon, sold all the basic provisions and business
was so brisk, they could not keep up. The wagon loads of goods
from the east had to be doubled and re-doubled because of the
demand. Giles and Stevenson were becoming rich men, very
quickly. The Oneida Nation had moved to the east of the camp
they had when the cousins were in their midst and it was nearly
a hundred mile trip for Giles.

Giles was anxious to see his children and his old friend
Shenandoh, and as he approached the camp, he could see that it
was much smaller than he remembered. The Oneida had been
devastated by cholera and many had died in the last decade.
They had moved several times trying to get away from the
disease, but finally realized that their only defense was complete
isolation of anyone who came down sick. Most of those that
got the disease, died because of isolation and lack of care plus,
of course, a natural lack of immunity. One of his children and
their mother had both passed as a result of the malady, leaving
an eight year old boy an orphan. The boy's name had been
changed to Kanti, which means "sings," by Shenandoh, because
of his astounding ability to sing. His clear and strong soprano
voice was perfect of pitch and vibrato. He sang the Indian chants
and songs so well that large groups of tribesmen would gather
from miles around and sit quietly just to listen. When Giles
arrived, one of the first things they wanted him to do was to
sing to the group. Before, he had sung as part of a trio, but now
it was solo, and it was the first time he had sung since Adie
had died. Slowly and surely he was able to put together the old
songs from his Mother and the tribe absolutely loved it. They
screamed with joy and delight and as he slowly warmed to the
crowd, he became more comfortable and his singing regained

the gusto he had in the old days. He and his son alternated singing songs to the Oneida crowd, he singing in English and Kanti singing in Iroquois. Watching his son sing brought the most pure joy and pride to Giles he had ever felt. He wished his Mother could hear her Grandson sing. Then he had the idea that he should bring his Mother to America, so she could share in his joy. He could arrange for her passage from Inverness to London, to Boston, and to Pitt. Why hadn't he thought of this before? So, he decided to write to his Mother and then to arrange for Kanti's education at a good boy's school in Boston. He and Shenandoh both agreed that the light eyed Kanti should have an education in an American school. So, he was a passenger on the next freight wagon headed east. He would be looked after by Stevenson and enrolled in the fall session of the local boy's school.

Letters were sent and Mr. Burton in Glasgow sent a courier to Inverness to inform Giles's Mother of the trip to America. Sarah listened to the courier with disbelief, and tears rolled down her cheeks and those of her sisters. She realized she was an old widow lady and felt this was something she must do while she could. It took months for word to travel across the Atlantic and Giles realized that it would probably be a year before he actually saw his Mom again.

America was roiling with dissatisfaction with the Articles of Confederation and many people were talking about a new type of agreement that would create a stronger government. The preferred type of communication was the newspaper and everyone read them daily. Out in Fort Pitt, Giles had to read the papers weeks after they were printed. The one copy of each of the papers delivered on the freight wagons were circulated around the fort and the neighboring community. They stimulated considerable debate over the issues and were rumpled nearly unreadable by the time they became fire starters. Giles was extremely impressed and proud of Harmon's grasp of the issues and his ability to convince folks of an opposing view to agree with him. Harmon was actually from Ireland, conscripted by the English and given an English name when he was 11. Because he showed exceptional intelligence, he was educated in England and forced under protest into the British Army and to America. Early in the war, he was captured by the Patriots and spent a considerable time in a prison camp where he was able to convince his captors of his true loyalty, and was released when the war was ended. He and Giles had become life-long friends; it was 1785.

The months rolled by and there was no word about Burton's arrangements for the travel of his Mother; he expected her on one of the summer cargo ships from Glasgow. He did receive regular reports on Kanti's progress in his new school. It turned out that he picked up English quickly and adjusted to the white man's life style easily. Of course, Stevenson treated him like a Grandson and this softened the shock of being away from Shenandoh. As the summer continued into fall, Giles' concern for the arrival of his Mother became more intense. With the arrival of every freight wagon, there was a note telling him that she wasn't there yet. He and Harmon were so busy tending to the business, it helped keep his mind occupied, but in the quiet times just before he went to sleep each night, he knew that something must have gone wrong and it caused him to worry about the welfare of his Mom.

The meeting hall at Fort Pitt rang with the sound of the trio singing all the old Scottish songs, and when the crowd cheered and clapped the place literally shook. It was a reunion suitable for a fairytale. The elderly woman, whose soprano voice was clear and strong, treated the crowd to a few songs in the old Gaelic, then was joined by her Son and Grandson to belt out tune after tune in perfect pitch and harmony. People in the audience wept openly at the sights and sounds of the three, then screamed and cheered wildly at the end. It was the kind of event about which, folks would tell their grandchildren. It started on a clear day in September when Kanti came running into Giles' small office in the Fort Pitt Stevenson building. He ran into his Father's arms and was yelling that his Grandma was there. Giles looked out the window in time to see Harmon helping an elderly woman from the wagon. She was thin, with rounded shoulders and short graying blond hair. She was much smaller than he remembered, and when she turned to look at him, her blue eyes were clear and her face covered with a smile. Tight hugs and tears followed as the three embraced each other. It was a dream-come-true for Sarah. Her little bastard Son was really alive and healthy; she had a Grandson and they were both in her arms. Harmon and the Fort Captain immediately arranged a big dinner at the meeting hall for that evening that was subsequently written about in the newspapers in all the major cities of America. They were referred to as the Three Generation Trio. During the next year or so, the Trio was asked to sing at many of the major events around the new country. They met governors and officials of all kinds, and without fail brought tears and cheers to all who saw them. Sarah fell in love with the new country and wrote to her sisters and children in Scotland that she was to stay there, forever. She encouraged all her children to go down to Glasgow and volunteer for the indenture program with Burton and immigrate to America, as it truly was the land of freedom and opportunity. "Leave behind the poverty and oppression of Scotland." During the ensuing years, and after her death, all three of her Scottish born children, their spouses and children came to America; all but one would be lost in the maelstrom of the new country.

The United States of America was finally formed, Kanti had decided to attend the college there in Boston, and Giles had started getting gray hair. He buried his Mom on a hill overlooking the little community of Fort Pitt and the confluence forming the Ohio River. He visited her grave regularly and sat and watched the pioneers embark on their float down the river on to the west and new lives of hope and opportunity. From time to time he had run across the name McGillivray and inquired about a possible relation to no avail. Occasionally during the remainder of his life, he saw the name in the newspaper, but was never able to make contact with any of his half brothers or their children. The steady stream of folks going west was slowly convincing him that it was what he wanted to do and he started listening to Stevenson and planning his own migration westward. Stevenson had encouraged him to start another distribution center for their house wares and tools somewhere farther west along the river. The question was, should they go clear to St. Louis, which was still controlled by the Spanish, or stop along the way. The fur trade from the west was just starting and the Ohio River was used as transportation for goods in both directions. For some years, the Stevenson's freight wagons were hauling manufactured metal goods and clothing westward and furs eastward. This was a chance for them to expand farther west and widen their markets. It was 1792.

Giles found that floating down the river was anything but smooth. It took a strong raft and a good captain to keep from getting into trouble. He stopped in Cincinnati for a few days and talked to some of the merchants and townspeople. It was a new city with a new name, and he could find no reason to start a new business there, so it was on down the Ohio to Louisville. Here the flat boats had to be unloaded and partially disassembled for road transport around the falls, and Giles felt it logical since the boats were unloaded anyway, why not actually warehouse the goods there. The problem was that nearly all the folks coming downriver already had purchased the products they felt they needed for the trip, so he proceeded farther to the Mississippi, then upstream to St Louis. The city, named after the French King Louis IX, was under control of the Spanish, and the local authorities were all appointed as such. English, French and Spanish were commonly spoken. Giles spent a week there looking over possible sites for a building and office and found a likely place at least 70 feet above the water line. This was truly the heart of the fur trade for beaver and buffalo. More and more, folks were coming to St Louis by boat either from the south or the east without the provisions they would need for the trip on to the great American west, and they needed a good source of supply. Giles resolved to be this source, and he started back, briefly down the Mississippi, then up the Ohio by keelboat, and finally had to ride horseback much of the way.

The trip back upriver was long and dangerous. The threat from thieves was constant and he had to arm himself and team up with several flat boat crews that were making their way back up river. A group of armed men could travel much more safely than one alone. One evening just before sunset, the group came across the scene of an ambush of a flat boat that had grounded. Somehow, it appeared that the flat boat had been lured to the shore then attacked and looted. All that remained were the bodies of the families and crew and the boat itself. It appeared that the women had been abused and their bodies mutilated. Giles and his group dug graves and buried each and marked the graves with crude crosses. It was a somber time, and the men were torn between rage and sorrow; each wished they could catch the perpetrators. They knew not that they were being watched and that a plan for their demise was being prepared.

Their camp was about 20 yards from the river itself, just at the edge of a grove of trees. The graves of the deceased, and the grounded flat barge were in sight of the camp, as was the river. They had just spent all day seeing to the proper burial of the unfortunate pioneers and were settled in for the evening knowing they were to head upriver in the morning. Giles' group had a small fire and lookouts had been posted. Someone shouted from the darkness of the forest, "hey you at the fire, put down your guns and we'll letcha live." The group immediately took cover and shots from the forest started coming from several directions. The only light was from the stars and the sliver of moon. One of the captains told the group to hold fire until they could see a target. It was going to be a long night. The raiders were not anxious to get into a close up battle with 10 armed men in the dark and Giles' group couldn't move without risking being shot. The situation was familiar to several men in the group that had skirmished with Indians or the British. Giles and one of the other men slowly crawled out to the river

and slipped in, Giles working slowly downstream and the other
slowly up. Giles had his bow and intended on circling around
behind the raiders and killing them one by one. The other man,
by the name of O'Brian, was good with a knife and would do
the same thing from the other direction. It took several hours for
Giles to get into position behind the raiders, who continued to
shoot sporadically into the camp. Their firing was a big mistake
because it gave the two attackers a location. Silently, Giles moved
through the forest, calling on his Iroquois training in stealth. He
crept up behind the raiders and had located three in the scant
light. Picking the one closest to him, he pulled up an arrow,
drew the bow, aimed at the man's back, and let fly. Pfffft, a slight
cry and the soft thump of a body hitting the ground, were the
only sounds. Then it was the next one's turn. Pfffft, .... Thump.
Someone called out several names, and there was no answer.
Pfffft,..... Thump again. Three were down. Giles continued on
his slow quest to find more. A shot rang out about 100 feet away
from Giles, then another, and then silence. After a while, he
heard O'Brian shout, "That's all of 'em." Back at the camp, it
made for a much more restful night. The next morning, Giles'
group found the three he had killed and four more with their
throats slit by O'Brian. They stripped the raiders of weapons,
put them in a pile for the animals, and continued on upriver. It
seemed it was good to have a man like O'Brian on your side.
The three captains all proved to be men of forthright character
and honesty and after weeks of traveling together, Giles asked
if they were interested in becoming part of the Stevenson
Company. So, by the time Fort Pitt was at hand, he had three,
three man crews hired and ready to start the push westward.

Harmon and O'Brian were both from the same vicinity of
Ireland and became instant comrades. When the time came for
the first flat boat to leave Pitt with a destination of St Louis,
O'Brian was the Captain and Giles a passenger. He had made the
trip back to Boston to confer with Stevenson and found him in
ill health. Having no heirs or relations, Stevenson advised Giles,
Doig and Jean Robert that his share of the business was to be

divided evenly between them at his passing. Doig and Robert were both actively involved in expanding their businesses westward and contributed to the requirement of two ship loads per month from London and Glasgow. Kanti McCumberland had grown into a lean and broad shouldered young man fleet of foot, with a clear baritone voice. He did acceptably well in his studies, but was so involved in the Stevenson business he had little time to excel. He loved to travel to Fort Pitt and accompanied his Father on what was to be his Dad's very last trip east.

# ST LOUIS

The first shipment of goods downriver was uneventful except for the portage around the falls at Louisville. It took nearly a week before they were back on the Ohio headed to the southwest. O'Brian and his crew spent much of the time on the river singing the old Irish songs handed down from his past. They had to be constantly on guard for river raiders and didn't succumb to the enticements of women and liquor, or the cries of children in distress along the shore for these tricks were used by the raiders to lure unsuspecting travelers to the shore where they could be robbed and killed. The trip by keelboat up the Mississippi was tedious, but was typical of the time as steam powered paddle boats wouldn't be invented for several decades. With the help of several St Louis townsmen, Giles, O'Brian and crew build a sizeable building with a small living area and places for the crew to sleep. When it came time to erect a sign over the front of the place, they found McCumberland to be much too long and shortened it to McCumber. The business and the name slowly took hold. The trips down the Ohio and the rides back up became faster as shortcuts were discovered. Then in the Spring of 1796, Stevenson passed and Kanti became the manager of the American operation that included distribution of goods through Boston, New York, Baltimore, Charleston and Montreal, plus the new and most profitable one in St Louis. He was a bright and attractive man with light brown skin, hair and eyes, and he modified his name to McCumber to match that of his Father. Letter pouches were sent west and east with every trip and it wasn't long before it became a regular letter delivery service along with the freight.

The flow of pioneers westward was never-ending and the demand for metal goods, clothing and blankets was brisk. They gradually added beans, dried or smoked meat and flour to the westward trips and furs to the eastward ones. The most expensive items they sold were crocks of the pickled vegetables, they made there in St Louis. They employed a half dozen local youths, both boys and girls, to plant, tend and water the very large garden on the low ground adjacent to their warehouse there in the town. Every fall, the peppers, onions and cucumbers were combined with salt, vinegar, honey and other secret spices then, wax sealed in hundreds of clay crocks. The crocks were made by a family just down the hill from the warehouse and used Mississippi clay as their raw material. They were known as *McCucumbers* and were hauled all the way up the Oregon Trail and distributed to traders along the way. Once empty, the crocks could be used as general kitchen containers and were bought and sold for decades along the trails west of Missouri.

Giles finally married a young German woman when he was 50. She was newly widowed when her husband drowned in the Mississippi just south of the town. All her belongings and money were lost with her husband and all she had were the clothes on her back when she walked into the warehouse and asked for a job. Ilse, whose German name meant, "God is My Oath," turned out to be a hard worker and natural manager of the young folks growing vegetables for the recipe. She showed them how to gather the droppings from the horses and cattle and till them into the soil of the garden and nearly doubled the harvest. One of the biggest jobs was hauling water to the garden, so she had the local blacksmith make a small wagon that could be pulled by a horse or mule and contained four large empty whisky barrels that could be filled at the river and wheeled up the hill to the garden.

Finally St Louis became part of the United States with the Louisiana Purchase. It had little effect on the nature of the small city but the number of immigrants heading west was increasing greatly every year. Giles' new family was growing rapidly and Ilse insisted they go to school, so she started a small one for them and some of their neighbors. They hauled in books from the east and finally had to hire a permanent teacher so skilled in the art. The great migration to the American West was just picking up steam and the McCumber clan was right in the middle of it. Giles' physical energy was on the wane, but his mind was still full of ideas on how to improve the business and how to prepare those pioneers headed west for the travails that awaited them. What he didn't anticipate was that the business was due to fail from lack of supply of goods from Europe.

Turner and Burton were both elderly men and had no trusted employees or relatives that could take over the business. Without their constant tutelage, the business would fail because of incompetence and dishonesty on the part of their employees. Without warning, both passed within months of each other in 1810, and the ship owners refused to do business with the new managers of Stevenson, Turner and Burton. The company quickly dissolved and the flow of manufactured goods to America and to the distribution centers there disappeared almost overnight. By the time Kanti found out what had happened, the company in Europe was gone and the manufacturers had other shippers in contract. He had no sources of supply and when their inventories were gone, each distribution center would also be out of business. A way of life for Jean Robert, Doig, Harmon and Kanti was suddenly gone and they found themselves drawn to the promise of the American West.

The desire to seek a new life in the West didn't happen overnight. For years, they had spoken almost daily with folks that were going west, full of happiness and hope for their futures, and this had an effect. They caught the fever and now that the company was gone, and they had a pocket full of money, they decided to pursue the dream themselves. Doig and his family took a ship around to New Orleans and struck out west into what is now Texas only to be lost. Giles received a letter from Doig that described a dream of owning a cattle ranch in Texas, and that was the last anyone ever heard. He and his family were apparently killed and forgotten in one of the dry ravines that lie across the landscape like a spider web. Jean Robert and his family had better luck as they traveled westward through the Great Lakes by boat and ended up in what is now Wisconsin. They stayed there several years then struck out westward again into Montana Territory where they too were lost in the immensity of the west. Giles kept the letters from both Doig and Robert safe in a tin box and until he passed, occasionally he would pull them out and stare at them for a long time as if he was reliving every moment he had with them.

# ON WESTWARD

Harmon was intent on going all the way to the Pacific. For some reason, he had this desire to go and find his future there. Giles couldn't talk him out of it and to make matters worse his oldest son, also named Harmon, wanted to go with him. At the same time, Kanti was preparing to travel up the Platte to the confluence and start another store that sold all the same food stuffs and basic supplies that Giles did in St Louis. It seemed that everyone was going west and even though Giles was in his sixties, he wanted to join them; so in the spring of 1812, he and Kanti headed up the Missouri River with a keel boat loaded with goods. Within a week the two Harmons set out on horseback following the Missouri west. This left Ilse with her 16 year old son Joseph and two young children a girl and boy along with a half dozen employees to continue their business. The boy's name was Domhnall, (pronounced Donnal) which was Gaelic for ruler. Young Harmon had his Dad's old compass and a copy of the recipe sewn into his pocket. Neither he nor Old Harmon was skilled at shooting, hunting or the like, but they were prepared with several pack horses loaded with provisions and weapons. What they lacked in experience was made up for in enthusiasm. One thing at which Young Harmon was very good was shooting a bow. When his Dad showed him the techniques, some years earlier, he took to it quickly and became very, very proficient. He didn't try to shoot an apple off his little sister's head, but he could have. Young Harmon was also extremely fast of foot, and it was these two skills that would save his life several times.

As they climbed up out of the Mississippi River valley, both the Harmons paused and looked back, because something in them said they may never return. Their route generally followed the south bank Missouri River westward until it turned north, then on west along the Kansas River. They had been warned about trail thieves and Indians that would be lurking along the way, so they avoided any contact with people. Their intent was to follow a river straight west for as far as they could. They had been told that most of the rivers began in the mountains, which they could cross, then find another river and follow it to the ocean. They knew there were settlements near the ocean and hoped they could make their lives there. It was a simple but somewhat naïve plan; that ignored the plethora of bad people along the way. They would have to travel through country controlled by a half dozen different Indian tribes. The Kansa were a relatively small group that controlled the eastern part of Kansas and western Missouri. West of them were the Kiowa, Arapahoe and just to the southwest, the Comanche. All of the tribes had access to horses; generally the farther west they went the more horses the Indians had. The Harmons didn't know it, but they would have to travel through all these areas to make it to the coast, and their only chance was to remain unnoticed.

Kanti and his Dad stayed close to the shore because the river moved more slowly there. Progress against the current was very slow, but picked up speed as they moved farther and farther upstream. Giles had trouble getting accustomed to sleeping on the ground. He took every opportunity possible to teach Kanti the ways of the wild; where to stop, where to camp, where the game was, and most importantly, where to expect trouble. Every evening they practiced shooting their bows, because they knew they would eventually run out of gun powder. The muskets they had were good for hunting but broadcast their location to possible troublemakers. The muskets would be used primarily for self-defense and not hunting. A good shot with a bow could feed them, and do it quietly. They were to follow the Missouri up to the point where it joined the Platte, then go west. The main pioneer trail from Independence followed the south bank of the Platte clear up into what was to become Wyoming Territory, and from time to time they got a glimpse of long trains of pack animals or small herds of cattle and horses on that route. The route would not open up to wagon travel for another decade or so.

It was about there that one evening, a group of Omaha Indians simply walked into their camp. The Omaha were heavily armed and were apparently on foot. Giles tried to converse with them to no avail and fell back on sign language. The Omaha tribe had been devastated by small pox, and they were wary of any incoming whites. They inspected Giles and Kanti closely for any sign of the red spots. The four Indians shared a meal of pickles, which they loved, beans and dried meat and seemed very interested in what was in the boat. Giles realized that he and Kanti were expected to give them some kind of gift for passing through their land, and he gave the Indians what was left of the pickles and the crock that contained them to the Indians. The delighted Indians gave them two dozen finely made arrows in return and, with a pat on the shoulder, disappeared into the darkness. Neither Giles nor Kanti slept well that night as they took turns sleeping. Going west on the Platte was different because there were so many sand bars and shallow places; they were limited to the deeper part of the river where the current was stronger. So the struggle upstream continued. It was mid-summer by this time and the mosquitoes were horrid. They had taken to covering any exposed skin with a light coating of mud and as a result were a sight to behold.

Several times they encountered small groups of whites along the bank. Usually, the groups were friendly and simply interested in making their way west, but on one occasion, a group of menacing and nasty, dirty men were seen that had four captive women with them. The bedraggled women had their hands tied and were being pulled along behind the horses. The group looked to be made up of six bearded men of middle age all on horseback and a two wheeled cart loaded with provisions pulled by a single scrawny horse. They were taking a break along the bank about mid-day as Giles and Kanti slowly moved upriver. One of the women secretly signaled that they needed help, and the men of the group simply watched silently until the boat moved around a bend. Kanti advised his Father that something had to be done, that they could not sit by and have the women abused and killed or sold into slavery. Giles was reluctant to agree and cautioned Kanti to be wary that there were probably more of them out of sight somewhere along the bank.

Rather than six opponents there were likely to be many more. Upriver several miles, they pulled the boat up on the opposite shore and hid it in a grove of willows. They took their bows, arrows and a knife and hatchet apiece and set out across the river and up the southern bank into the brush. They positioned themselves where they could see back along the route they thought the raiders would take and covered themselves with a light coating of black mud. Their plan was to follow the group until dark, then, one by one kill the men. The group had grown to ten, and was moving west along the southern bank and came right past Giles' position. This kind of thing was not new to Giles, but Kanti had never killed a human. His Dad was watching him closely and he never hesitated or wavered in his intent to do the right thing. One of the raiders was trailing the others by a100 yards or so. They would take care of him first and tie his horse to a bush. The group didn't stop for camp until it was completely dark. They simply stopped in a small grove of cottonwoods and plopped down in a crude circle and started drinking and abusing their captives. The straggler kept looking back along their trail for signs of followers and failed to see Kanti move up on him from the side, then shoot him in the throat with an arrow. He fell roughly from his horse and it bolted only to be caught by the reins. Giles was on him

quickly and made sure he didn't make any noise. The raider
was gurgling and twitching and pulling at the arrow in his
neck, to no avail. The stench of the man was almost more than
Giles could stand as he held him down and allowed him to
gradually stop struggling. They removed the raider's guns and
knife and put them with his horse, then moved slowly through
the darkness to the cottonwood grove. Some of the women
were screaming and others were quietly enduring the rough
treatment. Kanti and Giles separated and took positions about
90 degrees from each other. There was a lot of confusion as the
men were drinking and staggering around and fighting over the
women. Whenever a raider would stand up he would be hit by
an arrow and fall as if overcome by the whiskey. They killed
five before another raider noticed the arrow protruding from his
buddy. The alarm went up and the other four took cover, several
behind the women. Shots were fired wildly into the darkness
without effect. Giles and Kanti held their positions quietly and
this unnerved the raiders even more and they started to panic.
Two more stood as if to run toward their horses, which still had
the saddles on them and were dropped with two quick arrows.
One was groaning in pain and this made the last two even more
desperate. They stood up, and holding women in from of them,
made their way to the horses. Both Kanti and Giles moved closer
for better shots. They were totally black and could not be seen.
Suddenly, they dropped the women and tried to mount their
horses only to be mortally wounded by several arrows each and
falling off the other side of the horses. There they laid screaming
and groaning in pain. Several of the women came over and
kicked them in the face and other tender parts. After several
moments, they too succumbed to their wounds and died. Of
course the women thought they were taken out by Indians and
that realization terrorized them even further. Giles and Kanti
waited several minutes before they moved in just in case one
of the raiders survived enough to pull off a shot, and during
that time the women grouped together under the two wheeled
cart in preparation for possible abuse by Indians. Then Giles

spoke and told them they were safe and that he and his son were friendly. Slowly he and Kanti came out from the darkness. They started a fire and pulled enough food and blankets from the cart to make the women comfortable for the night.

There turned out to be five women as one was tied up naked in the wagon. They were all fairly young and were the wives of a small group of travelers that had set out on their own for what would become Oregon. Four days back, their trusting husbands had allowed the group of raiders to come right into them and without warning, were shot down. The raiders took the women, the money and what food they could carry and left the wagons and oxen behind. So, the next morning, Giles and Kanti stripped the raiders of their weapons and money, and tried to send the women back to civilization on the raider's horses. But, the women would not go. There was nothing to go back for; their husbands were dead and by now probably half eaten by animals. Giles explained that he and Kanti were traveling by boat and that it would be difficult for the women on horseback to keep up with them. He told them they would be going through Indian country and it would be dangerous. He tried his best to scare them into returning, but they would not budge; their resolve was firm. After much discussion, they decided that Giles, Kanti and two of the women would take all ten horses and return to the scene of the killing, bury the dead and salvage anything they could that would help the women on their quest for the west.

The trip was quick as the raiders horses were of good quality. Six of the horses were bareback and ran along on their guide ropes without effort. In two days time, they found the scene of the massacre. The oxen had broken loose and were not to be found. Several of the wagons, which would never have completed the trip, had been dragged until they encountered an obstacle that would not allow them to go farther. But the wagons were largely intact and the four travelers removed the canvas covers and made them into packs that could be tied onto the six extra horses. The two women proved to be extremely able and strong and took to the hardships well. In the evenings,

Kanti and Giles sang to them as they sat quietly with tears
rolling down their cheeks. The younger one realized that her
husband was but a week dead, and could still not resist her
attraction to Kanti. He sensed something was happening with
her and returned the warm looks of mutual admiration. Giles
and the other woman also took notice of the mutual attraction
between the two. The evening before they arrived back at the
boat site, the four of them had a talk around the fire. Kanti told
the women of his intent to build a trading post at the confluence
of the Plattes and that he would be depending on goods carried
by boat up from Independence or St Louis. He said he would be
growing a large garden and firing crocks as containers for the
sweet and spicy pickled vegetables for sale to passing travelers and
Indians. He would purchase furs from the traders and Indians for
transit back downriver on the boats. At least that was his plan.

The four travelers arrived at the grove of cottonwoods,
where they left the other three women, about mid morning.
There was nobody there. It had rained the previous night and
there were no tracks. Kanti rode off south to see if he could find
anything while Giles crossed the river to check out the boat and
then rode north. The boat was fine. Several miles north in a
ravine, Giles came across a recognizable piece of fabric caught
on a bush. The three had apparently been taken by Indians. This
was Pawnee territory and they were known to be peaceful. It
may have been a scouting party from some tribe farther north,
but without a trail to follow, it would be fruitless and probably
dangerous to try to follow. He returned with the news. The
four were quiet as they loaded the horses for the trip west. They
kept all the saddles for the time being. With eight pack horses,
they loaded six so the other two could rest. Then on the trail,
they could rotate horses so all would last longer. It was a good
plan. The only problem was that the younger woman and Kanti
seemed inseparable and in the evening, he would insist on
making camp on the southern shore so he could be with Elsa.
The very first evening when they were making camp, Giles
told the rest that he was going back to find the three missing

women. He had thought on it and could not go on without trying. The women had been through so much abuse with their first abduction and now they were prisoners once again, and he could not live with himself if he ignored it. He didn't even know their names. "It was beyond the tolerance of a civilized man not to try to help, and if it cost him his life, so be it." He knew the Elkhorn River was some 50 miles north of the Platte and told them he would search that far north before turning back.

The Harmons continued their trek west. It was summer and they made camp in low places away from the river and the mosquitoes, without a fire. They stayed off the ridges of the hills and within sight of the river. A few dozen miles into what is now the state of Kansas, the trees ran out except for the river valley and the going was pretty smooth. More and more they were seeing Indians on horseback in the distance and occasionally they could smell the smoke of fires. Then, about mid-day they crested a small hill and before them several miles distant was an Indian camp. Of course, they knew not what to do and had no reason to fear the Indians. Had they been farther west and suspected the Indians of being Comanche, they would have been concerned. To go around the village would require them to pass many miles to the south into plain dry prairie. They were careful to stay just below the hill crests except for momentary reconnaissance missions, and managed to completely miss whatever Indian village it was. After several days, they turned more westerly hoping to again run into the river valley without success. They were without water and their horses were beginning to suffer, so they turned back to the north and still there was no water. Here, they had barely begun their trip and were on the verge of losing their horses to thirst. They didn't know that the river had turned to the north for several dozen miles and had they gone either east or west they would have come upon it within the day. They put all their water into a shallow pan and gave it to one of the horses and the plan was to have young Harmon take that horse and strike off northeast in search of water, fill his containers and come back.

Young Harmon was smaller than old Harmon, so he was the one to go. Sure enough six or so miles away he ran into the river, filled the containers and returned without incident. During his climb out of the river valley, he was spotted by a small Indian hunting party, but they were not on horseback and he left them behind without notice. The Indians took note of his direction, which was southwest, and continued on their hunt. The problem the Harmons had was, do they go back to the northeast and find the river or strike out to the west and hope to find another. There was no guarantee that the river they had followed would ever go back to the west and they could be wasting their time, but they needed to get the horses to water and let them fill up before the set off into unknown territory. So it was back to the river they went, and back into the midst of the Indian hunting party.

It was nearly dark when the Harmons crested the hill that led down into the river valley loaded with trees and bushes and the fresh flowing water. As they got down into the bottom, the mosquitoes were horrendous and they stayed only long enough to let the horses fill up on water. In complete darkness, they struggled back up the side of the valley and onto the flat ground above where there was a slight breeze and few mosquitoes. As they settled down for the night, they could smell the smoke of the Indian fires up-wind. They decided to hobble the horses and reconnoiter the source of the smoke and determine whether or not they should leave immediately. Off into the darkness they went. Neither had the training of Giles or Kanti in sneaking soundlessly, but they were careful and slow and after an hour or so, came upon two smoky campfires with roughly a dozen Indians around them. They were 50 yards away and could clearly hear the Indians talking and laughing. The Indians had something oily and shiny on their skin presumably to keep the mosquitoes away, and the smoky fires coupled with their unpleasant body odor also helped in this regard. Their inclination was to walk into the camp and make friends, but why take the chance as they were unseen and downwind. They made their way back to their horses, set off the north and decided to follow the river for two days; if it did not turn back to the west, they would. Unseen hiding in the bush was a young brave that was supposed to be a lookout, but fell asleep. When they passed within feet of him he woke up and quietly watched them take off to the north. When they were out of sight, he hustled back to his camp and spread the word. The next day a mounted war party came through the Indian's camp and was advised that two white men with horses and pack horses were following the river north. They knew the river went north then turned west and back to the south in a big semi-circle, so to head off the white men, all they had to do was go west and sit by the river and wait, and they did.

Kanti refused to let his Dad go after the three women alone. With six of the horses, so they could trade off every hour and make good time, they were back at the point on the river where the women were abducted within several hours. In another hour they found the ravine where Giles had discovered the small piece of fabric. Meanwhile Elsa and her friend were hidden down in a willow grove next to the river and the boat. They covered any exposed skin with mud to keep the mosquitoes away and had no fire. They were told that after a week, they should load up the four remaining horses and head back to civilization. Of course, they would not; it was west they would go. Giles and Kanti decided it would be best to zigzag back and forth and try to find the trail. The entire day went by without clues. That evening they proceeded about five miles straight north and made a dry camp. At first light, they started their zigzag and after several hours came upon a footprint in a pile of soft dirt. It was small one made by a leather soled shoe. There were no horse tracks with it, indicating the band was on foot; good news. Kanti, being the better tracker, took the lead and Giles followed several hundred yards behind with the horses. He tried to keep Kanti in sight but it was difficult in the rolling terrain. The tracks led almost directly north. Giles figured there were about six men in moccasins and three smaller folks in hard soled shoes. One of the women stepped in soft dirt mounds left by gophers at every opportunity knowing she was leaving an obvious track for anyone following. It was probably her only hope and she was faithful to it. Giles figured they were 25 miles or so south of the Elkhorn River and they should be coming upon the group at any time, but it was getting dark and they would have to stop for the night.

With a breeze out of the north, they could faintly smell cook fire smoke, and the Indians had to be within a mile or so. They had to be careful not to kill the Indians before knowing whether or not they were hostile. It could be that the Indians came upon some stranded women and volunteered to help them. How could they tell? They would have to make contact with one of the women before they took down the Indians. They decided it would be best if they could observe the group and try to determine the intent of the Indians. If one of the women went into the bush to relieve herself, they might be able to find out. So they covered themselves with mud, picked up their bows, knives and hatchets and set off following the breeze. This was not a new experience for either of them and surely six Indians with bows and knives were less dangerous than ten white men with muskets and pistols. As they came into view of the camp, there were two fires burning and the women, who didn't appear to be tied, were all sitting together between them. None of the Indians were within sight and this greatly concerned Kanti and Giles. They squatted on their heels and sat silently for a long time. Every 15 minutes or so they would slowly rise and take in a glimpse of the camp. When Giles tried to straighten his legs, they resisted and he thought to himself, he was becoming too old for this. Several hours later the Indians came dragging a small deer back from the northwest. Two of the Indians that had been left behind to guard the women came into view from the shadows. That settled it, they were hostile or a guard would not have been needed, and the women would have been moving around. The Indians seemed to have no interest in abusing the women in any way and treated the women with some modicum of dignity. Kanti and Giles became concerned that maybe they had made and incorrect decision to kill the Indians without warning. They decided to wait a while longer until the fires burned down, before they took action. It must have been midnight before the Indians settled down to sleep. Giles and Kanti moved slowly into positions to shoot arrows into the camp at 90 degrees to each other. They took these positions to eliminate any possibility of an errant arrow striking one of them.

As they moved closer, Giles noticed that one of the women was awake, lying still, but with open eyes. He moved slightly to his right so he would be directly in her eye sight. He knew that one of the Indians had to be awake and sitting in the shadows, and he had to stay out of sight until he found the Indian guard. When he did see the lookout, the guy was on the opposite side of the glowing coals from him and much closer to Kanti. There was no way he could signal Kanti where the guy was without revealing his hiding place. The Indian was sitting with his back to a small tree, wrapped in a blanket. Giles simply remained stationary and stared at the man, hoping Kanti was sneaking up behind him. Another hour went by and the Indian's head slowly fell forward in slumber. Giles slowly rose up and took aim with his bow. Just he was about to release the arrow, he saw a hand come around the guard from behind and cover his mouth and simultaneously another hand with a knife slit the throat. The guard struggled unsuccessfully make noise for a few seconds then went limp and was allowed to slump to the ground. Kanti and Giles moved into the camp, knives in hand with the intent to take the lives of the sleeping Indians. The woman that was awake saw Giles as he came into view and blinked compliance as he held his finger up to his lips indicating to her to remain quiet. One by one the Indian men gave up their lives quietly and without struggle to the slashing blades of the rescuers. When it was all over, the women cried in relief as they helped drag the bodies into a little hollow and cover them in branches and grass. They would have been destined to a life of slavery, to be kept pregnant constantly, beaten by the squaws of the tribe, and forced to work hard every day from first light to after dark. Their lives would probably have ended while they were still quite young more than likely from complications of pregnancy or child-birth. As the group started back to where the horses were tied, day was starting to break over the horizon to the east. The pink and maroon sunrise in the east was appropriate as it was the start of a new life of hope for the three women and Kanti and Giles, tired as they were, felt even though they had taken six lives, it was the right thing to do.

The Harmons headed straight north as the nearly full moon rose over the eastern horizon. Old Harmon had an ominous feeling about their encounter with the Indians and felt better moving at a ground eating lope. The moon flooded the landscape with eerie light, the air was cool and the horses moved along easily, so they kept going hour after hour. The river was turning around to the west then to the south and could be clearly seen by the Harmons as they put distance between them and the Indians. They changed horses several times and tried to keep the horses moving as quickly as possible without doing them harm. The river finally completed its large semi-circle and turned to the west again and about day break, the Harmons found a nice nook in a small arroyo filled with fresh grass and settled in for a few hours of rest.

The mounted Indian party made their way straight to the west trying to cut off the two white men and about mid morning reached the edge of the river valley. They took up positions of ambush and waited for the white men to fall into their trap. But, it was not to be as the Harmons were already past that point and headed west. Had the Indians been more observant, they would have seen the tracks of the Harmon's horses. The Indians waited most of the day, before they realized the white men were not coming. When they started back along their trail, they discovered the Harmon's tracks going off to the southwest. They argued among themselves whether or not to go after the white men and another hour passed. The Indian group finally broke into two with one going east and the other following the Harmons' tracks westward. The five Indians took off at a gallop and had visions of catching up with the whites quickly, but after several hours of horse draining speed, they slowed to a walk. The Harmons' tracks were still going west paralleling the river, and the whites were nowhere to be seen. The sun had gone down in the west, and the Indians were tracking by twilight. Finally they had to stop for the night as darkness fell and the moon was not due to rise for several hours. The Harmons, on the other hand, had already resumed their trip and were walking their horses in the darkness. They planned to lope their horses once again when the moon rose as they felt safe traveling fast at night when their dust would not be visible. The landscape was fairly smooth except for an occasional buffalo chip and as the moon again flooded them with light, they put miles between them and their pursuers. This continued for several days; the Indians moving in daylight and the Harmons moving at night. Of course, the Harmons didn't realize they were being followed and since it was the hot part of the summer and they had a full moon to travel with at night, they became comfortable with the situation covered many miles rapidly. The Indians, on the other hand, were astonished at how fast the white men were traveling and disagreement broke out among them. Three more of the Indians gave up and turned back to the east leaving two to follow the Harmons. As inexperienced as the Harmons were, they were still tough and formidable men when it came to fighting. The two remaining Indians would regret their quest of the white men as shortly their life's blood would drain into the dust of what is now middle Kansas.

Giles and Kanti were finally back to hauling their goods up the rapidly dwindling Platte. It was mid-summer and the flow of the river had diminished significantly. The women were following the river several hundred yards away on the south bank and easily kept up with the boat. The women begged Kanti and Giles to sing to them each evening and that provided a good ending to each day. They had the advantage of short-cutting the river's many bends. The five of them turned out to be tough as nails, could ride horses with the best, and easily endured the hot days and the ground soaking thunderstorms of the great-plains. There was no doubt in Giles' mind that the five would be able to continue up into Wyoming territory without a male escort. They seemed set in their resolve to fight on all the way, but it was not to be, for nobody could anticipate the hardships ahead. The Indians during this period were usually friendly, but enough of them were dangerous to cloud the issue. The land itself was dangerous as Mother Nature was parsimonious with game and liberal with bad weather. None of them had anticipated the terrible blizzards that would keep them hunkered down for weeks at a time in the winter. Then there were the predatory white men. They were the worst of all. They had no scruples and would kill, ambush, lie and steal without remorse. They used and abused all women, Indian and white. The presence of five white women together was very unusual in a country where there were none. This could draw men like flies on a fresh buffalo chip. The predatory white men travelled around the country in gangs and preyed on anyone in their path, man or woman, Indian or white. They particularly liked small groups of horse or mule trains going west with a dream and a prayer. Their plan was simple; just ride in, act friendly, then suddenly shoot the men, loot the train, and abuse then abduct the women for sale to slavers headed southwest. Word of the women somehow traveled across the plains. They must have been sighted by Indians, who told white travelers, who told other Indians or white travelers, etc. Before summer was over, there were at least three groups of white raiders headed for the Platte. They would find that was a mistake, however, as the women were tough, had fortitude and could shoot and ride like the best man, and were more ruthless than any man.

It must have been luck that Giles and Kanti started the first McCumber store at the confluence of the Platte's when they did, because it was about that time that the entire trail west to

Northwest Country opened up to wagon traffic. After several hundred miles of traveling, a typical train of wagons would have a lot of goods they needed and in return, lots of stuff they needed to dump. Over the years, the store had to expand several times just to keep all the goods left behind out of the weather. That fall, however, Giles helped Kanti build a sod shelter because of the general lack of wood. Most of the trees by the Platte were cottonwood or willow and weren't straight enough for building. Giles wanted to leave by the end of October and float the boat back down the Platte and on home to St Louis. The five women, including Elsa, continued on up the Platte still determined to make it to Wyoming Territory by winter. They did leave two of the horses with Kanti in partial payment for their lives. Several small groups of unsavory looking men came through in the weeks after the women had left. Giles knew what they were up to, that they would never catch up with the women and if they did there would be big trouble. He always felt the attachment of Elsa and Kanti was strong and that somewhere down the line they would meet again. During one of their baths in the river, Giles noticed that he and Kanti the same unusual middle toes.

The day of farewell finally came for Giles and his Son. The boat was loaded with a little food and provisions, after a quick hand shake Kanti pushed him out into the current. The river was very low and he had to pay attention to keep the boat in the deep part. Going with the current was almost a joy, but the sadness of their parting haunted Giles. He planned to send at least 10 boatloads of goods upriver to the confluence each summer and would have to hire men for that purpose. It couldn't be done in the spring because of the fast current and floods. So, all the trips had to take place in mid-summer and early fall. He would try to find someone that could stay with Kanti year round to help with the work and protection. O'Brian would be ideal and when he arrived in St Louis he would put the word out. He figured it would take him about a month to finish the trip downriver and started to think about how much he had missed Ilse and the kids.

The two Indians following the Harmons knew the river turned abruptly south some miles ahead and could save some time if they shortcut on a diagonal to the southwest and perhaps catch the white men unaware. There were no white settlements in the Missouri Territory, now Kansas, and the Harmons knew they were entirely on their own. After roughly a week of traveling at night, they decided to switch to daytime. They assumed the Indians had been left far behind and had become less watchful underestimating the resolve of the two followers. The Indians had been successful in getting ahead of the Harmons and watched from cover as their two victims approached. The Harmons intentionally stayed 50 yards or so away from cover to avoid being shot from ambush. So they turned and maintained a safe distance from where the Indians were hiding. The Indians had to let them pass and try to follow and ambush them after dark. Old Harmon had developed a good sense of the prairie and had gotten several whiffs of the Indians when they passed. The Indians were notorious for their odor as they covered themselves with grease and oil and only bathed by accident, and he recognized their scent from the previous encounter. He didn't let on what he smelled until several hours later when they were slowing down for camp. The plan was, at sundown, to turn into the cover of the river valley, and have young Harmon drop off his horse with a musket and bow. He would then wait and shoot one of the Indians with the single shot musket and try to get an arrow into the other one's horse. Meanwhile old Harmon would stop and tie off the horses then backtrack on foot and try to get a shot also. Once he was in place hidden beside the trail, young Harmon decided he was more comfortable with the bow and could get off two arrows within a single second and take both Indians down, so he laid down the musket in the deep grass. Sure enough after a half hour, here they came, heads down following the trail. The Indians would stop every so often and look around to get a feel of the terrain and cover, but their attention was centered on the ground. Twilight was waning as young Harmon stood motionless, bow half drawn, and let the two walk their horses directly in front of him. Pffffft, the first arrow caught the front Indian square in the side of the chest and before he could react the second arrow was pfffft on its way. The second arrow hit that Indian in the shoulder above the heart. The first Indian was dead when he hit the ground, but the second screamed and charged his horse at young Harmon. They were so close together, all young Harmon could do was jump behind a tree and let the Indian go on by. By that time, young Harmon had another arrow strung up and ready and when the Indian turned for another charge he caught that arrow in the neck. Grasping at the arrow and gasping for air he fell off the horse and struggled for several moments his blood draining into the dust, while young Harmon stood and shook. When all was quiet, young Harmon covered them with brush, collected their arrows, lances and horses and was walking down the trail when old Harmon saw him. It was dark and old Harmon had quite a story to hear. This had been the first time young Harmon had seen a man die and was both upset and relieved it was over. Several days later young Harmon realized that in all the excitement, he had forgotten the musket.

Giles' trip downriver had been largely uneventful and almost boring compared to the trip upriver. He stopped at the Independence settlement for several days and sized up the competition there. An overly fat, oily, middle aged woman and her skinny associate were selling goods from a rundown shack in front of a cave. They kept the trade goods in the cave and seemed very suspicious of Giles and his load of furs. He wasn't the typical mountain man they had encountered, who usually got drunk and then relieved himself between the legs of the fat woman. Giles was clean shaven and well kept and had them sized up as crooks from the second he saw them. It was obvious Independence needed an honest merchant who had the best interest of his pioneer customers at heart. The fat woman and her partner would quickly go away in the face of any competition and that was exactly what he intended to do.

His two little kids were running to meet him as his boat touched the crude dock. Giles just stood and watched them come toward him yelling, "daddy" and smiling. Donnal and Lydia were the youngest of all his children. Joseph stood smiling in the doorway as he was at the stage where a good hand shake would suffice. The faces of those he had lost flashed through his memory. The memories of Kanti's two small siblings that had perished with their mother from disease, then Adie, Doig, his Mom, Stevenson and Robert all appeared then disappeared as Donnal and Lydia jumped into his arms. Ilse stood in the door, tears in her eyes, and watched her husband approach carrying the two youngsters. Winter was coming on and she had worried every day he had been gone. She realized his advanced age, even though he did not. She had a pot of stew hung over the fire and looked forward to hearing him tell the story about every detail of his trip into the unknown. He was a good story teller and one of the things that attracted her to him was his personality and ability to converse. It was such a compelling tale, that in the following days after his return, she wrote a long letter to her Mother and retold the story. Then at the last minute, she decided rather than mail it, she would put it into Giles' metal box for safekeeping, and she wrote another letter to her Mom.

The first snow fell on the sod house and lean-to with about a half-foot of snow driven by a strong wind. The wind was what disturbed Kanti as it howled relentlessly most of the night. Fortunately much of the ground was blown bare and the horses could still find something to eat. They had located the sod house about 20 feet above the river on the north bank looking south. A small hill behind the house helped break the north wind. There was an abundance of dead cottonwood in the grove just to the west to burn for heat. The deer in the area made regular trips down to the river and liked to browse in the grove, so Kanti felt there would be plenty of meat to last the winter. From the soddy, he could see several miles to the south up the opposite side of the river valley and enjoyed sitting in his homemade chair in the doorway and watching the animals trail down to the water in the evenings. Inside the soddy, he had a number of sacks of beans, several dozen crocks of the recipe, and several hundred pounds of dried and smoked meat. This stuff plus a variety of tools and clothing were all for sale, but he hadn't seen a single customer in the several months he had been there.

The winter had just started and Kanti was already itchy for something to do, so he decided to go hunting. If he could bring in a deer or even a buffalo, which he had never seen, he could spend the time drying and smoking the meat and working the hide into something to wear. He was on horseback and a dozen miles to the northwest up out of the Platte valley in a area of broken hills and arroyos, when he spotted a footprint; then after further investigation a single track of footprints going southeast, roughly paralleling the river. These were not the tracks of an Indian, as they were made with a hard leather shoe. It was a small line of tracks that didn't sink into the soft places very far and were obviously made by a woman. A ridge of clouds moved in from the west and covered the sun while it dropped the temperature quickly. He looked back up the tiny trail of tracks and thought he could see the dark spot of a person on horseback following.

Something was amiss, but he had to head back to the soddy as he didn't want to be caught in a storm after dark. He picked up speed and followed the small track as best he could because it took him the correct direction as it turned down toward the river he followed. A gust of wind brought large flakes of snow and now the storm began. Even though it was only mid afternoon, the sky was dark and the temperature was dropping rapidly. He hunkered down in his coat, pulled up the collar and tried to follow the track but quickly lost it. Fortunately the wind was at his back and was blowing him in the right direction. He knew he had to follow the river to find his way back to the soddy and became concerned for the welfare of whoever left the tracks. From ahead of him he heard someone yell, "Kanti." He could barely make out the sound coming from downwind. Again, he heard it; then, again. Who was it? He slowed his horse to a walk and peered into the snow. There was the call again, "Kanti." The voice was much closer this time. Suddenly out of the white, appeared a person wrapped in a blanket, standing directly on his path. He still did not know who it could be, but they obviously knew him. It had to be one of the women that struck out west months ago. He stopped and dropped to the ground, pulled back the blanket covering her face and it was Elsa.

She was cold and disheveled, but still strong as she gripped him in a bear hug. They didn't have time for talk, so he put her in the saddle and sat behind with the blanket wrapped around them both; off they went uncertain as to where they were. Kanti knew if they missed the soddy, they would be in serious trouble. He tried to follow the river but it was difficult because of the heavy brush. The wind and snow grew heavier into a full-fledged blizzard. It was a new experience to both of them. They couldn't see 20 feet ahead and if the wind changed, they would be lost and certainly perish, as the wind direction was their only guide. After several hours it became even darker and Kanti knew the sun must have gone down. They should have run into the soddy or the lean-to by now. But, if they had walked the horse at only three miles an hour, he calculated it should have taken them two or three hours to reach the soddy. If they didn't find it in another half hour or so, he would turn to his right and find the river to see if he recognized anything. At least if they were lost they might find some shelter in the brush down by the river. It was time to turn and find the river. He then realized the wind must have changed direction to more out of the west and they were too far north of the soddy and the river. Going cross wind was much more difficult and they could see even less. He resigned himself to finding shelter in the river brush and trying to survive the night. He was dressed warmly and could probably have survived unhurt, but Elsa was wet and only had a blanket for protection and it was getting wet so there would be little hope for her. He would have to share his clothing and that would jeopardize both of them. They continued cross wind for nearly an hour and hope was on the wane. Then, the faint whinny of a horse came up wind. Then another; and he realized it was his horse left in the lean-to that picked up their scent and was calling. They were safe.

It took nearly a week to bring Elsa back to strength. She hadn't eaten in days and was dehydrated. It was a wonder she made it this far, but she was tough and was a survivor. The soddy was well insulated and tight to the wind and with a little fire, they were comfortable. The storm had lasted two more days and finally broke into sunshine. The snow drifts were head deep in places and the river was almost totally covered. Kanti had to shovel away the snow, then, cut through the ice with an axe to get water. The temperature was considerably below freezing day and night. Kanti wondered how any living thing could survive out there on the open prairie. The summers were hot and dry and the winters seriously severe. Yet the Indians called this their home; they had adapted and so would he.

The following spring they found the lone white man's remains north of the soddy several miles. It was apparently the one that had been following Elsa when the storm hit. No horse was found and it must have survived. The women had followed the north fork of the Platte up into the sandstone butte country of what is now western Nebraska, and had been ambushed by a group of white, trail bandits. It was a cold day and Elsa had wrapped herself in a blanket; then just as they were crossing the river, her horse was shot out from under her and she fell into the current. As she drifted downstream, she heard more shots and yelling, so she stayed in the river for over an hour before she crawled out on shore. The only thing she knew was that she was alive and suspected her fellow travelers were not. With no food, weapon, or provisions, she knew she couldn't save her women friends so she set out down river and back to Kanti. It must have been at least a hundred miles, and she had to constantly hide from the bandit that followed her. She learned to walk on solid ground and on the short grass to minimize the tracks she left. This, pure luck, and her indomitable spirit had saved her life.

The other four were swallowed up in the vastness of the west and probably killed and forgotten. Further, their abductors were also probably killed either by more ferocious men or the severe conditions of the summers and winters.

The Harmons continued on to the west through Osage country and into that of the Kiowa. On several occasions they had short visits from hunting parties that were more inquisitive than hostile. They followed the Smoky Hill River until it petered out, then struck off to the southwest. It was fall and they figured south was better than north. This was the dry high plains and there were no trees and certainly no sign of human habitation within sight in any direction. The creeks had gone dry and water was scarce, so every time they crossed a ravine they inspected the bottom of it carefully. They could still remember the last time they nearly ran out of water. Game was parsimonious and rabbit became their main source of food. Prairie Dog had to be eaten several times, but they avoided its bad taste if possible. They had to start thinking about where to hole up for winter, and had been warned by the Kiowa to beware of the Comanche.

Finally, they came upon the Arkansas River and it was flowing strong so they followed it westward along its north bank. They knew not where it would lead them, but as strong as it was it had to be mountain fed. It wasn't long before they started seeing tracks of horses and men, many of them coming down from the north and turning west along the river. There had to be hundreds of them, and the Harmons became so concerned they decided to cross the river and go on to the south. They knew if the Indians spotted their tracks, they would be in trouble, so sticking to the hard ground when they could, they found a river crossing and took a heading on young Harmon's compass that was directly south. It was late fall and they were headed into some of the driest country in the west toward what was to become the panhandle of Texas. They had filled every container they had with water and felt comfortable for the first few days, but as the country became drier, they became quietly worried. They began to travel at night again as the moon was bright and the ground relatively smooth. The nights were actually cold and it was much more comfortable to sleep in the warm sun of daytime. There was just enough water in the bottoms of the arroyos and half dried creeks to sustain the horses, and it wasn't drinkable for the Harmons. They were putting miles behind them rapidly and made it to the Republican River valley just as a snowstorm hit them from the north. They were able to get out of the wind in a small hollow in the river bank. That's where they stayed for several days as the early blizzard kept them pinned down with little to eat, but plenty of water.

When the storm broke, they had to find food and ventured both east and west along the river in search of an animal of some kind. The Harmons were on foot, creeping along the river just below the bank, focused on the brush and scrub trees ahead when they heard a grunt come from the ground above them. They looked at each other in surprise as this was a unique sound with which they were unfamiliar. The crept up to the top and peered over the edge right into the eyes a buffalo. The buffalo didn't flinch and they stared at the giant animal in awe. The animal was no more than ten feet from them and seemed unconcerned about their presence. The Harmons were motionless as they stared over the edge at the hundreds of the giant animals that apparently had been driven there by the storm. They ducked back below the edge of the bank and tried to decide what to do. If they shot their musket, it would probably startle the herd and they might be trampled. But, could a mere arrow bring down an animal of this size? If it was carefully placed, they had a chance. So, young Harmon picked out his sharpest arrow and drew the bow back to the arrowhead and let fly. He had aimed at a spot just behind the shoulder and knew if the arrow could get through the ribs, the heart had to be there. But the slight sound and movement of the arrow leaving the bow-string caused the buffalo to flinch and the arrow struck it in the neck instead. It didn't seem to have any effect as the buffalo just stood there; then after several minutes it started breathing hard, staggered several steps and fell down. The Harmons didn't know what to do, and after a half hour or so, they slowly crawled up and started to butcher the animal. The rest of the herd moved away, totally unconcerned. It took them a week to strip the best parts of the meat, cook it over a smoky fire and pack it into bundles. This rest was good for the horses as there was plenty of grass in the low ground next to the river. The buffalo hide was so heavy and stiff, they had to leave it behind, but they eventually got everything loaded onto the pack horses and set off again on the compass heading south. The snow on the ground quickly thinned then faded away completely. They hoped they could find a nice river flowing to the west because they must be close to the western ocean, but it was not to be.

South of the Canadian River, the Harmons kept up a regular pace consistent with the health of their horses. The horse was a hardy animal and could survive on its own through all kinds of hardship, but it you overworked them, they would slowly deteriorate to the point where they would just lie down and die. The canyon, now called Palo Duro, looked to be about 10 miles across and stretched to the west clear over the horizon. The Harmons were amazed that this oasis existed out here in the midst of a dry and level plain. But there it was about 500 feet deep with a freely flowing creek, grassy meadows and gigantic groves of both deciduous and evergreen trees. It was just what they were looking for and skirted the northern edge until they found a way down. Loaded with the smoked buffalo meat, they planned to stay the winter and ended up enlarging a small cave in the northern cliff of the canyon. They spent several weeks enlarging it so it would hold the four horses and them. With dirt from the interior, they built up a mound of dirt in front of the cave to hide it from the canyon floor. What they didn't know was the Indians from hundreds of miles around all came to the canyon for the winter. The Harmons would spend the winter trying to stay hidden.

The first slow rain of spring was a welcome sign that the winter was over. Elsa and Kanti had been able to kill enough deer during the winter to keep them busy drying and smoking the meat and preparing the hides for bedding or clothing. Kanti had told her they would take the horses and investigate the territory up river to the sand buttes country and try to find a sign of her friends. He was sure that his Dad was preparing several boat loads of goods for transport up the river and they needed to be back by June to receive them. He hoped his Father's friend O'Brian would be one of the boat-men. Also, he expected trains of pack animals headed west to start showing up by June or so and didn't want to miss a chance to sell something. Another chore for spring was the planting of a garden of onions, peppers, and cucumbers. They would have to squeeze the juice from the local chokecherry trees, of which there were thousands, to make wine then vinegar. He figured to be back at the soddy in three weeks.

The trip upriver was easier if they followed it half way up the side of the river valley. The whole valley was about five to ten miles across, so there was plenty of open ground, and they traveled without delay. The creeks were all full this time of year and crossing some of them meant getting wet, but they had both become hardened to traveling in open country and moved northwest quickly. They carried enough food for the trip and didn't need to kill any game along the way, and saw their very first buffalo and sat for nearly an hour and watched hundreds and hundreds of them pass to the north. The buffalo were a majestic animal and both Kanti and Elsa became admirers. When they finally found the scene of the women's ambush, all that was left were the remains of three of the women and four of the ambushers. After Elsa fell into the water, the remaining women had four shots and made each of them count. Animals had been at all the bodies and all that remained were a few bones and clothing. They had all been stripped of weapons, which meant that someone survived, as Elsa had no idea of how many ambushers there had been. They couldn't even tell which of the women had survived. Whoever it was, the chance that she was alive after nearly six months with the abductors was slight. After a quick burial of the remains of the women, Kanti and Elsa stood over the graves for quite a while silently looking off into the vastness of the west. They came to realize how insignificant humans were out there and how easily lives were lost and forgotten. They thought about how each of the women was the daughters of someone, somewhere. Each had then married and set off full of hope to the west, ran into unbelievable hardship, and were lost to their loved ones and history.

With the breeze at their backs, they set off down the northern branch of the Platte to its confluence with the southern branch. Kanti noticed the faint smell of smoke coming from upriver, but never said anything to Elsa because he didn't want to add to her mourning. She smelled it as well. Each thought to themselves that they could outrun any possible trouble from that direction. The upriver strangers were renegade Indian and Mexican slavers from the south that had come north the previous summer and got stuck for the winter. Every year they came north to abduct Indian women, and now a white woman too, for sale in the south. Four had been killed in their skirmish with the women, one went down river and never returned, that left three plus their prisoner. They had holed up by digging a small cave into the south side of one of the sandstone buttes, and had been able to kill enough game to survive the winter. The Platte was raging and there was no chance to cross it for they would have been drowned for sure. They would have to wait for it to subside, which could take them clear into June or July. So, in the meantime, they scouted the surrounding area for Indian camps killing any they could and trying unsuccessfully to abduct women. Their presence was, of course, known to the Arapaho and Cheyenne and it would take little for a small war party to find and kill them all. One of them had gone down river to see if there were any Indian camps there and had seen Kanti and Elsa going southeast at a fast lope. They were out of sight in a dozen seconds; but now the slavers knew there must be white folks somewhere down river. The slavers spent the next day packing up to head off down river and collect the other woman for the trip south. They should have known they would not get away with the killing of several small hunting parties and both the Arapaho and the Cheyenne were coming after them. The slavers were more vicious than smart, and a group of eight could afford to be much more arrogant out alone in the west than the three that remained.

But, unfazed, the raiders headed southeast with one thing in mind. An Arapaho war party was waiting for them about one day down the river. On top of that, a Cheyenne war party was following behind them. As they were making camp at the end of the very first day, the three slavers were hit with several arrows each. They didn't die immediately and moaned piteously, as they were scalped alive. Finally, after several hours, they had bled to death, were stripped of their weapons, money and horses and left to the animals of the prairie. Their female prisoner was allowed the use of a horse, given some food and pointed on to the southeast. It was common knowledge among the Indian tribes that a sod house had been built at the confluence. Further, the owner of the soddy appeared to be a good and considerate neighbor and would be allowed to stay unthreatened.

Winters in St Louis were quite mild compared to those at Fort Pitt. Several boat loads of goods had arrived in December, and Ilse and Giles had their hands full storing it all so it was dry for the winter. O'Brian had finally gotten the word that Giles needed him and was on one of the boats. He brought word that Giles' stepfather, Shenandoh was over 100 years old and nearly blind, but sharp of mind. They immediately started planning to expand the business up to Independence and after outfitting several boats with the tools and provisions they would need, Giles and O'Brian set off up the Missouri in the dead of winter. If they ran into a storm, they would have to hole up somewhere until it passed. O'Brian's two trusted lieutenants manned the other boat. So, Ilse was alone once again. She had resigned herself to the fact that Giles had a limited time to live and that she would encourage him to be adventurous and active in the mean time. Even in winter, she had plenty to do caring for the animals and arranged their mercantile goods for sale come spring. She was interested in politics and formed a local council of elders to oversee the rapidly growing little city. She saw to it that a sheriff was hired that could keep the cardsharps, drunks, thieves and pickpockets under control, and she organized a merchant's group that promoted honesty and fair play toward each other and their pioneer customers. Most importantly, she secured an agreement among the town merchants to pay some of the unemployed men to remove the horse manure from the streets, pile it away from the town where the odor would not be a problem, and where it could be used for gardens.

When O'Brian and Giles reached Independence, they quickly located a strategic spot and put up two tents for living while building a trading post. The dwelling itself would be much larger than any they had before, primarily because of the abundance of straight, tall trees. It would have ten foot ceilings with an upstairs for sleeping up to 20 people. When the overly fat woman and her skinny partner saw the size of the building the four strangers were building, they immediately planned to go south on the next boat. She started frequenting the work site, offering herself for the pleasure of the men, and when that didn't have any effect, she tried to sell her odd collection of goods to Giles. She needed money for the trip to New Orleans. Giles surprised her and paid a fair price, and for his fairness, gained an unlikely friend. Upon completion of the post, and at the first sign of spring, Giles was again headed south and home. He was feeling nostalgic as he floated down river and had time to think about his life, and its many hair-raising experiences. He had been lucky just to survive. As he became older, he also became more retrospective and thankful for God's help. He would make it home in time for the spring planting of vegetables. This year, they planned to add corn and potatoes to their garden. He was filled with thanks for his life and hope for his short future, and when he cleared the last bend the tears came.

About half way through winter, the Harmons realized it was just a matter of time before they would be discovered. The canyon was hundreds of miles long and surely they could find a spot where they wouldn't be under the constant threat of exposure. In their first cave, there were two major encampments of Indians within ten miles or so. In the dark of early morning, they carefully left their little cave and crept up a ravine and out the top of the canyon. They skirted the canyon rim for dozens of miles frequently peering carefully down into the bottom searching for Indian villages. Toward the western end, they found a spot. It was easily accessible from the top, along the northern side for full sunshine, and close to water and wood. They constructed a small lean-to for the horses and dug a cave in the cliff face as a place to sleep. Their nearest neighbor was at least 30 miles to the east. In several months they would be able to set off to the west into unknown territory. What they didn't know was, that to the west of them was the Llano Estacado, one of the largest, driest most desolate and unforgiving areas in southern America.

The creek, later known as prairie dog town creek, never froze over and the Harmons could see a multitude of fish swimming therein. They tried spearing the fish, but the distortion under the water kept them from hitting any. A needle bent into a semicircle and some gut pulled out into a thin string for line, finally started to give results. The Harmons had to creep up to the edge of the bank and with the line tied to the end of a willow branch, then slowly lower the hook and bait into the water. If they were visible in any way, the fish would scatter and hide under the overhanging banks. The pair couldn't even allow their shadow to hit the water. Nearly every evening they had fresh fish for supper, and they smoked a large quantity for later.

It seemed that early morning and late evening were the best fishing times, and it was late afternoon that the two were lying along the bank when they heard then saw a large party of mounted Indians coming up the canyon. If they stood to run, they would certainly be seen. They remained motionless on the ground for several moments. The route the Indians were on, appeared to take them within easy view 50 feet or so up opposite bank of the creek. The Harmons hadn't been spotted when they slowly rolled over to the edge of the creek bank and eased down into the water. Then as the Indians continued closer, they eased under the overhanging bank and found an air pocket. The water was beastly cold and they knew they could only stand it for several minutes. From their hiding place under the bank, they could look out into the stream and see the shadows of the mounted Indians. They had left their fishing pole on the ground. They hoped the Indians wouldn't be observant enough to notice the tiny string of gut tied on the end. The Indians had paused for some reason at that very spot, and the worry intensified in the hidden pair. Even though they could breath, the air was dank and cold and only added to their desperation. Finally, the Indians moved off to the west, and the Harmons slowly crawled out of the creek and pulled themselves up on the grassy bank and into the warm sun. They removed their clothing without standing up and let the fading sun warm their bodies. Even though they had eluded trouble, they knew the Indians would surely come across their tracks somewhere in the area, and that was exactly what happened. Within a quarter mile upstream, there were clear tracks of horses lingering in the grassy areas and drinking from the creek. The Harmons' horses were unshod and unsaddled and left the tracks of wild horses and unless the Indians saw the actual tracks of humans, they would be uninterested. After a brief search, and a ride to the top of the canyon rim, the Indians decided to move on. It was enough of a scare that the Harmons knew they would have to go also. That night they packed up all their provisions and smoked fish, and at first light they set off to the west along the canyon rim. They intentionally stayed away from the interior of the canyon because that was where the group of Indians had gone.

In several days, they had left the canyon behind and were entering the dry, flat Llano Estacado. Fortunately, it was the spring of the year, and a few of the creeks had water, and the temperature was still tolerable. The land was tilted, and going west it seemed they were always going up-hill. The further they went, the hotter and drier it became. A small water hole here and there had saved them, but even those disappeared. It had only been a week or so from the time they left the canyon and they were already in trouble. Not knowing they were only a hundred miles or so from the Pecos River, they turned to the north hoping to cross a river or creek. But it was not to be. There were none. They knew that within days, the horses would fail and if that happened, they would probably perish. So, they turned back to the east, they would have to find another way across the high plains. On they went, their horses were starting to stumble and they were walking, each pulling their horses behind.

Once again they had to pool their water and let the best horse drink it. Then young Harmon, mounted the horse and with all the empty water containers and his bow, rode on to the east to the nearest water. Old Harmon would wait alone with the three remaining horses out on the open plain knowing if young Harmon didn't return, he would die of thirst. After a day went by, old Harmon decided to walk with the horses slowly to the east. If he could cut down the distance by just a few miles it may save him or the horses. Two days to the east, young Harmon was starting to get desperate. His horse had faltered and he had to dismount to keep it from falling. He was so dry, he was starting to see hallucinations of animals, trees and creeks in the distance. Off to his right he thought he saw the canyon where they had wintered in the distance, but he couldn't be sure his eyes weren't tricking him.

A group of Indians was riding directly at him. He was unconcerned because he knew they weren't real. As they got closer, one of the Indians yelled and then he knew they were real, but there was nothing he could do to defend himself, and he just stood and watched them ride up and surround him. They discussed whether or not to kill him and take his horse. He of course knew not what they were saying, but realized they were looking for some redeeming sign that they should allow him to live. One tossed a water bag made from the stomach of an animal to young Harmon, and rather than drink himself, he poured some in his hat and gave it to his horse. When his horse had a good drink, he finally had some himself. This impressed the Indians, was the sign they were looking for, and saved his life. Young Harmon insisted that he shake the hand of each of the Indians, and they took this unusual gesture as a sign of friendship. They sat around young Harmon for several hours until both he and his horse were fully hydrated and during that time pointed out the quickest route to water. They were also curious about the bow he carried and set up a small leather shield a couple feet in diameter, some 30 steps away and started shooting at it and gestured for him to join them. After his first shot hit the shield dead in the center, the Indians all cheered. Then one of them went out and retrieved his arrow and scratched a six inch circle in the middle of the shield. All the Indians gestured for him to shoot again, thinking he must have been lucky. So he held the bow and five arrows in his left hand and drew back and launched an arrow, then another and another until all had hit the target in the circle in about five seconds. The Indians were astonished, and this time each had to shake his hand again as they slapped him on the back and talked furiously among themselves. This small group of a dozen fit and ferocious looking Indians, had just become life-long friends with the first white man they had ever seen. They called him "Hummmunn," gave him another skin full of water and sent him on his way. Through sign language, he pointed them at his track to the west and told them to go help old Harmon as it would take him at least three more days to get water out there.

Old Harmon had just about given up. All three horses would not move and he had unloaded them of saddle and provisions. He was sitting on his heels looking to the east. He could have walked, but didn't want to leave the horses to wander away and die. If, by some slim chance young Harmon had found water and was on his way back, they would still need the horses to continue their journey. Old Harmon was seeing hallucinations and could swear there was a lake just a mile or so away. He had been seeing mirages most of the last several days, but now they were more vivid than ever. Out of the mirage it looked like a group of horses were running directly at him. He almost smiled at how real they looked. They kept coming and he could see people on the horses' backs. Then he realized the people were Indians and they were not hallucinations. He had no place to hide, couldn't run and certainly couldn't defend himself. He tried to get his musket loaded, but was so uncoordinated was unable to. This was going to be the end of his life, and he was resigned to leave this earth with dignity. He sat on his heels, too weak to move anything but his eyes. An Indian dismounted and came over and looked directly into his face. Two of his horses were lying down and the Indians lifted their heads and gave them water. Then Harmon felt someone hold his head and gently put water in his mouth. At first he couldn't swallow and the water ran back out on the ground. A few drops trickled down his throat and gradually he began to swallow. After several hours of care by the Indians both old Harmon and his horses were up and moving around slowly. The Indians pointed to the east and said, "Hummunn." Slowly, old Harmon got the point, and smiled at his newly found friends. Then he too, had to shake the hand of each of the fierce looking men helping him. Old Harmon shared his smoked fish with his friends and a while later, they took off to the west, and he mounted his horse and started east.

Shortly before sunset, he spotted young Harmon coming from the east at a lope. It was completely dark when they finally descended back down into Palo Duro Canyon. They had gone in a giant complete circle, and nearly perished. Old Harmon couldn't get over the fact that the Indians had used up a lot of their water reviving both he and young Harmon, and then headed straight west into the Llano. They must have known where they could find water. He had no confidence that he and his young friend could do the same, so he suggested they again go back to the north and pick up the westward course of one of the big rivers.

The young woman found herself with food, water, and fur clothing, riding a good quality horse with a loaded musket in the holster. She couldn't believe her luck and hoped she could remember the faces of the Arapaho warriors that had saved her life. She had been abducted three times in the last year and had survived them all, unhurt except for her pride. Before she left her Arapaho friends, she had given each man a hug and a kiss on the cheek, and told them she would be a friend for life. Of course, they didn't understand a word of what she had said, but felt her friendship and gratitude through her gestures. She set her horse into a ground eating lope and followed the north fork down-stream. Every little hill she came to, she paused and looked back and for a while could see a faint trail of dust disappearing over the horizon. Finally, there was nothing left but a memory of those magnificent men and their painted horses. Bella decided that once she got to Kanti's soddy, she would take the next boat back downriver; "to hell with this pioneer stuff."

Kanti and Elsa were in the middle of their garden when they heard Bella yelling and galloping toward them. Elsa screamed with relief when she saw that lone rider slapping the horse wildly and yelling with joy. At first, Elsa couldn't tell which of her friends had survived, but when she recognized Bella, she started screaming her name. Kanti just stood and watched the emotional spectacle; he was happy for Elsa, and even happier for Bella. When they weren't working in the garden, they were trying to keep the birds and ground animals out of it. Another soddy, a smaller one, was about half completed. Fresh sod was cut to finish it and repair the first sod house. Sod was a good building material for the winter when everything was frozen, but the rain in spring and summer slowly washed the dirt out of the root matrix and would cause it to collapse. So the sod houses required constant repair. Bella had camped in a stand of evergreen trees up-river a half day's ride and suggested they go up and cut the

logs then float them down the river so they could use them for
building.

Nearly a dozen groups of pioneers came through the camp
at the confluence that summer. The three intrepid inhabitants
were busy from light to dark every day with the garden, the
new log trading post, firing clay containers for the recipe, and
hunting just enough for their needs. They had several visits from
the Arapaho and Bella outdid herself with kindness for each of
them. She insisted on giving each of the ferocious looking men
hugs and kissed their cheeks. They didn't know quite how to
accept her admiration, but clearly liked the attention. When they
finally rode over the last hill and out of sight, they would always
stop, and shout their friendship and wave goodbye for now. She
was quite the charmer. The boats that brought their goods up
river were well received and went back with letters detailing the
events of the winter. Bella fell in love with her work and her two
partners and decided to stay. Sometimes at night, she would cry
and Elsa would get up and hold and soothe her. They became as
close as two humans could possibly be.

The chokecherry bushes were thick with berries and Kanti
was nearly hidden trying to reach what had looked like the ripest
ones. He heard several horses walking nearby and then the voices
of men speaking a language he couldn't understand. Peering
out, he saw a two mounted, rough looking men trailing several
more horses with what looked to be Indian women tied and
slung over their backs. He knew immediately, that he had to
get back to the post and warn the women, but if he moved, he
would surely be seen. Their route would take them somewhat
east of the buildings and if they looked up river at just the right
time the raiders would see the new log house. The two slavers
stopped and watered their horses in the river and pulled their six
prisoners off the horses and let them drop roughly to the ground.
They were still not in sight of the trading post and Kanti was
able to slip out the opposite side of the bushes and back to get
his bow. He signaled to Bella and Elsa there was danger. It was
very unusual for slavers from the south to adventure north in

such a small group. Either the rest of the raiders had been killed, or were waiting to meet this pair somewhere down the trail. It looked as if the pair wanted to take a long rest as they pulled the saddles off their horses and partially untied their captives so they could drink from the river.

In short order, Elsa and Bella each had a loaded musket and Kanti his bow. The three had decided they had to kill the slavers where they were and could not let them get away. For if they did, they might join up with a larger group and become even more dangerous. Further, the women appeared to be in bad shape and were begging for something to eat. It was nearly noon and Kanti knew time was short. They had to move quickly, but the slavers were down in a little hollow and it was unlikely anyone could get a clear shot without being seen. Someone would have to draw them out into the open. Bella and Kanti were to take up positions for a clear shot, while Elsa would lure the cutthroats out of the hollow. Elsa smeared dirt on her clothing and face so she would look like she was lost and needed help. She was to come over the ridge up-hill from the hollow and yell for help as she fell to the ground, seemingly injured or starved. When Elsa thought her partners were in position, she went into her act. Immediately, the two slavers trained their rifles on her and yelled for her to come to them. But, she couldn't get up and began crawling slowly toward them. The slavers smelled a trap and stayed put. So Elsa collapsed and laid on the ground waving weakly for help. The raiders untied one of the Indian women and sent her up to Elsa with water. The Indian woman tried to help Elsa to her feet, but was so weak herself she could not. So there they sat.

After a long time, the slavers figured it was OK to come out, so one of them trudged up the hill toward the two women. He roughly slapped and kicked the Indian back down toward the hollow and bent over to pick up Elsa when an arrow struck him in the center of his buttocks and penetrated deeply into his abdomen. He fell immediately screaming in pain from what was a mortal wound, but would require some time for death. His partner yelled at him to get up and come back, not knowing what had happened as he was far enough away that he could not hear the pffffft of the arrow. All he knew was that his partner had fallen and was screaming in pain, for no reason. The slaver on the ground didn't even know what had happened as he had suddenly felt this immense pain in his lowers. He didn't see or hear anything; all the guy knew was the pain was overpowering and he passed out. He wasn't dead but would be in several hours. Elsa crawled over to the motionless stranger and slowly took his musket, cocked the hammer, and laid it across his body aiming at the raider in the hollow. If he moved or raised to any degree, she would nail him. She knew he would have to do something soon as he was sounding desperate and she was the only one with a decent shot. The odor of the wounded slaver was overpowering and she began to breathe through her mouth to avoid it. It seemed like hours passed, the raider in the hollow had given up trying to arouse his partner. Kanti had crept up so he was only feet away just barely out of sight over a mound of soil and grass. He had his hatchet and knife and was waiting for his chance. He could hear the slaver cussing under his breath and breathing loudly. Suddenly the slaver began yelling again. Then a shot rang out and the Indian women screamed, for he has shot one of them. Another shot boomed, this time from a musket and the women screamed again. The stranger was killing his hostages. Now, Kanti sprang and caught the slaver before he could raise a third weapon, hitting him in the top of the head with the hatchet. The slaver dropped straight down, stone dead. The four remaining Indian women began weeping loudly at their ordeal, as Kanti untied them. The slaver with the arrow in his innards, regained consciousness and moaned for a long time. Grabbing him by the feet, Bella and Elsa drug him down into the hollow where they could cover both him and his partner with dirt and sand. The Indian women took the needle sharp ends of some soap weed and pierced his eyes, which made him scream even more. Finally after many hours the slaver passed, and Kanti returned that evening and covered the two with dirt, knowing the animals would find them within hours.

Several days later, the Indian women were fairly well recovered. Kanti put them on four of the horses with provisions for a week or so and sent them off to the north back to their homes. They tied the two dead women across one of the horses for eventual proper burial. Finally, our three intrepid pioneers were back to the trading post preparing to make as much of the recipe and smoked meat as possible. In several months, winter would be roaring in again and before they knew it they would be pinned down to reading the dozens of books sent up-river on the boats. Each of them looked forward to the boredom of winter.

Young Harmon wanted to go all the way across the first river, which would be named the Canadian and take the second, the Arkansas, to the west while staying on the southern bank. The Arkansas was much bigger and certainly must have its beginning in some kind of highlands. Of course they realized there were mountains in the west, but had no comprehension of their size. It was early in the summer and the streams and rivers were raging torrents. They couldn't cross the Canadian and had to follow it to the west, which turned out to be the direction they wanted to go. Several hundred miles to the west the river turned north. The Harmons were picking up glimpses of the snow capped Rocky Mountains and thought they must be seeing clouds down on the horizon. The river was taking them parallel to the mountains and as the elevation increased, the river rapidly dwindled until it finally was so small they crossed and continued on to the north. Snow capped mountains filled the horizon, west, north and east and they became apprehensive about their route. Once into the mountains, the going was very difficult and they repeatedly had to backtrack and find another route. The canyons were impassable, the mountains too steep. They finally found their way up to the Arkansas River deep in the heart of the mountains. They realized they must stay in the large valleys and avoid the deep canyons, and made their way up into what became central Colorado, home of the Ute Indians. There was plenty of wood for fires and shelter under the giant fir trees. The nights were cold and the days warm and sunny. They saw multitudes of beaver dams, elk, and deer, and had thoughts of staying there, but there were no humans. They had never seen nor heard of elk before and were astounded at this great animal, three or four times larger than the largest deer. Occasionally they caught a glimpse of a catamount, usually standing in plain sight, watching back. Moose were there too, but in smaller numbers, and then there were the wolves. It seemed everywhere they went they were followed by the wolves. But, some of the sounds in the forest and the flickers of motion back in the trees weren't wolves; they were something much more sinister.

One sunny morning in late summer, old Harmon went off into the trees to do his daily toiletries. Young Harmon thought he heard a slight gasp coming from that direction, and called out to old Harmon. There was no answer. After a few minutes, young Harmon called out again, this time louder. Again, there was no answer, so he went looking. There was nothing, no sign of a struggle, no blood; only the stools were left behind. Young Harmon yelled loud and long without response. His first thought was that old Harmon was taken by one of the animals. It could have been the old Harmon simply walked off investigating something and fell into the gorge or the roaring creek. Young Harmon spent the next several days looking for his partner without success. Coming back to camp after a long fruitless day of searching, Harmon saw the clear track of a moccasin in a soft place. Then on close inspection, there was another track, and another larger one. The hair stood on the back of his neck as he suddenly realized old Harmon had been killed. But why didn't the intruders simply attack him, he was alone and all he had was a bow for protection. The Ute had seen his extreme skill with the bow and didn't want to take a chance that he would kill one of them, so they waited for the best opportunity, but he took it everywhere he went, and that probably saved his life. When he was in sight of his camp, he could see the horses were gone.

As he crept closer, he saw that someone had taken everything, and he squatted and sat on his heels in the brush, motionless. Over an hour went by before the Ute began to move around. They knew he was approaching, but had lost track of his exact location. Slowly and one by one they came into sight. They were big men and all of them carried weapons. Harmon held his hiding place and didn't dare move for they would have been on him in a flash. After a brief search, the Indians disappeared into the trees. Harmon thought they had given up looking for him and felt it safe to move about, but it was a ruse. The Ute had gone into the woods and slowly fanned out knowing that sooner or later Harmon would show himself and they would have him surrounded. As Harmon, slowly turned his head, he could see two of the Indians behind him. They were stationary each standing with a tree at his back, simply watching for movement. It was late in the day and Harmon's only hope was to wait until complete darkness and try to creep away.

Hours went by and Harmon remained in motionless in his hiding place. The night was passing and occasionally he could hear soft movement around him. He was determined to out wait them. At first light the next day, he looked around and didn't see anyone. It was the twilight before dawn, and he couldn't be sure, but it seemed that they were gone. He knew it was now or never, and with only his bow and the clothes on his back, he moved very slowly out to the northeast away from the camp and away from the Indians. When he was several hundred yards away from the area, there was a sudden shout. An Indian had spotted him and was running directly at him. The race was on. Harmon was quite tall and long legged and could run like his Father and Uncles. The Indians were close on his heels and he couldn't afford a fall. They were good runners also, so he would have to keep up a fast pace to stay out of their grasp. The ground was rough, covered with trees and brush and marshy places. He could leap the creek, flying from one bank clear over to the other barely breaking stride. The Indians could not and had to struggle splashing into the water, falling down, and then struggling up the opposite bank. His headlong flight quickly took Harmon out of the valley bottom and up the mountain to the east. He knew not where he was going; he did know that he would have to run all day to lose them, and he did.

It was midday when Harmon slowed down and looked back for some sign of his followers. He kept going at a good pace, but not frantic, for several more hours; when he finally paused and ate the last of the jerky in his pocket, he realized his perilous situation. He had no provisions, no skins for protection at night, no way to carry water and most of all no companion. He thought old Harmon was dead but couldn't accept it. He had looked for him for several days after old Harmon's disappearance, without success; he couldn't return to the area because of the risk of being killed by the Ute's. By that time he had come upon the upper waters of the South Platte and had given up on his quest for the west. He knew he had to survive and return to St Louis somehow, someway. He spent that night in a dry space under a big spruce, buried in branches, grass and pine needles. He was high up on the east face of a mountain looking down a 1000 ft or so on a sizeable river. He took inventory in his pouch and had his flint, compass, and a piece of cloth with the recipe stitched in. He had his skinning knife, hatchet and bow with six arrows. His well worn breeches and shirt would have to do until he could kill an animal and prepare the hide. His shoes were in bad shape and one of the very first things he had to make was a pair of moccasins with a padded sole. So, the first order of business was to kill a deer sized animal.

Old Harmon had just finished his daily toilet, and as he stood up something hit him on the head and everything went dark. When he woke up, he was bound and had a thick, foul tasting strip of leather tied around the back of his head and in his mouth. He was sure he could hear young Harmon calling his name, but could not respond. After a while several good sized adult Indian men quietly sat down beside him and checked and rechecked his bonds. Harmon couldn't recognize where he was located, except that he was the captive of some severe looking men. They pulled him to his feet; it seemed to be about mid-day, and prodded him along a very faint trail that led off to the west. One was ahead and the other Indian was behind. Their pace was quick, and the trail was well hidden to the casual observer. In the distance, old Harmon thought he could hear young Harmon calling his name, and as they passed over the crest of a ridge, it faded away. He couldn't figure out why they had captured him and not his young friend. Long after dark and after many miles, Harmon and his dual guards, stopped for the night. They untied his hands and let him wash in the stream. The two Utes gestured for him to sit down by the fire and handed him several pieces of some kind of animal fat mixed with berries and seeds. As he was eating, one of the Indians looked him in the eye, smiled and asked, "What the hell are you doing here?" He spoke in perfect English.

Young Harmon was successful in his quest for meat and hides. The Utes had not followed him and he was truly alone. He hoped old Harmon was alive, but was slowly coming to believe in his demise. He knew his only chance for survival was to make his way downriver away from the mountains, so he followed the river on its tortured route around impassable gorges and into the foothills of the eastern edge of the Rocky Mountains. By this time it was well into fall, and he began to worry about the coming winter. This would be his second, since leaving St Louis, and he resigned himself that it would be his last. The path of the river finally left the last mountain ravine and broke out onto the flat lands of what was to become north eastern Colorado. The flow of the river was slow and the main channel was fairly narrow. There were large shallow areas over most of the river bed, but the main flow of water was in the main channel. He set out to make a small raft that would float him down river at three or four miles per hour, 12 hours a day. The river was quite comfortable and the mosquitoes mild. Young Harmon figured to simply let the river carry him all the way to St Louis.

The country side through which the river passed was very desolate and covered with desert bushes and cactus. Other than a tiny dry creek that joined the river every several days, there was no sign of any break in the desert country. The river valley was quite wide and deep indicating that in the spring, the waters multiplied many times. A steady supply of animals came to the river for sustenance, and young Harmon was well fed and clothed. He stopped regularly and camped in likely sheltered spots along the river for days at a time. He had squandered any chance he had to make St Louis before winter. Actually in mere weeks, he would be faced with digging into the side of the river bank for protection from the early season blizzards that raced down from the north. If he continued on down the south branch of the Platte, he would eventually run directly into the Kanti's trading post.

Young Harmon had a simple five log raft tied together with strips of green bark. He had to constantly repair it, but it was easy to guide and kept him and his hide bundle mostly dry. He had used animal fat to coat the smooth side of several of his animal hides so they were water proof and stitched them together with narrow strips of hide, into a crude but effective poncho. He enjoyed stopping a number of times each day and climbing up on the bank to look around the countryside. He salvaged an animal stomach and bladder as water carriers.

A sizeable cloud of dust was being stirred up some miles to the east and it looked as if it was coming his way. He went down and pulled his raft into a place where it was partially obscured. As the dust got closer he could see horses and riders moving fast and coming parallel to the river and the bank on which he stood. He jumped down beside the bank and peered over the edge, watching apprehensively. As they approached closer, he ducked lower and lower. The riders were white men each pulling a short string of pack-horses. They were obviously running from something or someone. Young Harmon didn't know whether to reveal himself or not as it looked like the riders would be passing right on by. Their horses were laboring and some were lathered, but the men whipped them relentlessly. They were definitely afraid of whatever was following, and Harmon didn't need the trouble, so he stayed hidden below the bank. After several minutes the riders had gone off to the west and all was quiet. It would be impossible for the heavily laden horses to elude a group of mounted Indians. But sure enough, an hour later, here came a group of several dozen Indians loping along saving the strength of their animals, and knowing the white men would soon exhaust theirs. It was an impressive group; the horses were painted in one way or another and the Indians rode them effortlessly almost as if they were a part of the animal. Young Harmon was glad they weren't after him as he watched the spectacle go out of sight to the west. He knew that if the Indians had ill intentions for the white men, there was no hope for them. If he could just get a hold of one of their horses though, it could save his life.

The Indian that had just spoken to old Harmon had brown hair and light brown eyes. There was some patchy facial hair much different from any other Indians Harmon had ever seen. Harmon stared at the young man of about 20 and introduced himself, then shook the man's hand. It turned out that this was one of the many half Indian children of Thomas James$_r$, one of the original responsible mountain men. The two sat for several hours and talked and each told his story to the other. Old Harmon couldn't understand the man's Indian name so he called him Jameson. The man explained to Harmon that the Ute had no reason to attack the Harmons, but they feared most white men and didn't want them to encroach on Ute territory. Several mountain men had come through in the last several years that had been antagonists of the Ute and indiscriminately killed all they could see. Jameson made it clear they didn't like that kind of behavior and would not tolerate it. The Ute had followed the Harmons for several weeks to determine whether or not they were just passing through. They had seen young Harmon shoot his bow with astonishing accuracy, and knew they didn't want to be on the receiving end of any arrows. Jameson didn't know the welfare of young Harmon, but reassured old Harmon that their intentions were not deadly, and they simply wanted to let him know to move on. The Ute had been seeking a friendly white man, and wanted old Harmon to come with them to act as a go-between and negotiator with any white men that might encroach on their land. Old Harmon was faced with a decision. Should he stay and survive or go back and try to find young Harmon, who most certainly had perished or was completely out of the area? Jameson finally convinced old Harmon that he would be comfortable and well respected among the Ute. Harmon's power of persuasion would finally be used in a place and time nobody could have anticipated. Many years would go by before he would see familiar faces.

A letter had arrived via the fledgling mail service of the time. It was worn and dog-eared and had been wet, but there it was. The date on the front was nearly a year ago, and as near as Giles could see it was from New Orleans. Could it be? Yes, it was a letter from Doig; he was alive. He had made the mistake of taking his wife and children with him and set out straight into the middle of what is now Texas. But, it was controlled by the Mexicans and was part of their country. Doig's letter was damaged so badly, Giles could only decipher several sentences. Doig's wife and children had been killed and he had survived by literally out running his attackers. He was in New Orleans and wanted to start up the business, and that was all that was readable. Giles had never been to New Orleans; so come summer 1813, he would set out on what could be his very last adventure.

The Mississippi was so large in the spring, boat traffic was sparse. A few danger seeking souls rode it downstream, but Giles wasn't willing to take the chance. It finally fell to summer levels and river traffic picked up to a fever pitch. The raft Giles was on was actually more of a boat as it had some crude structures that could be used for sleeping and protection from the weather. Most of the deck was loaded with freight and the passengers had to find a place to sit either on or between the bundles and wooden boxes. The raft would be taken apart and used for wood once in New Orleans. One of the women on the raft, sang to the other passengers from time to time and Giles finally joined in. She was a Spanish lady and there were few songs common to the two. But gradually they both adapted and were able to combine their talents and win the hearts of their fellow passengers. Giles noticed when he sang he had to breathe more often and this became a small worry.

New Orleans was a place to get lost, and it reminded him of Glasgow. There was no pattern and the streets ran helter- skelter in all directions. Giles knew two people there, Doig and the overly fat woman from Independence. He knew Doig would be involved in some sort of mercantile enterprise and that the fat woman would be in prostitution, so he started going into every one he saw. Everywhere he asked, people looked at him as if he was stupid, as few folks actually spoke English. It had been years and years since he heard French, but slowly the words came back into his memory. After several weeks, he thought he had been into every place of business that sold supplies or food. But there was no Doig. It was such an unusual name, he thought people would remember it. He did finally find the overly fat woman; she was the manager and proprietor of a large house of ill repute, and insisted that he take a nice room on the second floor at no charge. It was an odd friendship between the straight laced, honest and loyal Giles and the devious, deceptive and dishonest overly fat woman. The women, that worked there, tittered privately at the contrast, and at the same time showed the greatest courtesy and understanding to Giles, who was old enough to be their grandfather. In the evenings, Giles sang to the women; his voice was weak and husky with age, but they each fell in love with the old gentlemen and wished they could have known him years before.

Try as he might, though, there was simply nobody in New Orleans by the name of Doig or McGillavry. It had been more than a year since the letter was written, and maybe Doig had moved on. But surely someone would have remembered the name. It finally occurred to Giles that Doig too was in his sixties and he might have taken sick. After a week of searching out doctors of all kinds, he was finally guided to a thin old man setting in the evening sun, staring into the sunset. It looked like Doig, but the man was so severely thin, he couldn't be sure. The thin man didn't respond to Giles' voice, and he simply stared through Giles' face as if he could not see him. Dejectedly, Giles returned to his room and spent the evening trying to think of something that would help him determine whether or not it was Doig. Then in the middle of the night, he remembered that Doig had a deep scar in his shoulder from a Seneca arrow; when morning came he was off to see the thin man once again. The chair in which the little man sat was empty, and Giles questioned everyone around as to the whereabouts of its user. He found that the man had expired during the night and was at the undertaker's emporium. It was there that Giles discovered that his last cousin had passed; the scar was there. Without someone he could trust in New Orleans, the chance of starting a new business diminished substantially. In the process of looking for Doig, he discovered the city already had a plethora of mercantile shops, so he returned to his room and prepared to leave on the next boat north.

Young Harmon made a serious mistake in thinking some of the horses would get away in the melee that was to follow the white men. He was nearly desperate in his quest for a horse as he couldn't be certain the river he was following would ever take him anywhere of benefit. He set out on foot to the west following the river and short cutting many of the bends. He had his weapons and as much of his fur bundle as he could comfortably carry and maintain a good pace. He knew the white men's horses would give out in several hours at the most so he only had to go 20 miles or so to find the scene of the coming massacre. If he could reach the scene of the battle in three hours, it would be about sundown and he could scout the area without being seen.

It appeared as if the white men had set up an ambush for the Indians, in hopes to kill enough that it would discourage the rest. It hadn't fooled the Indians though and the battle must have been brief. Once the white men had emptied their weapons of the single shot, the Indians overwhelmed them. Harmon counted thirteen white men killed and stripped of anything useful including their hair. The white bodies had been drug into a crude pile. There were no Indian bodies, though some must have been killed. He scouted around for any sign of horses that may have strayed during the confusion, but it was nearly dark and he was going to have to hole up for the night. He found a spot down by the river bank that was dry and out of the wind. There was a small hollow in the bank where he could snuggle down in his skins and be hidden from any scouts that may be around. It was logical that when the white men were being overrun, some of them fled into the brush by the river, and several Indians might have stayed behind until daylight to be sure none got away. He had been quiet and avoided silhouetting himself against the western horizon by staying low.

He was awakened by a scream and some groaning that came from upriver. It was beginning to get light in the east, and an Indian had surely come across a white man. The fracas continued for several minutes as it sounded like a desperate fight. Then, he heard a horse pounding off the east. It was exactly what he was hoping for. The fight became quiet as one or the other must have won, he couldn't be sure which. After a while, a voice cried out in English, calling several names. There was no answer. There were more cries for help. Harmon was not going to compromise his position until he knew he would not be attacked. After an hour or so, he slowly crawled out of his hollow and very slowly moved in the direction of the cries. He discovered a red headed boy with a fearsome gash in his head, crying and moaning, next to an Indian with a spear through his chest. The boy's scalp down to the bone had been torn partially loose and he had bled badly. Harmon dragged him away from the dead Indian and wiped the boy's face so he could see. He took out several long leather thongs and tied the flap of scalp tightly to the boy's head. The boy's name was Roidh, which meant reddish in Gaelic. Even though Harmon was born in America, he recognized an old Gaelic name and inquired as to the background of the boy. For several hours while the boy was recovering, Harmon scouted to the east looking for the horse he heard headed that way. He figured it had to stay in the river valley for food and water, but he had no success and returned for the boy. All the boy had were the clothes on his back and the spear he pulled from the dead Indian's chest. They took off to the east at a good clip, because Harmon anticipated some of the Indian party would return to see what happened to their friend. They walked in the shallow part of the river for the first day, to keep from leaving tracks. Early the second day, they reached the place where Harmon's raft was hidden, and there standing on the upper bank was the horse with saddle. It was puzzled and frightened and would have nothing to do with either Harmon or Roidh (pronounced Roy).

The boys tried repeatedly to get hold of the horse, but it was skittish enough that it would stay just out of their reach. So as if to say the heck with it, they got on the raft and started floating eastward. The horse followed. Going with the current was pretty smooth, and Roidh reassured Harmon that the river would take them all the way to Independence. The nights were growing very cold and each evening the boys would stop by the river down over the edge of the bank out of the wind and before a crackling fire, tell their individual stories. During one of those evening episodes, the horse came up behind Roidh and nuzzled the back of his neck. Roidh told the story of how he survived the attack of the Indians. He was instructed by his father to hide in the brush by the river from the beginning. He said the Indians came at the ambush from all directions and once the arrows started flying, the skirmish only lasted a few minutes. The Indians yelled and screamed ferociously as they finished off all the white men and Roidh knew he must remain hidden. Several of the white men tried to use the river for refuge and escape but were found out and slaughtered. Early the following morning Roidh was discovered by one of the Indians that stayed behind to finish any white men that may have survived. He said the Indian was creeping through the brush and was coming straight at him, so he suddenly stood up and yelled. This startled the Indian who slipped and fell in the middle of throwing his lance, which narrowly missed Roidh. He was able to get hold of the lance just as his feet slipped out from under him and fell flat on his back. The Indian jumped through the air, hatchet in hand, only to come down on his own spear which impaled him right through the chest. The Indian's hatchet came out of his hand and struck Roidh in the head glancing off his skull and tearing a chunk of scalp loose.

After they caught the horse, one of them rode it while the other stayed on the raft. The horse was relatively small and couldn't carry the both of them plus their bundle of skins. The South Platte River continued through dry country east and north for hundreds of miles. Late in the fall it was very low and sometimes the raft became stuck in the shallow water. After nearly dying of thirst several times, Harmon insisted they stay in the river valley and follow it back to civilization. So, the strange procession proceeded downriver, day after day, until winter displayed her fangs. It was mid-afternoon, the day was partly cloudy and suddenly a cold gust of wind out of the north struck the boys. They looked at each other and the cloud bank to the north and immediately pulled the raft up the bank adjacent to a ten foot overhang on the north bank of the river. By the time they had a small hole dug into the wall of the bank the snow was coming down hard and the wind had picked up out of the north. Their horse was smart and found it a spot out of the wind down below the edge of the river bank next to their cave. The Indian spear came in handy to loosen the soil so it could easily be scooped back out the mouth of the cave by hand. In an hour they had a cave large enough for the two of them and their bundle of hides. They had no time to gather any wood because the storm was so sudden and severe they couldn't venture beyond the protection of the river bank. They did have food and certainly water from the river was available just feet away. In the next several hours, the temperature dropped massively and the boys tied some of their hides over the horse's back to help protect her. They pulled the raft up to partially cover the opening to their cave and tied the horse to it. The sun should still have been up, but the storm was so severe, it was nearly dark. Each boy was frightened, but wouldn't reveal it to the other. The storm slowly intensified during the night and by morning the snow was so deep, they had trouble getting out to relieve themselves. Only a tiny bit of the river remained uncovered by the drifts, and this storm was just getting started.

The same storm hit Kanti and his friends sending them scurrying for cover in their new log cabin. Several of their horses were too far from the lean-to and were quickly lost. Fortunately Bella and Elsa were close to the trading post when the cold front hit but Kanti was a half mile away, and had to run for it. By the time they all got into the cabin and the windows closed, the snow was swirling and seeking every crack. This was going to be a bad one, and except for the horses, they were prepared. They had plenty of wood stored just outside the door and plenty food was stacked on makeshift shelves. Kanti still didn't feel the least bit comfortable, because he knew how severe these early storms could be. It was not a good way to start the winter. If there were any mule trains that were on the track along the Platte, their only hope would be to get down by the river out of the wind and try to hole up and last it out. Chances are they would lose half their animals and when the weather broke, they'd have to turn around and go back. The wind howled and moaned and snow found every tiny crack in the loggy. Bella and Elsa packed small strips of fur into the cracks in an effort to stop the intruding cold drafts. The day grew dark and it was difficult to keep candles lit because of the drafts, but slowly the women got all the cracks stuffed and they settled down to listening to the loggy creak and shake in the wind gusts.

The storm seemed to let up the following morning, but only for an hour or so. Then the sky darkened and the wind picked up again only it was out of the east this time. New drifts formed as the snow was redistributed. It was a total white-out. They had to brace the door shut, and for the first time Kanti was concerned about the integrity of the log structure. Fortunately there was a heavy load of snow on the roof or it would have been blown off. The wailing of the wind was becoming frightening to the three; they could see it in each other's faces. They just sat quietly, bundled in furs, and listened to the wind. Occasionally they thought they could hear someone or something calling from deep in the storm, and they would look at each other questioningly. They couldn't sleep, and each sat staring at the front door rattling against the braces they had placed to keep it shut. They lost track of time as the hours dragged on, not knowing when it was daytime or night. They finally fell asleep as the storm wailed and moaned.

Elsa woke with a start. The wind had stopped, but it was still dark. She slowly opened a window and the opening was completely covered with snow. She could see light coming through the snow and poked a big enough hole that she could see bright sunshine. She yelled at the others and in a few minutes Kanti had a big enough hole broken through the snow drift that he could get out. The door had been completely covered with a drift that went up over the roof of the log house. It was packed in so hard he had to use his metal shovel to cut a big enough tunnel so they could use the door. He looked in the direction of the lean-to and could only see snow that had drifted ten to twenty feet deep. It was a catastrophe; if the horses survived, he would be surprised. From the location of the sun, it looked to be about mid-day. The three would spend the next week cutting paths in the snow to the river, the lean-to, the soddy, root cellar and the outdoor toilet in reverse order. The four horses in the lean-to had survived by huddling together in the back corner. The ground was bare between drifts, and many of the monstrous piles of snow were so hard they could walk on them. They found if you stayed on the upwind side of a drift, the snow was packed in hard enough to support your weight. But if you ventured into the downwind side, it was soft and would completely cover you.

Eventually Kanti made his way up to the top of the hill just to the north of the cabin, and from there in every direction all that was visible was drifted snow. Down in the river bottom, the snow drifts were immense and most of the brush was completely covered. The river itself was covered except for a patch here and there. He became concerned for their future. Surely, no wildlife could have survived; they would be running out of food in mere weeks, and this was the beginning of winter. They couldn't go back downstream and couldn't set off across country on horseback, they were stuck. The first order of business had to be; find food. Kanti scouted on horseback as far as he could both up and down river. The only thing he saw was a few rabbits and squirrels. They were far too crafty and were safely out of sight by the time he came within range. The three had put up a small stack of grass to feed the horses in winter, but never anticipated anything like this, so they took to pulling up any grass that was exposed and taking the horses out to find grass on their own. It turned out the horses were very good at foraging. Gradually their food ran out. Kanti stopped eating first and after a few days the women did as well. They were going to have to kill one of the horses to survive and tried on several occasions to agree which one. Finally, without agreement from the women, Kanti decided to shoot the oldest horse, a mare, the following morning.

He absolutely hated having to kill the horse, but they were desperate, and he could see no other solution. That evening sitting quietly listening to the crackle of the fire, they were startled by shouting in the distance. It had become the greeting of the Arapahoe warriors they had befriended. They were shouting their friendship for the three settlers. In minutes, four warriors were at their door, were greeted warmly by the three and kissed and hugged by Bella. One of them, a particularly magnificent warrior, was among those that saved Bella from the slavers, and when she recognized him, he was showered with special kindness. It was obvious he reciprocated the admiration. They had two deer with them and immediately started preparing one for eating. Kanti stoked up the fire a little and in a few minutes more they had venison cooking on the spit. Even though they couldn't communicate directly, sign language sufficed. The Arapaho had come from down river some 40 miles where the storm was much milder and the game had survived. They had been a party of six, but the other two, had taken several more deer and headed at a gallop for the Arapaho village, where food was critically low. The small group sat drinking chokecherry wine and staring into the glowing coals of the fire late into the night, finally warm, fed and together. The friend ship between our three settlers and the Arapaho was deep, yet in the coming years would be sorely tested.

Roidh and young Harmon had no choice but to stay in their cave. The wind screamed and moaned for days and many times it was difficult to tell daytime from night. They started to wonder if the storm would ever quit, but it did. The drifts were so deep across the river, it would be spring before the water could be used for transport. The boys realized they must move with all haste, and loaded all the furs they could on the horse and set out on foot. Roidh's boots were nearly gone, so young Harmon made him some padded, water proof moccasins similar to those used by his Dad in the old days. They thought they should stay in contact with the river, and made a beeline to the east, northeast thanks to Harmon's old compass. Most of the time they were able to avoid the deep drifts and stay on relatively clear ground. There was plenty of exposed grass for the horse, but their food was going quickly. They had traveled for many days and had seen no animal tracks other than a few rabbits, and when their food was nearly gone, Roidh showed Harmon how to snare a rabbit. It turned out that rabbit was good eating and they came to living on them. The only problem was that setting snares was time consuming and their pace slowed considerably. Winter was setting in with a vengeance and the night temperatures were always well below freezing. They had taken to digging caves in the snow drifts down by the river for sleeping and covered their horse every night with furs. They tried to keep several rabbits in storage in case another storm pinned them down. All they had to do was persevere and they would make it back to civilization. Roidh recalled the small trading post at the confluence with a half Indian man and two attractive women. It was a long way off, but became their goal.

The trip north from New Orleans was slow as the flow of the Mississippi was heavy for that time of year. He wanted to get back to St Louis for the fall harvest and preparation of the next batch of McCucumbers. He knew Ilse would be apprehensive about his absence, so he talked the boat captain into several more hours each day on the water. The current was easier to handle close to the bank and it was there they encountered trouble. River raiders were common and it was standard procedure to have several heavily armed guards on each boat going north simply to discourage thieves. Out of the blue, one afternoon, came the shout, "Duck." Suddenly there was firing from the boat and from the shore. The captain and one of his men were hit as was Giles. The boat immediately turned sideways and started drifting back downriver. Another volley of lead balls hit the boat causing it to start leaking. They finally floated back out of the range of the shore raiders, but with three wounded people and a leaky boat continuing the trip was out of the question. They drifted with the current for several hours while those who were unhurt tried to help those that were. Finally they grounded far enough downstream they felt safe. The captain and his crewman were both seriously wounded and died within hours. Giles had a painful rib injury as the bullet apparently hit him a glancing blow and did little serious damage.

The next morning, the two bodyguards repaired the boat, pushed it back out into the current, and they floated out of control most of the day. Getting back to New Orleans without an experienced pilot was going to be difficult because of the dozens of channels that divided the great river near its end. If they took the wrong one it could take them into a dead end swamp or bayou or even worse into the open gulf. It would be a few days before they would have to select a channel, so maybe they could hire a new pilot from one of the northbound boats. Giles' wound had become infected and he was down with a serious fever. The festering in his side was oozing bloody puss and all they had was a little whiskey for disinfectant. They were told by a northbound captain to stay in the middle channel and to look for trees on which all the branches had been removed except one, and to go in the direction the lone branch pointed. Then New Orleans would be on their right. On their arrival in the city, Giles was nearly out of his mind with fever. The body guards took him to the overly fat woman's house where he was bedded in his second floor room. A doctor disinfected his wound and had to remove fragments of the lead ball from his rib and the surrounding tissue. If he survived, it would be a slow recovery. The overly fat woman wrote a personal letter to Giles' wife in St Louis and paid a boat captain she knew to deliver it personally without delay. One way or the other, he would miss the fall harvest. What an unlikely friend the overly fat woman was.

Giles had a fever for several more days, and the doctor returned to change the bandage and partake of the women every day. Changing the bandage was probably an excuse. He gradually got to the point where he could move around on his own, and he began singing to the women in the evenings. On one of those occasions a young Scotsman was visiting one of the ladies, and heard Giles sing one of the tunes of Inverness. It was a song his dad and uncle sang to his family and had been passed on to all the children. After the singing was finished for the evening, the young man approached Giles and inquired about his name. The name Giles McCumber didn't ring any bells with the youth, but when in the course of their conversation, "Macum" was mentioned, the boy blurted out that he was Brendan McGillivray and that Macum was his uncle. He spoke of Great Aunt Sarah and how she had gone to America and written back demanding that the entire family follow her. The letters Macum had written to Aunt Sarah, had described the freedom and hope of America so well the entire family was inspired. He said that a man by the name of Burton had arranged their indenture agreements with a merchant in Nova Scotia and that his father and uncle with their families still lived there. He had become infatuated with the promise of America and had taken a ship from Nova Scotia around to New Orleans, where he had hoped to find work that would take him on to the open country of the west. Giles listened intently with glistening eyes, remembering that he had spoken that very way, decades ago. He felt bound to Brendan even before he found out they had the same blood. The boy had little money and was looking for work to support himself, so Giles insisted he move into his room and sleep on the floor. The overly fat woman gave him a job cleaning the place in exchange for food and a few clothes. In the evenings, Brendan joined his uncle in song much to the delight of the ladies and their customers. With winter coming on, the river flow was down and a trip north would be much easier, so plans were made for Giles and Brendan to arrive in St Louis before the heavy snow hit. Giles never really recovered from his wound; he seemed unable to stand quite as straight as before; his hair looked grayer, and his voice was slightly raspier. On their departure, all the women in the house had to give each a big hug and kiss as the two men, one old and one young, had won the hearts of everyone in the house. Even though the women were prostitutes, the two men treated each with polite respect and understanding that was not taken for granted nor forgotten.

The winter storms young Harmon and Roidh encountered were simple single day squalls containing several inches of snow and northeast breezes. They continued to live on rabbit and Harmon shot several turkeys with his bow. Occasionally they ran across the tracks of horses with riders that came down to the river for water. Some of these contained 15 for 20 horses while most were two or three. The tracks were left most likely by Indians traveling to and fro across the plains looking for game, but the big blizzard had killed all the large animals. Then they realized they were being followed. If they looked carefully back up river, once in a while they could glimpse a horse and rider following their tracks. This concerned them and they didn't know whether to stop and confront the tracker or increase their speed and try to elude him. They couldn't veer away from the river and lose the follower as their tracks would be too easy to follow. Perhaps it was someone like them simply going down river. It was difficult to hide in the brush because there were no leaves to obscure you. There were some fairly large cottonwoods next to the river behind which one of them could hide, so they decided that young Harmon would drop off the trail and hide behind a tree and wait for the tracker, then try to ascertain his purpose. They crossed some shallow parts of the river several times and during one of the crossings young Harmon stopped and worked his way back up stream 50 yards or so, then eased out of the water up behind a big dead cottonwood.

It was an Indian with a deer carcass slung over the horse in front of him. He seemed to be alone as he came along the track the boy's had made. He had his head down and was certainly not looking for an ambush. Young Harmon stayed hidden by the tree and listened to the horse as it slowly passed by. Then once it had its back to the tree, he moved out and drew his bow only to see the Indian was no longer on the horse. Someone slipped their arm around his throat and squeezed hard enough to take his breath away. Harmon dropped his bow and tried to pry the arm loose from around his neck, but shortly lost consciousness and went limp. The Indian slowly laid him on the ground and sat quietly beside him. In a few minutes Harmon revived to see the Indian sitting quietly on his heels holding a lance to his chest. Harmon slowly put up his hands as if to surrender and indicated in sign language that he was a friend. The Indian surprised him and said, "Me friend." He held out his hand to help Harmon up and shook it as white men customarily do. This gave young Harmon the feeling that he just might survive and using sign language again, determined that the Indian was taking the dead deer to some friends just a short distance down river.

Roidh had begun to walk very slowly beside the horse intentionally so Harmon could catch up easier. He was slowly becoming concerned for his friend's safety. But if the intruder had killed Harmon, what chance would he have? He stopped frequently to look back and finally saw a horse and rider with someone walking beside. The walker had to be Harmon, so he stood and watched the unlikely pair approach. When they got close enough, he could see that both were grinning.

Kanti heard the shout of the approaching Indian and was watching that direction when over the hill appeared Bella's Indian friend with two white boys. Both looked like boys, one a mid teen while the other, a red head, looked to be about 12. Harmon recognized Kanti, but Kanti did not recognize Harmon. Bella ran out to meet her Indian friend and ran right by the two boys, barely saying hello. Her main concern was obviously the man on the horse. Kanti introduced himself to the teen aged boy that was suddenly hugging him as if he were a long lost friend. The boy exclaimed loudly, "I'm your brother Harmon."

The McCumber trading posts at St Louis, Independence and Confluence, flourished for several decades while the recipe was slowly modified both in chemistry and style. Roidh stayed out on the Platte with Kanti, while young Harmon went back to Independence and worked with O'Brian. Bella ended up going off with her Indian warrior as his wife and bore him seven sons. Finally a preacher came through on one of the first trains that were actually composed of wagons, and married Elsa and Kanti. Brendan McGillivray and Giles made the trip back to St Louis on a steam powered boat; where Brendan with the help of Donnal, took over managing the store. Brendan then shortened his name to McGill. Ilse passed away from influenza in 1819, leaving Lydia to look after Father Giles, who had taken to writing the family stories down on paper. Missouri became a state in 1821. Joseph married and went to Vermont. The overly fat woman opened new houses of ill repute in both St Louis and Independence, and was killed by accident in a shootout between two customers. Reports of a white man named Harmon, living with the Ute in the western mountains, filtered back to Confluence and Independence. Upon hearing about his friend's survival, young Harmon and brother Donnal started making plans to resume the quest of the west and reunite with old Harmon.

# WEST AGAIN

The two brothers were fully grown men astride good horses; each pulled two pack horses with plenty of provisions. They knew their Father would disagree with their trip to the mountains to find old Harmon, if he was still living. Even though he experienced a number of life threatening situations during his lifetime, he didn't like the same for his sons. Giles was almost relieved when Joseph decided to follow a woman to whom he was smitten to the east. He would have looked on this trip west as an unnecessary risk. The great migration to the American west had begun and thousands of people in great trains of wagons were leaving for Oregon and California every year. The routes west typically took them right past the growing settlement of Confluence. It was a town of multiple buildings and nearly four dozen stubborn citizens. They were their own law as most of them were armed and ready to gang up on any thieves that happened to venture into their little city. They knew if they stuck together they were a formidable deterrent to the unlawful; while alone they were none. Young Harmon and Donnal selected the route that would take them past the home of their half brother. They wanted to personally deliver the message that their Father had recently passed. The small metal box with all the old letters, deeds, the recipe and writings was to be kept in a bank vault in St Louis and they wanted Kanti to know exactly how to claim it if they failed to return.

They left Independence early one morning in April 1820 and followed the main track of the wagon trains on the south side of the river to the northwest. Young Harmon still had the old compass his Dad had given him many years before and he enjoyed checking the direction frequently. The main trail was easy to follow and there was no real reason for the compass; it simply brought back a flood of good memories. He remembered his first trip west with old Harmon and looking at the compass and not believing it; of course it turned out to be right. He recalled the time he and old Harmon had almost perished from thirst and were saved by a group of Indians the identity of whom he knew not. And he remembered when he had to run for his life, leaving old Harmon behind. Now, he was going to rectify what he thought was a misdeed. There were all sorts of crooks, thieves and slavers that lurked along the main trails west hoping to find a small group of slow moving settlers heading west. They avoided the large well armed wagon trains and fast moving groups of men on horseback. But two men, even though they were well mounted, could be vulnerable. They made good time and passed a slower moving wagon train every week. They tried to time their contact with the trains at supper time, because this was a chance at a good home cooked meal. This early in their trip west, the trains had plenty of food. About the time they reached Confluence they would be running low and would need to take on the essentials.

The trip was almost boring until they were well into Nebraska Territory, when the pioneers that were faint of heart started turning back. Every few days a wagon or two could be seen going back down river, the owners looking scared and disappointed. The trip was dangerous even without the bandits or Indians; serious accidents were frequent. A simple creek crossing could turn into a nightmare when wagons got stuck, ropes snapped and men fell under the wheels where they were horribly injured. When the husband or father of a hopeful family was killed, the wife had no choice but to turn back. It was these wagons largely driven by women, the raiders liked. It was one of those wagons that would change young Harmon's life forever.

The days slipped by as Harmon and Donnal became disheartened with what they were witnessing. So many people had dreams of better lives waiting for them somewhere in the west, but they had no idea the difficulty they would have to endure to find them. History teaches us this was a good thing as only the toughest and smartest survived the trip. It took people of fortitude and perseverance to build western America, just as it had the east. They finally delivered the news of their Father's passing to Kanti and Elsa. Both were deeply moved, and around the glowing coals each evening, recalled the details of Giles' dedication to saving Elsa and her friends from both slavers and Indians. They told Kanti and Elsa about the bank in St Louis that held the metal box with all the family history.

Finally, the brothers had to say goodbye and turned their horses to the southwest following the South Platte toward the mountains. The wagon tracks were almost faint going that direction and they didn't pass any trains for several weeks; those were small and contained only a dozen wagons or so. They each pulled only one pack horse, the others being left with Kanti. Young Harmon recognized the route and recalled all the little escapades that he and Roidh endured. His favorite stories were of the raging blizzards he ran into and how they howled and moaned for days. It was difficult for Donnal to understand what 15 foot snow drifts would do to the countryside, as the weather was hot and the countryside dry and covered with soap weed and cactus. Dust devils twisted in the distance, and sundogs appeared in the sky most days. He teased Harmon's great exaggerations about the snow. Little did he know what was ahead?

Just as they crested a hill and the distant mountains came into view, a lone wagon appeared far in the distance. It came along steadily, faithfully following the faint wagon tracks eastward pulled by a pair of bedraggled horses. The wagon was driven by a young woman with an old rifle across her lap. She warily approached Harmon and Donnal, slowed the horses, and took the rifle in both hands. "You know how to shoot that thing?" Harmon inquired. Without saying a word, she pointed out a foot sized rock 40 yards or so away and shot it with a crack. "I'll take that as a yes, but now wha-da-ya do with an empty rifle?" She looked Harmon in the eye with disdain and started loading her rifle. Donnal stepped in and explained to her that he and Harmon would be no problem, and that they were concerned with her safety all alone in the wilderness. He introduced himself to her and inquired as to her name and what she was doing. It turned out that her father and mother were dead in the back of the wagon and she was going to take them back east for burial; her name was Lydia. Her father had his arm pulled off in an accident with a stuck wagon and had bled to death before anyone could help him. Then her Mother blamed the wagon master, took after him with a knife and was shot. Lydia decided to turn back and had been on the trail less than a day.

The McCumber men knew that sending a young woman off on the trail alone was the kiss of death and convinced her to stop and camp with them to discuss the situation. They explained that she could not take her parents all the way back to New York for burial because they would start decomposing quickly. She appeared to be a bright and well spoken woman and finally settled down to the reality of the situation. They all sat around the fire as the sun drifted down over the mountains in the distance, and got to know each other. Lydia had washed the dirt and dust off her and her clothes and had combed her hair. Harmon was, for the first time in his life, infatuated with the very attractive younger woman. She explained that they had started in New York, traveled by boat through the Lakes to the west then down the Mississippi and up the Missouri to Independence. They stayed there over the winter then purchased an old wagon and six horses. Then joined a seven wagon train headed for the mountains of the South Platte where they heard fertile land was available for farming. It was a lot closer than

Oregon or California and could easily be reached in a single season. Four of the horses came up lame and had to be shot, and as a result they nearly emptied their wagon of everything except a few clothes, food and weapons. The wagon master of the train turned out to be a lustful man and was constantly after both she and her Mother, much to the chagrin of her Father. There were only three other women in the train and this was the cause of a lot of aggravation along the way. The unattached men were regularly making suggestive comments about the women, to which the husbands or fathers objected vociferously. There were regular arguments and pushing matches, encouraged by the wagon master that slowly separated those that had women from those that did not. The animosity had grown to the point that, when Lydia's Father was killed, the first thing the wagon master did was approach her Mother, which ended tragically. Lydia knew she could not continue west with the group and immediately turned around and headed east. Several of the men threatened her with rape, but it was the loaded rifle plus the fact that she was a dead shot, that finally discouraged them.

Harmon told the entire story of his experience with old Harmon. He spent several hours over the glowing fire that evening detailing how they had narrowly survived, thirst and Indians and how he finally had to run for his life leaving old Harmon behind. His blue eyes, glittering in the firelight entranced Lydia, and it was then and there she fell in love. He told her how his Father had come from Scotland, was held by the French, then was grounded at Chesapeake and found his way west to the Oneida Indians where he lived for a decade and fathered his brother Kanti. He told her about his Mother and brothers and sisters and the trading posts they started in St Louis, Independence and Confluence. And he told her about the recipe that had always been a good source of income for the family. When the three awakened the next morning and could see the mountain tops gleaming pink in the morning sun each knew that something special had happened to Harmon and Lydia. The men were faced with an uncomfortable decision;

they didn't want to have to travel east to Confluence to see Lydia safely to help, and they couldn't just go off and leave her to the will of the west. Harmon wouldn't have any part of any plan that separated him from Lydia, so they decided to discard the wagon and take her and her two downtrodden horses with them. So, that morning the unlikely group started west toward the white tipped mountains. Harmon and Lydia rode slowly side by side and talked the whole time. When they stopped, Harmon demonstrated his super skill with the bow. Donnal finally fashioned a crude saddle for Lydia from some hides and an old blanket that made it easier for her to ride. She refused to use one of the men's saddles and gave Donnal a vigorous hug for his trouble. After several days, they were catching up with the small group of wagons that had killed Lydia's parents, and they decided to veer to the south and avoid a confrontation that could get someone hurt or worse. Harmon knew the route of the river and by turning south then west he could intercept the point at which the river left the mountains.

Several of the men from the train, had glimpsed our three riders far in the distance behind them and decided to see who it was and whether or not there were any women. So, as Lydia and friends turned to the south, so did five of the more ruthless members of the train including the master. The countryside was dry and the cloud of dust coming from the five riders could be seen in the distance. Harmon was wise in the ways of the west and quickly recognized the threat as more than just a dust devil. The three increased their speed to a lope, but the two old horses from Lydia's wagon were having trouble keeping up. They knew they couldn't outrun the oncoming men and decided to try to elude them. The first creek bed they came to, had a reasonable amount of water flow, so they took their horses into the stream and followed it to the northwest, hoping to pass unnoticed in front of the five men who would be going south. They walked their horses quietly downstream in the creek that had cut deeply into the countryside, constantly studying the rim above them for an ambush. Every quarter mile or so, Harmon dismounted and climbed on foot to the rim of the stream bed and scanned the countryside. As he slowly rose up over the rim he saw two of the raiders coming down the hill not a hundred yards away. They would surely be found. He ducked back down below the edge and motioned for Lydia and Donnal to dismount and bring their weapons. He sent Donnal downstream 25 or so yards and Lydia upstream to spread their fire and told them not to shoot until he yelled. The sound of gunfire would certainly bring the rest of the gang down on them. He needed to take the intruders out with his bow.

Peeking over the rim of the creek bed, Harmon could see the two men were headed directly at Lydia's position. He signaled her to stay low and quiet, and that the two were coming directly at her. His position was perfect for a bow shot as he could hit the nearest man with an arrow in the left side of his chest and by the time the other could figure out what happened, he could hit him with an arrow also. He hoped it would be sudden enough they wouldn't manage to get a shot off to warn their friends. When they were no more than ten feet from the rim of the creek bed, Harmon slowly rose up and calmly sent an arrow into the left chest of the left intruder, pfffft. The guy let out a low gasp and fell from his horse that shied and caused the other horse to shy. Harmon ducked back below the edge and watched for another chance once the remaining rider's horse calmed down and he could dismount. The rider finally got off his horse and jumped to the aid of his buddy when, pfffft, another arrow was launched that hit him under his armpit. He lurched back and fell over the rim of the creek right into Lydia's hiding place. He grabbed for his pistol and was trying to get it out when Lydia buried the muzzle of her rifle in his belly and pulled the trigger. His ample belly completely absorbed the muzzle blast and the only sound that escaped was a deep liquid pop. He was nearly dead and she was shaken; she stared at the man bleeding his last and staring back in wonder at what happened. Harmon quickly checked the other man who was moaning his last also and dragged him down over the edge out of sight. Donnal had come running and took control of both

horses and pulled them down also. Both men were a flurry of
activity, while Lydia stood staring in shock at what she had just
done. They removed her things from the old horse and tied
them on the best looking of the two new ones. They took the
halters and such from the old horses and let them go, mounted
the good horses and took off at a lope down the creek bed.

They hadn't gone a quarter mile when suddenly a rifle shot
rang out and Lydia's horse was hit in the front shoulder. It went
down and rolled on the ground taking her with it. The horse
couldn't get up and she was stunned by the fall. Harmon and
Donnel jumped off their horses and grabbed all the reins, tied
the horses to a bush, and took cover. More rifle shots rang out
from several different directions. "Hey you in the creek, give us
the woman and we'll let-cha go."

"Not a chance." Harmon shouted back.

"We gotcha pinned down an-ya got no choice."

Harmon didn't answer as he patted Lydia's face gently trying
to bring her back to her senses. He was willing to wait until
dark, and take them out with arrows. After an hour or so, Lydia
was back to normal and they were checking their weapons. In a
few hours it would be dark. Harmon had heard his Dad explain
how to creep up on intruders and kill them, and that was all
he had for experience for that sort of thing. He slipped on his
moccasins and the three hunkered down and watched the rim
of the creek bed as they knew their antagonists would try to
creep around to a better position for a shot into them. Donnal
and Lydia both had their rifles trained on the edge of the bank
waiting for a target. At first, Lydia thought she was seeing
things. The barrel of a gun, then the top of a head very slowly
appeared up over the edge just where she was aiming. When it
got down to the eyebrows, she let go with another shot. She saw
chunks of someone's head fly; then there was complete silence
again. After a few minutes, they could hear horses pounding off
to the north, and as they looked over the rim, the two riders, at
full gallop, crested a hill about 100 yards to the north and went

out of sight. The crisis appeared to be over. They mounted the three remaining good horses and set off to the south at a gallop.

After a while, the three slowed to a lope then a walk. They couldn't help looking back to see if they were followed. The wagon master was not only a lustful man, but vengeful and Lydia knew he would not give up that easily. She knew he would go and get help and be right back after them. Women were scarce in the west and some men would do almost anything including murder, to get one of their own. They continued on south roughly following the river and when it turned into the front-range of the mountains, they followed. Their camp that night was just inside of the first hog-back, one valley north of the river. They were there for two reasons, first the river canyon was far too steep and rocky to traverse, and second they could see any followers coming at quite a distance. Harmon knew from experience that the best route into the mountains was one valley north of the river. The next morning, sure enough, a fairly large group of men on horseback were raising a cloud of dust in the distance just east of their position. The group would surely cut across their trail and within hours would be after them again. Going up into the mountains with a group of antagonists following was extra dangerous; frequently a back-track was necessary because of the terrain. Harmon was aware of this and decided to follow the hog-back north to the first stream, then walk the horses in the water downstream to the east as far as they could; turn back north and follow the next stream to the west hopefully losing the wagon master and his crew.

What they were unaware of was, after Lydia left the train, full scale mutiny broke out and the three married men that remained decided to leave the train and strike out on their own. The dozen or so men remaining shot the three and proceeded to abuse the women. Two were able to commit suicide right away and the third followed the next morning. Now the group had turned into a mounted, bloodthirsty gang hell bent on finding another woman they could use, and didn't mind killing to get her. The gang stripped the wagons of anything useful, set several oxen and draft horses loose and set off to the south at a lope, blood in their eyes and rape in their minds.

The gang picked up Harmon's trail and followed it west past the hogback, found the spot where Harmon had camped for the night, and tracked the trail north to the first creek. They split up; some went upstream and others downstream, but they couldn't find where Harmon had left the creek. After a few hours of searching, they met back at the point where Harmon had gone into the stream and sat and drank the last of their whiskey, called each other names, scratched themselves and napped in the warm sun. By that time Harmon was headed west on the very next creek just to their north some 10 miles. Had the gang simply followed the hogback north, they could have intercepted Harmon, but they decided to go east and find, then pillage the settlements in the area. Having given up finding the woman with Harmon, the gang traveled east following the creek then turned northeast. They knew there were some settlements along the river just to the north, and were taking a shortcut when they ran across Harmon's track. One of the trio's horses had relieved itself and left a fresh pile of excrement right in the path of the oncoming gang. Once again they were on the right track and galloped wildly to the steam where Harmon and turned west. They were on the right track several hours behind Harmon and they knew it. The gang prodded their horses to run up the creek and several stumbled spilling their riders and injuring both horse and rider. Nobody stopped because at that point, each man looked on the others as adversaries, as competitors for the favors of the woman.

Our trio was walking their horses up the creek and had just passed the hogback leading them into the heart of the mountains. Donnal suddenly stopped and listened. He thought he could hear the rumble of horses running behind them. After a few seconds, Lydia and Harmon could hear them too. Harmon could see the fear in Lydia's eyes. They needed to leave the stream in a spot where it would not be obvious and maybe they could ambush the horsemen galloping pell-mell upstream. It was obvious that the trio was going to have to fight for their lives. Harmon told Donnal and Lydia to continue on upstream, and that he was going to try to get an arrow into as many horses as he could. If he could bring down half the horses, he thought they might have a fighting chance against the rest. He found a spot with a good view of the creek, out of sight from the onrushing gang and waited, bow in hand. He planned to aim at the rear flank of the horses, so the riders wouldn't know what happened until they hit the ground.

Pfffft, Pfffft, Pfffft, the arrows were launched a second apart, six in all. Horses squealed and fell; other horses fell over them. Someone yelled, "Injuns." More were screaming in pain. Harmon kept launching arrows, at the riders themselves. Only two made it through the melee untouched, and they made a beeline upstream to where Donnal and Lydia were waiting, guns loaded and cocked. One by one the gang members were taken down either dead or mortally wounded. Some were firing wildly into the brush; some shot each other. They never did see where the arrows were coming from. Several tried to get away, but their horses had shied and bolted, so they started running downstream panic stricken. Pfffft, Pffft, two more arrows found their marks and the last of the gang went down seriously wounded but still dangerous. Suddenly the booms of rifles shocked the air from upstream. Donnal and Lydia had both fired; Lydia hit the wagon master in the neck and Donnal missed. One rider was left, mounted and armed; he turned and rode directly at Lydia, screaming and cussing what he was going to do to her. Donnal jumped in front of the horse and caused it to veer sharply. In the process, he was hit hard and thrown to the ground, dazed. The rider was thrown from the horse, but was up and stumbling toward Lydia, screaming mad. She had her hands on the pistol calmly waiting for him to come into range. Donnal was rolling on the ground, trying to collect his wits, and Harmon was running upstream. When the rider was mere feet away, Lydia lifted the pistol, aimed at his chest and pulled the trigger. Misfire, nothing happened. She tried again, but by then

he was on her. She could smell his rancid breath. He was big
and strong and forced her to the ground, ripping at her clothing.
Donnal was trying to crawl to her aid, but he had lost his pistol.
The big man slapped her hard several times and Lydia went limp.
He grinned and yowled in joy as it would only be seconds before
he started his rape. As he was standing over Lydia pulling at his
pants; pfffft, a sudden pain developed in his rump as the arrow
struck him high in the buttocks and sliced its way up into his
belly. He blanched and stiffened and fell on Lydia screaming.
Harmon ran up and threw him to the side and kneeled to help
Lydia. She was motionless.

Donnal staggered to his feet and made his way over to Lydia;
he feared she was dead. In the chaos, he couldn't be sure the
rapist hadn't shot her, but he couldn't see any blood. The front of
her shirt was open and Donnal pulled it shut covering her chest.
Harmon was speaking softly to her telling her to wake up. He
patted her cheek, and slowly she blinked, then jerked and started
to fight him, not knowing who he was. He quieted hers, spoke
softly and held her in his arms for the very first time, and she
hugged him back. Tears formed in both Harmon's and Donnal's
eyes as they had both fallen in love with the spunky woman.
They both silently thanked God, they were all safe.

The wagon master was dead and his partner in the last stages
of life with only minutes left. The arrow up in his gut had cut
major arteries and he was bleeding internally. The group downstream was motionless as Donnal and Harmon approached. They
kicked each in the foot or leg to see if there was any response.
Several tried to raise a gun but were unable to fire before it
was kicked away. Most were still alive, but mortally wounded
and it may have taken days before some of them died. Harmon
set about retrieving his arrows, as they were precious and hard
to replace. He had to cut them out of most of the men which
caused them to groan and plead for death. All the weapons and
healthy horses were rounded up. Several of the wounded horses
had to be shot. They kept the two best saddles and discarded the
rest. Four good horses were loaded with weapons and utensils

plus the little edible food they carried and our trio went on upstream to make camp for the night. Just as the sun surrendered to the mountain, they all fell asleep. An occasional scream came up from their back trail, but nobody heard.

The next morning, they rearranged the loads on the horses and headed into the mountains. Harmon made a quick trip back to the ambush site. All the men there were dead and scalped. He decided to keep it from Lydia and Donnal for the time being. They were each mounted on splendid horses and pulled another six loaded with everything of value. They thought they may have to buy old Harmon's freedom and had plenty of stuff for trading. Their progress was marked with fits and starts and back-tracks. There was no good route for horses and they had to find their way, but perseverance paid off and they slowly made progress. Lydia and Donnal hadn't seen anything like these mountains. Towering walls of granite, torrents of water blasting down the ravines and thick forests were everywhere. They rode along looking up at the peaks in awe. Donnal or Harmon would take one horse and try to find a route all the horses could make and frequently had to turn back and try another direction. Harmon used his old compass repeatedly, and every time he pulled it out, he thought of his Father. Even though he had been there once before, he didn't recognize a single thing. He sensed they were being shadowed, but didn't see any signs of such. He did know there were some big valleys ahead and hoped to run into the Ute there. In the evenings, before the glowing coals of a dying fire, Lydia described the green fields of rural New York, she and her parents had left behind years before. Life there seemed comfortable and simple and you didn't have to worry about losing your life every day. She told Harmon she loved him, but she could not raise a family out in this wild country where she would have to worry about their well being day and night. She couldn't live where they didn't have access to a doctor or regular food and shelter. She wanted a simple garden and a kitchen, a family and the sounds of love and laughter. With a lump in his throat, Harmon agreed for he knew not his future.

They finally came upon one of the big open valleys in the middle of the mountains and made a good camp where they could stay for a few weeks. Each day Harmon and Donnal could strike out to the west and see if they could pick up some sign of the Ute. On one of these forays, Harmon started to recognize the surroundings and thought he had found the route old Harmon and his captors used to pass on to the west. Summer was on the wane and he knew they at least wanted to return to Confluence for winter. On the way back to camp, he started seeing fleeting glimpses of someone through the trees. He repeatedly stopped and called out, without result. When he returned to Donnal and Lydia, he told them he was being followed. Then he heard someone shout, "Harmon." Again they shouted, "Harmon."

He answered, "Yes, it's me." Out of the trees walked old Harmon. Young Harmon screamed his name and ran to him with a gigantic hug that picked him completely off the ground. Old Harmon was clean shaven and dressed completely in heavily decorated leather. He looked happy and fit and had three friends with him. One of them, he called Jameson was a large, lean, and light skinned man that spoke perfect English. Old Harmon told him how they had watched them kill all the gang that was after the woman. The only thing that kept them from coming forward was the fact that old Harmon did not recognize young Harmon. They didn't seem to need any help. Then when old Harmon saw him shoot the bow, he was sure who it was. They had sent a runner to the Ute camp and asked for permission to invite young Harmon and his group to visit. And, so it was that our trio was welcomed into the Ute camp, where a good number of the elders could understand English. Old Harmon had become a valued and trusted member of the nation and had negotiated numerous deals with white men from Canada for the fur trade. He had taken a wife and between them produced four children, two of which survived. He had named his boys Giles and O'Brian, two of the toughest, smartest men he had ever known.

One of the first things old Harmon did was arrange a bow shooting demonstration by young Harmon. He challenged the very best bow shots to see if they could duplicate young Harmon's skill. Young Harmon shot last in the contest, all the others had hit some targets that were set up out about 30 yards, but rarely in the center. Young Harmon put five arrows in his left hand along with the bow and drew back on the sixth. Pffft, Pffft, Pffft, Pffft, Pffft, Pffft, the bow went as he launched all six in about six seconds, and all struck the target in the center. The crowd of Ute erupted with applause and admiration. Young boys ran to retrieve his arrows for him, and old Harmon remembered the times this skill had saved his life. When young Harmon broached the subject of coming back to St Louis, old Harmon looked him in the eye and explained that everything he loved was with the Ute. He had a good life, and even though he knew his sons would live to see the Ute Nation disappear, he wanted to stay. He appreciated his association with old Giles and O'Brian and every time he looked at his boys, he would think of them. Most of all he appreciated young Harmon's dedication to return to find him and if necessary save him from slavery. But, he was so logical and likeable the Ute elders had taken to him and treated him like a son. He knew he would be needed more and more as the white men migrated to the west and gradually took over all the inhabitable areas. He just could not leave all these people in this time of struggle for their very existence. Young Harmon sat quietly and held Lydia's hand for a long time looking into the flames of the camp fire. He reached out and shook old Harmon's hand and said, "I will always remember you, every evening of every day." With that he stood and led Lydia off to their last night in the Ute camp; for at sunrise, they would start their trek of thousands of miles back to the green fields of New York. When our trio left the camp, old Harmon, in the Indian tradition, shouted his friendship. Slowly the sound of old Harmon's shouts faded and all the trio could hear was the breathing and footsteps of the horses. Young Harmon's eyes glistened with feeling as Lydia reached over and patted his hand. They both knew it was goodbye forever.

# NEW YORK AND OREGON

Their objective was to make it to Confluence before winter broke. Harmon was aware of what the early winter storms were like and didn't want to have to spend the winter in the settlements at the base of the mountains. Donnal wasn't sure what he wanted to do. He could stay at Confluence or go on down to Independence and work with O'Brian, or go all the way to St Louis and combine efforts with cousin Brendan McGill. Each would welcome him, but he was still a young man and had the spirit of adventure in his genes. Now that he'd had a brush with death, he appreciated the unmerciful west and how only the strongest survived. He would go on down to Confluence and make his decision.

The trip back out of the mountains was much easier than the trip in. They didn't encounter any humans along the way and were glad for that. They thought they should avoid the settlements at the base of the mountains, because they were usually hangouts for local thieves and thugs. So, they proceeded straight east and then turned to the northeast on a route that would intersect with the South Platte, which they would follow on up to Confluence. A century later the little settlement at Confluence would become the small city of North Platte. They were able to avoid travelers going both directions along the river, and made good time as a result. They were well mounted and knew how to take care of their horses. The pack horses were also of good quality and had no problem keeping up. The days were growing short and every night they had to find a spot down out of the cold wind to make camp. Then one night it snowed. Harmon was happy there was little wind and the snow ended up to be about a foot deep. It was still easy for the horses to negotiate, but would leave tracks that would be easy to follow.

In the next several days, a couple groups, one Indian and one Mexican, crossed their trail. The Indians counted the tracks of six horses that all looked to have riders. They weren't looking for trouble and kept to their own business, but the Mexicans were interested enough to follow. If there were a number of armed men, the Mexicans would back off, but when they saw it was only three and one was a woman, they were very interested. Harmon had seen the oncoming Mexicans in the distance and figured to outrun them. They stopped quickly and grabbed the absolute necessities from the pack horses and turned them loose. It might confuse the followers for a little while and allow Harmon the space to get away. The Mexicans couldn't pass up three good horses and took the time to catch them. Then one stayed with their new horses while the rest continued to follow Harmon at a lope. Now it was a question of horse quality and Harmon knew he had the advantage. They rode the rest of that day and into the night. After a brief stop to allow the horses a drink and rest, they were off again, alternating a gallop, lope and walk, which they kept up all night. The Mexicans thought they should have caught the trio in a few hours and sometime during the night, they gave up and turned back. When the sun finally rose in the southeast, Harmon crested a tall hill and looked back many miles along their track and could see nobody coming. They stopped and had a good breakfast and let the horses crop what grass they could find, and were off again. They kept up the fast pace all day and as the sun was passing in the southwest, found a good spot down out of sight and slept the night. Just before first light a blast of cold wind buffeted the open plain and that frightening moan of an approaching storm woke Harmon.

He recognized the signs and woke the other two; they needed to find shelter for them and the horses as soon as possible.

The snow that was available quickly became a ground blizzard as the trio struggled to get their horses under control. They needed to find a south facing river bank overhang that they could dig into and hole up. Following the bank on the north side of the main river was their only hope of finding a safe spot for them and the horses. The wind was in full roar when they came upon a likely looking place and Donnal and Harmon leaped off their horses and started digging into the side of the bank. Lydia held the reins of the horses and squatted down between them in an effort to soothe them. She could tell they were frightened as their eyes were wide and they snorted and stamped. She kept a tight hold because if one got loose it would certainly run wildly into the storm and get lost. When the snow hit, it was suddenly dark and the horses pulled to get loose to no avail. Donnal and Harmon were soaking wet by the time they got a cave big enough for the three. Lydia and Donnal got in the cave with all their provisions and used the saddles to block the entrance. Harmon tied some of the animal skins over the horses' backs and wrapped hobbles on their feet. It was just as frightening to Harmon as the first one had been a dozen years ago. Our trio looked at each other with concern, because if they lost the horses, their lives would be in jeopardy. They had food for several days, but were almost out of water, even though the river was only yards away. Lydia cried softly to herself and wondered how anyone in their right mind could come to this country and survive. In the short time she had been in the west, she had nearly lost her life several times and now she was in the middle of another threat. All they had was their combined body heat to dry Harmon and Donnal, but the shelter of the cave would save them. The storm screamed and moaned for hours and hours; it seemed as if it would never stop. It had been early morning when the blizzard hit, but it was so dark it was difficult to tell day from night. Each of them shifted and groaned in an effort to find a comfortable position.

The dirt of the river bank had combined with the moisture on their clothes and made a muddy coating over everything but their faces. Donnal recalled the description Harmon had given him of the first blizzard. He remembered how he had teased Harmon about exaggerating its fury and duration. It all was true. Even though they were uncomfortable and cold, each knew they would survive. Harmon and Lydia dreamed of the green that awaited them in the east, and were thankful that this was the last of the life threatening trials they would have on the open plains of new America. Unfortunately their struggle had just begun.

Lydia awakened to the sun shining in her eyes. What a blessed feeling, she thought as she stirred and groaned at her stiff and sore muscles. Donnal and Harmon opened their eyes to the sun also and sighed with relief at the end of the storm and the warming rays of the sun. It was only November and the winter on the plains had started off with a blizzard that piled the snow in great drifts that would last until spring. Slowly, they pushed the snow out of the way and uncovered their horses. After a good drink by all, they mounted and wound their way to the east avoiding the deep drifts and sticking to the bare ground where they could. Harmon looked back at the little cave they had dug. It was a pathetic little hole and helped him recall the previous one a decade ago, and said to himself, *that's enough of digging into the ground to survive, never again*. He agreed with Lydia, this was no place to try to have a stable life and raise a family. Between the weather and the uncivilized men, Indian, white, or Mexican, he had had enough. It would probably take a year to make their way back to New York, but that is exactly what he was up to. He now understood why his brother Joseph had gone east, and kicked his horse into a lope.

Lydia didn't look back, the quicker she could forget that stinking little hole, the better. She thought about the colors of the tree leaves this time of year in New York and about how next year at this time she would be there to see them. Donnal on the other hand was already thinking about his next adventure. He didn't know which way he would go but it was either west, southwest or northwest. He planned to spend a year or so at Confluence and get more information about what was happening and where before he decided. It was winter, 1820.

In spite of the huge drifts of snow, they made good time travelling at a lope basically following the South Platte as it wound its way to the northeast from what eventually became Colorado into Nebraska territory. The Missouri Compromise that admitted Missouri as a slave state and Maine as a free state was passed. The great migration of the American west had paused for the winter and a few poorly informed souls tried to travel across the northern plains only to perish in the harsh weather. It was one of these groups that Harmon and his partners stumbled upon late one harsh, windy day in December. Lydia thought she heard a child crying upwind somewhere. She motioned for her comrades to stop momentarily while she listened. Sure enough she could hear someone crying, and it was coming from the river channel just north of them. She asked Harmon and Donnal if they could hear it. In between gusts of wind they could surely hear a child crying for help. Reluctantly, they investigated and found two wagons stuck in the river. There were horse tracks all around them as if someone tried to help them out. Our trio couldn't see anyone around, and except for the sound of crying, there were no human signs. Harmon led his horse down the riverbank and into the shallow river and as he approached he could see blood on and around the wagons. He could make out marks in the snow where several people had been dragged behind horses. He shouted his approach to the wagon and got no response as he approached the first wagon and slowly raised the cover and looked in the back. There was a half dressed, dead woman that was still warm. In the other wagon, were two little kids along with two deceased men, both of whom had been partially stripped? The two little kids were about four or five years old and appeared to be OK. Who could have done this, was his first question? Someone had, just in the last few hours, killed some adults, dragged some others away with them, and left two defenseless children alone to perish in the weather. He motioned for Lydia and Donnal to scout around the area to see if they could come up with anything. Other than a trail of tracks heading off to the northwest, there was nothing. They agreed they had to bundle up the kids and get on the trail the other way as fast as they could. Someone had killed the men and taken at least two people with them, probably both women. The intruders had taken the horses, food and weapons along with most of the clothing and blankets. They left one blanket for the kids. Harmon rode to the top of a sizeable hill just to the north and looked west where he saw a band of a dozen or so horses and people on foot. He couldn't make out who they were, but knew this couldn't stand.

Lydia didn't want him to go, she told him to simply take the children and go on to the east and forget the whole thing and that he could not right all the wrongs of the west. Harmon and Donnal wouldn't have any part of it. They put the kids and Lydia on her horse, wrapped them in blankets and sent them off to the east. She had instructions to continue on to the east for several hours then find a spot down out of the wind and hole up for the night. It was getting dark when they set out at a lope to rectify the situation. Figuring there must have been four horses per wagon; that meant there must have been four or so raiders. Harmon and Donnal were confident they could handle the situation. Lydia was concerned for their safety but was so proud of both of them she could only cry as she walked her overloaded horse off into the night wind. The two kids were in shock but held on tightly the smaller in front of her and the older behind. They frequently broke out into sobs and she spoke to them in a soft voice and told them they would be OK. The wind blustered and blew the snow around on the ground, but the sky was clear and the star light showed them the way.

Harmon and Donnal crept up on the camp of the intruders and peered over the river bank down at them. There in a stand of cottonwoods, were five men both white and Mexican and three women they had taken from the wagons. They had a large fire shooting flames five feet into the air and were sitting around sententiously treating the women and drinking. The terrified women were huddled together by the fire trying to warm up as they listened to the descriptions of what the men were going to do to them. Harmon knew the men would have to go into the brush and relieve themselves and when one did he would drill him with an arrow. Then when someone came to investigate he would pop that guy also. That would leave three to deal with. He positioned himself so he would have a shot at the most likely toilet spot next to the fire. It wasn't long until what appeared to be the leader got up and went into Harmon's bushes, dropped his breeches, and squatted. He heard a pfffft, and looked up just in time to take an arrow in the eye. Without a sound of any kind, he simply fell over, twitched several times and died. After a few minutes one of the other raiders called to the dead one, and when there was no reply, called again. They jabbered among themselves in concern, and finally one got up to investigate, and when he discovered his dead comrade, started to yell out a warning only to take a pfffft, in the throat. A gurgle was all that came out, but that was enough to alert the other three. Donnal shot one as he stood, then fell into the fire, but the other two took cover behind the women and shouted for Harmon and Donnal to stop firing or they would kill the women. Harmon quickly moved around behind them so he would have another clear shot with his bow. The snow on the ground made it possible to move without any sound. The women were bawling and calling for help, and the raiders were shouting their threats when pfffft, another went down with an arrow in the back. He tried to raise his gun to shoot the women but was paralyzed by the pain of the arrow he had taken in the lung and one of the women kicked his gun from his hand. The remaining raider tried to run for his horse, but slipped and fell in the river. Just as he got up, Donnal caught him with a ball in the breast bone that shattered it and continued into his chest, killing him instantly. In the space of several minutes it was all over. The three women huddled together as they knew not who their rescuers were. Harmon called to them that he and Donnal meant no harm and were there to help them. One of the women had picked up the dead raider's gun and had it pointed into the darkness. She was so frightened that she would surely try to shoot anything she saw. Donnal called out from the other side that he and his friend had found their wagons and kids and were going to help them and that she should not shoot. She slowly put the weapon down.

They gathered the horses, put warm clothes on the women, packed up the weapons and food and set off to the east into the night. Several of the raiders had large sums of money in their leather pouches indicating the extent to which they had robbed others on the trail west. An hour later they passed the scene of the wagon attack and stopped to bury the dead men and the woman. It was dawn the next morning before they caught up with Lydia who had just fed the children and loaded everything on her horse to continue on to the east. They all went down by the river, started a fire and had a hot breakfast. One of the women was the mother, the other two were her teenage daughters and the two children, both boys, were her sons. The group had now grown to eight, and fortunately they had eight saddle horses plus eight others. The young boys turned out to be good riders as the ungainly collection of forlorn souls made their way eastward toward civilization. Reports from the west propitiated opportunity and promise, but at what expense? All, but Donnal, were fed up with the west and its endless dangers. There was something in him that told him this was just training and preparation for his future. Lydia looked at Donnal and Harmon with even more respect; they had ridden off into the dark willing to risk their lives to save another; they were truly men of probity.

A week's travel without incident brought them to the village of Confluence and the warmth of good meals and protection from the winter. Harmon gave all the money he had taken from the raiders to the woman who with the help of her four children started a boarding house and laundry. They decided to stay in the west after all. People on the big wagon trains coming upriver realized by the time they reached Confluence that they could not carry their furniture with them and sold much of it at a low price or traded it for beans and flour, and as a result there was a plethora of beds, bureaus, chairs and tables in the little village. Kanti had a large supply of cloth and blankets shipped up by wagon so there was no shortage of those either. He and Elsa tended large gardens of potatoes, cucumbers, peppers, carrots, corn, dill and onions, some of which he pickled with the recipe and some of which he stored in the root cellar. They used the horse manure from the streets of the village for fertilizer in the sandy soil, and paid local boys to haul water from the river, so their gardens were the envy of everyone who saw them. Kanti had heard from Cousin Brendan McGill that everything was going well with him and O'Brian in Independence and that Brother Joseph had sent word that he was happy with his new wife and the farm back east. Their little sister Lydia had passed through Confluence earlier that year, married to a young pioneer headed west.

Harmon and Lydia left just after the spring floods had passed and had their first rides on the new steam powered flat boats that became popular on the rivers of the Midwest. They stopped in both Independence and St Louis and renewed their friendships with O'Brian and McGill. While in Independence they got preacher married; it was 1821 and Harmon was 21; Lydia was 17. In St Louis they visited the grave of Father Giles and went down to the bank and read all the letters and documents in the metal box. He also found, and kept, a bedraggled piece of fabric with the recipe stitched into it Father Giles brought from Scotland. Occasional letters were exchanged between Harmon and each of his brothers in the coming years, but those gradually petered out and contact was lost. He never knew what eventually happened to Kanti, Elsa, O'Brian, Sister Lydia, old Harmon or McGill, but received long letters in the next several decades from Donnal telling tall tales about escapades along the Oregon and California trails. Donnal would mention his older brother Kanti occasionally, but that finally stopped also. Harmon's letters rarely caught up with Donnal because he wasn't in one place long. He lost track of the metal box in the St Louis bank that contained all the original family letters and documents of his Father Giles.

Harmon and Lydia made their way up the Ohio River all the way to Fort Pitt, which had been renamed Pittsburg and visited the grave of his Grandmother Sarah. It had been moved to a little cemetery farther away from the three rivers junction so more buildings could go up for the growing town around. By that time it was relatively safe to transit the rivers as most of the river thieves had been run out to the west. Late in the year they finally ended up in Saint Lawrence county New York, working on a farm owned by one of Lydia's relatives. They stayed there and parented thirteen children in the many decades to come, while Donnal traveled the western trails a number of times always in search of the excitement he had experienced on that very first trip into the mountains with Brother Harmon. It was typical of the times, that families were spread and separated by circumstances, never to see each other again.

The first decade or so in Saint Lawrence County, Harmon and Lydia both worked for other farmers in the area. Harmon learned the trade and saved his money to buy a piece of land of his own. He and Lydia had five girls from 1826 through 1834. Finally in 1836, a boy William$_r$ was born alive and well. They were overjoyed. It was about then they were able to purchase a small farm with a rundown house near Parishville; he was now working for himself. The living children following William, were, Jane$_r$, Adolphus$_r$, Romelia$_r$, Mary$_r$, and finally Giles$_r$ in 1850. Little Harry was born and died from a fall into the open fireplace. By then his farm, which was by far the smallest in the area, had grown to 60 acres, about 1/3 improved. Many times over the years, Harmon and Lydia sat and watched the sun go down in the west and talked about the old days when they had to fight for their lives against either weather or other white men. They both wondered what life would have been like had they stayed in the west, in Confluence. Surely, it would have been protected well enough they wouldn't have to scratch and scrape to protect their family. Surely it would have been better than the hard-scrabble farming in which they found themselves. They all worked from daylight to dark just to grow enough to live on; there was no time for schooling and the kids grew up unable to read or write. When he had time, Harmon regaled his three youngest with stories, probably exaggerated, of the terrible blizzards, the slavers and other bad men that chased them. He told young Giles about the Ute and the Arapahoe and how grand the warriors were. He told him of the trek he and old Harmon made across the deserts and into the mountains where old Harmon was captured by the Ute, and how he and his brother Donnal had saved a woman and her four children from the certain death in the hands of slavers. He showed his youngest son how to make and shoot a bow. Harmon frequently took the old compass of his Father's from its wooden box and held it in his hand as he sat quietly and closed his eyes in deep thought. He felt moving to the east had been a mistake. Young Giles was impressionable and constantly played good guys and bad guys and dreamed of the time when he too would go west and ride horses, chase bad guys and herd cattle. His dreams would come true.

Donnal stayed in Confluence several years and worked at odd jobs. He watched the trains of horses, mules and wagons get larger and longer all the time. At that time, wagons couldn't make it all the way to Oregon; so many pioneers stopped along the way and slowly populated what were to become Nebraska, Wyoming, and Idaho. If they were lucky, they could transfer to mule trains and finish the trip clear to western Oregon. The trail branched off to the south into Utah on what was later called the Mormon Trail, and further to California. Until 1869, when the transcontinental railroad went into service, these trails carried roughly 400,000 hardy folks to their dreams. A shorter trail broke away from the North Platte and followed the southern branch of the river down into Kansas Territory, what is now Colorado, with smaller branches continuing on south to Mexico. Donnal's first trip was as a guide along this very trail that he, Harmon and Lydia had traversed each direction several years earlier. A small group of wagons had gathered in Confluence having heard that wagons could not make it all the way to Oregon, and decided to take their chances on the South Platte but needed a guide. Donnal talked the deal over with Kanti and decided to go ahead and show the folks where the headwaters of the South Platte broke out of the mountains. He knew there were small clusters of homesteaders in the area, but there was no protection from either marauding renegade Indians or whites. His little 12 wagon train of hopeful folks seeking their destiny would fit right in. In the creek basins and river valleys large tracts of fertile ground could be found that would be good for dry land farming or gardening. The surrounding land wasn't good for much more than running cattle, so his settlers would be able to raise their own food in gardens and cattle on the dry land. This area was on the arid side of the mountains and usually didn't get much rain or even snow, but if the settlers carefully located their farms and ranches close to the rivers and streams, they could prosper. So, in June 1823, the little wagon train pushing nearly 200 cattle and several dozen un-mounted horses, set off to the southwest.

Donnal proved to be a capable wagon-master and quickly earned the respect and trust of his pioneers. The river was still quite high and he kept the train on the southern bank far enough away to limit the mosquitoes, but close enough that water for the animals was easily available. Donnal had scouts out on the flanks of the train several miles ahead of the main group looking for horse tracks, creek crossings, and low places with good grass. Both were experienced men and could be trusted to be both careful and thorough. They gained altitude rapidly and had to steer off to the south several miles frequently in search of crossing for some of the major creeks and ravines, but always came back to the main river. In weeks, they were in view of the mountains low on the western horizon and glistening in the sun. The out riders usually came back around noon for lunch and when one didn't, Donnal became quietly alarmed. He gulped down his food and chose three other men to go with him, and then set out in the general direction that should cut someone's trail. They found their scout staked to the ground, scalped but still alive. He confirmed it was a group of about a dozen renegade Indians. They left the scout alive to warn the main group to turn back as this was not the white man's land and they were not welcome. The scout would be dead in weeks from infection. A dozen probably would not attack the train directly but would constantly kill anyone separated from the main group and would try to steal as many horses as they could. They had little use for cattle. All of the men and several older boys took turns doing guard duty at night. They kept the horses inside the circle of wagons, but had so many cattle they had to leave them out. Several times the Indians ran off most of the cattle and they had to spend the better part of the next two days rounding them up. So, Donnal decided to set a trap and see if he could kill enough of them to discourage the rest. He would use himself as bait to lure the Indians into an ambush, but the first thing they had to find out was the exact whereabouts of the Indians. The little train and their sizable cattle herd turned and took off straight to the south away from the river and out into the open plain just east of the mountains. The terrain was barren and treeless so there was nowhere to hide, and if the Indian renegades followed, they would have to keep quite a distance away. Then, the first night, Donnal sent a pair of scouts out several miles directly to the east and another pair directly west. They had instructions to find a spot down in a high arroyo or draw where they could watch for the Indians following the main group. They were not to disclose their hiding places or take action of any kind, but to simply keep track of the renegades. Then after dark, return to the main group with the Indian's camp location and set up the ambush for the following morning. Sure enough, the renegades slowly followed the train keeping several miles behind it and staying off the hill tops so they wouldn't be seen. They hadn't noticed the two pairs of scouts' tracks breaking off from the main group because the ground was so sandy and the jumble of horse and cattle tracks covering a wide swath. The renegades sent scouts ahead to keep tabs on the wagon train. Their plan seemed to be to follow and look for opportunities to steal horses or take a shot at one of the cattle outriders. If they could cause panic of some kind and separate the train, they could actually attack the smaller groups successfully. Of course, everyone on the train knew they had to stay together at all cost. But the renegades were clever and could be counted on to be unpredictable.

Late the next evening, all four scouts returned with the location of the Indian camp, which was about three miles directly north of them. Donnal wished Harmon were there because of his extreme skill with a bow, and he was sorry he never learned himself. But he was a good shot as were many of the men in the train, and that would suffice nicely. Before first light Donnal set out on his fastest horse headed directly at the Indian camp. He had to be careful because they would surely have scouts posted and one might take a shot at him. The breeze was coming directly in his face and he could smell the faint odor of buffalo chip smoke. He peeked over a ridge and could make out the camp in a slight depression and could see the group of Indians packing up for the day. Donnal waited until they were all mounted and slowly made himself visible at the top of the ridge. He sat still in plain sight and after several minutes they spotted him. They were wary of tricks and walked their horses directly at him. Finally one of the Indians couldn't restrain himself and took a shot. Indians were notoriously poor marksmen with rifles and he missed badly, but the sound startled the rest of the group to charge; the race was on. Donnal's horse was far faster than any of the renegades' mounts and he stayed ahead of them relatively easily as he wound his way off to the west slowly descending into a creek bottom where eight of his friends, each with two loaded guns, lay in ambush. His route was indirect as he rushed back and forth stirring up the renegade's desire for blood. They thought their quarry was running in abject panic and this spurred them on, but actually Donnal was toying with them and luring them closer to destruction. The Indians were taken totally by surprise as they rushed down the ravine into the creek bottom; it seemed as if there were explosions everywhere. Indians and horses were both hit with the balls spitting in flames from the muzzles of the rifles. They didn't have a chance, only one made it through untouched, some were killed outright and some fell from their stricken horses, while those in the back fell over and trampled those in the front. The single survivor didn't slow down or look back as he knew his group had been destroyed. After the first fusillade hit the renegades, the men frantically reloaded so they could finish the deal. Donnal had mixed feelings about finishing off the injured Indians, but he knew if he left them alive, they would return and cause more grief for the settlers somewhere down the line. It was a nasty business that Donnal never forgot. They buried all the Indians and put the injured horses out of their misery. Donnal's party caught three of the horses that were uninjured and added them to their horse remuda. The next morning, the train turned directly to the west toward the mountains that glowed pink in the pre-dawn light.

In several weeks, the wagon train finally reached a permanent destination and had taken refuge in one of the small canyons just east of the Rocky Mountains along what is now called Castlewood. The canyon was deep enough and wide enough to accommodate the entire group with timber for building, good grass, fresh water and enough fertile ground for large gardens. The remains of their dwellings still exist nearly two centuries later nestled in the protection of the canyon walls. Donnal knew he must return to Confluence before November, because of the possibility of early season blizzards. He never forgot the one he, Harmon and Lydia had endured some years earlier, and in all his travels, he never again got caught in one.

The very next spring Donnal signed on with a 200 mule pack train headed up into Wyoming Territory, hoping to go all the way to The Dalles. He was a wrangler and scout, but his real reason was to gain experience on that route. Their route took them past what came to be known as Chimney Rock and then Scottsbluff as they followed the North Platte until it turned sharply to the south. Then they went straight west past Split Rock, through South Pass and on to Tortoise Rock. South Pass was the point at which many turned back. Wagons had to be dismantled and carried on the backs of the draft animals, then re-assembled on the other side. They had constant trouble with losses of both horses and mules to the Indians who took pride in being able to steal an animal from under the noses of the trail bosses. The mule train had too many well armed men on horseback to be in any real danger. But the outriders had to be careful not to be ambushed by small groups of warriors watching the train from a distance. The trail was well worn with the tracks of thousands of animals and wagons that went before. The distances between water holes or creeks were well understood by the guides as the trail was established on the basis of avoiding mountains and following sources of water. Donnal spent a lot of time as an out-rider and hunted for edible game along the way. His favorite was the grouse and wild turkey, but occasionally shot a deer or two. They made good progress until about old Fort Hall where previous wagons that arrived there realized that was the end of the road. Most of the wagons were sold or dismantled and used as building materials; some made the trip back with disappointed settlers. They picked up the southern bank of the Snake River and continued on to the west, but the going was definitely much more difficult and the trail was one animal wide in many places.

The Snake turned to the north, and they continued to follow it for nearly a month more before turning to the north-west straight at the Blue Mountains and Lee's Encampment. Once clear of the mountains they turned true west at Echo and found the Columbia River basin and The Dalles. At that point the train broke up into a half dozen smaller groups each going to a different destination and leaving many of the wranglers with a pocket full of money, a good horse and plenty of free time. Donnal wanted to get a look at the ocean and continued on west with one of the small groups. When he finally got a look at the ocean he was astounded at its immensity. The monster waves breaking on the shore were frightening in size and power and he couldn't comprehend how anyone could survive in a wooden boat out in that maelstrom. He took a job as a hand on a ferry boat crossing the river from what is now Astoria. It was a steam powered boat that used wood as its power source. He frequently led wood cutting parties into the adjacent forests to find, cut and haul the dead stuff suitable for burning. His Captain, a middle aged Scottish gentleman with the name of McCovey, took a liking to Donnal and taught him how to operate the boat. He enjoyed the job so much; he stayed for a number of years until old McCovey's young wife got involved. She also took a liking to Donnal but in a different way and it wasn't long before she had enticed him onto her paillasse. He was inexperienced at that sort of thing, but she obviously was not, and it wasn't long before he couldn't stay away. He knew it was a sordid deal and at the first hint of the next spring, shook old McCovey's hand and was off, back to the deserts and mountains and away from "that woman."

It was fall by the time he returned to Confluence. The town was empty and most of the buildings were in shambles. The threat of Indian attacks had driven all of the residents either east or west to the protection of the forts. He was dismayed to find Kanti's buildings abandoned. There was no sign that a garden had been grown the previous summer. The original sod house and the root cellar had caved in. Half the buildings had been burned and there were signs that a fight had occurred some months back. He looked through Kanti's house for some sign as to their whereabouts, but found none. He looked around for graves and found quite a number of possibilities but none were identified. Once more the chaos of the west had swallowed a friend or family member never to be heard from again. It was 1828.

Lydia was a healthy woman and had no trouble with child bearing. Their daily grind was grueling; they were up at first light, tending the chores, washing clothes, and hand watering the garden. Chickens were their only source of meat and she killed, plucked, gutted and cooked one every day for dinner or supper. Harmon spent every hour he could in the fields trying to grow enough to sell. He insisted that Lydia rest several times each day. The area around Parishville had a traveling doctor or sorts that told her she must eat meat and vegetables every day. As the years slipped by, Harmon became slowly more bitter about his situation and his failure to properly provide for and educate his children. Lydia secretly longed for the old days, when they had adventure and economic security. Her life had turned into a never ending struggle to survive. There was always something that ate up the small savings they managed to hold together. Their older boys William and Adolphus worked part-time for their neighbors to bring in extra food or a pair of shoes. Charlotte and her older sisters married and moved away the first chance they got. Their farm was incapable of furnishing them with an adequate living, no matter how hard they worked. The ground had lost its fertility years before. Poverty and hopelessness slowly overtook the family.

The dozen years or so before the Civil War was a turbulent time. The issue of slavery had become divisive and everyone had an opinion one way or the other. Then when the South attacked Fort Sumter in the fall of 1861, military units all over the north were being formed. Adolphus, shortened to Adolph, saw this as a chance to get away from the hard work and poverty in which he found himself, and implored his Mom to let him join up. The 16th Infantry Regiment was forming over in Pottsdam and a couple of his friends were urging him to come and join Company B. Harmon didn't like the idea and flatly refused to let him go. His life had become full of bitterness and disappointment and if he lost a son to the war, it would kill him. But Adolph was 19 and strong headed; he rolled his meager clothing into a ball, kissed his Mom on the cheek and ran to Pottsdam.

# CIVIL WAR

There were tables set up in the main street of Pottsdam, each with a line of 50 to 100 young men all eager to sign up for the war. Behind each table was an officer of the newly formed 16<sup>th</sup> Infantry. Adolph couldn't read the signs so he asked his buddy where to go and he said it didn't make any difference. They got into the line that had the most impressive looking officer which happened to be Major Bull Palmer. When he finally got to the front of the line, he was asked to sign his name, but he could not. So his friend signed it for him, Adolphus McCumber; it was September 11, 1861. They were put up in tents and each given a uniform; their training commenced the next morning. Adolph was amazed at the number of young men that had volunteered. He couldn't put a number on it but it was more people than he thought were in the whole state of New York. They marched and marched and marched some more and after a week received orders to join other units of the 16<sup>th</sup> down in Fort Lyon, Virginia. It was the first time Adolph had been away from home and he was amazed at all the towns and farms they passed along the way. Young women and girls stood by the side of the road and threw kisses to them as they marched by. When he saw them he strutted his best and tried to look straight ahead as if he hadn't seen they were there. His friend Willy on the other hand insisted on smiling at them which got him in trouble with the sergeant and at the end of the day Willy was put on latrine duty. Finally at Fort Lyon, they were mustered into Company B and attached to the Army of the Potomac. By that time it was November and the fighting had pretty well subsided; so his unit was sent to winter at Camp Franklin near Fairfax, Virginia.

Compared to the farm back home, winter camp was easy. They got to eat every day and had warm little log cabins each with a fireplace, to sleep in. They spent most days practicing their marksmanship and battle formations. The one that impressed Adolph the most was the formation in which they would line up six ranks deep, the front rank would all fire, then each soldier would turn to his right and scramble back behind the last rank and the second would fire, and then scramble and so on until all six had fired. By then the first ranks would have reloaded and would fire to start it all over. Other groups did it differently, but the result was a nearly continuous stream of firing. The problem was the noise affected their hearing and they couldn't hear much for several hours after. Adolph used his free time to practice his reading as several of the soldiers in his cabin were willing to help those that needed it. The winter went by quickly and they kept hearing about the tough times other units were having. The biggest problems they had were washing clothes, bathing and toiletry. The latrines filled quickly and the smell was overwhelming even for winter. In early April they were sent to Catlett's Station and prepared for their first battle. Adolph was glad to get away from the winter camp because of the odor of both the latrines and the cabins. He was glad to be sleeping in a tent in a different place each night where the air was fresh. A few weeks later Company B was thrust into its first battle at West Point.

Confederate General Joe Johnston had suddenly disengaged the battle of Yorktown and was rushing back up the peninsula toward Richmond. Company B was part of the Army of the Potomac that was put aboard transport ships and sent to Ethan's landing to try to head off Johnston's troops. They had been held in reserve during Yorktown and were yet to see any shooting and Adolph could see everyone was up tight as a bow string. They tried to sleep where they sat but could not because of the sounds of battle in the distance. When they finally arrived at the Landing everyone rushed off the boats and formed up into their companies, ready to march. The sergeant said they were to form a skirmish line in the woods on each side of the landing to protect it from Confederates that were coming up from the south under General Hood. They had just found a good spot to hunker down in the heavy woods, when ahead of them they could hear the approaching Confederates. Balls of lead started flying and zipping over head psssst, pssst. Before they could shoot back the sergeant yelled to pull back. Adolph was astonished, because they hadn't even engaged the enemy and he wanted to stay, but everyone was running past him back out of the woods onto the bare ground of the landing. The gunboats from the river started shooting their cannons over the heads of Union troops holed up on the landing into the woods were the advancing Confederates had set up some cannons of their own. The Union gunboats had more range than the Confederates did and made quick work of the situation driving them back away from the landing. It was frightening to hear and see balls of flame screaming overhead back and forth. Adolph rolled over onto his back so he could look up and watch the exchange and for the first time wished he was back home. Just after noon, the Confederates could see the situation was futile and withdrew, so Adolph and his Company went back into the woods. Before evening, they had orders to form up as they were going up the peninsula to Mechanicsville. They marched into the night into a light rain. Adolph and his buddies could hear the lightning and thunder up ahead of them. Some thought it was more cannon blasts, but Adolph was just trying to stay dry and at that point it didn't matter. The situation was confusing, it was dark, cold and wet and they didn't know where they were or where they were going, but they did know they were headed for trouble. Finally they received the halt order and fell out and tried to erect enough protection from the rain that they could sleep.

They were at Mechanicsville and didn't see any actual battle, then Chicahominy, and into the part of the war called the Seven Days' Battle in which an entire week was spent exchanging fire with the Confederates. Nobody got hurt or wounded and they seemed to stay out of all the major fighting around them. They went through Oak Grove, and Beaver Dam Creek, then on the third day of the Seven, the battle was at Gaines' Mill, and that was the first real battle Company B would see; everyone was apprehensive. The Union General McClellan had ordered General Porter to which Adolph's Company was attached to hold the ground at all cost. Confederate Generals Magruder and Jackson had 50,000 men assembled and intended to run over the Union lines under Porter. Union General Slocum helped Porter avoid a complete rout but Porter ended up in full retreat. The 16th Infantry Regiment had 231 men either wounded or killed that day, June 27, 1862 and had to leave most of them behind. Adolphus McCumber, age 20, was one of them. No one knows whether he died quickly or was wounded and died slowly. We hope it was the former as the battle was ferocious for a little while and the injuries were gruesome. The point of the Confederate charge was right at Company B and it suffered most of the casualties of the day.

Word of Adolphus' death finally filtered back to the farm. Harmon was especially broken over the news and he grew more bitter about the war and his failures in life. He could hardly remember his times out west when he had felt alive and in control. Four decades of toil with the soil had beaten him down and he could barely walk or bend over, but he insisted on working in the fields each day with his two remaining sons, William and little Giles. Thirteen pregnancies had taken their toll on Lydia and she was frail and coughed constantly. Jane then married and left home, and Mary was about to. Romelia died of tuberculosis. They couldn't watch the deterioration of their parents and what the war and a life of struggle had done to them. By late 1863, the word was out that the Union needed more soldiers and units were forming in Parishville for the 14th New York Heavy Artillery Regiment. In December William said goodbye to his Mom and left. His Father wouldn't talk to him and refused to let him go. William was 28 when he left that run down little shack of a home, the two frail and beaten down parents, and young Giles, barely 13. William was to receive a bounty of $100 from the federal government and another $150 from the state when he mustered in. He thought it was a chance to get his folks out of debt and pay for a doctor to tend his Mother. So, when he mustered in on December 29th, he walked back out to the farm with the cash, handed it to his Dad, and turned around and ran back to Parishville. Harmon shook with grief as he watched his son slowly run out of sight, for he felt that was the last time he would see him. And it was. He was sorry that he had not been a better Father; shaken William's hand firmly and wished him God Speed.

The 14th was involved in seven battles during 1864 into 1865. Somewhere along the line William picked up an injury to his right leg and it festered for over a month until he was finally removed from battle in May 1865. They had been through, Wilderness, Spotsylvania Court House, Ny River, North Anna, Totopotomoy and Cold Harbor. He had been promoted to Corporal then demoted back to Private. He was sent to the US General Hospital in Chester Pa., where his right leg was removed. More than a year later in 1867, he made his way back to the farm at Parishville and found it abandoned. The field was grown over with weeds and the house had been emptied of everything of value. He inquired about the whereabouts of his parents in Parishville, and was told Harmon had passed over a year ago and was buried in the yard by young Giles. He could see where Harmon's grave was, as the dirt was soft and only partially grown over with weeds. He dug up the box and took it to the Chapel Hill Cemetery and buried it properly. Nobody knew the whereabouts of young Giles for he had set out to fulfill his dream of going west. The bank owner gave William several hundred dollars for the farm. He had a friend in the 14th from Erie County and walking on one foot and one crutch, he headed southwest not realizing it was hundreds of miles away.

# DEATH OF CONFLUENCE

The conflict of the Civil War wasn't restricted to the east. Folks in the west formed small groups sympathetic to one side or the other and fought and killed each other all the time. The scale was much smaller, but the brutality was the same. Donnal was clearly on the side of the Union because his brothers lived there. In the intervening years he had been up and down nearly all the trails of the west, including a steam boat up the Missouri into Montana. Everywhere he went he asked about Kanti and Elsa or anyone with the name McCumber. He saw countless clay jars that once contained the recipe and inquired about their source. Occasionally he would run across someone that had heard the name McCumber, but every lead was a dead end. In the early 1850's, he had stopped writing letters back to New York as he had never received anything in return and thought Harmon dead. What once was a large and closely knit family had fallen apart; scattered to the wind. When Donnal thought about it, he became lonely and decided to go to St Louis and try to find the metal box his father spoke of. He was in Fort Laramie at the time, the trail back was well traveled and many good sized towns had grown up along the way. Donnal had never married and now that he was approaching the last half of his days, thought if he had the chance to do it over, he should have married somewhere along the way. He was a

tall, broad shouldered, lean man with light blue eyes, balding
blond hair and still attractive to women, but there were so few
women in the west, he just never had the opportunity. Donnal
slowly came to the realization that he needed a wife. His friends
laughed at him and suggested that they knew female animals that
would make him a good wife. This kind of talk only made him
more determined and he decided that on his trip to St Louis, he
would keep his eyes open for likely widows. He said farewell
to his demented friends for the last time, as he intended never
to return, and with a good horse under him and a strong pack-
horse behind, set off alone down the Platte.

The hills of southeast of the Fort along the river were green
with knee high grass. It waved in the incessant breeze and as
Donnal rode he realized he had come to love this land. He loved
the wide open spaces and the threat of danger. He loved sitting
by a warm fire in the evenings and watching the western sky
glow pink, red and lavender. He had to think of the future and
he had to think of settling down and "sinking roots" as some
called it. He was right in the middle of Arapaho and Cheyenne
country and bands of each were watching the Oregon Trail for
trains of wagons they could plunder. He would have to keep a
low profile and avoid smoky fires. He was wise in the ways of
the Indians and could read the land, the breeze and the weather.
He knew where the trail watchers would be holed up and where
the main groups liked to camp, and was confident he could
avoid trouble. He passed the Scott's Bluff, then Courthouse
and Jailhouse rocks, Chimney rock and on down to where
Confluence once thrived. Each time he had passed in the last
several decades, the place had deteriorated more until it was
little more that small piles of decayed logs and sod. He always
made camp there so he could sit and remember the old days
when the place was full of activity. He recalled Bella and how
she was such a pretty thing and wondered what ever happened
to all her half Arapaho sons. They were probably among those
raiding the settlers on the prairie. And then there was Roidh,
the kid with the crooked hair. A big chunk of his scalp had been

knocked loose by the glancing blow of a tomahawk, and when Harmon tied it back on it was a little crooked. It knit OK but looked odd. That kid could sure catch rabbits. It brought a smile to his face. Kanti and Elsa were always so serious in those days, they never took any days off; there was always something that needed attention. He couldn't imagine that they weren't alive and thriving somewhere. If they were, they would have sent word to Brendan McGill in St Louis. Donnal had nosed around the ruins and the adjacent area on several occasions, but he never noticed two small posts sticking a foot or so straight up out of the ground on top of the hill overlooking the town. One side had been flattened and burned into the flat with a hot iron, one said KM and the other EM.

Donnal passed several large trains of wagons, each with a hundred or more wagons and hundreds of cattle and horses. He also passed a few wagons headed back to the east with forlorn looking folks who had come to the realization that the west was too tough for them. Usually someone in the family had been killed, and the disillusioned remainder decided to go back. These were the wagons the Indian raiders liked because they were easy marks. He recalled that was the way Harmon and Lydia had met many decades earlier; how feisty and what a good shot she was. He had tried to talk them out of going back to New York to no avail as he was sure they had the stuff to succeed in the west. He never knew what happened to them. Every wagon he came upon going east, he hoped there would be a woman like Lydia driving. Most of the other wagon masters knew him personally and every time they crossed paths, he was invited to supper with them. He insisted on compensating them in some way and usually shot a small animal of some kind that he could contribute to the meal. He saw a few healthy and interesting women but they were always going the other way. When the Platte finally drained into the Missouri River, he pretty much gave up, sold his horses and much of his gear and took a boat to Independence.

O'Brian was still in business in his two story building and had a booming trade in tools, weapons, blankets, food staples and the recipe. He had two different clay pot makers make his jars and paid a family to raise a gigantic garden of vegetables. He had vinegar and cayenne pepper shipped up from New Orleans and used local honey for the sweetener. O'Brian told Donnal that Brendan McGill had pulled up stakes and set out across Kansas Territory for the southwest. Someone had convinced him that there were thousands of cattle running wild that could be rounded up and sold. As far as he knew McGill had never ridden a horse, so it must have been quite an experience. He had set off to the southwest at least five years ago in the company of three other hopeful souls, all green but able. O'Brian had not heard anything back, and he had not heard anything from Kanti and Elsa for decades. He had concluded, correctly, that they had been killed somewhere along the line. Donnal stayed with O'Brian for some months and they became very fond of each other. He enjoyed O'Brian's hair raising stories about his Dad. O'Brian was looking for someone that could take over the business as he was ready to hang up his store keeper's apron and sit around and enjoy talking to all the travelers that came through town. So Donnal agreed, but first he wanted to go to St Louis and retrieve the metal box.

The trip to St Louis was an easy one by this time as the giant paddle wheel flat boats were charging up and down almost daily. Donnal went directly to the old trading post his Father had built decades earlier. There were strange faces in the place, but all the goods were still for sale except the recipe. The sign on the front still said, "McCUMBER." The big garden that furnished the vegetables was still active, but they sold the produce locally and to the paddle boats. They also cut and stacked piles of wood for sale to the paddle boats. The building was just as he had remembered; several windows had been added to let natural light in. He spoke with the owners for quite a while and inquired about the details of the transaction McGill had made with them. He was advised that a sizable sum was waiting for him at the bank as his share of the deal. He had to go to the bank anyway and thought he could kill two birds with one stone. He stopped in one of the local drinking establishments on the way and was instantly taken with the owner-bartender of the place. It was called Lucy Heart's Palace and featured dancing girls, small plays on the stage, with food and drink. He had seen the woman a year or so earlier going to the east after her husband and son had been killed, and had struck up a friendship with her at that time. Out of respect, they had only exchanged kindnesses, but he had ridden with her for several days until she could hook up with others going the same direction. He hadn't remembered her name until he saw it on the sign out front. She instantly recognized him as a man of probity, and pulled him to a table to renew an old friendship. She got right to the point and asked him to become her partner and stay with her. He was a little bowled over by her proposal, but interested. Within a half hour, he asked her to marry him. And, she said yes. His head was spinning with infatuation and the whiskey he had just downed, and after kissing her on the mouth, excused himself to continue his walk to the bank. He was looking for a wife and found one in a single hour; he couldn't believe it. He shook his head to clear it a little as he entered what he thought was the bank that had the metal box. After he was informed there was no metal box anywhere in the bank, he inquired about the deposit that had been left by Brendan McGill and was given a large envelope stuffed with bills in exchange for his signature on a strange paper. He was told that the bank had moved three or more times in the last several decades and that the metal box had been lost along the way. What nobody knew was that one of the bank employees had taken a liking to the box and had emptied the contents into a waxed leather bag, put it on a shelf, and absconded with the box. The papers were on a shelf in the back room where they would remain for decades more and nobody realized it. Donnal left disappointed, but much richer. Now he had a dilemma on his hands, he had made two separate and conflicting commitments.

Back at Lucy's, he immediately penned a letter to O'Brian. The wedding was the next day in the dance hall. Several hundred folks attended as the beer was free. Lucy was a busty woman a few years younger than Donnal. She never dressed provocatively and always showed poise and respectability even if some of her dancers did not. This was one of the things Donnal liked about her. It wasn't long before Donnal found himself serving drinks and beer at the bar. He liked to talk with the men and heard all kinds of wild tales about what was happening on the trail west. The coming Civil war was a hot topic and more than a few fights broke out over the situation. Donnal had to use his oak stick to control a few of the more hot headed gentlemen from time to time. He found that a firm stroke across the head of the antagonist usually settled the issue quickly. He settled down to the humdrum of working six days a week. The bar was closed on Sunday and Lucy insisted that they go the church, much to the chagrin of some of the prim and proper ladies of the city. But he survived and bowed and removed his hat to the tight lipped ladies who slowly began to enjoy his gentlemanly attention. Lucy was enjoying the slow transformation from bar owner to respectable merchant.

Donnal especially liked to chat with the old trail masters and fur trappers. He always questioned them as to the whereabouts of Kanti, little sister Lydia or Brendan McGill. He found one old timer that heard Lydia had married to a Mormon in Utah Territory, and had a bunch of kids. But there was never any word on Kanti or Elsa. Until, one stormy evening in late-summer one of the real, bearded mountain men came in and proceeded to get loose-lipped. He had been up in the mountains of the South Platte and brought down several bales of beaver and sold them so he could have a good ole time then return for the winter trapping season. He told Donnal of his dealings with a white man that lived with the Ute, and how he had always been fair with them and split his fur haul. Donnal immediately asked if he knew the name of the man and he replied, "Harmunnn." Donnal knew it was their family friend that he, young Harmon, and sister-in-law Lydia visited some 40 years ago. When the trapper met him, old Harmon was an old man and could barely take care of his personal needs, but he really liked to talk about the old days and "spun yarns that would curl your hair." Donnal knew those yarns were most likely true. The old trapper stayed in St Louis until his money started to run out and went down a bought all the stuff he'd need for another season. But, before he left he said he wanted to tell Donnal something he had been holding onto but felt he had let go. So, he and Donnal went over and sat at a corner table and while the old trapper sipped on a beer, he told Donnal the story of how, many years ago, he came upon Confluence just after it had been raided by the Arapaho. He thought it was the Arapaho, but couldn't be sure. He was coming down the South Platte with several big bundles of beaver fur in his little boat. Two more trappers were in a slightly larger boat behind him. They had seen signs of large bands of Indians crossing the river, and had looked forward to the relative safety of the small town. They could see smoke coming from where the town should have been, so they pulled their boats up into some willows and crept through the brush to where they could see what happened. Everyone had been tortured and sliced up. Some were disemboweled, some mutilated while alive, and some burned. Most of the dead were men and boys, although some were the older women that were of no use to the raiders. All the dead looked to have been molested and defiled except two, Kanti and Elsa McCumber. They were dead all right, but simply had been shot and laid out next to each other with respect. Kanti had been the founder of the town, so they buried him and Elsa up on the hill overlooking the place and marked their graves with small posts with their initials burned into the surface with a hot iron. The old trapper said they spent a week there burying everyone, but only marked those belonging to Kanti and Elsa. Donnal immediately knew it had to be the Arapaho. Kanti and Elsa were spared the torture and disfigurement because of their long friendship with the Arapaho and their association with

Bella and her seven sons. Not much of a consolation for the only school educated McCumber.

At first, Donnal was reluctant to believe the story, but after he asked a few questions about details only someone that had been there could answer, he accepted its truth. The years started becoming comfortable and the Civil War came and went. Lucy and Donnal didn't have any children, but they had built their circle of friends into the hundreds. He financed dozens of trappers, prospectors and young merchants with a compelling sounding story. Once in a while he would get something in return, but more likely was the chance that he would never hear from them again. Donnal visited his elderly friend O'Brian in Independence many times and finally bought the place. He turned it into a saloon and dance hall similar to the one in St Louis. It was much less work and much more profitable. He paid a young couple, who claimed they were teetotalers, to run the place. Lucy and Donnal grew respectable and old together. He had known adventures young men only dream about; he had been places and seen things few folks could even comprehend, and he relished and remembered every one.

# WEST, THE FINAL TIME

Young Giles was alone on the farm with his failing parents. His Dad had taken the money William gave them for enlisting down to the bank in Parishville and paid off their loan, leaving a few dollars left for the doctor. Harmon's injuries from a fall and the resulting arthritis were so severe by this time there was no relief for it. His hands and feet both were horribly bent and deformed and it left him unable to walk more than a few steps at a time. Lydia was coughing day and night and couldn't lie down without going into a coughing fit. So she had to sleep sitting up, which of course, added to her rate of deterioration. The doctor told them she must have total rest and had to be kept warm and breathe the steam of boiling water, but she wouldn't give up on taking care of her men, and between the two therapies, started improving. It was Harmon that quickly failed because of his maladies; he slowly lost his ability to walk, and then sit and finally passed. The local preacher came to the house, said prayers and, because they had no money, told young Giles to dig a grave out behind the house. Giles pulled some boards off the old shed and made a box just big enough for his Dad. The next morning, he put him in the box and dragged it to the edge of the hole and slid it down some boards into the bottom. He brought out a chair for his Mom, who read from the Bible, and they had their own burial service. She sat in the chair and watched young Giles fill the hole with dirt; tears streaming down her face. She continued to sit there, watched the sun go down and remembered all the times that she and Harmon shared at sunset, then stayed in the chair until late that night when young Giles had to literally pick her up, carry her into the house, and put her to bed. Her daughter Susan Goodale, from Colton came and took Lydia home to live with her where she finally passed years later in 1887.

Giles paused at the top of High Flats, a small group of flat-topped hills a few miles to the southwest of the farm, and looked back at the farms around Parishville. His eyes were moist as the years flashed through his mind. He had seen years of hard work and poverty from the time he could first remember; they were always one day away from being thrown off their place. He would miss his parents, his brothers and sisters, but he wouldn't miss the bad times, the nights of hunger, and the depression of his Dad. He gathered everything he thought he would need for his trip west, including his Grandfather's compass, rolled it and the fabric recipe up in an oilcloth around his bow and set off to the southwest before dawn. It was spring 1866.

Unable to read signs and totally dependent on word of mouth from the folks he met along the way, Giles walked directly across country through farm fields and past houses. He stopped at several and asked for water from the farmer's wives and was given smiles and offers of friendship. He was a tall, broad shouldered young man with large, long arms and huge hands. He had blond hair and blue eyes just like his Grandfather. He insisted that he work for the meals he received; refusing to take charity. At Colton, after a brief stay with his sister and a final goodbye to his Mom, he picked up a two track wagon road going his way and stuck with it most of the day and the next. He slept in barns and hay stacks and bathed in creeks. Everywhere he stopped, when he offered to work for food, his proposition was accepted. In the years after the war, thousands of young men returned to abandoned farms and homes and had to strike out for themselves. It was common behavior to offer to work

for a meal; a tradition was created that would last for a hundred
years. Young Giles finally ran into Lake Ontario and followed
it around to Oswego. A branch of the Erie Canal connected to
the lake there and he was able to get a job as a "hoggee" and
drove horses that pulled the barges. He worked there most of
the summer and finally got the same job on the main canal to
Buffalo.

Buffalo was a gigantic and confusing place to Giles, and
he had to be extremely careful not to get lost. He stuck to the
neighborhood where the Erie Canal actually connected to Lake
Erie. He had his favorite boarding house that provided plenty of
food and comfortable beds. It was the first time he had actually
slept on anything but a paillasse. Once in a while he had a half
day off and would venture over to the main wharf where the big
boats that sailed the Great Lakes were loading and unloading.
They were hundreds of feet long; some were paddle driven and
some had sails. He loved to take a lunch and watch the big
steam powered hoists lift the cargo from the wharf to the ships
and vice versa. Workers swarmed the loading process to well
orchestrated voice commands of the dock boss. One day he
happened to be there just as lunch was taken by the workers and
liked to watch some of the bigger men arm wrestle each other.
One of the men invited him to try it, but he declined saying
that he had never done it. The workers involved in the contest
were some of the larger men with bulging muscles and Giles was
intimidated, but he never forgot the challenge and asked some
of his older cohorts to show him the proper techniques. After a
few dozen impromptu contests with his friends, he found he was
quite good and easily beat anyone his knew. He was very careful
not to be overbearing and took his time about challenging folks.
He slowly accumulated a reputation up and down the canal and
started having unknown men with pockets stuffed with money
challenge him, while others bet on the outcome. As he became
better at it, one of his older bosses started lining up little contests
in which handfuls of money changed hands. He made lots of
money for his friends, but didn't have enough himself to do any

betting. Starting small, he slowly began betting on his skill and after a while had more money than he knew what to do with, and he was just a kid.

Giles was doing well and was slowly learning to read. He started with the signs along the canal, then signs over businesses and finally street signs. He learned to decipher a map and relate it to the physical characteristics of the city or countryside. He couldn't actually read a book or newspaper, but he could make out enough to get the drift of the story. His friends devised things for him to lift and exercises that would strengthen his arms and he finally reached the point in his arm wrestling where nobody would bet against him. He beat men much larger and heavier. Even though he was happy with life there, he was drawn to his original dream of going west and becoming a cowboy or marshal. In the winter of 1867, he signed on with the great lakes steamer Morning Star$_r$ as a freight loader and general hand. It was a 243 foot side paddle steam powered ship with 38 foot diameter paddles. It made regular trips from Cleveland and Buffalo to Detroit and all the way around to Chicago. Captain E.R. Viger$_r$ had noticed Giles in one of his arm wrestling contests and admired the tenacity and good mannered perseverance the young man possessed. Giles loved the ship and the water and he drove himself to be the hardest worker in the crew, so he wouldn't lose his job. Even though he was the youngest, he had the respect of the other crew members, because of his ethics and strength. Whenever they would make a new port, his crew friends would go ashore and line up some arm wrestling contests for him. Then when he showed up, the opponents would laugh at his youth and size and give his friends a chance to double the bets, which they usually did. Giles was nearly maniacal when the contest judge would slap the table for the match to start. He broke several men's arms and injured many more. Gradually his reputation got around and everyone in the port cities refused to match up with him. In the process though, he pocketed hundreds of dollars for his place out west. This was even better than the canal job, because he got to go to new places and learn to read more signs and meet new people. He was slowly realizing just how big America was and this stimulated his growing need to move on.

It took a dangerous accident to push him to continue on west. In late June 1868 about midnight, the barque Cortland, and the Morning Star collided. Giles was in his bunk just behind where the Cortland broadsided the Star. Before he could figure out what was happening, he was thrown from his bunk and submerged in water. The Star was mortally injured and sank in less than 15 minutes, while the Cortland took over an hour to go down. It was dark and the water was black; Giles didn't know how to swim. Water rushed into the Star as she broke in half and the stern and bow both went down first. She was loaded with pig iron, nails, stone and machinery so the sinking happened fast. Giles was trapped, and thought he was done for when suddenly the ship tilted so the open hole was up; he was released and floated to the surface. He thrashed around there and grabbed onto some pieces of wood for buoyancy. He could hear his shipmates screaming for help as some that had surfaced were injured; all were frightened. The lake was rough and the waves high. It was the longest night of his life as the water was cold and the waves washed over him every few seconds; but he hung on. Gradually the screaming stopped and all was quiet, except for a few that shouted to be calm and help was on the way. About 3 AM, the R.N. Rice, arrived at the scene and rescued all the survivors that were in sight including Giles. The Star had 32 crewmembers and about 40 passengers; roughly half were never recovered. Captain of the Rice, William McKay,, took everyone to Detroit and offered to keep all of the Star's crew on for the trip on around to Chicago. Giles promised himself that he would depart the open water for dry land as soon as possible. Once in Chicago, Giles limped down the gangplank with borrowed clothes on his back; his money and all his belongings, including the recipe, had gone down with the Star. McKay had given him the few dollars pay he had coming. There he was, young and disheartened in a city he had only visited briefly several times. He basically would have to start over, but he was alive.

He walked down the street toward the middle part of town and contemplated his plight. First, he would find a place to stay and pay them in advance, then he would find a bar and use what little money he had left to finance his arm wrestling. He walked past several seedy looking joints and finally settled on one that seemed to have a lot of people inside. When he walked through the door the bartender yelled at him to leave because they didn't serve kids. Several burly bouncers walked menacingly toward him to help his exit. He was able to tell one of them he was not there to drink that he was there to arm wrestle. The bouncer laughed and yelled to the bartender that the kid wanted to arm wrestle and everyone had a good laugh. They let Giles in thinking they would take his money, then, throw him out. The larger of the two was willing to take him on and they sat down at the nearest open table. Several of the bar ladies crowded around Giles and mussed his hair and bet their services against his money. But he would only bet money for money and after some belligerent discussion among the crowd around the table, they finally settled on a bet. Giles got 2 to 1 odds against the big bouncer. They sat facing each other and when the bouncer grasped Giles huge hand he started having second thoughts. Giles' grip was so strong it hurt the bouncer and the contest hadn't even started. Everyone around was trying to bet more when they saw the look of pain on the bouncer's face, but the bartender slapped the table and "bam," Giles broke the bouncer's arm. The bouncer screamed in pain and everyone around started yelling for their money. Giles grabbed his small pile of money that was lying on the table and jammed it into his pocket. Pandemonium broke out for a few minutes as Giles simply sat as if saying, "Who's next?" Several people helped the broken bouncer out the front door as Giles looked around the room sizing up his next opponent. Now the other bouncer felt duty bound that he should avenge his friend's injury and decided to challenge Giles. Giles pulled out his little handful of money and placed it on the table, but the bouncer didn't have enough to cover it, even one to one. A big busted bar lady dug a handful of cash out of her cleavage and smacked it on the table looking Giles in the eye and said, "You young bastard." That's all it took, Giles motioned for the bouncer to take a seat and held out his huge hand. The bouncer was intimidated at the young boy's hand. He took hold of it slowly and could feel the unbelievable grip Giles had. The bouncer had done some arm wrestling and was so big he had beaten everyone easily, but he wasn't what you would call a practiced professional like Giles. When the bartender slapped the table, Giles let him push his hand back a little ways to give the bouncer some encouragement, then held and slowly went the other way. When he had the bouncer's arm at about a 45 degree angle backwards, he slammed it down hard and that bouncer cried out in pain. Everyone went nuts; there was pushing and shoving and yelling from both men and women. Giles pocketed the money on the table and made his way out of the place. Several older gentlemen followed him and offered to put him up in their homes if he would arm wrestle for them. He declined. In the space of ten minutes, he made more money than he did in a month of work on the Morning Star.

After a good meal and a peaceful night's sleep, Giles was ready to move on. Several more gentlemen were waiting for him in the lobby with propositions, but he was determined to go on west. As he walked straight west down the street, the men prattled on about all the money he could make and the high life he could live, but he never fell for it. Even though he did enjoy his arm wrestling, he realized it was simply a way to raise money in tight times, and that once people knew of him his betting advantage would evaporate. Besides that, his Dad always told him that no matter how tough you were, there was always someone tougher. He knew that sooner or later he would lose.

William, Giles' older brother, had a crude wooden prosthetic leg that fit onto the bottom of his stump, he could use to walk short distances, but when he had to go farther, he used his crutch. He had mastered the technique of kind of swinging from his good leg to the crutch and could make good time, but his right arm got tired and he had to stop and rest regularly. When he finally hit a road headed south west, people were kind in offering him a ride on their wagons and he quickly accepted. He inquired about the location of Erie County and people either didn't know or looked at him in amazement and told him he had a long trip ahead. "Just keep going southwest toward Buffalo," they would say. He slept out in the open most nights and bathed in the streams. When it was too windy or cold he would rent a room or offer to work for a room at a farm. Folks took pity on him and accepted him into their homes without question and pampered him with food and warm blankets, but he insisted on always leaving a small bit of money with them when he left. He passed over the branch of the Erie Canal that ran from Oswego down to the main line to Buffalo and from the bridge watched the "hoggee" drive the horses slowly pulling a giant barge. It could have been his younger brother Giles that was driving the horses; he didn't notice. He slowly and surely made his way to Erie County, but could not locate his friend. At the end of the Civil War, thousands of service men returned home only to find it gone, or abandoned, or occupied by some strangers. That had apparently happened here. Finally, one evening in a small hamlet called Colden, he gave up and resigned himself to the fact that he was stuck and would have to find a temporary job. It was that money that allowed him to continue on to the west all the way to Lincoln County Iowa, where he bought land, and settled down to family life with his wife Harriet.

He was good with mechanical things and understood how things went together and why they worked the way they did. While he was eating one day he overheard one of the townsmen complaining that he had nobody that could fix his mill. It turned out the man was the owner of a flour mill there in the town and William offered his services to look at the mechanical monster to see if he could fix it. As you would expect, William was able to diagnose the problem in short order and told the owner exactly what he had to do to get the thing running. He was offered a job on the spot, and accepted. He used part of his money to purchase a small house in town and with a steady job, became the town's most eligible bachelor. The old farm in Parishville seemed a long way off and his memory of all the hard times faded quickly. He always wondered what ever happened to young Giles and never knew that his little brother was working the Erie Canal and resided in Buffalo. After some months went by, one of his friends there in town brought a handbill back from Buffalo that challenged all comers to arm wrestle the young iron man; his name was Giles McComber. The last name was spelled differently, but William was sure it was his brother. Young Giles had worked the farm from the time he could walk and was strong as an ox; much stronger than his older brothers. This had to be him. He carried the old handbill and hoped to find someone that could lead him to Giles.

News of the sinking of the Morning Star was in all the papers late that June. William was able to find out that about half of the people on board had been saved and once again he made the trip to the office of D&C in search of information on his brother. He was relieved to discover that Giles was among the survivors and had been taken to Chicago, paid and released. With no method of making contact with young Giles, William returned to Lincoln County where he wrote letters to the Chicago newspapers searching for word of a young arm wrestler by the name of Giles McComber. Months later he received a reply with a clipping from the newspaper dated August 1868, about a young arm wrestler that broke the arm of a burly bouncer, and then injured another in one of the popular dance halls in Chicago. The reporter that contacted him was told that the young man had stayed but one day in the city, then went on to the west; but where? William became even more determined to find his Brother. He had lost track of the remainder of the family and didn't want to lose this one.

Giles was able to catch a ride on a freight wagon going almost straight west out of Chicago. The bearded old driver was a big talker and needed someone to listen to him other than the mules. Giles got a big charge out of the old timer and shared his escapades about the arm wrestling and the sinking of the Star. He did have a goodly sum in his pocket and kept it a secret. They finally came to St Charles and stayed in the boarding house for the night. The old timer liked Giles and told him if he wanted to go all the way to Rockford, he would have to take another road that drifted off to the northwest. Over supper that evening the old driver told Giles about the woman friend he had in Rockford and how she wanted him to settle down and marry her, but he was resisting. He was a heavy, hairy, sweaty old guy with a tobacco stained beard and Giles was interested in what kind of woman would like to marry him. The old fellow wanted to stop at the local saloon for a drink after supper, so Giles agreed. He was told that he could sit with the old timer but could only have sarsaparilla. Giles' friend tried to get him to arm wrestle, but he was content to watch and told the old guy he wasn't interested. The arm wrestling matches in the saloon were becoming more and more interesting, and Giles could see that their technique was crude and followed the matches thinking that he would challenge the winner with the most money in the end. As the evening wore on, more and more new challengers came through the door and money started flowing freely. This was getting interesting and Giles bided his time. Everyone was talking about some monster of a man that was expected to show up within the hour.

Finally a gigantic man burst through the door with an entourage of flashily dressed men with hands full of bills. The giant looked to be well over six and a half feet tall and 300 pounds. His arms were the size of most men's legs, and his hands seemed small in comparison. He had a big black beard and a mouthful of rotten teeth that showed as he challenged the crowd to a match. Nobody took his challenge as things got very quiet in the saloon. He stomped and cussed and called everyone cowards. His handlers slapped piles of money on the table. Then they started offering odds. They started at two to one, then three and finally reached six to one. Giles pulled his money out and held it below the table where nobody could see it and counted out $96. It was a lot of money for Giles and he hesitated for a few minutes. Then he thought he would bet $90 and keep six. But he kept quiet as the handlers tried to goad various men into a match. So, Giles slapped the $90 down on the table and the crowd roared; they had a match. Black Beard sat down across from Giles and glared at him. He talked constantly telling Giles how he was going to injure him for life. The bartender made sure they put down the $540 to match Giles' bet, and he re-counted it. It was more money than most of the crowd had seen in one place in their entire lives. It was enough to buy a good sized farm most anywhere in the country. Black Beard put up his hand and Giles could tell he was a relative novice to arm wrestling and won through intimidation and sheer size. The bartender told him to put his elbow on the table, as Giles placed his elbow and grasped the man's hand. He squeezed hard and he could see Black Beard blink with surprise and concern. The crowd was jammed in close around the table as Black Beard roared at Giles who just sat and stared into his eyes. Giles could smell his rotten breath and knew he had to get it over with quickly. The bartender slapped the table and the match was on. Black Beard was stronger than any man Giles had ever wrestled and the giant tried to cheat by lifting his elbow and crowding the table. But Giles was experienced and held his position. Black Beard screamed with effort as he could not put Giles down. Beads of sweat appeared on Black Beard's face as Giles started getting the advantage. Giles could feel him tiring and started his final push. Black Beard was howling with effort as Giles slowly moved his arm farther and farther down toward the table. Suddenly Black Beard's bicep tendon snapped with a pop and his arm slammed back against the table. He moaned in pain and bawled like a baby as Giles and the old timer scooped up the money. The crowd was slapping Giles on the back and the women were offering their services free to the winner. But Giles and his old friend quickly made their exit and hustled directly back to the boarding house, much richer. For the first time,

Giles' arm hurt. The next morning they were on their way to Rockford. The old driver couldn't get over what had happened the previous evening and he talked about it for hours. It was an experience he would remember for life. He was beside himself with excitement and kept asking Giles to show him the money as if he wanted to be sure it hadn't been a dream.

Sycamore was a tiny hamlet of a dozen or so buildings. The old timer had to stop and get a wheel fixed at the local smithy, and while they were waiting, they strolled over to the only place in town where coffee was available. On the wall next to the door was handmade poster advertising for a hired man at one of the local farms. Giles knew what it was but couldn't read it very well and had to have the old timer help him. He finally got the drift of the poster and thought he should take the job. So, he got directions and walked out to the farm. James Ashcraft$_r$ had just about given up trying to hire someone to help him on his large farm. He had quite a bit of equipment and horses to pull them as well as a nice big house and two barns. Giles had never seen a farm so big or well kept and was favorably impressed. A boy about 10 saw Giles and went running out to the field to get his Dad. The farmer's wife Lucy$_r$ invited Giles to sit in the shade of the porch and told her oldest daughter Alice$_r$ to fetch him a fresh glass of water. Giles and Alice looked into each other's eyes; Giles felt his heart skip and he had to take a deep breath. About that time the Father, James appeared around the corner of the house and introduced himself, his wife and all the kids. Giles shook each of the seven children's hands, except the baby's, and when he came to Alice, it was electric. He was smitten and so was she. James got right to the point and offered Giles the job and was accepted in a second. He told James that he had to go to town and get his stuff and tell his friend that he would be leaving him and he would be back by sundown. And he was. A new chapter in his life was about to begin.

The farm was prosperous and the soil fertile. James used horse and cow manure in his fields to keep the soil in top condition. Giles asked James' help in depositing his money. They had to go clear to Rockford to find a bank James was happy with. James was amazed that a boy like Giles, who could barely read and write not a letter, could accumulate that kind of money, and Giles had to finally tell him about the match in St Charles. James got a big kick out of the story and shook Giles' hand and told him to squeeze hard. Giles nearly broke James' hand and when he winced in pain, Giles let go. James became a believer. What's more he was amazed at the strength the kid had so Giles described for him how his friends on the canal devised all kinds of exercises that would strengthen his hands and arms. Giles told him that he really didn't like to get involved in arm wrestling as a sport because of all the shady characters it attracted. It was the start of a friendship that would last until James passed many decades later. One of the first tasks the Ashcraft family had was teaching Giles how to read and write and do his numbers. Giles loved his work and looked forward to lunch when Alice would bring him some sandwiches wrapped in a cloth plus a big bottle of cold water. She would hang around and wait for him to finish the food and talked to him about her dreams and how she wanted to move to the city and make something of herself. He warned her about big cities and told her what usually happened to young girls that went there unattached. They became fast friends and traded dreams. He told her how he wanted to go on to the west and become a cowboy or marshal so he could chase cows and bad guys and she laughed at him. He decided that he should keep his dreams to himself.

William acquired a map of Chicago and points west and had Harriet write letters to the newspapers in the area requesting the names of more newspapers and inquiring about a young man that was an expert arm wrestler. It was a slow and laborious way to try to track down his brother, but it worked because the newspapers of the day were known to be cooperative in matters of that sort. There was an article in the Rockford paper that described the match between the Black Bearded giant and the young farm-boy. It was a David versus Goliath situation and everyone in five counties knew about it. The people of Sycamore finally learned the story, connected it to Giles and he became their local hero. William was excited and had Harriet write more letters to all the surrounding towns and finally received a letter from Lucy Ashcraft advising William that Giles worked on their farm. William immediately started making plans to go to Sycamore to visit his brother.

When Lucy Ashcraft received the letter from Harriet McCumber, she read it to Giles and could see tears form in the corners of his eyes. He didn't say much, but was touched that someone cared enough to try to find him. In the letter, William's wife told the story of how one legged William came home from the war and found the house abandoned and a grave in the yard. She explained how the town sheriff had helped William dig up the box and move it to the cemetery. With no place to go and no way to work the farm, he decided to look up an army buddy in Erie County. She described their farm and home in Lincoln County and told him that he always had a place to go to if needed. But Giles had no intention of going there; his dream was in the west. He tended to his work and knew in his heart that someday he would go to the west and make his fortune. He didn't realize that by the time he went there, it would have changed and caught up to civilization. The love between Giles and Alice grew to the point that they asked James and Lucy for permission to get married. In late summer of 1869, they tied the knot in the small church in Sycamore. It was a gay affair in which the old folks all cried, the young girls swooned and the men envied. Nine months later Agnes$_r$ was born and Giles was thinking it was time to go west.

When he mentioned that he thought it time to move on, James and Lucy disagreed and tried to talk him out of it. He had plenty of money to buy a farm and felt that he and Alice should start a place of their own. Alice agreed with Giles and it wasn't long before he was headed west again. With a wagon full of stuff, two good horses and a pocket full of money the young couple and little Agnes set out to the west. Lucy made Alice promise to write and let them know where she ended up. They hadn't been gone a day when the clouds opened up and it rained off and on for nearly a week. They tried to travel but the road was so muddy the horses couldn't make it, so they found a spot with some protection from the wind and made a crude camp. They had to sleep under the wagon to stay dry and sat under oil cloth covers during the day.

But, they struggled westward. Either it was too hot and humid or it was cold and rainy. Baby Agnes was unbothered by the rough ride in the wagon as she slept most of the time. Alice was enjoying her first trip away from home and wanted to stop to talk with everyone she saw. Giles was frustrated that he couldn't seem to find a good farm at a good price and they kept going west farther and farther. At a small place called Boone, there was a sign in town about a farm for sale, so Giles rode one of the horses out to see the place. It had been abandoned several years earlier and was overgrown with trash bushes and weeds. In the front door, a message was scratched that said, "Gone to Coal Town." Dejectedly, Giles rode back to town and hitched the horse in preparation of leaving. While doing so, he was approached by the town leader who informed him that half the farms in the area had been abandoned and the people had all gone to work the mines. He could probably buy three or four farms for the price of one. The town leader told him they were looking for hard working young folks to come there and sink roots. He continued to try to convince Giles to stay even as he slapped the reins against the horse's backsides and the wagon moved ahead. Giles was going to Coal Town too.

It was only a 20 mile trip and the very next day they entered the helter-skelter town that was growing too fast and without any kind of plan or control on the types of buildings. It was bustling with construction and men were lined up in preparation of entering the mines for their shift of work. Giles saw what looked to be 100 men of all sizes and shapes lined up ready for work. When the whistle blew, the gates to the mine opened and another 100 poured out into the town. He had never seen anything like this and had to be a part. This was the Climax

Coal Mine$_r$ and there were dozens of others. The four to five foot thick coal seam was over a hundred feet underground and part of the men went down to actually dig out the coal, others raised it to the surface, and still others ran steam powered crushers that broke it into small pieces. The coal was loaded on wagons and taken to the Minneapolis and St Louis Rail Road for transport to the cities. There was lots of noise and black dust; men were yelling and whistles were blowing. It was the most extraordinary thing he had ever seen. Wagons of coal were going out and empties were coming back by the dozens. He was hired instantly to drive the coal wagons. Small houses were going up by the score and he purchased one for $88. It was completely new, had two windows, a wooden floor, and a front door all made from rough cut lumber that was hauled in on wagons also. In several months, Giles and Alice had accumulated a bed with springs, a stove, several chairs and a table, some wash tubs to wash clothes and bathe in, a sink and dishes and a special lid for the outdoor john that was much more comfortable than sitting on the bare rough wood. Giles had several hundred dollars in the bank and the town was continuing to grow every day. Life was good. Alice posted a letter to William and Harriet, letting them know about their new life and how happy they were. At that point, more coal seams were being found all over central Iowa, and the rush to mine them was just starting. In less than 25 years they would begin to run out and all the small towns that supported them would nearly disappear.

Giles was such a good worker he was transferred to the maintenance crew that kept everything running and the wagons fixed. Taking care of the mules and horses that pulled the wagons was a gigantic job as they were constantly worn out, malnourished or injured. Climax Coal paid local farmers to raise hay for them and it was a boon to the surrounding area. Giles bought several hundred acres of adjacent land and produced hay for the company. He worked a full ten hour shift at the mine; then worked the hay fields another eight hours or more. Three more children, Lydia$_r$ in '74, Mable$_r$ in '76 and little Harmon$_r$

in '79 followed. Letters from William finally petered out. Giles was seriously injured several times over the years and spent weeks in bed at home recovering. Slowly his dream of going west came back to him and he grew dissatisfied with the grind of 120 hour weeks, sick children and a quickly aging, angry wife. His dream of herding cows in the west wasn't fading; it was getting stronger. Coal Town changed its name to Angus and the coal seams either disappeared or became so thin it was impractical to mine them. Lydia and Mable married and moved away. Alice finally got fed up hearing about Giles' dream; took little Harmon, and moved the several hundred miles back to Sycamore. They were finally divorced in 1897 when Angus had withered from nearly 5000 people to 1000.

# CHERRY COUNTY

$G$iles hitched a wagon ride south to the Chicago and Northwestern Railroad, jumped the train and rode it west. He was elated and the wind blowing past the open car in which he rode was exhilarating. He would miss little Harmon but realized Alice needed her son's help running the farm back in Sycamore. The train quickly passed into Nebraska and the landscape gradually changed from farms and forests to open prairie. He saw cattle by the hundreds roaming through grass next to the rails. This was a land of 50 to 100 foot tall sand hills separated by large, flat bottomed meadows of knee high grass. His dream was coming true and he stared at the passing countryside in wonder. This was truly the land of opportunity. A hundred years before, his Grandfather Giles and Uncle Kanti had explored the same land and now it was his turn. He had very little money and had given up arm wrestling years ago after his right arm was partially crushed in a mine accident. He finally got so thirsty and hungry he left the train when it stopped for water in Cherry County, Nebraska. The town of Merriman was just another dusty little group of well weathered buildings and a sprinkling of struggling trees planted by the inhabitants in an effort to give the place some summer shade. It was surrounded by miles and miles of open prairie in every direction. Surely, he could find a job there, and if he could not, it would be back on the train and west.

Merriman consisted of a church, a café-saloon, a mercantile store, black smith, hotel, and jail. The streets were sandy with a generous coating of manure. The era of open grazing was just about over and the surrounding land was broken up into finite ranches. A few fences were used to separate them but were not very popular and the ranchers aggressively branded their cattle for identification. There were several dozen private homes clustered around the main buildings of various sizes and age. Several looked new but most appeared to be a dozen or so years old. Giles took an instant liking to the place as it was similar to his home town of Parishville and most importantly, it was not the big city. As he walked down the street a small funeral procession of mourners passed by on the way to the church. He went to the town water well and took a deep drink and sat on the bench beside a middle aged woman who was also watching. She was dressed as if she was prosperous in some way and struck up a conversation with Giles. He found that the funeral was for a man by the name of Dahlgrin, who had been killed by a roving band of renegades out in his pasture. This sounded like the old west his Father Harmon described when he was a child, and he liked it. He asked the woman if anyone in the area needed a hired man and she replied that everyone did. There was more work than there were men to do it, and she suggested he first ask the dead man's widow Rachael. She would be needing help on the ranch of several thousand acres and hundreds of cattle. Giles was amazed that one ranch could be so large and he asked the woman if it was really true that the Dahlgrin Ranch had thousands of acres. She repeated that it did, and suggested that he wait several days, out of respect, before applying for a job. She replied that the Dahlgrin ranch was just a relatively small one and that most were much larger. Giles sat in silence for a long time, thinking that he had found heaven. He then asked the lady which ranch was the best one in the area in their treatment of hired men. Her answer was not encouraging as she told him the hours were long, most were spent out in the weather, the living conditions were crude, and the pay was low. If he received $20 a month, he would be doing well. Something didn't add up, if help was needed, why wasn't the pay higher? So, she said if he lasted a year or two, the pay was much better and that the problem was that the work was so difficult that few men would tolerate it and quit quickly. Those that stayed with it were then quite well paid.

Giles had no money and had to sweep floors, shovel manure and empty slop buckets to pay for a room and a few meals. After several days, he got to know a few people and put out the word that he was seeking a job as a cowboy. One of the first to approach him was Rachael Dahlgrin. She sat with him on a bench just outside the blacksmith shop and explained that her husband had been killed and she needed a hired man to help out. She said that she was looking for a man of "probity." Of course, Giles had no idea what that meant and he replied with something he had heard from a preacher. "I am not a wicked man ma'am, for the wicked shall perish from this earth. Additionally, I would prefer if you would call me *Mack* ma'am." They reached an agreement shortly thereafter. Those closest to him, henceforth, would call him by his nick name taken, on the whim of the moment, from his understanding of his own Grandfather's original name.

They fixed up a place in the barn to sleep and put his things. He had no cowboy gear and started the job with a common pair of shoes and woolen pants to protect his legs. He had never ridden a regular saddle horse. So it took him a little time to get used to the relative comfort compared to bareback on a draft horse. He knew not, how to throw a rope or drive cattle and learned quickly to let the horse make all the decisions and all he had to do was hang on. Rachael was a little upset at his lack of any knowledge about being a cowboy, so the first months were spent on other chores and fixing fence. She became impressed with his work ethic and willingness to do nearly anything to accomplish the job. Her teenage son and daughter were less thrilled about having an "old man" at the ranch, but gradually came to respect him also. He used all his pay the first few months to purchase some boots, a broad brimmed hat, leather chaps, a rifle and a slicker for the rain. Slowly he became the cowboy he had dreamed about since he was a boy. It had been a long and difficult journey, he had lived nearly five decades, but he finally felt content with his life. He came to recognize a number of the cattle and spoke to them all the time. A quite a few other men arrived on the train and some came to work for the Dahlgrin Ranch, but few could handle the work and without notice, most moved on. Some stayed and the work went well except for the spring branding and fall roundup for steers to sell. During those times other ranchers sent over hands to help with all the work. The arrangement was reciprocal, so he went to other ranches for several days also. He enjoyed it immensely; the work was hard and the food good, and he got to know quite a few of the other cowboys in the area. One of those, who became a life- long friend, was William Fleischman$_r$. (Mack) Giles played the violin, the accordion and sang in a mellow baritone, and was always quick to be chosen by other ranch bosses as he would serenade the crew late in the evening after it was too dark to work. Songs like, "Red River Valley, Casey Jones, and Red Wing the Indian Maid," were popular, but his favorite was "Wild Irish Rose."

The new fences didn't completely encircle the ranches and there were numerous places where the cattle could intermingle with those of others. Giles was about five miles from the main ranch house looking over the newly branded calves for those of other ranches when he smelled smoke coming from a draw upwind. There had been a small rainstorm the evening before and he assumed it was a lightening fire. Fires of the time were a serious business as they burned without control until they ran out of fuel or reached a river or stream they couldn't cross. He set out at a gallop into the wind hoping to find the source of the smoke. He couldn't see any significant smoke plume in the distance and thought it a small smoldering fire that he could probably put out. He carried a small shovel on his horse he used to dig holes for fence posts that needed mending, and if he could get to the fire quickly he could stop it before it had a chance to spread. As he crested the rim of the ravine, he abruptly turned his horse into some brush to get out of sight, for down in the bottom several hundred feet away, was a band of renegade Indians that had killed a calf and were roasting it over a small fire. He didn't know what to do as there were at least ten men sitting around the fire drinking whiskey and enjoying the smell of roasting beef. He didn't think he could get back over the rim of the ravine without being seen, so he sat back on his heels and watched the situation unfold. It wouldn't be long before the sun dropped below the horizon and he could sneak away and get the sheriff then be back before morning. He noticed their horses were tied up about a hundred feet away up the ravine in a natural corral closed on three sides. A rope was tied across the opening. He couldn't see anyone posted around the horses and thought if he could just drive them off, he would leave the Indians on foot and impotent. If he was caught, he would be slowly and painfully killed.

This was a situation he had dreamed about since hearing some of the hair raising tales about his Grandpa Giles. The longer he sat, the more he thought he had to drive off the horses as it was what his Grandpa would have done. The ground was soft and sandy and the grass parsimonious, so it would be easy to sneak down to the little corral without being heard. But what would he do when he got there? Maybe he'd better sit back and be patient and develop a good plan. Hours passed quietly; the Indians all got drunk and ate gigantic quantities of beef, then fell asleep. Giles moved around to get a better look at the camp to see if anyone was awake. He concentrated on the shadows looking for someone sitting awake with a loaded gun, but none were there. Finally, when it was pitch dark and the fire had burned down to glowing coals, he made his move. He knew the folks back at the ranch would come looking for him when he didn't return for supper, and expected someone would arrive at any time. He had to work fast. Step by step, he slowly led his horse toward the corral. He was worried that the ponies in the corral would smell his horse and start nickering, so he tied his by the reins to a bush along his escape route. He planned to sneak down to the corral, untie the rope across the opening, mount one of the Indian ponies and drive them all out in a rush. As he passed his horse, he would grab the reins as he went by and jump from the Indian pony to his horse, then drive the ponies away from the camp. He expected the Indians would be shooting at him in the process, so he would have to stay low. He would need both hands, so he wouldn't be able to carry his Winchester.

Giles couldn't wait a moment longer, if he did, he would falter. He very slowly led his horse down an adjacent ravine and tied it off in a slip knot. Then he crept around the main cluster of sleeping Indians, one step at a time. He hesitated five to ten seconds between each step to be sure he was not seen. As he approached the Indian ponies, several stirred and nickered lowly. He spoke to them in a low voice as he untied the rope that held them in. Running his hands over their noses and necks soothed them and he slipped astride one of the larger stallions. He gripped its mane with both hands and urged it ahead slowly; the rest followed without hesitation. He slowed the stallion and let the other horses pass him by, and then when they were about 20 feet from the sleeping Indians, he screamed so loud he startled himself. The skittish ponies stampeded right through the middle of the sleeping Indians horribly injuring some and trampling the rest. The renegades were so dazed and disoriented; they didn't find their guns until Giles was almost out of range rounding the corner past his waiting horse. With his right hand twisted in the mane of the stallion, he reached out with his left and snagged the reins of his horse as it twitched and strained to join the stampede. His horse nearly pulled him off the stallion until it could get started and match speeds. Just as he let go with his right hand, he heard a gunshot and felt the stallion falter under him. He dropped the reins on the stallion and grabbed for the saddle horn on the other horse with both hands. For several seconds his horse drug him until he could pull himself up to where he got a foot in the stirrup. Then as the stallion stumbled and went down, he swung his leg over the back of his own horse and screamed again driving the rest of the Indian ponies up out of the ravine. He chased them for another 20 minutes at full gallop howling in joy all the way, then slowed down to a trot and let the ponies spread out into the surrounding arroyos where the Indians would have trouble finding them. He let out another yell as the adrenalin was still pumping into his system. A rider was galloping directly at him and yelled back. It was Fleischman. As Giles went by riding by, he yelled to William to follow him and soon he was describing his encounter with the renegades.

Rachael sent son Andrew into Gordon to notify the Sheriff about the renegade Indians. And he sent a telegraph to Fort Niobrara some 60 miles to the east to get the soldiers. Two days later, a contingent of 12 mounted Negro soldiers jumped off the train and headed for the Dahlgrin Ranch. When they found the Indians, four had died from the slashing hooves and three more couldn't walk. The rest had scrapes and bruises and were forced to carry their injured comrades all the way to the Ranch where they were loaded into wagons and taken to the Fort. They had been the bunch that had killed the rancher a month before. Over the course of the next week, Andrew and his sister Grace scoured the area and caught all the Indian ponies. The first chance she had, Rachael grabbed Giles and firmly hugged him as she kissed him on the cheek. It had been a while since he felt the attraction to a woman; he was touched and speechless. Word got around the county about their local hero and when he went to town or to other ranches, he was back slapped and treated to all he could eat and drink. When Giles had a chance to sit quietly and reflect on the whole deal it reminded him of his Grandpa and he was glad he sat back calmly and developed a good plan to deal with the Indians. He felt sorry for the poor devils, but realized they had brutally murdered Mr. Dahlgrin and who knows how many more. The world would probably be a better place without them, and for this he was glad. On the other hand, had he been detected by the renegades, he would have met a painful death. Was there something he did wrong or would change if the circumstances were repeated? Probably not; he was sure his Grandpa would have approved. He had no idea that the big test was yet to come.

The Bowring Ranch was north of Merriman several miles, and discovered they were losing cattle at a noticeable rate. Several other ranches reported losses also. Someone was downing the fence on the north side and driving the cattle miles and miles up into South Dakota. Whoever it was, they were very clever because they were unpredictable; both their escape route and the time intervals between thefts were highly variable. The land to the north was still basically open range so it was easy to drive cattle through it and get lost in the plethora of tracks crisscrossing the surface. Tracking the drives of what looked to be anywhere from 20 to 50 cows at a time over sandy dry ground was nearly impossible. Virgil Musser$_r$ worked for Bowring and was making the rounds of the ranches seeking volunteers to try to get to the bottom of the rustling. Rachael asked Giles if he was interested in taking several weeks off and going to help Musser. About a dozen volunteers finally were assembled from the surrounding ranches. The plan was to spread out along the northern border of the Bowring property in a slowly circulating pattern several miles apart and try to catch someone driving cattle north. If one of the volunteers saw something suspicious, he was to follow and mark the trail so the rest could follow also. The cattle would be moving so slowly, it should be easy for everyone to catch up. It was William Fleischman's plan and seemed reasonable to Giles.

Several weeks went by with no results and four of the volunteers gave up and went back to their ranches. More weeks went by and it seemed as if someone must be watching as there were no attempts at rustling. Finally everyone but Giles and Fleischman gave up and were released back to their ranches. William was getting itchy as he was partner to a large chunk of land southeast of Merriman and wanted to develop a ranch of his own. The vigil on the northern edge of the Bowring was down to the three of them, so they decided to stay within the sound of a gunshot as they circulated back and forth. Then it happened. Giles saw the tracks of what looked to be three or four shod horses heading from north directly into the Bowring. From the depth of the tracks, he could tell they were big horses carrying large men; certainly not Indians. If he fired his Winchester into the air, it would alert them and they would disappear, so he stayed on their tracks and waited for his partners to come by. Will and Virgil appeared in less than an hour; they decided to go to the highest ground around and get down over the horizon and watch. But hours went by, then overnight, then the next day without seeing anything. It was obvious the rustlers were not coming back the same way so the three followed their tracks. Sure enough they could see where the rustlers came upon a group of several dozen cows and calves and started driving them, but it was west, not north. The raiders came to the fence on the west edge of the Bowring and pulled it loose from the posts then held it down on the ground while the stock crossed, and then put it back up. Except for the tracks, nobody would have known what happened, and the tracks would fade with the first wind.

Giles, Will and Virgil were at least two days behind the rustlers, but decided to follow anyway. If they could just figure out where they were going, half the battle would be won. The trail left by several dozen cattle was easy to follow even in the soft sandy soil, but they could see a storm on the western horizon and knew their time was limited. After crossing the fence using the same method as the rustlers, our three men set off at a lope directly northwest toward the open range of South Dakota and the black thunderstorm in the distance. They had one more fence to cross as they were on Gardner Ranch property. The rustlers used the same trick crossing the north fence on the Gardner, so our three pursuers did also. The wind was picking up blowing toward the storm. The tracks indicated that the rustlers were not letting the cattle stop and were driving at a good speed. The tracks were slowly disappearing in the growing wind, but Virgil thought he knew where they were going. After a brief stop to put on their slickers, Virgil's trio picked up speed trying to catch the rustlers before the rain hit that would completely erase the tracks. But, their chase was fruitless and they had to stop when the rain started coming down hard. The pulled down into some trees in a ravine, dismounted and sat on their heels while their mounts shied and pulled on the reins every time the thunder clapped. Virgil let them know that he knew the rustlers were headed for the badlands. It was a maze of hills valleys and canyons mostly without vegetation roughly a hundred by two hundred miles in size. Unless you knew where you were going, there was no water or grass for the horses, and you could get into trouble fast. Virgil wanted to continue directly northwest to see if they could pick up the trail again. Will was reluctant and wanted to return to his new ranch, while Giles was ready for the adventure. So, it was decided that Will would return and advise the folks at the Bowring and Dahlgrin Ranches as to the whereabouts of Giles and Virgil. If they didn't return in seven days, send help, but the two were supposed to observe only, not engage. They figured two more days to the Badlands, two there, then three days to return was about right.

Will felt apprehensive that his two friends were going into danger without him, and they were concerned also, but wouldn't let each other see it. After the thunderstorm let up, Virgil and Giles headed straight for the Badlands. They would be going right through Indian Territory, and the probability of encountering renegades was considerable. Giles didn't realize that he was going straight into trouble, but Virgil knew it and he was uncomfortable. They absolutely had to find out what was happening to all the cattle from Cherry County, and once he knew enough about the location of the rustlers to send the troopers from the fort, he would turn back. Most people assumed the rustlers were coming from the northeast away from Indian country, not directly into it. Giles was realizing another part of his boyhood dream; chasing the bad guys, and he was about to find out that these guys were more than bad. As they loped along, he was exceedingly happy and oblivious to the stark surroundings. They had to pass through about 20 miles of near desert, where there was no obvious water and little vegetation. Virgil kept his eyes peeled for any tracks of any kind, but there were none; the rain had washed the landscape clean. They rode most of the day making good time riding in a zigzag pattern in an effort to cut any trails made after the storm. But, there were none; how could anyone hide the tracks of two dozen cattle and four horses?

They persevered and rode until there wasn't enough light to see the ground. Then made camp down in the bottom of a ravine where a small patch of green grass survived on the seepage from a spring. It had enough water to fill their canteens and give the horses a good drink. During the night, Giles thought he could hear a cow bawling in the distance. There was a slight breeze out of the northwest and when he held his ear into it he could hear something that he had heard on multiple previous occasions, the sounds of cattle. He woke Virgil, but by the time he came to his senses, the sound was gone. Before first light they were up and ate most of Will's jerky, took a big swig of water and were off. They tried to follow the natural contours of the land sticking to the higher ground where they could see ahead for a good distance. That day's ride was also fruitless, but they came within view of the Badlands. From a distance they looked ominous, but with the evening sun on them, they were beautiful. As they went down into the bottom of the network of arroyos and ravines to make camp for the night, suddenly they found tracks. Sure enough it looked to be two dozen cattle and four horses.

The Badlands were an area of roughly 400 square miles of ancient sea bed exposed by ages of wind and rain. It was largely devoid of any trees or bushes. Plots of grass survived down in the bottoms of ravines that could be as much as 300 feet deep, where rain water collected. It was an endless maze of multi-colored canyons and eroded hills with no visible trails, roads or rivers. Neither Virgil nor Giles thought of the place as dangerous, but they had never been there. More importantly, why would anyone make this place home? Why were they called Badlands? Parts of these forbidding hills were religious for various tribes of Indians. There were, however, places where the pools of water and stands of grass were big enough for life to survive year around. Prehistoric people left traces of villages that contained dozens. The Badlands were unusually cold in the winter and hot in the summer, and it attracted people looking for a sanctuary away from dangerous or nosey neighbors.

The cattle rustlers were part of a sizeable gang of killers and thieves, Indian, Mexican and white alike, that had made a permanent camp about 10 miles into the Badlands. They stole cattle to eat, women for entertainment, and money to purchase clothing and weapons, from all parts of northern Nebraska and southwestern South Dakota. They were clever enough about it that nobody in law enforcement or the army suspected it was an organized gang. They had built crude dwellings of mud bricks and canvas roofs with forced, kidnapped labor. Most of their victims were travelers making their way across open territory that weren't missed for weeks or months. They used people up regularly and then killed them, so a constant flow of new victims, beef and whiskey was needed. They spent much of their time preying on the folks in the area around them and fighting and killing each other for a bigger share of the spoils. They had a crude tribal form of government where three of the older members passed judgment on disagreements, which were loud and frequent.

When there was a tiny hint of dawn down over the eastern horizon, Giles and Virgil were on the trail following the tracks. As the sun rose behind them, they realized how vulnerable they were down in the bottom of a ravine along which were hundreds of hiding places. If they were getting close to the rustler's destination, there would be lookouts along the way. So they slowed down and each watched the canyon sides carefully. The bottom of the canyon had a lot of soft sediment in it but there were stretches where the ground was solid sandstone and the tracks disappeared. They found themselves backtracking and investigating alternate branches of the canyon. But they were able to follow the cattle tracks well enough that most of the entire day slipped by without any contact. They were using up their week quickly and both of them were concerned about finding their way back out of the maze. As long as it didn't rain they would have tracks to follow. They had just come to a dead end and were backtracking, when suddenly a rider galloping full tilt, came out of the mouth of one ravine and shot up another. It had to be a lookout and they had to catch the guy before he could pull up and fire his rifle. Giles had the bigger and faster mount so he jumped out ahead of Virgil and was closing the distance between he and the lookout. Virgil's horse stepped in a hole and went down with a broken leg causing him to fly over the front and land on his face and chest on the rough ground. The poor horse thrashed around trying to get up to no avail and Virgil couldn't shoot it for fear of alarming the rustlers, so he took out his knife and plunged it into the horse's throat. It had been a good horse for years and it broke Virgil's heart to have to do such a thing.

Giles had glanced back when he heard Virgil cry out when he fell, and knew he was alone in trying to catch the lookout. He could see why the lookout didn't fire his weapon, he didn't have one. In all the excitement the guy apparently dropped it. Giles continued to close the distance because of his superior horse. After a few minutes he came up alongside the fleeing lookout; they were side by side bumping legs as they flew through the canyon. Giles reached out with his huge left hand and wrapped it around the lookout's neck, ripped him out of the saddle, and let him fall screaming between the horses to the hard ground. He continued on and grabbed the reins of the now rider less horse, slowed it down and turned around. He figured Virgil would need a horse to get out of there. The lookout was sprawled on the ground not moving so Giles dismounted and rolled him over. He could see the man's neck was bent askew and figured he had a broken neck. That was fine because if the main group found the guy, they would think he simply fell off his horse, and Giles and Virgil could get away clean. Giles had to mark their trail some way that wouldn't be noticed by the rustlers. At the entrance to each branch of the canyon, he left two rocks about the size of his fist, one atop the other. Unless the gang knew where to look, they would never have noticed the markers. The rocks naturally were the exact color of the surrounding rocks, but in a position completely unknown in nature. Weeks later he would be able to lead the army into the maze without error.

He was finished with that whole deal and wanted to get the heck out of there, but not Virgil. Virgil wanted to go on up the canyon branch the lookout had been in to see if it led to anything, then they could go. To be so close and not actually see what was going on didn't make sense to Virgil and in about ten words, convinced Giles. They tied their horses in a little alcove where they wouldn't be seen by a passerby and lit out on foot up the base of the canyon. It was nearly dark by that time and their senses were on hair trigger. They had shells in the chambers of their rifles and the safeties off ready to shoot. If they did shoot, they would surely be killed as they knew not about the three dozen killers ahead.

It was completely dark, as the night was cloudy, when they started hearing the sounds of a camp ahead. They stayed in the deepest part of the canyon and moved slowly. The trail was wide enough for several wagons abreast and they could see wagon tracks in the faint light reflected off the canyon walls. The sounds became louder and the firelight brighter, and when they peeked around a corner of the canyon there was a group of several dozen mud brick huts all lit by about six small campfires. A man was screaming in pain as a group of men sat in a circle around him laughing and drinking and encouraging the torturer to make him scream again. They had some poor soul strung upside down hanging over a small fire while an antagonist peeled strips of flesh from his body. Blood had run down and completely covered his face. He was holding his hands up to keep them from burning over the fire. Every time he relaxed even a little and let his hands fall, they would burn a little more, but he had been hanging there so long he couldn't hold them up any more and slowly had to let them hang in the flames and burn. The blood in his hair was sizzling and smoking and Giles could smell the burning hair. The prisoner wasn't long for this world and his torturer knew it, which caused him to peel even larger pieces of flesh. But the man stopped screaming and was either dead or passed out, so the torturer put more wood on the fire to finish the job. The show was over and Giles and Virgil were dumbstruck. There was nothing they could do without being caught and tortured, so they backtracked and got the devil out of there.

They had barely started their retreat, when gunfire erupted behind them which stimulated them to move faster. They were reasonably sure they hadn't been seen and they couldn't hear any horses pounding the canyon floor. Virgil was less than half Giles' age and ran down the canyon leaving Giles behind. There was more gunfire and Giles could hear the bullets thump against the sides of the canyon next to him. Now behind him the pounding of horses' hooves on the canyon floor made the hair on the back of his neck stand up. He had to get out of sight and fast. It was so dark he knew the killers hadn't seen him as he couldn't see anything behind. The zzzipp and thummmp of bullets striking the canyon walls fell behind him as he rounded a bend and dove into a small nook away from the main trail. He was exhausted and could go no farther and as long as it was dark he felt secure in his hiding place. His heart was pounding in his ears so loud he was sure everyone else could hear it also. Out of the darkness galloping at top speed a horse and rider appeared and thundered past Giles. He couldn't make out who the rider was, but the horse was bareback. A minute later, more riders on saddled horses charged past firing wildly down the canyon. Someone had escaped and was being chased and the whole thing was happening right in front of him and Virgil. He wished there was some way he could help, but he was on foot and exhausted. The melee noisily raced on down the canyon and in a couple minutes, it was quiet again. He wondered whether Virgil was able to hide or got involved. He decided to follow and moved quietly down the canyon concerned that he may get lost. If he did, he had no water or food. *How did I get in this mess?* He asked himself. Giles wished it would start getting light as he was really confused and it would be pure luck if he was on the correct route out. He couldn't hear anything coming from ahead or behind him, and he assumed he was lost.

The clouds thinned slightly and let some moonlight through and it was enough to allow Giles to see the horse tracks in the soft places of the canyon bottom. This relieved him and he suddenly felt better about his chances of survival. He walked as fast as he could and knew that the hiding place for the horses should be just ahead. He searched for footprints that would indicate Virgil was OK, but saw none in the turmoil of tracks from the charging horses. When he finally got to the place where his horse should have been, all that was left was a pile of fresh manure and lots of tracks. Virgil had taken both horses. "Here, up here," a voice came out of the darkness farther up the little canyon branch. It was Virgil. He slowly walked out of the shadow leading both horses. Without saying a word, they mounted and proceeded at a lope down the main canyon leading to open country. As the day dawned, they could see the tracks of the procession that had preceded them and they sped up wanting to get completely away from the maze of canyons before the group of killers returned.

Giles and Virgil stayed on the high ground just to the south of the route they had previously taken the other way. There was a little more jerky in the saddle bags, so they had some breakfast with big drinks of water and felt quite a bit better after their hair raising night. Toward noon they decided to pull down into a ravine and take a nap in the shade of some stunted pine trees. They couldn't see anything except for the draw below them and they were exhausted beyond caring. There was just enough seepage to keep a small patch of grass alive and their horses helped themselves. Each man sighed in relief as he lay down and put his head on his saddle. The day was warm and the breeze gentle; their troubles were forgotten quickly; but not for long.

Giles could feel someone jostling him and telling him to wake up. It was Virgil, and he was pointing down the ravine a hundred yards or so below them at a group of four horses. Three had men and saddles on them and the forth had a naked person tied over its back, with the head on one side and the feet on the other. It had to be the escapee and killers that made the mad dash the night before. The little procession was making its way up the ravine adjacent to the one in which they were hiding and as it got closer, it was obvious the person tied over the fourth horse's back was a young woman. Giles and Virgil looked at each other; they were both thinking that they couldn't let this happen. There was no way in hell either of them would let these killers take that woman back to face years of abuse. They pulled out their rifles and readied them for battle. Giles was to take the front one and Virgil the second. Then, they would both shoot the horse out from under the third as he would surely bolt with the first shot. When the killers were about 30 yards away, Virgil quietly counted down, "three, two, one, fire." The two targeted killers pitched off their mounts without a scream, both mortally hit. The other did bolt only to take two bullets into his horse that stumbled and pitched him over the front. He immediately turned and started firing in Giles' general direction, but knew not where he was shooting. He rose up and was taking aim at the young woman when Virgil shot him in the side of the head killing him instantly. Giles ran to get control of the young woman's horse with Virgil right on his heels. He cut the rope and eased the lady to the ground and took off his shirt and put it around her. She looked to be about twenty and was bruised and beaten. He held her in his arms and thought of his own daughters, as she cried with relief and kept saying, "thank you." Virgil took the pants off the cleanest of the three and gave them to her to cover her legs and lower parts. They found a relatively clean shirt and some socks in one of the dead man's saddle bags. Their boots were so disgusting, she decided socks were enough.

In a few minutes, she was mounted on the best of the outlaw's horses and they were off to the southeast and Cherry County. Virgil removed the saddles and bridles from the other two horses and let them go, but they decided to follow our three intrepid survivors back to safety. One of the killers was still moaning when they left. Once they got to Merriman, they would be completely safe from any killers that decided to follow, but the lady was worn out from her night of trying to escape and they had to stop early in the evening. Again, they camped down in a ravine out of sight and away from the hot wind that had come up out of the west. She sat and cried and tried to tell her story, but couldn't while the two men talked calmly to her and told her that with time it would all pass. How could the murder of her husband and child followed by weeks of brutal treatment ever pass? In the coming years, she did recover and eventually married Virgil Musser and helped him begin a chain of ranch families that would last to the present.

The young woman moved in with an elderly couple in Merriman and worked in their store on Main Street. Giles and Virgil went back to their ranches for several days until a contingent of soldiers could arrive from Fort Niobrara. Several dozen hard bitten veterans of many skirmishes arrived via train and accompanied by Virgil and Giles set off for the Badlands to clean out the pack of killers. It turned out to be the Bill Newsome, gang of outlaws plus various independent killers and thieves. The little stone on stone markers the led the way and while Virgil and Giles waited at the mouth of the entrance to the Badlands, the soldiers killed about half the bunch and captured the rest. The outlaw gang had 16 captives, men, women and two kids of various ages that had been beaten, starved and abused and required months to recover. Many eventually found family around the territory and some stayed in Cherry County. Most of the killers ended up hanging gruesomely as the captives eagerly participated in testifying against them. Several of the captured gang swore if they ever got out they would kill Giles and Virgil, and at the time, it seemed like an idle threat that could never be carried out. From then on, every time one of the male captives saw Virgil or Giles they shook hands and thanked them, while the women kissed them on the cheek. The two were local heroes once again.

Giles felt relieved to be back to the hum-drum of everyday cattle ranching. It felt good to sleep in a bunk and have two good meals every day. He thought back on the recent events to the moments when he realized he was in mortal danger, and he finally knew how frightened his brothers Adolphus and William must have felt when they were engaged in life and death battles four decades back; it was not a good feeling. But it was over and he could stick to talking to the cattle, fixing fence and rounding up strays; he loved it. The chasing bad guys part of his dream, he didn't love. After working most of his life at hard labor tilling the soil or shoveling coal, riding around the countryside listening to the meadowlarks sing and smelling the air of the seasons was like heaven. He did miss his ex-wife and children and often wondered how they were and what happened to them. Being unable to write a simple letter, he completely lost track of them, and them of him. Time flew by and Will Fleischman, with the help of his partner Shadbolt, got their ranch going, and then convinced Giles and Virgil to start working for them. So Giles said good bye to the Dahlgrins, packed up his stuff into a pair of saddle bags, and moved some 20 miles southeast of Merriman to the Churn Ranch. He was nearly 60, could carry all his belongings in his two hands, and that's the way he liked it.

Harry Swain was slow of mind, and a brute in stature. And it was because he was judged to be feeble minded, that he was given a single year sentence in the Federal Prison in Lincoln for his part in the Bad Lands caper. It didn't take him long after his release to find other men that agreed with his disdain for society, and before he made his way back to Cherry County there were three in the budding Swain Gang. They had stolen much of what they had and were always looking for someone they could intimidate or abuse. Harry had always remembered Giles and Virgil and was one of several that swore to take revenge. He was far too stupid to have remembered their names, but still felt drawn to perpetrate harm upon, if not kill, the two. He had enjoyed his time with the Newsome gang and had talked several other half wits into going back to start up another hideout from which they could raid the territory. Harry didn't realize that his course of action would precipitate his end with the vise-like grip of Giles' huge hands around his throat.

There was a wagon road that roughly paralleled the rail line of the C&NW from east to the northwest, and that was the route Harry and his pals used. Along the way they intimidated farmers and ranchers into free meals and overnights at their houses. Sometimes, outright rapes took place along with frequent beatings and pillaging of household valuables. But, they moved fast enough that by the time the ranchers got to town to report their crimes, they were long gone. They were clever enough always to take off to the north or south before turning back northwest thereby throwing the law off their trail. A warning did go out in every direction via telegraph to officers of the law, for three large scruffy, bearded men heavily armed and on horseback. Their descriptions were pinned up on the walls in every town up and down the line. Word of their possible return was passed by word of mouth in every direction in Merriman, so Virgil and Giles were aware of the possibility of danger, but neither thought it serious as they were 20 miles away from Merriman and it may as well have been a thousand.

Harry and his partners had to veer away from the main roads and towns when they started to notice warnings about them hung up on walls, and posts. They couldn't read the details, but recognized their names and assumed the rest. They elected to follow the Niobrara that wound its way roughly 20 miles to the south of the main line to Merriman. The ranches and farms were few and far between and whenever they came to a fence, they simply cut the wire. It was common for cowboys to take care of a task, whether fixing fence or rounding up strays, by themselves, and this is exactly what Giles was up to when the chance meeting between him and the Swain gang took place.

It was mid afternoon and Giles was taking a break sitting under a box elder tree down in the river valley. He had just dozed off when he heard his horse nicker softly and knew another horse or a sizable wild animal was about. Coyotes were common in the area and a few wolves were still around. Deer were common also which brought the mountain lions down from the west. Less frequently elk were seen following one of the river valleys. When he slowly stood up, he could see a trio of riders and recognized them as part of the Newsome outfit, slowly picking their way across the Niobrara not a hundred yards downstream. It was mid-summer and the river was fairly low, so it could be crossed easily. They stopped their horses and let them drink while they talked loudly to each other amid wildly waving their arms and pointing different directions. Apparently there was an active and disagreeable discussion going on over which direction to go. It was Harry Swain. Giles squatted so they wouldn't see him, but his horse was in plain sight. He then realized if they saw a saddled horse, it would get their attention, so he very slowly crawled over and unbuckled the cinch and pulled his saddle off onto the ground. The horse still had a bridle with the reins tied to a branch and when the trio looked in that direction, they spotted it. The deep grass and low brush came up to about the horse's belly, so they hadn't seen Giles and his saddle, but they were slowly on the way.

Giles checked to be sure he had bullets in his rifle and crawled as far as he could away from the horse and remain unseen. He heard them first, talking to each other to keep a sharp eye out for a trap. Coming upon a lone horse tied to a branch was unusual and there had to be someone around somewhere. Two of them fanned out each going on a 45 degree angle while the third continued directly at the tied horse. One of the outriders was going to spot Giles in another 30 yards and he had to do something fast. He couldn't hide from them, so it was going to come down to a fight. Giles' heart was pounding in his ears just like it did up in the Badlands; it was so loud he was sure everyone could hear it. With them spread out, it was going to be impossible to shoot more than one at a time. He took dead aim on a spot just ahead of his outrider and waited for the guy to come into his sights. Bam! And the outlaw hit the ground; his horse bolted and ran. The other two spurred and turned sharply away and galloped up into a grove of trees where they couldn't be seen. Giles knew it wasn't over because the one he shot was not Harry Swain.

Virgil thought he heard a gunshot in the distance. He knew Giles was in that general direction and was alarmed because even though they all carried rifles, they seldom used them. He set out at a lope, rifle in hand, scanning ahead for any sign of horse tracks or riders. He couldn't hear any more shots and after going a half mile or so, started thinking he must be hearing things. Harry and his outlaw friend decided they had to kill whoever attacked them as they couldn't take a chance of getting the army or the law on their trail. They separated and started in Giles' direction moving quietly from tree to bush to log and crawling in the deep grass listening intently for any sound. They were coming at Giles from two different directions and he really didn't have much choice but to remain silent and let them come. After nearly an hour, his horse nickered again. Giles was sweating so hard, it was running down his forehead into his eyes. He had just about given up thinking he was in for a shoot out, when he heard a shuffling sound come from the brush not 20 yards away. He found a tiny opening in the bushes and aimed his rifle at the sound. His horse stamped nervously, and Giles knew they were coming for him. Slowly a hat appeared in his sights, and then a pair of eyebrows, then an eye and Bam, Giles fired. The outlaw pitched silently backward, half his head gone. At the same instant Harry said, "turn around you son of a bitch, so I can shoot you in the face." Harry had the drop on him. He was ten feet away next to Giles' horse standing with his rifle pointed directly at Giles' head. The saddle was at his feet and in another step, he'd trip on it. Giles turned around slowly, his rifle still in his hands, and when he saw Harry right next to his horse, he dropped his rifle, waved his arms and yelled,

"Heeaawww." His horse reared and its front hooves hit Harry in the back pushing him over the saddle. As Harry fell, he shot and Giles could feel a sharp pain in his side where the bullet had gone through the skin, caromed off a rib and exited. Giles knew he had to act before Harry could collect himself and in spite of being 60, moved like a cat. He dove on Harry and hit him with his fist only to take a blow from Harry right in the eye. Harry was strong as a bull and was getting up in spite of being pummeled by Giles. Giles could feel his grip on Harry slipping and knew he had to do something or he was going to die. He slid around onto Harry's back and slipped an arm around his neck. Harry's neck was thick and fat and he shook and squirmed and flailed his arms, but Giles held on cutting off Harry's breath. Harry backed up slamming Giles into the tree and crushing his breath out, but Giles held on, wrapped his legs around Harry's middle, and tightened his grip. Harry was getting desperate and Giles felt him weaken. Harry collapsed onto the ground causing Giles to let go temporarily, and as Harry rolled over onto his back, Giles was at his throat with both hands. Giles had a death grip on and Harry knew it. He tried to poke Giles eyes and break his grip but could not and finally he started to go limp. Giles could feel something in Harry's throat breaking under his grip and held it on until Harry simply stared off into space. When Giles tried to loosen his grip, he couldn't get his hands to open. After a few seconds of trying, his hands finally relaxed enough he could let loose and he got up off of dead Harry just as Virgil rode up. Giles was still shaking with adrenalin as Virgil pitched off his horse and grabbed him to keep him from collapsing. The sun was low in the sky by this time, and they sat and stared at the sunset for over an hour before Giles could collect himself enough to speak. Virgil patted his back, held his neckerchief against Giles's side, and spoke in soft tones to him. Giles thought of the wild stories his Dad had told him about the old west. How his Dad and Grandfather and Uncles had fought and killed Indians, thieves and outlaws, struggled against the weather and thirst and survived. He then realized that they must have all been true, and slowly he became proud of what he had just done and that he was too a survivor. Virgil got him back onto his horse and they headed for the ranch house at a lope, leaving the three dead gangsters lying in the dust until the sheriff could come out and take care of them. That night, in spite of his wound, Giles slept more soundly than he had in years.

Several days later the sheriff showed up with a couple helpers and went out and buried the three thieves, collected everything of value plus their horses and brought them to the Churn Ranch. He wanted to give all the stuff to Giles, but he would have no part of it. Giles wanted to forget the whole thing and looking at the thieves' stuff would only remind him of the whole unpleasant deal. If he could have run away, he would have. He didn't think of himself as a hero and only fought to save his own life, but in the coming months, he had plenty of time out on the range to think about his life. He remembered how his Father loved the west, but went back to New York to raise a family because of the relative safety there. It had cost his Father his self respect, and now he understood the years of bitterness. Giles was convinced that the west was a dangerous place. In the short time he had been in there, he thought he was nearly killed three times; was it inherent in the west or the curse of the McCumbers? He started thinking about some line of work a little more sedate. Riding a horse at breakneck speed over rough ground chasing a stupid steer, was looking more and more like foolishness. He'd had his share of the wide open places, grass knee deep to the horizon, lightening on the prairie, and stars that scored the sky from horizon to horizon. He longed for the smell of frying pork chops eaten with boiled potatoes and gravy with those spicy-sweet pickles from the recipe and for the smell of a woman's freshly washed hair once again. His dad had told him about the metal box in St Louis that contained all the family papers including the pickle recipe, and he wondered if anybody had ever claimed it. Winter was coming on and maybe he should pull his wages, collect the reward for Harry Swain, and head for St Louis. Maybe he could find an inside job or at least a job on a farm, where the winters were spent mostly indoors and not out on the range in the wind and cold sitting astride some stubborn horse. He had fulfilled his childhood dreams; he had chased and killed the bad guys, herded cattle on the back of a horse, and now he was looking to settle down to a more sedate existence. Find a good woman and start again; was he too old? The school teacher, by the name of Fanny Jensen, and three decades his junior, had showed interest in him; maybe he should marry her and settle down to farming for the rest of his days.

The trip to St Louis was a little bewildering. Traveling was a problem for Giles because of his inability to read most of the signs. He could recognize the names of the major cities but all the rest were gibberish. By that time trains crisscrossed the Midwest and he was able to solicit enough help that he finally made it to St Louis. It was a raucous city, growing by leap and bounds, and when he walked out of the train station, he was confused and concerned that he would never find the correct bank. By then there were dozens of banks and finding the proper one, would take time. A woman at the boarding house, he chose to stay in not far from the train station, befriended Giles and offered to help him find the correct bank. She had assumed from the way he talked that he was looking to collect a large sum of money and if she could help him find it, maybe she could lift it from him and be gone. Giles was unwise in the ways of thieves, crooks and devious women and was totally unaware of her motives. But, he was no fool either and kept his money well hidden. He didn't have a plan other than to walk up and down the main avenues one at a time and go into each bank as he came to it. He was asking for the metal box and did not know that years ago the papers were taken and put into a waterproof bag and put on a shelf. But he was determined to continue and walked into bank after bank giving them his name and inquiring as to the box. The helpful woman stuck to him like glue the first few days, but tired of it quickly and was content to hang around the boarding house and check him out each evening. Up and down the streets he went encountering one bewildered or blank look after another; nobody was able to help him until finally a decrepit bank manager recalled a strange bag on a shelf in the old bank he worked in many years ago. It had a metal tag attached that had a name stamped into it saying MC something, but it wasn't a metal box. The old gentleman had a failing memory for things in the present, but seemed to soundly remember things from his distant past. Giles finally persuaded the gentleman to help him, so that afternoon they took a carriage ride to a little bank on the southern edge of town. It was a two room affair; the front containing the teller window and the back being the manager's office and safe. There on a shelf, was the bag with the metal tag. The tag was barely readable and said "MCu_b_r." But, the bank manager wasn't convinced of Giles identity and wouldn't let him have it. Giles and his decrepit friend finally convinced the manager to at least open it and let Giles name the people that might be recorded on the papers. After an hour of studying the papers and letters, who they were from and the names of the folks in them, and questioning Giles, the bank manager finally gave in and let him take the bag. It contained a few letters from his Grandfather Giles to his Great Grandmother in Scotland and several from her. One small scrap of paper had the recipe for the spicy pickles. It also contained pages and pages of stories written by Grandfather Giles about all his travels and adventures from Chesapeake, Boston, the War (of Independence), Fort Pitt, St Louis, Independence, Confluence, New Orleans, cousin Doig, and his sons Harmon (Giles' Father), Kanti, Dohmnall, Joseph, and daughter Lydia. Grandfather Giles wrote about near escapes from death and encounters of all kinds with slavers, Indians, and river thieves. He described the rivers, the trips, and the severe weather out on the prairie, the travels of his son Harmon and his friend Harmon, his friendship with the Oneida Indians and his trip from Scotland to America with his cousins. He told of the singing with his son Kanti and mother Sarah after she had made the trip back to America. It took the helpful woman several days to read all the documents to Giles as he sat quietly, eyes closed, intently listening to every word. He asked her to read several parts over again as he tried to commit the entire history of his family to memory. The following day he was gone, on his way back to the prairie.

The folks in Merriman were glad to see Giles again, and he was greeted with cheek kisses, back slaps and soft handshakes. By then, all the men around knew not to squeeze Giles' hand very hard because of his bone crushing strength. Fanny Jensen Roberts, who was a little woman and barely came to Giles' chest, was in town and gave him a tight and suggestive hug. He stayed in the boarding house for several days, rested from his trip and looked over the papers he had found. He felt lucky to have them, but couldn't read more than a few words. By accident in casual conversation, he discovered that the Roberts family who lived eight miles east of Gordon was looking for a good hired man to help with the farm work, so he was on the next train west.

Charles and Elsie Roberts had moved from the tiny hamlet of Dannebrog in Brown County Nebraska, to Ainsworth in Howard County, then on to the big farm east of Gordon several miles west of the Cherry- Sheridan County border. They had worked as hired labor on farms for years and finally saved enough money to make a down payment on their own farm. Fanny was the oldest of five children. She had the name Jensen because, when at age 28 and nearly considered a spinster, had run off with and married a traveling con man by the name of Jensen. When she insisted on writing to her parents to let them know she was OK and where she was, Jensen abandoned her.

Antone "Slim" Jensen was over six feet tall, with dark wavy hair, had a pencil mustache and the hint of a beard even after a fresh shave. He traveled for a mercantile house in Chicago selling goods to stores along the major railroads. He had married a number of times and always quickly abandoned his brides as he considered them an encumbrance he could not abide. He especially liked the very young women, but never passed any opportunity and had married several women of nearly 50. He was smooth with the language and quoted poetry and the classics with ease and appeared to be a highly intelligent man. The Chicago and Northwestern train usually didn't stop in Irwin, but late in August 1892, it did for some reason. This chance stop was to alter the life of the aging Fanny Roberts in a way that she would always regret. She taught at the local school and happened to be at the train station when Slim stepped off and gave her his irresistible smile. He came over to the well where she was standing and sat on the bench while she took a drink. She offered him the ladle filled with fresh well water, and he looked into her eyes while he slowly drank. He introduced himself as a lonely traveler and recent widower and invited her to set with him. Several hours went by as he told her of all the exotic places he had been and those he would share with some lucky woman. She was entranced and didn't resist when he put his hand on hers. Her younger sisters Elvina$_r$ and Louise$_r$ giggled as they peeked around the corner of the station at their gullible sister. Finally the train blew its whistle and slowly chugged away to the east. Elvina came around the corner of the station expecting to see Fanny, but she was gone. It scared the girls and they told the station manager that the man had taken Fanny. But the manager said the man had purchased Fanny, who was a grown woman, a ticket and that he had seen her get on the train voluntarily; there was nothing he could do. He asked Fanny if she really wanted to go with the man and she said yes. So, the sisters ran all the way home and told their dad. It took him until well into the evening to get to Gordon and send a telegraph to Valentine sheriff, but the train had already passed and was on its way to Chicago. The Roberts' were devastated; their oldest child had just run off with a drummer and they didn't know what to do. Charles got on the next train east and stopped at all the towns along the way and inquired about the drummer and his young daughter. Several had seen them, but didn't think anything was amiss as the young woman seemed happy and attentive. Charles finally returned empty handed and broken hearted; he refused to believe that Fanny could abandon them voluntarily.

During the next few months, Slim married Fanny using one of his many aliases for a first name on the license. They traveled all over Minnesota and South Dakota and finally got on a Great Northern train to Montana then Washington. In October, the Roberts family received a letter from Fanny in Spokane asking for money so she could return home. Charles was on the next train to Chicago then on to Washington and by Thanksgiving was back with Fanny. Jensen had abandoned her for another woman and seriously crushed her heart. She knew she had been a fool and wanted to start over with her life, but that was not to be, as her reputation had been tarnished and no man in good standing would have anything to do with her; until, several years later when Giles smiled. In the mean time, she taught at the Barley school on the Churn Ranch, and that's where she met Giles the first time. He was a local hero and even though she was half his age, she thought of him as a "possible," for she perceived herself a spinster.

The new job at the Roberts farm took Giles back to his life in Parishville with its endless plowing and tilling of the soil, then hoping for rain. He had a warm bed and two good meals every day, but most importantly no horses to ride or stubborn steers to chase and no bad guys to fight. He worked hard at the job and became a close friend to Charles and Elsie. At the end of the school year, Fanny moved back to Irwin so she could teach there again. Soon Giles and Fanny married and their first child; Robert Giles$_r$ was born there at the farm; it was December 1913. Nearly four years later in August 1917, Mabel$_r$ (spelled differently from his first daughter Mable) made her debut on the scene, at their home on Elm Street in the town of Gordon; Giles was 67. He worked as a hand at the local livery stable and proudly kept the place well organized and clean. He rediscovered that he could sing extremely well, when Fanny coerced him into going to church. His booming baritone voice and throbbing vibrato were the delight of the entire congregation. Somewhere along the line, he lost the bundle of family papers, so he spent numerous evenings telling young Robert the names and stories of his ancestors. Young Bob was concerned about his "funny" toes so Giles showed him, his own feet and the toe deformation that many of his ancestors carried. Giles and Fanny insisted that their kids get an education and both graduated from the local high school. Giles worked up to the last day of his life when he finally passed in the spring of 1931; he was 81, and his last two children were still in school. He died shoveling horse manure, a fitting end for the now severe gentleman.

# SHERIDAN COUNTY

The owner of the livery knew Giles' passing would impoverish the family, so he told young Bob to take over the work of his Dad. He went down both before and after school to help take care of the place. He wasn't as big and strong as his Dad, but he had youthful vigor and sometimes worked until nearly midnight to finish. As he worked, largely alone, he thought about the stories and the names of his ancestors and wondered if his future would be as colorful. Times had changed so much that the opportunity for high adventure was vanishing. America had become an organized country; states, counties and cities had been formed, and each had its own government. Keepers of the peace were everywhere and the chance of breaking the law successfully was becoming tiny. Telegraph and telephone along with indoor toilets and running water were becoming common. Newspapers still were the best method of getting out the news, and every town had a local printing office that produced advertising handbills plus a local newspaper. Many houses had oil burning stoves instead of wood or coal, and some people even had automobiles. It was the early 1930's and the country was just going into hard times. Work on the main road connecting all the little towns that sprang up along the C&NW Railroad had started and the wages were good, so the minute young Bob graduated, he applied for a job and got it.

The roadbed for US highway 20 was constructed largely using horse drawn scrapers and graders. In some cases, sections had to be hand dug by the workers with shovels and this was the gang, of about three dozen, on which young Bob found himself. He was younger than the rest of the men and was constantly teased about his youth and inexperience in life. Most of the men there were thankful to simply have jobs and worked furiously to keep them. Young Bob followed their lead, worked right along-side them and slowly gained their respect. As the months went by, young Bob finally worked his way up to the job of grader driver, first with horses, then with the new fangled gas powered, smoke blowing steel wheeled graders. The gas powered graders were quickly shown to be far superior to the horse drawn kind and the construction bosses were constantly pushing their owners for more of them. The horse drawn gravel wagons were slowly replaced by gas powered trucks that also proved to be much more efficient and took far less maintenance. Young Bob quickly learned there was more to driving one of these mechanical monsters than simply turning the steering wheel and stomping on the pedals. Each truck had its individual idiosyncrasies and there were numerous joints and points that required daily grease or oil or adjustment in order to keep it rolling. The construction bosses became dependent on Bob's ability in keeping these mechanical marvels running and had him instruct other drivers on all the fine points of the task. This was a skill young Bob would continue to utilize throughout his entire life.

That first summer, the highway construction gang was harassed by the summer heat, the mosquitoes and the weather. Repeated rains left the freshly opened ground a sea of black mud and it did no good to drag the equipment around in it. The work crew missed several days of work each week because of the wet conditions, but that was nothing compared to the wrath mother nature was about to unleash. The roadbed required that the tops of the hills be cut through with a slot wide enough for the road and shoulders and the dirt be moved to the draws between the hills. A small culvert, up to four feet square and fifty feet long, had to be constructed in the base of the draws to prevent them from becoming dams in wet weather. These culverts were usually made of hand mixed concrete. Most afternoons the storm clouds built up in the west and charged across the prairie pounding the countryside with heavy rain and hail, and it was common practice for the men on the crew to take shelter in the small culverts. When the hail was large, the horses took a pounding and if the men had a chance before the storm hit, they would turn them loose to run fruitlessly about squealing, bucking and looking for shelter. There was none.

The last afternoon before the fourth of July was a payday and all the men were looking forward to several days off. They normally worked six days a week, but this particular week, they got two days of rest. As usual, the storm clouds came out of the west, but this time they were a wall of swirling black and green. The crew boss warned the men with his bull horn about the time the wind picked up and you could smell the moisture in the air. The men were running for the culverts when the first torrents of rain hit like a cow peeing on a flat rock. It rained so hard that the culverts became flooded and some of the men were flushed out the downstream end. The wind was so strong and the rain came down so hard, you couldn't see a thing and most of the crew didn't realize they were about to be hit by a tornado. When it hit, it picked up horses and empty wagons and carried them away to be found the next day. It had the sound of a hundred trains and the men of the crew later said, "It came up from the middle of Hell." Several of the men had been sucked up into the funnel and were found dead with their clothing torn off, miles downwind. Young Bob was the last man in the downstream end of the culvert and would have been sucked out if the next two men inside hadn't been hanging onto his belt. The water was rushing through the culvert trying to wash the men out the end and if they slipped and slid out, they would have been pulled up into the funnel and killed. But they desperately gripped the inside seams of the culvert and each other; none of them were hurt. Young Bob survived, beaten bloody by the hail and soaked to the bone by the rushing water, but he was alive. That evening, riding back to Gordon in the back of the engine powered truck, he was having second thoughts about his line of work. The men sat packed together for warmth in silence; realizing that four of their crew were lost and hadn't been found. Young Bob dreamed of following the tradition of his Grandfathers and heading west as he'd heard there was work out in the oil fields of Wyoming. He liked and was adept at driving the big trucks that hauled dirt and gravel and he possessed the skill to keep them running reliably. The close call had scared him thoroughly enough that he remembered the details of that day and would relate them to his own son, decades later, roundly embellished of course.

Young Bob saved and saved so he could purchase a truck of his own and it wasn't long before he had that truck with rubber tires and found himself married to a college educated music teacher. Fernella Bateman$_r$ (went by Fern Ella) grew up in Merriman, went off to university down east at Nebraska Wesleyan, graduated in 1932, then came back to Gordon, started teaching music, and abruptly married Young Bob. Her Father Fred and both brothers were big, broad shouldered men accustomed to heavy, hard work. In the coming years, this strength would help the brothers survive European World War II. As the depression deepened and jobs disappeared, Bob had trouble finding hauling jobs in Sheridan County and scraped together enough money to buy gas for his truck so he and Fern could head west. Highway 20 was intermittently finished nearly all the way to Casper Wyoming. In most places, it was smooth gravel and in others was but a pair of tracks across the dirt field. They passed through all the towns along the way; Rushville, Hay Springs, Chadron, Crawford, then Harrison on the border of Wyoming and suddenly they were out on the high and dry plains and there were no towns for miles. Bob thought they should have filled up in Harrison, but he knew they carried two five gallon cans of gas in the back along with all their belongings. If they averaged 15 miles per hour, they were doing well and frequently found themselves eating or sleeping in the shade of the truck with no sign of human habitation in sight. During the hot part of the day, they had to stop regularly to let the truck engine cool down. Then, sure enough, before they could make Lusk, it chugged to a stop, out of gas. They waited for an hour or so and no other vehicles came by, so Bob set out on foot to the west carrying a five gallon can. It was late in the day and he hoped he could get a ride and return before it got dark. Just before dusk, a local rancher picked him up and took him into Lusk and agreed to take him back when the rancher finished his business. Bob waited until well past dark at the filling station and the rancher didn't show up. He was starting to worry about his new wife and what she would think about his ability to take care of her. About 10 PM, a pair of headlights came jerking down the street; it was the rancher and he was swimmingly drunk. After running off the road several times, he let Bob drive and promptly fell asleep on the passenger side of the seat. It was OK with Bob and he drove all the way to his truck, poured in the gas and had Fern drive it along behind him back to the rancher's turn off. He parked the rancher's truck along-side the road, and let the guy continue to sleep and snore loudly. He jumped into his driver's seat and they were off, once again headed west, it was just before dawn, July 1933.

Lusk at dawn in July, pathetic as it was, was a welcome sight and it wasn't long before they found the city park, washed and filled up on fresh water. They fell asleep in the truck for several hours, but then it started to get hot again and they had to head on west. Just as they were beginning to stir, the local cop was rapping on the truck door with his night stick. Bob and Fern were advised by the acerbic gentleman that they didn't allow vagrants and bums and that it was time to move on and never come back. Bob didn't have time to inquire about any possible work that might be available, as the cop kept rapping on the door until it moved out of reach and they were again headed to the west. Fern was greatly disturbed by their treatment as she was a sophisticated and educated woman and had "read more books than the cop had probably even seen." She kept whispering about it under her breath to the point that Bob became amused at her which didn't help the situation. They stopped in Manville for badly needed gas and food, and were told there were oil jobs in both Glenrock and Casper, as they were low on money and needed relief soon. Later that day, they made it to Glenrock and drove out to the oil refinery that was under construction only to be told there were jobs in Casper. The foreman asked them to carry a big motor that didn't work in the back of their truck up to Casper for repair, and Bob quickly agreed. When they got to Casper and dropped off the motor, the owner of the oil equipment company asked Bob if he would make regular runs back and forth with his truck and haul parts and supplies to the oil fields around the territory. They quickly reached a handshake agreement and that evening Bob and Fern enjoyed their first bath and bed in over two weeks. Once again a McComber was in the metal goods business, of sorts.

Bob enjoyed traveling all the back roads in the area and finding the oil drillers, then listening to their complaints and sharing a shot of whiskey. The drillers were a wild bunch, punching holes in the earth seemingly willy-nilly and seldom were successful, but just enough were to keep the business alive. Slowly though, the areas of success were slowly taken over by the bigger operators and the wildcatters disappeared. Fern did laundry at the hotel during the day and worked as a piano player in the hotel restaurant at night, and between them they had plenty of money saved for the rough times ahead. But oil wells came and went and it wasn't long before the business matured and Bob's boss told him that he too was being bought out and the closest hauling work was down in Wheatland.

The highway south was one of the few that were paved in those days. The paving process consisted of alternate layers of gravel and hot liquid asphalt that worked well but required constant maintenance. Bob was able to get the truck up to 30 miles per hour going down-hill, but had to keep a sharp eye out for holes because if they had hit one at that speed, something would break or they would blow a tire. The gravel pit at Wheatland was gigantic and served as a source of gravel for all the roads within several hundred miles. The boss of the pit had over 30 trucks hauling in every direction and paid spot cash for each load delivered. It was a constant race among the drivers of trucks of all kinds and sizes to make as many round trips as possible. If you didn't have the correct signature on your delivery ticket, no cash was forthcoming; this precipitated numerous arguments, and many truckers simply gave up. If they returned for their cash with the wrong signature, they couldn't get enough money to buy gas for the next haul. You were paid depending on the distance and the tonnage of gravel and the pit boss had a tendency to try to reduce both, or round the math down, in order to cheat the drivers. But Bob thrived and consistently made more cash than any of the others. He knew his truck inside and out, maintained it like a mother caring for her baby, never overloaded it, and knew the location of every bump and pot-hole in the region. He saw driver after driver break down their trucks by trying to go too fast or carrying too heavy a load. Some tore the suspension out from under their trucks on the holes, and some burned up their engines by overheating or tore out the transmission gears, but not him. Inevitably, winter approached the region and the business was due to slow mightily. The road crews would be lucky if they could work several days a week, and Bob and Fern had spent one winter in Casper. That was enough; Fern thought she was pregnant, and it was time to go south.

They headed south without a clue as to where they could find a job, let alone shelter. Bob then knew how his Father Giles and Grandpa Harmon must have felt when they failed to provide proper food and shelter to their loved ones. He knew they had gone through rough times, why Grandpa Harmon and his wife stayed in a dirt hole for several days waiting out a prairie blizzard. Now he was going through his own difficult time. Every town they came to he inquired around for hauling jobs or any jobs period. Cheyenne, Greeley, Fort Morgan and all the tiny burgs in between were passed without results. Several times they ate in the local town café, and mostly, they slept in or under the truck. Bob stopped by all the pool halls trying to get up a game in which he could win some money, but folks were touchy about that sort of thing and he wasn't successful. This was the middle of the depression and those without food and shelter were desperate, and those with, compassionate. Several times they were invited to eat a meal with a farmer or townsman in return for a few hours work. Akron, Otis, Yuma, and Eckley were checked out and next in line was the town of Wray. They had heard of trucker jobs there and were hopeful. Bob was slowly becoming more and more concerned that they were on the road to nowhere and there was no way to get off, stop or turn around.

Wray was down over the horizon to the east and storm clouds were blowing up with the east wind. It was the middle of the morning in the late fall and black clouds were coming out of the east? Bob knew something was wrong. He watched the cloud grow slowly toward the sun; it was the blackest thing he'd ever seen and he stopped at the top of a hill and watched it. Sheet lightening flashed constantly within the enormous cloud. The more he watched the more panicked he felt and he decided they had to find shelter. There was a dry creek down in the draw at the base of the hill and the highway bridge spanned it. If they could make it down there under the bridge they would be better off. The cloud suddenly covered the sun and it got dark instantly. He turned on his headlights and sped down the hill. They could see that the storm cloud itself was less than a mile away. It went all the way to the ground and completely obliterated the countryside. Bob thought it had to be a tornado, and his previous close call flashed through his mind. Without hesitation, he drove the truck down off the road and around into the dry creek bed. They went down over several drops deep enough that there would be no way to get back up, but they were frantic and concerned for their lives. The truck cab fit under the bridge without much room to spare and if the bridge stayed put, they would be protected. Fern could get her door open just enough to get out, but Bob's door was too close to the bridge pilings.

When the storm hit, it shook the truck and instantly it was pitch black as if someone had pulled a tarp over the cab. They couldn't see each other and they just sat holding onto each other huddled in the middle of the seat. The truck shook and jerked and dust forced its way into every little crack and hole in the cab and there were plenty. They started choking and had trouble breathing and Bob took off his shirt and pulled it over their heads. He reassured Fern that the storm would pass in a few minutes, but it didn't. It was one of the gigantic dust storms of that era that blew across Texas and Oklahoma and removed millions of tons of precious top soil for redeposit up in Kansas and Colorado. It was hot down there and they were sweating along with choking; as an hour ground by, then another. The wind wailed and moaned, and the sand blew against the truck so hard it tore off the paint. They grew thirsty and were able to find the jar of water they carried on the floorboard before it all leaked out; it had been turned over on the rough trip down. A few drinks of water revived them greatly; more hours went by. It seemed like it was the end of the world. Fern prayed and Bob listened intently to her pleas for deliverance. She prayed for their unborn baby and Bob silently cried. The storm lasted nearly 12 hours and it was dark when it blew out. It suddenly grew quiet and the truck stopped shaking. Bob removed his shirt and slowly rolled down the window to shake it out only to realize they were completely covered by dust; so he rolled it back up. The dust was a foot deep in the cab and covered most of the truck on the outside. Fern was able to roll her window down without dust rolling in and Bob crawled out only to sink into the talcum like dust completely over his head. He couldn't breathe and fought to get higher in the bridge structure. Fern's prayers flashed through his mind and he thought he would surely die if he couldn't get a breath of air. He climbed the structure with all his strength and finally burst into the fresh air. It was a cold night, the sky was full of stars and the full moon was bright. He could see that the hole in the dust he made getting out had filled back in and was surely pouring directly into the truck window. Again he panicked and he furiously brushed the dust away from the window with his hands and arms. It was a little like light snow, but it was dark, dirty and warm and smelled of death. After 15 minutes of thrashing around in the dust, he had enough removed from her door to get her out and up onto the road above. The countryside was covered in dust in drifts three and four feet deep. Everything was covered. The road was clear right where they were, but it would be impassable for days because of the drifts. There they were, stranded without a bush or a tree or a blade of grass in sight; all were covered. Bob had no shirt and fern had only a light cotton dress. She did bring the water jar that had several mouthfuls left. There was no way to get the truck out as it was buried and the engine surely wouldn't start without some serious cleaning. They would have to spend the night, so they crawled down under the bridge but above the truck and found a place to sit comfortably. Bob thrashed around and found their suitcases and bedding and was able to cover them for the night, as it would be very cold. Hopefully, sometime the next day help would find them.

They were awake off and on throughout the night and both were up at first light. Bob drug out his scoop shovel and broom and they proceeded to uncover the truck. When he pulled back the side covers to reveal the engine, he was startled as it was not visible. Dust was packed tight all around it and slowly but surely, he was able to clean it off. He removed the generator and cleaned out the dust. The starter was sealed, but the air cleaner was packed also. It was an oil bath style cleaner and the oil was contaminated, so he dumped it and replaced it with a little that he drained from the crankcase. They were both completely covered with dust and only their eyes and mouths were recognizable. Fern's auburn hair was gray as was Bob's sparsely populated head. The entire morning went by without a single vehicle coming down the road. So, Bob started shoveling a path backward through the dust drifts up to the highway. He started the truck engine to check it out and turned it back off because he knew it would not make it on its own. He knew he would have to back up onto the road as the truck had more torque in reverse than in low gear forward. It was common in those days to back up an exceptionally steep hill.

A few hours later a snowplow came by and with some help from the crew and a long chain they finally got the truck back on the road. They followed the snowplow on into Wray where the townsfolk were cleaning it up. Huge heaps of dust were piling up on the outskirts where folks were dumping it. They used buckets and wheel borrows, and pickup trucks. Horse drawn wagons and farm equipment did their share. Bob and Fern had enough money to rent a room as they needed a bath and had to wash out all their clothing. The town mayor hired Bob on the spot to haul the dust down and dump it in a ravine a mile or so out of town. The city had a front end loader they used in the winter to remove the snow from the streets and put it to good use scraping up dust and dumping it into the back of Bob's truck. Two weeks later, with the help of a couple brief rains, the town was back to normal. With the mayor's help, Bob found a job hauling dirt from the new irrigation ditches that were being dug to funnel water from the river down into the low lands south of town. Slowly their lives returned to normal and in March their first of five children, a girl Lois Fern$_r$, was born. Their lives changed overnight.

In the coming months, Bob realized they needed to settle down in one place, so his little family could establish some normalcy. All the moving from town to town of the previous years would have to stop, so they moved back to Gordon and he started hauling gravel for the highways that ran both north and south of town. He also hauled for the C&NW railroad. Slowly those jobs ran out as the roads were completed and he and Fern had to move to Rushville where he took a job hauling fuel to the farms around the area. Four more children followed, Donald$_r$, who was named after Bob's Great Uncle Dohmnall, Billy$_r$ and Betty$_r$ the twins and finally the youngest, Raymond$_r$.

Bob was able to start his own business hauling fuel for the Carter Oil Company, which later became Exxon and their lives settled down to raising children, working, playing pool and fishing.

During those years World War II was thrust upon the country and lean times continued for most of the people especially those in small towns. Most of the young men volunteered for the army, as it was the only job they could find, but those with families were discouraged from joining. Friends and neighbors went to fight the evil in Europe and a significant number never returned. Fern's two brothers volunteered and almost immediately found themselves in the thick of the fight. Myron, who had red hair like his sister Fern, was the first to go in. He was plugged directly into the fight in North Africa as part of the II Corp offensive under Patton that eventually drove the Germans out. He then fought in Sicily, up the boot of Italy and on into western Germany at war's end. Francis ended up in the battle of the bulge and the relief of Bastogne; then his unit pushed into the heart of Germany in the final thrust that finished the war in 1945. Francis returned to the States with a backpack full of stamp collection books for his Mother, he saved from certain destruction in a burning building. He took flak from all his buddies for discarding his belongings, except for his dry socks and underwear, and replacing them with the heavy books of stamps, which he then had to lug around for months. Francis returned physically and mentally healthy, but Myron suffered from the delayed effects of the atrocities he's witnessed and passed within a generation.

Bob delivered fuel of several kinds to folks in town for heating their houses and to farmers for both heating and equipment fuel. It was these trips to the farms that little Donnie liked the best. He enjoyed the trips along dirt and gravel roads and liked to look in the rear view mirror and watch the dust roll up behind them. Most of all he liked to play with the kids on the farms and each was a special adventure. They fished in the creeks, played on the stacks of hay, climbed in the barns and chased chickens. But one day when little Donnie was gently chasing chickens he came upon a big old tom turkey. It was all ruffled up and looked twice as big as it really was and when it saw little Donnie, who was only four at the time, it make a beeline for him. Donnie stood his ground thinking the turkey would stop or go around him but it didn't and it knocked him to the ground. It pounced on him and proceeded to peck him on the chest every time Donnie would make a sound. The farmer's wife was wise to the old turkey as it had done that before, so she was watching the whole deal and came running when the turkey got on top of Donnie. She smacked it with a broom several times and the feathers flew; the turkey gobbled and took off around the corner of the barn and took up a station so it could attack again the moment the wife disappeared. And it did.

Donnie saw the turkey coming that time and ran for the truck with the turkey right behind. He jumped up on the running board of the truck and yanked at the door handle just as the turkey fluttered into him gobbling and pecking furiously. He threw open the door hitting the turkey and knocking it to the ground just long enough for him to get into the truck and slam the door behind him. Bob saw that part of the attack and smiled to himself as he took his time filling the farmer's tanks. By the time he got into the truck to fill out his papers for the job, Donnie was calmed down and was watching the old tom standing on the ground just outside his door. Donnie told his Dad that he didn't like this place because the old turkey just wanted to knock him down and peck him, and it hurt. So, Bob came up with a plan.

Bob didn't want to seriously hurt the turkey, so the next time they went to that particular farm, they stopped at the Niobrara River and cut a pair of thin willow switches about three feet long. Little Donnie was enthralled with his new weapons and couldn't wait to get out of the truck and try them out. When they drove into the farm yard several dogs came out barking and chasing the truck just like usual. The old tom turkey was watching from his hiding place around the side of the barn. The farmer's wife ran out cussing and chased the dogs away with her broom and went back into the house presumably to her chores. Donnie piled out of the truck with his switches and swished them around like a pair of swords and smacked them against the front tire of the truck. The switches made a sharp smacking sound which pleased little Donnie immensely. The turkey continued to watch from his hiding place and waited for its chance to catch little Donnie away from the truck. Sure enough after a few minutes, little Donnie looked around and didn't see the turkey and headed for the meadow and a big haystack. Bob was busy filling the tanks taking care not to fill them too full so when they warmed up, and the fuel expanded, they wouldn't overflow. Turkeys are pretty smart compared to chickens and this old tom was especially wary of both the farmer's wife and her broom and the door to the truck. He slowly followed little Donnie and waited until they were several hundred feet away from the farmyard. Little Donnie had laid his switches down and had just started to climb the haystack when he heard the chilling sound of the turkey gobble. He turned and saw the turkey all fluffed out and swelled up in a dead run straight at him. He slid down the several feet to the ground and picked up his switches and stood with his back to the stack and started to cry as the turkey gobbled and charged. Donnie was scared to death and his crying only served to enrage the turkey further. When the turkey got within reach, Donnie whipped one of his switches out and smacked it on the head. It stunned the turkey and stopped it just long enough to get another blow across the neck. The turkey's feathers went down and he became disoriented, just as he was smacked several more times. Little Donnie wasn't going to stop hitting the turkey until it ran away, which it did. Bob looked up just in time to see little Donnie chasing the turkey back to the farmyard as fast as he could go, still whipping the turkey on the back. Bob yelled for him to stop. Little Donnie made his way to the truck where he sat down and went to sleep. Sometime later, Bob shook Donnie awake so he could enjoy a fat piece of warm pie and a glass of milk the farmer's wife brought out to celebrate the defeat of the turkey. Over the years, they repeated their trips back to the farm multiple times and the old tom turkey was never to be seen as it watched little Donnie play with the dogs from a safe distance. He always hoped the farmer's wife would bring out another piece of pie, but she never did. Many decades later, Donnie visited that farm only to find the place abandoned, the house had been torn down and the barn turned into a crude shelter for the cattle. His memory was vivid and in his mind, he could see the wife, the turkey, the haystack and the two little willow switches. He could hear the swish they made as they cut through the air and the dull smack as they hit the turkey.

In the mid-forties, the pool hall in Rushville was off limits to kids because they served liquor next door and it was common for adults to bring their drinks over into the pool hall with them. The place was filled with smoke, especially on Saturday nights when folks were crowded around all the tables watching and betting on the games. It hung like a cloud in the place and streamed out the door like the place was on fire. It was common to chew tobacco and brass spittoons were lined up against each wall where folks simply spit their wads in their general direction. Bob was an excellent pool player, but was so busy during most of the week his only time to play was Saturday night, and when he and Jack Hannah locked cues, it was a brawl. Folks always showed up early at the pool hall so they could get a good spot to watch the oncoming match between the two very best players around. Neither Bob nor Jack could get anyone to play them for money, but everyone liked to bet on whether or not they could make the next shot. The billiard table was at the end of the hall next to the front door where there was a little more room for bettors and supporters.

Bob and Jack never actually bet each other on a game, they made their money by taking a small, voluntary cut of the winnings of the bets on each shot they made. The bettors would put their bets on the outside edge around the table and if someone wanted to match the bet they would put their money next to it; so the table rim was usually covered with money except for where the shooter would have to put their hand or lean on it. Then after the shot was made, the winners would peel off a couple of bills from their winnings and hand them to the successful shooter. If the shooter missed the shot he received no cut, so he had great incentive to make the shots. They liked to play three-cushion-billiards, which is by far the most difficult game in pool. The way it was set up, neither Bob nor Jack would ever lose any money, and they each had their own avid supporters. Bob's most avid supporter was his young son Donnie. Young Donnie was, of course, barred from going into the pool hall, but he found that the best place to watch was by standing on the window sill just outside the open front door. He had a difficult time actually seeing the surface of the pool table, but he could tell who was shooting and also could tell by the yell of the crowd, whether or not the shot was made. The window sill was brick and was tilted at a slight angle to let the water drain off. This made it difficult for young Donnie to stand there for long periods at a time, so he had to get up and down constantly. In addition, he had to be home at 9:00 PM, and the pool match was usually just getting up a good head of steam by then, so he missed most of the action that continued until well after midnight. Young Donnie loved the excitement, the anticipation of a well bet shot and the cheers or groans that resulted. He was impressed by the free flow of money and the next day, he would push his Dad to show him all he had won the night before. It seemed like a lot of money to Donnie as it was usually a roll compressed with a big rubber band, bigger than you could put your hand around. What he didn't know was, it was that money that allowed the family to survive. This was the WWII forties and the hard times were still with all the small towns around the country, and with five kids to clothe and feed, Bob needed every cent. Rather than buy anything new, everyone fixed the old one. This applied to houses, cars, clothes and shoes. Fixing something that had broken down was a way of life and everyone was good at it. It was that under-the-hood mentality that contributed to the American's love for cars.

One of Bob's fuel customers started another hobby for him and the family by trading him a fishing pole for a five gallon can of fuel. It was an old pole and casting reel that had seen its better days, but still worked and included a complete tackle box filled with hooks and sinkers and do-dads of all kinds. Young Donnie was impressed with all the stuff but had never seen or heard of people like them actually being able to catch real fish. This was a new adventure that was to end badly. Neither of them could wait to try out their new pole, and when a customer trip took Bob past Alkali Lake, they stopped and "drowned" a few worms. Bob put a small weight on the end of the line followed by a hook-with-worm about a foot up, then with a red and white bobber about three feet above that. It took him a half dozen tries to finally stumble on the technique of casting, but finally they had the rig out in the lake a dozen yards or so. It took less than a minute for the first fish to strike and the bobber suddenly disappeared from the surface. Bob hastily reeled the fish in and young Donnie was clapping his hands with excitement. It was a small bullhead and when Bob pulled it up out of the water, he grasped it in his hand and was promptly horned, by one of the stingers just behind the gills. He let go, the fish flopped and fell off the hook into the water and was gone. Bob's hand was bleeding slightly in the palm and their moment of joy changed to disappointment in an instant. But, undaunted Bob put on another worm, and cast the rig out again, this time a little farther. Again, a few seconds later, a fish took the bait and this time was reeled in and dragged upon the bank a few feet before it was carefully grabbed and the hook removed. They slipped a short rope through its gills and tossed it into the shallows next to them. Before they were finished, they had caught their limit of a dozen or so, and took home a nice string of fish to clean for supper. Floured and fried with hush puppies, they were a definite hit with the family. It was an event young Donnie would remember his entire life.

They stopped by the lake several times in the coming weeks and each time took home a nice mess of fish. Bob bought another rod and reel so they would each have one and wouldn't have to alternate casting and reeling in the fish. They always went back to the same spot on the lake. The road that skirted the lake looped around to the west and south and ended at a large farm house and barn on the southeast side. Bob would pull the truck as far off the single lane road as he could without getting stuck in the soft ground, and they would walk a hundred or so feet over to the lake. They had just started fishing when Bob realized he had forgotten something in the truck and sent young Donnie after it. Just as he got to the truck, he paused and sat on the running board to remove his shoe. He pulled off his sock, noticed his funny toe (known as Morton's toe) and repositioned his sock so his big toe didn't stick through the hole. As he was tying the shoe, a beat up old Mercury pulled up beside him. A stringy haired young man jumped out, smacked young Donnie on the head and threw him into the back seat. He got back into the car and it drove off. It only took a couple seconds. Since it happened on the far side of the truck, Bob didn't see what happened and after a few minutes, went to see what was holding up young Donnie, only to find that he was gone. He then realized that the car, that had come by slowly, had abducted his son. He was panic stricken and jumped into the truck, leaving all his fishing gear down by the lake. He tried to turn the truck around on the narrow gravel road and got stuck when the rear duals sank into the soft soil. Down the road several miles, when the two abductors could see nobody following, they stopped and tied young Donnie's hands behind his back then threw him into the trunk along with two young girls they had stolen. The girls were tied and gagged and looked to be in their early teens. They had been roughed up and were crying. Dust covered everything as the trunk leaked as was typical of cars of that era. The abductors had been driving on all the graveled back roads to avoid being seen on their trip south. They had seen the farm from the main gravel road a quarter mile to the east, and went over to steal some gas. When the farmer turned his back momentarily, they knocked him cold, beat his wife senseless, then took their 12 year old daughter. On their way back to the main road they had to go back past the lake and saw the chance to add a young boy to their catch and took it.

The two abductors drove onto the south as Bob went north. After 15 minutes, he had been able to extricate his truck from his predicament and headed out as fast as the truck would go on the old gravel roads. Only he had gone north back toward the main highway, while the kidnappers had gone the other way, and then planned to cut to the west and pick up the main southbound highway and drive steadily to Texas. Bob got to Highway 20 and went west several miles to Hay Springs and called the sheriff. The word went out to all the surrounding towns to look for a dark car, going away from the area. It wasn't much to go on and the abductors were able to continue on to the south through Alliance, Bridgeport and on into Kansas where they found a southbound gravel county road and stopped for the night. By that time young Donnie had awakened; he was covered with dust, didn't know where he was, was terribly thirsty, and had to pee. Suddenly the trunk lid opened and he could see the two grinning men as they dragged the three prisoners out and slid them down into the grassy ditch beside the road. It was then that young Donnie realized that his hands were tied behind his back and that he had a headache. The abductors untied the three and retied one leg of each to the car door with a single piece of rope. They gave some bread and water to each of the prisoners and waited a few minutes, while they were gulped down. The two abductors then abused the girls one at a time. Donnie lay on the ground facing away from the slapping, crying, and thrashing and held his hands over his ears so he couldn't hear the pitiful cries of the girls. He didn't know what was going to happen to him, but it wasn't going to be good. After a while, things quieted down and the men pulled some blankets out and covered themselves for the night. The three prisoners were left lying in the ditch uncovered, hurt and frightened. It was summer and warm, but the mosquitoes were having a feast. In spite of the poor treatment, Donnie was able to fall asleep while both girls were softly crying.

Early in the morning at first light, Donnie was awakened by the snoring of the two kidnappers. When he realized where he was, his first thought was to get away. He knew not their location but it didn't matter; all he wanted to do was to get away from the two grinning men. He wasn't able to untie the knots in the rope that held him and started to cry in frustration when he rolled over and felt his jackknife in his pocket. He always carried a small jackknife and most boys did at the time. It wasn't very sharp, but had a rough edge from the crude sharpening stone he had used, and after a minute of sawing on the rope, he was free. The girls had quietly watched him get free and held up their own ropes, which he cut through in another few minutes of high drama cutting. He knew the two abductors couldn't catch him, but he wasn't sure that the girls were able to run for the several hours it would take to free them. He also knew they must stay off the road, and not knowing which direction to go, the three quietly slid under the barbed wire fence and headed off to the west toward a tree lined draw a half mile away. Donnie had enough sense to stay to the low ground and off the ridge lines where they could easily be spotted. He had to tell the girls to watch where they were stepping and not to look back. They couldn't afford a sprained ankle or worse at that point; the girls responded.

The girls were fast of foot, and stayed with Donnie easily. The three were miles away from the car by the time the sun came up and the two stringy haired men woke up. Immediately, the two were enraged that their prisoners were gone; they blamed each other as they drove frantically up and down the road trying to get a glimpse of the children; but there was none. The two went back to the spot where they slept the night and one set off to the west while the other went east. They weren't skilled in tracking and had no idea what to look for, but they wouldn't give up easily and the westward heading man ran as fast as he could toward a distant hill, where he hoped to get a view of the countryside and the missing children. After a quarter mile or so he was unable to run any longer and began walking. Then he went slower and was about to turn around when he spotted a fresh footprint in a soft prairie dog mound. Then, he saw another, going toward the west. Suddenly, he was encouraged and started to jog in a westward direction. By that time, the three children had turned to the north as they had sighted a farm house in the distance. The abductor lost the trail as quickly as he had found it and continued on west far past the point where the children had turned north.

It was about mid morning when the three escapees trudged into the farm yard. The wind mill was turning furiously in the morning breeze and the stock tank was overflowing with cool clear water. The house had been abandoned several years before, so the yard was overgrown with weeds and the front screen door nearly torn from its hinges. Donnie ran his fingers over the tender lump on the back of his head and wished he could hit the guy back some way. But the kids saw the water, took off their shoes and socks and immersed themselves in the tank. It was only two feet deep, but was wonderfully refreshing. Donnie found several empty bottles in the vacant barn and filled them with water as they prepared to follow the little two trail road on to the west from the farm. They were just over the Kansas state line south and east of Haigler, Nebraska and Highway 27 was a few miles to the west. The country was hilly and treeless; the sun was hot and the air dry. Their abductor had given up and was headed back to his car. When he got there, his buddy was nowhere in sight, so he slumped into the car and just drove off. Those blond haired kids were worth a thousand dollars each, the girls a little more, down in south Texas or northern Mexico. A week later the partner was shot with buckshot trying to steal a local farmer's old pickup truck. It took him two days to die, and in the meantime, he told the sheriff the complete story.

Donnie and the girls were picked up by a local rancher on his way into Haigler and dropped off at the sheriff's office. It was almost exactly one full day from the time they were abducted when the phone in the Sheridan County Sheriff's office rang with the news. A friend of the Sheriff's was dispatched to make the drive down to Haigler and pick them up and a phone call was made to each set of parents. Bob didn't cry often, but when he got the news, he walked out behind the gas station where he could be alone and quietly "dropped a few tears." When Donnie got home late that evening, he was treated to his infrequent but favorite meal, hamburger steak and french-fries. From then on, Donnie's jackknife could always be found buried deeply in his pants' pocket.

Fishing became the family hobby. Every pond, stream, reservoir, and puddle was fished, some with great success and many with none. Pine Creek, White River, Box Butte Reservoir, Walgren Lake, Smith Lake, and even Rush Creek Bridge frequently gave up their best fish. Catfish, bullheads, perch, trout, crappie and bass all became family favorites and when combined with hush puppies doused in syrup, everyone smiled. Occasionally one of the kids would get a bone in their throat, so a major operation would take place in which Fern would hold a flashlight and Bob would use a pair of long needle nosed pliers to yank the bone free in between gags from the victim. Sheridan County was known for its hot and humid summers and snowy, windy winters. Of course, the folks that lived there thought it was much more severe than the rest of the country. The old house was gradually modified; a toilet and running water were added along with a refrigerator, kitchen sink and an oil burning stove. The upstairs of the house was hot in the summer, so the boys slept in a tent just south of the house under the big old American elm trees. Summers were spent playing cowboys and Indians and baseball, and the winters going to school. Fern taught many of the local kids how to play the piano for a buck a lesson.

Early in January 1949 a sudden blizzard hit that part of the country, the likes of which hadn't been seen for over a century when Harmon and Lydia had to dig into the side of the river bank to survive. It was the single event that changed the course of the family forever, and it happened again. Bob was out north of town delivering fuel to one of the farms, when the wind started strong out of the northeast. He always told the kids, "When the wind comes out of the east, it's time to hit for home, and when it comes out of the northeast, run." By the time he had finished filling the barrels and tanks, it had started snowing and the wind was howling. The problem getting back to town wasn't the depth of the snow, but the visibility. He only had to go a dozen miles straight south, but with the ferocious cross wind, he had trouble staying on the road. It was a gravel road with deep ditches on both sides and if he drove into one, he would surely be stuck or even turn over. He didn't, of course, know it but the storm was going to last for over three full days, and if he got stuck, his chance of survival was slim. The temperature plunged to around zero and the wind was moaning at a steady 60 miles per hour, and gusting above that. A man out in the storm with no protection had no chance. Herds of cattle were driven into ravines and frozen solid. It killed nearly all the wild animals in the region too large to get underground. It took decades for the deer to return. Driving completely blind, Bob had to feel for the edge of the road with the front tires and could only make three or four miles an hour. In the four hours it would take him to get to town, the snow would become so deep he would never be able to find the road. He knew he had to speed up while he could still feel the edge of the road with his front tires; it was his only chance.

He remembered the story his Dad had told him about Grandpa Harmon and knew he could dig into the side of the ditch to make himself a cave if it came to that. It was cold in the truck in spite of the having the heater going full blast. He tried to keep the truck going close to ten and prepared mentally for the fight of his life. Every time the right front tire started to go down into the ditch, he would wrestle the steering wheel back to the left, then drift to the right and pull back left. The windshield wipers were frozen solid, but with the defroster on full, he could see just a little bit out the bottom two inches or so. As long as he kept the wind blowing across the hood from left to right, he knew he had to be going south. He had been on this road a hundred times and knew every cross road and turn out. The road was also dead flat level with no hills except where it crossed the railroad tracks. The truck was starting to buck through sizeable three and four foot drifts and Bob's heart dropped every time as he thought he was off the road. But, he wasn't and finally the truck climbed the small hill going up to the railroad tracks then sharply slid down the other side into deep snow and bogged down right in front of old Sterling Stern's Carter Oil station at the northeast edge of town. Bob found himself stuck in a monster drift right in front of the only gas pump Sterling had. He could just make out the glass container at the top of the pump and knew he had finally made it to town. Those dozen miles had taken him the longest two hours of his life. He shut off the truck and scooted across the seat to get out on the downwind side, opened the door and slid out into three feet of snow. He knew the office to the station was 15 feet away but couldn't see it. He momentarily thought about staying in the truck, because if he set out for the office and missed it, he could wander off to the north and perish. Pushing through the snow was difficult as it was packed hard from the wind. He intentionally veered to his left so he would be sure to run into the building, and he did. He was south of the front door about eight feet so it was relatively easy to find it. When he opened it, the wind nearly took it out of his hands and flung it open into the hands of old Sterling who was standing just inside looking out the window. Instantly the inside of the station was covered with a dusting of snow and it took both of them to close the door. They looked at each other with fear in their eyes. From the single minute Bob was out in the raging storm, he was cold to the bone. His glasses were frozen over and snow had found its way into every opening. He had no idea how he was going to get home that night.

The electric power was off but the phones were working and he called Fern to be sure all the kids were home and that he probably wouldn't make it that night. She said all the kids were home and that eleven of his customers had called wanting burner fuel for their stoves. He told her he was going to wait until morning to try to come home and hopefully the storm would have broken. Sterling's hovel was in the small building just southwest of the station itself. He had converted the little shed into living quarters when his wife died. He made do with a simple hot plate for cooking and an outdoor toilet; he hauled water several gallons at a time from the neighbor's house. The only insulation it had was the air space between the weathered wood on the outside and the plywood on the inside of the wall studs, and the wind found all the little cracks to fill with snow, but it was shelter and he had a good wood burning stove in it, with plenty of wood. When they finally made it to Sterling's little house, they spent the next hour plugging up all the cracks with newspaper. Had they not, drifts would have formed several feet deep. Sterling heated up several cans of soup which they ate out of the can, and they sat down and listened to the wind moan through the forlorn little group of buildings. The high wind kept the draft through the stove much too fast and they had to turn down the flue damper to a mere crack. They were warm, fed and alive and when they finally had a chance to relax, Bob became frustrated about not being able to help his customers. In his mind, he went over each of those that requested more fuel and was sure they would have enough for at least a week, and he slowly thought himself to the realization that they would be OK. He didn't dream that he would have trouble getting them fuel in a week, but that was what was going to happen. During the night the wind shifted so it was coming out of the north. This served to reposition many of the drifts into new ones. By morning, there were drifts that were routinely ten feet deep and some were twenty. In places, the ground was blown bare by the wind and if you could have seen where to go you could navigate between the drifts quite easily.

The next day it was still so dark, Bob had to look at his watch several times before he could convince himself it was daytime. He was going to try to get home and had found several hundred feet of clothesline rope to help him. He had planned to tie one end of the rope to something close to the door at Sterling's house, then head off to the south to the next house and tie off the rope; return to Sterling's and untie the rope, then follow it to the next, etc. He would have to make the equivalent of three trips instead of one, but when you can't see more than a few feet, he thought it a good plan. Bundled up with all the coats he could get on, hip waders, and cloths tied around his head with only eye and mouth slits showing, he set off. He was able to tie off on fences and trees he recognized along the way, and quickly he made it to the highway then turned west and followed the line of trees on the north side. He'd been gone from Sterling's a half hour and had made it almost three blocks when he ran into a drift that he couldn't get around or through. The drift was far deeper than he was tall and he knew he couldn't thrash his way through. He figured he must have been across the street in front of the courthouse, so he tied off his rope on a tree adjacent to the monster drift and headed south across the highway. The snow was so deep, he got stuck again and began to search off to what he thought was the south for any sign of the court house or jail. He hit the end of the rope and knew he must be way off course because it was not more than about 100 feet across the highway. Had he wandered to the east or the west? he did not know. Should he let go of the rope and try to find the metal fence that surrounded the courthouse, or should he go back? His hip boots had filled with snow, and his feet were getting wet. He had to get inside somewhere and empty the boots, then try to tie something around them at the top to prevent the snow from filling them up. Reluctantly he went back to the tree where the rope was tied. He started to question whether or not he really knew where he was. The wind had changed and was coming out of the northwest, and he still thought it northerly. He was becoming completely disoriented and panic welled up in his stomach and he began to feel woozy.

He put his back to the tree and sat down exhausted physically and mentally.

It didn't take long for the snow to start covering Bob and he could see his body quickly turning white with snow. He moved a little and it blew away. He looked straight up and could make out some of the tree branches. The storm must have slowed slightly. He looked around and could barely make out the shape of the house to his north. Yes the storm was letting up. He instantly knew where he was and stood looking off to the south but could see nothing. He was some 100 feet to the east of the court house; to his west was a monster drift. While the storm was giving him a parsimonious glimpse of his surrounding, he took advantage and struck off to the south, crossed the highway and tied off the rope on the picket fence. He was back across the highway and untied the other end, then followed the rope to the fence, just as the storm intensified and he was again totally blind. But he knew exactly where he was. He was able to angle off to the southwest where he should run into the jail. There would be some gigantic old cottonwood trees in the yard. Sure enough they were there and before he knew it he was on the porch and knocking on the door. Dorothy Hills, opened it a crack and could see it was someone needing help and quickly drug Bob into the room. She and Wendell, who was the county sheriff, brushed him off and sat him down on the couch, where they pulled off his boots. Nearly three hours had passed since he had left Sterling's. He had gone three blocks and had about two and a half to go. Wendell brought him some dry pants, which were way too big, and socks as Bob was insistent that he had to continue. He called Fern to let her know where he was and learned that the list of folks needing more fuel had grown to 16. The storm had been moaning with vigor for nearly 24 hours when he set out the back door of the jail and went straight south down the alley. There were so many buildings along the way that the snow had nearly filled the alley and Bob couldn't make any headway and turned back. As long as his rope was tied securely, he could pull on it to help him stay on his feet.

So, he set off to the west cutting behind the court house and made it over to the old wrought iron fence. Retreating to get his rope, he was encouraged that he would actually make it before night fall. The storm was beginning to falter as there were short periods when Bob could actually make out the outlines of the buildings and homes. He continued on south then west, then south with only four houses to go. He persisted against the sisyphean storm; knew it was past sundown and that the house before him was his, but he couldn't get to the door. The snow was so deep it had covered the ground floor almost completely, windows and doors. He felt his way around to the back door and squeezed between a large drift on the back porch and the house to get to the back door. Fern was inside waiting for him. The kids were puzzled at her tears; they were just glad to see their Dad.

The next day, the wind went down slightly and the visibility lifted just enough that a person could see large objects 20 or so feet away. Bob knew he couldn't get his truck extricated from the snow drift in which it now slept, so he arranged to borrow a horse from Wofford on which he could sling several five gallon cans of fuel for his customers. The next two days Bob delivered enough fuel to keep folks going and the storm finally broke. The fourth day the sun came out bright and folks emerged from their buried houses to stand in awe of the size of the drifts that remained. Slowly the town dug out. The drifts on the roads were so large, the city couldn't handle them. The Army National Guard showed up and proceeded to dig out all the small towns in the area. One drift was over 25 feet deep and extended completely across Highway 20 between the Post Office and the Chevrolet Garage on the other side. Some drifts in the streets were so large the Army just left them. They remained until June. Opening the railroad was a different story. The Army couldn't get their big equipment up on the tracks, so it was up to the C&NW to clear their own. And they did. Young Donnie went down to the tracks to watch the gigantic Vee plow that had been attached to the engine pound its way through the drifts. Immediately behind the plow and engine was an extra long car that had a crane on it large enough that it could pick up the engine and set it back on the tracks. The odd looking train would get back a mile or so and run at a big drift and hit it with a thunderous crash. The ground would shake and the snow would fly. Sometimes it would break through and more frequently it would not. About every fifth blast into a drift, the engine would derail and have to be set back onto the track by the big crane. It took them several hours just to get from one side of town to the other and late in the afternoon it went out of sight off to the west. Young Donnie was impressed with the ingenuity of the crews and the size of the plow and crane. It was an impression that would affect his life course.

For the kids, the storm was great. First, there wasn't any school for at least a week and second, it was a wonderland of drifts, caves, paths and tunnels through the snow. Most kids spent every possible minute playing in the snow. In many places, the snow was drifted so hard they could walk on it, and cars and trucks drove on it. But there were also places where it was soft and you could sink in five or six feet. Gradually, things got back to normal, the children got bored with the snow, and finally when it warmed in the spring, most of the snow melted and faded along with many of the memories. Bob never forgot that feeling of complete bewilderment he had when he thought all was lost at the height of the storm.

The '50's in Nebraska was a time of growth and promise. Farming and industry were still exploding as a result of the start they got when the war ended. The atomic threat was raised as the Soviets tested their nuclear bombs developed with technology they stole from America. Both countries were building bombs as fast as they could and the intercontinental ballistic missile was developed. Numerous companies were vying for government contracts and were hiring engineers and technocrats by the millions, one of which was the oldest son Donald. Americans began to live under the threat of nuclear war. It was 1961, and Vietnam was festering with communism.

# VIETNAM

The buildup to war took nearly a decade when in May 1954, the Vietnamese attacked Dien Bien Phu and killed or wounded over 10,000 French. Disillusioned with a war on the other side of the world, the French ordered their troops home. By 1959, the North Vietnamese were actively building an invasion route down through Laos and Cambodia roughly paralleling their borders with South Vietnam. No one knows how much it cost the communists to bribe Prince Sihanouk for his complicity, but it was an agreement he to which he would stubbornly cling for the next dozen years, and was largely responsible for the protracted nature and outcome of the war with the Americans. By late 1961, President Kennedy ordered more help in the form of military equipment and over 3000 military advisors. In early 1962, operation Ranch Hand began. The goal was to defoliate the jungle hiding the North Vietnamese trails coming down from the north and expose them to the view of airplane observers. This was the mission that brought Bob's youngest son Raymond to Vietnam.

Many of the service men and women that found themselves in Vietnam were involuntary draftees, that didn't want to be there and did as little as possible. The specialists from the Marines, Navy and Air Force, however, were a different breed and were there on a mission; no matter how misguided it may have been by our politicians. Raymond volunteered for service in the Air Force and through a series of unusual, if not malfeasant, decisions by superiors, found himself training on Okinawa then in the Philippines and on to Vietnam where he was one of the crew on an AC-47 gunship. They were equipped with the new GE MXU-470 mini-gun modules that could spit out bullets so fast they shredded trees and brush in their path. This was a new tactical weapon developed primarily to support the spray planes, but was found to be so effective it was used in nearly all offensive actions. The Vietcong and North Vietnamese regulars both became deathly afraid of the low, slow flying AC-47's as there was literally no place to hide from the devastating shower of bullets. The mere sight of the slow flying plane in the distance caused most to flee in abject terror. The particular crew in which Raymond found himself went on approximately 300 missions that killed over 3000 VC and NVA; destroyed 320 trucks, transports and buildings in the 26 months they were in Vietnam. Approximately 120 medals were accumulated by the crew that included 38 purple hearts, 9 Distinguished Flying Crosses and one Air Force Cross.

Ray was confident that the crew were well prepared for the task at hand, but still had the uneasy feeling that there was much they weren't being told. At the very first briefing for their first mission, he was impressed with the precision of the proceedings and the information provided by each of the speakers. They knew the exact location, terrain and weather along with the probable locations of the NVA (North Vietnamese Army) along the way. There were to be three spray planes accompanied by a half dozen other support planes of which their AC-47 was one. The other planes of the group took down some of the targets on Ta Dung Mountain, adjacent to the spray area that could have been a problem for the low flying gunship and dusters. The secondary explosions indicated they had hit some weapons caches. When the group finally got to the defoliant area it was up the AC-47 to make its gun run to clear a path for the dusters, as the spray planes were called, they would fire each of the three gun modules separately in close sequence so it seemed as if it was one continuous flow of bullets. Each time a gun would open up, the back of the plane would buck sharply and had to be corrected by the pilots. The guns were fired in short bursts to keep the barrels from overheating. The plane directly behind them reported multiple hits of enemy vehicles as the banana trees hiding them also fell. As the end of the valley approached, Raymond could feel the heat of the hot guns building up inside the plane in spite of the open doors on the left side. He was too busy inside with the communications to see any of the devastation they were leaving behind. The sound of the guns ejecting the spent cartridges sounded like someone was pouring dimes on a metal table. The final pass up the valley was a three gun shoot in which the plane's tail lurched so violently to the right that everyone had to hang on, and when the three guns shut off the plane lurched back to normal. Each of these maneuvers required the pilots to make quick corrections in the controls to keep the plane stable. Follow up reconnaissance photos showed a dozen NVA trucks destroyed along with 72 supply cycles and 82 fatalities. Back at the base, they found the AC-47 had taken 51 small caliber hits plus a few from a 12.7mm anti-aircraft gun. The latter were armor piercing and would pass completely through the plane and anything in its path. This first mission was an eye opener for all the rookies including Ray. Yes, there was much they hadn't been told, but they had no idea what hair raising adventures were ahead.

Bob's middle son Billy joined the Army to avoid the draft, and after a few months of training, was shoe horned into a transport plane, destination Vietnam. Everyone around him, which included mostly draftees, was air sick or scared sick. They had been given puke bags before they took off from the American west coast, but one per person wasn't enough. There was a steady stream of young men proceeding to and from the head. They had seat belts but probably wouldn't have needed them as they were packed so tightly on the benches, no one could move except to get up, and then they had to step over an endless assortment of legs and packs to get to the head. It was a ride Bill never forgot until the day he passed nearly 40 years later. The entire place smelled of vomit and urine and Bill was glad to get out of that hell hole when the plane finally unloaded at Bien Hoa, Vietnam. He didn't realize he was out of one hell hole and into another.

It wasn't long before Bill's regiment was slogging through the Iron Triangle, in search of the Vietcong. It was Operation Cedar Falls. Snipers and booby traps were everywhere and one after another of Bill's comrades were injured or killed. It only lasted three weeks and in that time Bill's platoon lost almost one third of its members. Much of the time they were simply sitting on the ground waiting to get the all clear signal to move forward. The VC had tunnels all over the place and repeatedly surfaced behind them to pick off and unsuspecting American boy and disappear. They did have several fire fights and they finally got their first taste of actual battle. The noise during a fight amazed Bill. The endless explosions from the muzzles of their weapons combined with the pop and buzz of those opposing. He wondered if the VC were like them and simply wanted to survive and go back home. The shouting and screaming of the wounded on both sides prevented him from sleeping much during the relatively short campaign. At first, he generally couldn't see enough to get a good shot at anyone, but that would change. There was nowhere to clean up, but their commanders made sure they had plenty of water and they learned to get most of the slime and dirt off with a wash cloth. It was January and the weather was hotter than hell. Men were constantly trying to take off their shirts or cut the legs off their pants, but the bugs were everywhere and the only protection they had was their clothes. You just learned to sweat and sit in it. Bill often wondered if the VC could smell them the way the Americans could smell each other.

Several times they came across tunnel entrances that had been hidden under branches and grass and once he was assigned to sit next to one and kill anyone that tried to come out; then drop in a grenade or two and plug the hole. He sat there for hours and hours as his unit moved on ahead. Just at dusk, he heard someone breathing. He had dozed slightly and jerked awake to the definite sound of someone breathing hard. Bill slowly looked around to be sure it wasn't someone above ground. Then there was the sound of someone sliding in the dirt up to the entrance. Bill pulled the pin on the grenade and held the handle down tightly. He was already sweating, but now it started running into his eyes. He tried not to breathe as he was sure the VC would hear him. His heart was pounding in his ears and he could feel his pulse in his throat. Very slowly over the span of 10 or so minutes the VC took up a position in the tunnel entrance; it was more like a large hole in the ground. He had grass tied to his head that was coated black with mud. Bill could smell his body odor as he was only five feet away. The man's head was still below the level of the ground and he apparently didn't sense that Bill was there. Bill pointed his M14 rifle at the top of the VC's head and held it in his right hand, finger on the trigger. In his left hand he held the live grenade. In another minute the head would lift above ground level and Bill would have to act. Then, as the head started to move ever so slowly, he pulled the trigger and the blast blinded him temporarily. Blood and brains from the top of the VC's head blew out in the opposite direction. He dropped the grenade into the hole next to the dead man and took off at a dead run in the direction of his unit. Behind him, he heard a muffled boom and he knew that entrance had been sealed, body and all.

By the time he found his unit, they were bedding down for an evening nap. You had to get sleep when you could because this was a 24 hour a day deal. When they seemed to be out of harm's way, some of them took a nap while the others provided guard duty. As he sat down and finally took a deep breath and a drink of water, Bill wondered about the man he had just killed. Surely the guy had parents and loved ones too that would miss him when this business was finished, and for that Bill felt badly. But he also was reminded by his platoon leader that he had done the right thing and that it was part of their responsibility to stay alive at all cost and "kill the other guy." The next day, they slowly moved to the north searching the sector to which they had been assigned. Different units moved onto new ground as directed by the company commander. His platoon discovered a weapons cache buried in the ground up on a sparsely wooded hillside. It was about 15 feet square and 10 feet deep and literally filled with explosives and weapons all still in the Chinese crates. The crates were each about three by four feet square and were heavy. How in the world did these guys get this stuff down here? It was a long way from North Vietnam and there were no roads, at least that they knew about. The main unit was going to move on up the hill. Bill and three others were left at the cache to remove all the crates from the hole, and about the time they had all the crates removed from the hole and lined up for inspection by the commanders, they started taking fire from their rear. VC had apparently come out of one of the tunnels behind them and had taken up a position farther down on the hill in the heavier trees and underbrush. The bullets were buzzing around them, not in great quantity but enough to keep everyone down. His three comrades ran up the hill a hundred yards or so to join their unit, but Bill was still in the hole when all the noise started and he immediately scrambled up to the lip to retrieve his helmet and weapon. His platoon was now firing on down the hill over his head. They had scattered into whatever cover they could find, and he was alone in the midst of the fight. Bullets were buzzing and hissing from both directions. Slowly, the VC moved up as they gathered in numbers and volume of fire. They were hell bent to retake as much of the weapons cache as they could. Bill thought, *here we go again*. He hoped his comrades could drive back the oncoming VC, because if they couldn't, he was going to die. The VC weren't known to take prisoners. He dug into the side of the hole up high enough so he could see over the rim and started firing himself. There were two large tufts of grass that kept his head out of view with just enough space between them to support his rifle. The VC were moving, first up one side then the other, then back and he had to constantly change positions to take advantage of open targets less than fifty yards away. He was a good shot and took them down one at a time. Bam..., Bam..., Bam..., he continued to aim and fire and slowly the VC ducked and retreated as they couldn't see him. He fired again and again until he was nearly out of ammunition and suddenly, he found that he was the only one shooting. He was able to take down four more as they moved away. Bam..., Bam..., Bam..., Bam... and it was over. The only sounds, other than his heart beat, he could hear were the rumbles of bombs far in the distance. Bill's rifle barrel was so hot he couldn't touch it. He knew not how many he had killed that day, but afterward he counted bullets and decided that he must have shot 52 times and didn't miss many.

The main group of Americans came back down the hill moving quickly to follow the VC survivors and find their hidden tunnels, so they could seal them up. Many of them slapped Bill on the head in congratulations for fast shooting as they moved past. He was so relieved that tears ran down his cheeks, and he could only watch as dozens of his comrades moved down into the trees below. Sporadic explosions bumped from on down the hill as grenades were dropped into the entrances of the VC tunnels. The Operation went on for another week without incident for Bill and his platoon. In the end, about 20 tons of enemy supplies were captured; 72 Americans were killed along with 721 VC. Bill and his platoon were now considered grizzled veterans.

On a routine mission along the Laotian border near Dak-To, Ray was listening in on the radio's emergency channel to see if he could pick up on what was happening in the area, when he received a call from Firebase Veronica requesting help in the face of an overwhelming force of VC. An airborne spotter, called Spot 69, had the VC located just to the west of the firebase and said he would mark the VC location with smoke spotting rockets, so the AC-47 could come in and take care of business. The firebase set up smoke markers at their perimeter to show the gunship where they were located as the low-slow plane came into view from the south. The plane came in at 800 feet and cleared a line just 30 meters outside the firebase perimeter, firing one gun at a time in the familiar sequence they routinely used. The firebase wanted another pass farther out in the tall grass near the tree line so the AC-47 circled around again. As they made their run, the RatPack$_r$, as they called themselves, saw the VC running back up into the trees where they had heavier guns and equipment, so they circled around for a third run in which they used all three guns at the same time. Firing the guns in a sustained burst like that usually "burned the barrels," that could be changed in just a few minutes by the gun crews. The third run was devastating. The plane bucked violently and the ka-ching sound of the spent cartridges was nearly overwhelming. When it was finished, Spot-69 observed the area searching for pockets of VC, while the gun crews changed out the barrels and loaded the remaining ammunition into one of the guns. A fourth pass was unnecessary as dead VC, shredded trees and equipment covered the ground. There was no sign of life; any that had survived, fled. Thank you was passed to the RatPack by both Veronica and Spot-69 and the last thing they heard in return was, "we outta hea." From then on the gun crews were ordered to monitor all communication emergency channels and provide aid as needed. The action for the RatPack was going to heat up as they were to be used on rescue missions in North Vietnam and Laos.

In the first briefing for the rescue support missions, the problem of fuel versus ammunition load for the old AC-47's came up. The Remington Raiders, as the combat crews called the mission planners, had decided to cut the crew by three and reduce the ammunition by 25% in order to load on enough fuel to complete the missions. They were already short on ammunition, and they needed everyone in the gun crew to be able to function. The Nakhon Phanom Royal Navy Base$_r$ in eastern Thailand was known as NKP, and for good reason. All kinds of rescue and reconnaissance aircraft had been assembled there to support the anticipated rescue missions of the so called safe rescue zones in Laos. There was going to be a big increase in bombing North Vietnam that commanders hoped would bring about an end to the war, and pilots in disabled aircraft were instructed to make for the safe areas in Laos or the ocean to the east for rescue. Ray and the rest of the RatPack crew were becoming concerned about the suicidal sounding missions for which they were being briefed. They sounded a lot like one way trips as the crew would be used for offensive attacks on the Ho Chi Minh Trail in Laos and Cambodia as well as bomb crew rescue. More and more they got the impression that they were considered expendable and they didn't appreciate the attitude.

The North Vietnamese had anticipated the use of the Laotian safe zones and had built antiaircraft batteries at strategic points around them to take down the rescuing planes. The border between North and South Vietnam, Laos and Cambodia is paralleled by a mountain range known as the Truong Son, Annamite or Annam Cordillera depending on the country. Supplies from the north would basically follow the mountains directly into Laos then Cambodia where they could be moved into South Vietnam in dozens of different border crossings. The Ho Chi Minh trail was much more that a single trail or road; it was an interconnecting network of dozens of trails that gave the North Vietnamese hundreds of different combinations for transporting men and supplies south. If one trail was damaged or exposed by defoliant, they simply moved to another. Because of politics, American troops could not cross the borders of either Laos or Cambodia, but rescue missions were permitted. Many of the Laotian military rebels had allied with the North Vietnamese for reward and money and were glad to capture Americans they could sell to the North.

The RatPack and the other support aircraft had been in orbit around several "safe zones" when the call came through that a single seat F-105 with heavy damage was coming their way. One hour into their first mission, here they were in the thick of a ticklish situation. They hoped that all the antiaircraft guns had been taken down in the area, but you could never be sure. The entire group of helicopters and planes flew to their rendezvous point, but the F-105, known as the Thunder chief, was not going to make it to Laos and was going down across the border in North Vietnam. The smaller, faster aircraft swept the rescue site looking for anti-aircraft guns, in preparation for the AC-47 gunship run. North Vietnamese ground troops were flooding into the area and the RatPack was going to have to chase them off before the helicopter known as Jolly Green could actually pick up the downed pilot who was OK and had set off a smoke signal to mark his position. The observer plane sent a smoke rocket down in each of the four corners of the advancing troops so the gunship could make an effective run. As the gunship made its approach, the Vietnamese troops started to scatter as they knew what was coming. RatPack made a two gun run which devastated the troop formation and caused them to withdraw. Immediately the Jolly Green got low enough to winch down a para-rescue jumper. He slipped the harness on the pilot and off Jolly Green went as it reeled both into the safety of the cabin. Ray called into his radio, "we outta hea," and off they went back to NKP.

The little five day mission quickly turned into a month with no end in sight. The RatPack had been on a dozen or so rescue missions during that time and failed to get the pilot out safely only once. A large munitions plant outside Sam-Son about 80 miles south of Hanoi was going to be targeted by every available aircraft in the area. It was going to become one of the main battles of the war and every rescue crew was called to fly at the same time. The RatPack's assignment was the north end of the entire rescue area some 200 miles north of the DMZ (North – South Vietnam border). This was going to stretch their fuel-ammunition beyond capacity. Needless to say, the crew was apprehensive, but their Colonel cooled them off and told them they had been chosen for that end because they were the best, they used far less armor, more fuel and ammunition and could stay on station longer. By leaving behind two crewmen, their drinking water, survival gear and raft, they could add three, 75 gallon fuel bladders that would give them about three hours on station. So, Buzz and Tim along with Dundee the dog were chosen to stay behind. The dog was adopted by the crew back in Phan Rang and they took him everywhere they went. The plane ended up being 1600 pounds overweight, so the pilots Colonel Jim and Red, were going to have to back off on the throttles every chance they got. Taking off was hairy as they used every foot of the runway at NKP; then gaining altitude was very, very slow as the old AC-47, known in the States as the DC-3, would stall easily and "head for the dirt." On the way they topped off their fuel tanks with the bladders and cast them overboard, and by the time they were on station they could maneuver the 25 year old plane nicely. Ray looked at his watch, it was 0255, a mere five minutes before the big bomb run was to commence at Sam-Son.

At 0300 a glow appeared on the horizon in the distance. The RatPack crew knew the bombs were falling in earnest and it wasn't 30 minutes until they got their first call, a B52 based in Guam was coming their way with four of its eight engines damaged. The plane called Dallas01 was trying to make it to Laos but would come up short and the crew had to parachute over North Vietnam. When the unguided plane smacked into the side of Bu Cho Mountain, the NVA in the area woke up and back tracked its path to catch its crew. Jolly Green the rescue helicopter had four of the five pulled into safety in a couple minutes. Muzzle flashes from the ground marked the location of the oncoming NVA and the RatPack was going to have to make a gun run before the fifth member of the B52 crew could be picked up. All at once armor piercing antiaircraft rounds started blasting through the RatPack's plane. The shelf next to Ray's radio disintegrated and blew metal bits all over. Col Jim, the pilot, asked Ray to take a look in the back and report. It was a jumbled mess, the guns were trashed and the gun crew was lying in a bloody heap as the back half of the plane had hundreds of holes in it. Barry, the co-pilot, grabbed a fire extinguisher and put out the fire on and next to Ray, just as he unbuckled and jumped up to go to the aid of those in the back. Blood was all over the back of the plane and the men lying on the floor plates. As the AC-47 broke off its run and headed away from the area, Jolly Green reported they were up and away with the fifth member of the crew. Now, it was up to Barry and Ray to try to take care of the wounded. One gunner named Bill was the most seriously hurt as the others were just had superficial wounds from flying pieces of metal and hadn't been hit with any of the AAC rounds. Bill Childs, had a hole through his thigh just below his crotch that was spraying blood from both sides, and the application of gauze bandages would not stop the bleeding. They patched Ray directly to a doctor through their communications system and the doctor told him to thoroughly wash everything with alcohol then insert his finger into the wound and try to plug the hole in the artery with his fingertip. Ray could feel his cold finger being warmed by the meat of Bill's leg and sure enough there was the artery. He could feel the blood pulsing from a hole in the side made by the ACC round. He pressed his fingertip over the arterial hole and the blood stopped squirting. The next problem was that NKP didn't have any vascular surgeons and the nearest one was on an aircraft carrier out in the ocean.

With Ray's finger stuck in Bill's thigh, the plane flew to Da Nang where a blood transfusion was administered to Bill and they were transferred to a helicopter destined for the USS Constellation. Hours had gone by and Bill was now conscious and complaining about the pain in his leg. Ray told him that was a good sign as they both gritted their teeth and endured the long ride. Finally on the carrier, the surgeon had a nurse replace Ray's finger with his own and Ray was free to return to his unit. As Ray was about to leave the OR, Bill grabbed his arm and cried out a "thank you;" as he was going home. Ray's unit had to fly all the way back to Phan Rang to get their plane repaired and re-fitted with new guns. So Ray, after being fixed up for his own wounds, traveled to Da Nang, to NKP to get the dog, and finally all the way down to Phan Rang, before his could get cleaned up, tip a few and sleep in a bed. Ray finally felt he had been fully informed about this war. He marveled at all the people along the way that had treated him and Bill with the greatest care and caring. What a bunch these Americans were to go to such great extremes to save the life of a single warrior. It gave him a feeling of hope and put a lump in his throat.

The RatPack soon thereafter were in a crash landing and a ditch, the first in the Mekong Delta and the other on a training mission with a new crew in an AC-119 over the ocean. In the first crash, several of the crew were injured, pinned in the wreckage or stunned and several Viet Cong in black pajamas had come into the plane just as Ray was coming to his senses. With the help of Big Casino, his trusty shotgun, that was by the way illegal in war, Ray dispatched the VC with one shot from his damaged gun. They had just recovered from that crash when they were called upon to train another crew fresh from the states. The pilot of the new crew refused to cooperate with their advice and was quickly shot out of the air by ground AAC fire. They were able make it to the ocean and all parachuted into the water only to wait for nearly seven hours for rescue. All ten made it out safely.

The Vietnam War was unique in the world as it was the first of the nuclear age. American administrators were constrained in their strategy by the threat of escalation that would certainly include China, maybe the USSR and possibly nuclear weapons. They were overly careful not to militarily invade or endeavor to control the key areas of Cambodia, Laos and North Vietnam that were involved, so they settled on the flawed tactic of inflicting casualties as a goal. This resulted in a long conflagration that took the lives of over two million North Vietnamese and Viet Cong men at a cost of more than 60,000 American lives. Battles were fought and won to take control of a hill or area that was promptly abandoned back to the VC. Everyone involved questioned the lack of a sensible objective or strategy and kill ratios were not enough to actually bring the war to an end. In

1970, Nixon allowed several attack expeditions into Cambodia and Laos with the goal of taking over resupply strongholds that constantly fed men and materials into South Vietnam. Hope traveled through all branches of the armed forces that *finally* they had a strategy that would win the war. But Nixon folded at the first sign of diplomatic complaints and withdrew, leaving his troops hopeless and frustrated with the sisyphean situation.

In the central highlands, Pleiku was one of the main centers from which search and destroy missions were based. Bill was stationed at several of the firebases that supported these missions one of which was number 42, eight miles north. They were 60 miles east of the main border with Cambodia and about 80 miles southeast of Laos and as such were the recipients of constant threat of attack from fresh NVA. Bill and others of his company familiar with the area were constantly being called upon to join with other units on search and destroy missions to the border and on occasion "accidentally" crossed when it suited them. Helicopters loaded with troops would routinely leave at first light and drop them off in predefined locations that would give them access to NVA filtering across the borders. They knew the routes the NVA liked and regularly posted ground forces in strategic positions to prevent them from finding their bases. Every week, Bill found himself in hot firefights with bullets sizzling overhead or thumping around him. He was one of the rock steady fighters others with less experience looked up to, and he earned it. He had gradually shifted his opinion of the NVA and VC from that of innocent young men forced into the situation to that of remorseless killers. When he saw what they did to unarmed villagers that might not support them fast enough and how they used children to carry bombs into their camps; he began to hate them. He felt a sense of accomplishment when he was able to end their lives. Being taller than all the Vietnamese and most of the Americans, he slowly became known around the villages in the area as "khlong lo chien binh" or Giant Warrior. Villagers were quick to tell him where the NVA or VC was, or where they were going or when they had been there. He was very careful to conduct these conversations out of the sight of other villagers as they never knew who had sympathy for the other side. The villagers also knew he had a heart of gold and frequently gave all his food to them. He would load up on candy and give it to the children and medical supplies for the village midwives. He felt so sorry for the native folks caught in the middle that he frequently mourned for them when he was alone and had a chance to unwind back at Pleiku. He slowly became a marked but driven man.

One mission took them to a valley running north to southeast out of the hills of Laos, and they were informed of major NVA troop movements were headed their direction along several of about five routes that meandered down the valley. There appeared to be several dozen trucks loaded with fighters and about five more with equipment poised across the border in Laos ready to move at a moment's notice. The trucks then crossed the border late one evening hoping to travel mostly at night and wanted to be at their destinations by daylight. Bill's platoon had been in place for nearly a day waiting for them, but little did they know that spotter estimates of the size of the NVA convoys were greatly underestimated. There were dozens of trucks approaching them on each of about three routes through the dense forest. Before first light, some of Bill's group that numbered nearly forty said they could hear the sound of truck engines revving in the distance. The terrain was anything but smooth as numerous ravines ran down the sides of the valley into the small river, and the trucks were constantly either going uphill or down as the crude double trail roads negotiated the rough ground. When it was clear that trucks were approaching from multiple locations, the captain got on the radio and asked for air support. It was still several hours before first light, and people were starting to panic. It sounded as if the trucks would be on them before it was light enough for an air attack. Should they attack the convoy or should they allow them to pass and have larger American units take them on later when there was less cover? Since they were obviously outnumbered and surrounded, their commander decided to wait and radio in the size of the force, its location and direction of movement to Pleiku so more air support could be arranged. They sat in the dark with trucks passing on both sides. They could hear the engines whining and see the headlights flickering through the trees not more than fifty yards away, as it took nearly an hour for the trucks to pass. This was a gigantic movement of NVA south.

The captain of Bill's unit was trenchant and waited for nearly a half hour before ordering his men to follow the NVA convoy on foot and it wasn't long before they were walking down the same rough road the trucks had used. Bill and the captain were at the front of the group that trailed out a hundred yards or more behind him, when suddenly a number of flares shot out of the forest ahead and on both sides of them completely lighting up the area. Simultaneously they came under heavy fire from small arms and heavy machine guns mounted on some of the vehicles. Bill and the captain dove into a muddy spot and rolled down into a thicket of brush completely covered with mud and brush. The captain had been hit in the shoulder and whispered to Bill that it was a flesh wound. They could see a small section of the road ahead from their vantage point and watched as large groups of NVA advanced. Somehow the NVA had known they were there and had enticed them into an ambush. Some of the Americans had jumped into the brush and trees adjacent to the road and most had run in the opposite direction. Everyone knew they would be killed or captured if they couldn't get away, because to stand and fight was going to be a losing battle. Men were falling, stricken with gunshot, all over the place. Bill and the captain continued to lie under the brush and because they were covered with mud were nearly invisible. NVA soldiers were running by them as blood lust for killing Americans had set in. Vehicles with machine guns and small cannons were advancing up the road. A few Americans were firing back and were quickly overwhelmed and killed. Others took off cross country with groups of NVA in hot pursuit; if they were in good condition, they were able to get away, but most were caught, brutalized and killed. By the time the little battle was over it was solidly daylight and Bill knew it wouldn't be long before spotter planes would appear looking for the NVA column. He and the captain stayed in their hiding spot and several times soldiers came within feet of stepping on them. Fortunately they were completely covered in mud and the bushes over them had large thorns. Both were scratched up from their fall, and the wounds were starting to burn in the mud, but they remained still.

Finally, they heard the NVA trucks restart and head off to the southeast. When they could no longer hear the trucks, Bill rolled out from under the bush and sat up to clear the mud off his face and eyes. He looked up directly into the muzzle of a rifle pointed between his eyes. When the captain rolled out, there were more NVA there to greet him. They chattered among themselves apparently deciding whether or not to shoot them or take them back for interrogation. Several trucks were parked down the road with other Americans that had been captured. It looked as if they had been treated badly as most had broken lips and teeth or other facial contusions. Bill and the captain were washed off with buckets of water and it was then that the NVA identified both; the captain because of his bars and Bill because of his reputation. The commander of the group was gleeful that he had captured Americans of such high standing and he was likely to be rewarded in some way. They were crammed into a truck that was turned around and headed back to Laos. If the NVA could get them over the border before the Americans could organize a rescue, they could keep them forever and kill them at their leisure. The NVA knew the Americans would never give up when it came to rescuing their own. On top of that, several spotter planes had buzzed the area and were undoubtedly radioing back the situation, so they had to hurry. Two smaller vehicles with heavily armed guards accompanied the prisoner truck headed north, one in front and one behind. The entire day went by as the truck reached Laos and refueled and continued on north. It stopped at a river and the prisoners were herded out and given a chance to get some water and wash a little. Rifle butts slammed into some heads stunning the recipient or knocking them out. Their buddies quickly picked them up and put them back in the truck as several of the soldiers were looking for an excuse to shoot someone. Another day went by and the captain's wound had become severely infected. He had a high fever and had a difficult time standing without help. The captors had cut away his shirt and looked at the wound and laughed; one jabbed it with a dirty finger and they laughed some more. Bill sat quietly and bided his time because he knew his chance would come.

Just short of going to North Vietnam, a missile struck the vehicle in front with a direct hit. The vehicle flew up into the air in a ball of fire instantly cooking the inhabitants. The driver of the truck with the prisoners was blinded by flying glass and the guard in the passenger seat killed as the front half of the truck drove into the hole in the road and came to a violent stop. The vehicle behind rear ended the truck and slid under it. The inhabitants were injured and stuck under the wreckage. Several of the prisoners in the back of the truck sustained broken bones and everyone else escaped with bruises. They slowly crawled out of the truck box and climbed down over the squashed guard vehicle trapped under it. Some were moaning in pain and Bill quickly assigned several he knew to find sticks that could be used as splints for the broken bones. Water containers and weapons were lifted from the guard vehicle; Bill hoisted the captain up across his shoulders and off they went down the road to the south. Bill assigned several to venture a few hundred yards ahead and behind of the main group of 16 and warn them if NVA vehicles were approaching. They hadn't gone a mile before vehicles were approaching from both directions.

Their only chance was to set off cross country to the southeast and try to make it across the border into South Vietnam. So it was off through the forest with Bill still carrying the captain and others helping the wounded or hurt. The rag-tag bunch of Americans were moving rapidly up and down ravines, through swampy areas and brush so thick you couldn't fall down. Bill assigned three to bring up the rear and use branches to smooth out their tracks. Several times during the day others carried the captain who was delirious with fever. It seemed as if their escape was successful as the sun finally went down and they didn't seem to be followed. They spent a fitful night with guards posted around the main bunch. Other than an occasional moan, everyone was quiet. The second day a half dozen fell into holes and were injured so seriously on sharpened bamboo sticks that they had to be left behind as death was imminent. The third day more were killed in a small firefight with NVA scouts. Bill suspected that they had not killed all the scouts and some must have gotten away to inform on them. The group broke up as some wanted to go off to the south, thinking it would be a safer route. The original group was down to Bill, the captain and one other.

They traded off carrying the captain who was still unable to stand but was awake about one fourth of the time. Hidden booby trap holes with sharpened bamboo sticks were still all over the place and they had to be extra sure where they put each step. They were in extremely rough country and mountains were all around them. Bill knew the border was just southeast of the mountains. When his partner fell into a pit and was impaled on multiple bamboo spikes, it finally came down to Bill and the captain. Bill would carry for an hour or so, and then take a 15 minute rest. Using a stick to poke the ground before him, he took one careful step after the other and was able to find enough water to stay barely hydrated even though it was impure and he knew he would get diarrhea in the end. A week after the escape, Bill suffering badly from dehydration, finally stumbled into a South Vietnamese village where his reputation was known. As he laid the captain down on a crude cot and routinely reached up to feel his head for fever; it was cool. When he checked for a pulse, there was none. The captain had passed just hours before. Bill was given a bitter tasting drink to kill the bacteria in his digestive tract and a bucket of water in which to clean up. As he washed, he cried openly for the captain whom he really hadn't known, but to whom he had become attached because of the man's great will to live. They all had carried wound antiseptic, but were not able to use it because the NVA had taken it all and by the time they got it back, the captain was fully contaminated. It was so unfortunate and unnecessary he couldn't contain his grief. One of the old women of the village came up to him, firmly took him by the hand and led him to her paillasse. She motioned for him to lie down on his belly and she commenced massaging his back. Softly, with a weak and wavering voice, she sang to him including the words "khlong lo chien binh" in a language he knew not, but still enjoyed. Quickly he succumbed to exhaustion and slept. It was to be his last battle and, in the coming years, he often thought about all his nameless, innocent friends in Vietnam. In his mind, he could still see their faces.

On a later offensive mission on the Laotian-Cambodian border, whose objective was to strike a major NVA base, again, Ray's plane took heavy AAC fire and was seriously damaged. One of his friends was injured and died in Ray's arms with grievous wounds. The right engine and left landing gear and tire were damaged, leaving them no chance of landing safely. They were able to manually crank down the landing gear but the tire was shredded, so they decided, in order to have a reasonable shot at a decent landing, they would have to flatten the tire on the right side also. Ray proposed that he hang out the door on the left side and try to shoot the tire. With his parachute on and four people hanging onto his straps, he slowly descended and when he kicked the floor twice, the pilot lowered the right landing gear. He had taped a pistol to his right hand and was able to grab onto the UHF radio antenna with his left hand. Slowly he inched farther and farther. He had on his helmet with the visor down and the wind was howling by at a hundred knots. He was buffeted violently but was able to hit the tire in the tread the first shot. Then he shot more into the sidewall to be sure it was flat and kicked the floor multiple times for them to pull him back in. The next crisis was getting the big bucket of bolts on the ground without doing a nose-over. With so much drag on the main landing gear, the tail had a tendency to flip over the front. So on landing, when the pilot cut the engine, everyone raced to the tail and latched on to a floor strap. With the weight shift, they might have a chance. The five of them in the tail caused it to hit the ground simultaneous with the main gear. Then the tail started to rise, higher and higher and when it reached about 10 feet off the ground the plane came to a stop; the tail smacked down on the runway with heavy smoke boiling from the landing gear and damaged engine. Everyone jumped out as the ground fire crew started dousing it with foam. Once again, this group of intrepid warriors was saved by their own courage and ingenuity.

Accumulated flight time for the group went over 2600 hours, which was way over the normally allowed maximums and they had all lost a lot of weight in the process. They had all extended their tours several times and the Colonel was determined that they would not be allowed to continue. The AC47 was being taken out of service and replaced with the AC119 and the AC130, so they would have to completely retrain and by that time everyone expected the war to be over. They had one mission left and it was to take out supply depots and equipment at Ahn Son North Vietnam. It would turn out to be, by far, the most costly.

# N. VIETNAM ODYSSEY

Unexpected circumstances forced Buzz, Lew, Barry, Ray and the dog Dundee into an odyssey of survival across the rugged Annamite Mountains of southwestern North Vietnam and northeastern Laos. They had to cross several hundred miles of heavily wooded, rugged mountains. There were swamps in the low ground, large fast flowing rivers and the whole area was peppered with NVA. Everything except for a few farm fields of yams, corn, mangos and sugar cane was covered with dense forest and brush. Small farming hamlets were sprinkled in, all of which were hostile to the Americans. Their destination was NKP airbase in Thailand; they never made it.

The RatPack was to make a number of runs on each of three different primary targets at about 600 feet altitude. The first successful run was with two guns and the next was to be a three gun strike on the primary target. The first run was clean, and AAC fire opened up before they had even started the second, but they were still too low or out of range. As the run proceeded, dozens of holes were punched in the old plane. When secondary target was obliterated, they turned west and reloaded for stage two. Their support planes had taken down two surface-to-air missile sites and they got the all clear to start their next run. The AAC guns were firing in earnest and the RatPack requested 50 caliber support from their friendly jets. On the way into their stage two target they took out one AAC battery and continued on for a three gun run on the object building. It was destroyed with secondary explosions and very little return fire. Out of all the aerial confusion, a Russian MIG17 shot through the area headed west. RatPack ignored it as they were getting ready for another three gun run on the stage three target. As usual, AAC fire preceded their run because they could only shoot directly left and down and even though both the target and the AAC battery were destroyed they took a hit on the port engine. At that point the pilot notified the crew he was declaring an emergency and pointing the old "pig boat" home.

Coincident with that, the MIG17 had come back and was starting a gun run at the RatPack of its own. Two F105 Thunder chiefs, called Thuds, were on the way to intercept the MIG, but would be a couple minutes late; the RatPack prepared for a beating. Ray got the pilot of the MIG on the radio, who sounded Russian, and warned him in rough language to leave them alone. He figured that an irritated pilot might just make a mistake and miss or dive into the ground. The two Thuds were coming in low and would intercept the MIG just after it had it way with the old AC-47 and its stalwart crew. As the MIG got closer and about to open up with its 37MM cannons, the Russian pilot came on the radio and triumphantly told the RatPack that, "it is time to die." Steel jacketed shells slammed into the starboard wing and cockpit plus the gun area. They must have been hit 30 times; immediately Ray was on the radio calling a "MAYDAY." The two thuds were waiting as the MIG came out of its dive right in front of them and in seconds, exploded in a fireball. The 37MM cannon shell was about an inch and a half in diameter and destroyed anything it hit as it passed through the plane. A quick glance at the cockpit and Ray knew they were in trouble, Col Jim the pilot had been hit in the legs and was in bad shape and Red was fighting to keep the old pig boat in the air. The instrument panel was smoldering. Ray bandaged Jim's legs and gave him a shot of morphine. Two of the gun crew were lying on the floor plates in the back wounded with shrapnel. Lew bandaged them up while the others started unbolting the guns and the other equipment. Red had told them the plane needed to lose a lot of weight or they were going to hit the dirt. Everything was thrown out that was loose and they still needed to lose another 1500 pounds or they couldn't make it over the mountain range ahead of them; someone was going to have to parachute out of the plane. Barry, Buzz, Lew and Ray knew it would have to be them as they were the only able bodied folks left; everyone else except Red was injured and Red had to fly the plane. As Dundee licked Col Jim's hands and soothed him, they gathered up all the equipment and extra packs. Red came on the intercom and told them no rescue was available for that area and they would have to walk out. At that point, Ray was impervious to another threat of death and continued to get ready to jump.

The four asked Red to call their parents and let them know what happened. Red knew they were four of the toughest bastards he had ever seen and if anyone could make it, it would be them. They shook hands with Red and Col Jim, saluted and headed for the back door as Ray picked up Dundee and snapped him into his parachute. In a flash, the four were floating in the air. Ray was descending much quicker than the others as he was overloaded with the dog and extra equipment. He injured his ankle on striking the ground and smashed the locator beacon, so there was no chance of being found from the air; they were going to have to walk the entire 200 miles. Barry cut a hook shaped branch from a nearby tree and fashioned it into a crude cane for Ray while they taped his ankle with duct tape over his boot; he could walk quite well. They had a number of knives of various sorts and a 10 shot semi automatic 22 caliber pistol as weapons. With a good map, signal mirror, compass and binoculars, they felt they had a real shot of survival. They cut up the camouflage colored fabric part of the parachutes to use as shelter and bed rolls and rolled the cord for use as ropes. Since Lew was the largest, they had him and Dundee lead the group and set the pace as they set out for their first land mark,

Ba Mu mountain about 20 miles to their south. From there they could turn and head for Laos, then southwest to NKP. The first day was short but went well and soon they put up a crude shelter, settled down to a supper of jerky and water, then slept with Dundee keeping watch. Ray was awakened by Dundee's low growl and was looking back in the direction from which they had come. He took the binoculars and slipped out of camp back toward the north and found a spot where he could survey their previous day's landing site. Sure enough there were two trucks and about 20 men looking around the area, someone had seen them come down. Ray and Dundee retreated back to camp where they all decided to stay put until the area cooled down with searchers. When the searchers departed so did they. Lew in the lead along with Dundee were responsible to keep watch ahead while the second and third searched to the left and right and the last kept watch to the rear. Ray took Dundee off his leash and let him roam the area ahead, back and forth through the brush occasionally waiting for his masters to catch up. They wanted to stay under control and not get totally exhausted or rush into a bad situation. They refilled their canteens on water they drained from the large segments of bamboo trunks. In the wet season the bamboo fill the hollow segments of their trunks with water for use in the dry season. Young sugar cane stalks that had been peeled provided a good source of sweet high energy fiber. That, combined with bamboo water and jerky gave them all enough food to continue.

Buzz climbed a 60 foot tree to check their direction and the surrounding countryside for obstacles. They would have to change their direction to more southwesterly. Ahead was a good sized river and the approaches to Ba Mu looked to have a lot of farms. Once on Ba Mu, they could adjust their route toward Ban Kari Pass then west to Laos. Along their way they found a field of nearly full growth corn loaded up with large tender ears, and mangos. Both the corn and mangos were loaded with energy and water. They knew they would run out of jerky for Dundee and had to adjust his menu to include corn cobs and sugar cane mixed with bits of jerky. The dog ate it fine, just as if he understood the dire nature of their situation. They could hear the rush of the river long before they could see it. It looked to be about 70 feet across in most places and flowing deeply at a good clip. Using the parachute cord, they fashioned a way to get them and their packs across without a soaking. Ray tied the cord to a fist sized rock and pitched it across over a tree limb, then by sawing the cord back and forth, caused the rock to swing back and forth more and more until finally it wrapped around the branch. First, Ray strapped Dundee to his back and followed the cord rope across with one hand while searching for a foothold with the cane in his other. Inch by inch they crossed, successfully, and once on the other side they ferried the packs across followed by the other three members of the intrepid little group. The whole operation took over an hour and they decided to let their clothes dry before they continued. Inspection of the map indicated this was going to be one of the easier crossings as the oncoming rivers looked formidable and could only be crossed on a bridge. It was another more dangerous problem; they preferred not to think about. Again they foraged for food and came back with yams, corn, mangos and coconuts. They had four packs full of food and one with water. Dundee was carrying five pounds of jerky.

They finally started the ascent of Ba Mu and switch-backed up and up until the trees finally thinned and they could see miles into the distance. The mountain didn't have a sharp peak but was topped with a ridge over a mile long. They made their way around to the southwest corner where they would have a better view of the landscape. Looking west they were disheartened when they saw range after range of mountains running north to south between them and Laos. A route slightly east then south toward the border with South Vietnam would be much easier and a brief discussion settled them on the new route. Ben Kari Pass and loads of NVA would be in their path, but they felt they could avoid them by staying off the roads and going slow. Several days went by without incident and the small river they were following suddenly turned and went under a bridge on the main road. They had to wade in the knee deep water along the edge of the river hidden by fairly heavy overhanging bushes to make their way under the bridge and safely out of sight of the road which was heavily traveled by NVA. Then they came to a much larger river that was fortunately flowing slowly enough they could cross without guide ropes. As the days went by they needed to refill their food supply, so Ray and Barry took a little detour back to the north to a village called Phu Quan to forage.

They discovered fields of sugar cane and corn so they decided to split up and using a lone tall tree as their rendezvous point would fill a pack at a time then return for another until they had all their packs stuffed with food. Ray had filled several packs and could see nothing of Barry and went to find him. As he was about to come out of cover into a small clearing he heard Barry speaking in a normal voice, "Ray, they caught me, Ray get outta here. There's at least eight of them. Two out here and six hiding in the bushes." When Ray got to the edge of the trees, he saw Barry standing about 30 meters into a yam field facing him with his hands raised. He was talking normally as if directly to his captors, but was passing a message to Ray, to vamoose. Over and over he repeated his message until Ray flashed sunlight with a signal mirror across his eyes to let him know he got the message. When Barry saw the flash, he said, "Ray, don't try anything. It's a trap. There are six more in the bushes. Get outta here. Call my parents and Yvonne. They're taking me now. See ya buddy." Ray flashed Barry's eyes again to let him know he received his message, and the NVA tied his hands and took him away. As they took him slowly out of sight, Ray's heart cracked as he knew he would never see his friend again. Worse yet, Barry was doomed to the painful existence as a prisoner in the north. Ray was frustrated that he couldn't act and do something, but with no weapons plus a bad foot, he would either be killed or captured.

*(Decades later Barry Matson's remains were returned to America for burial in the Arlington National Cemetery. He had died between the*

*ages of 43 and 48 of diabetes and cancer, and was not repatriated with*
*the other American prisoners in 1973. He had dental fillings of Russian*
*origin and had lived as a prisoner in either North Vietnam or Russia for*
*the better part of two decades.)*

When Ray returned to Buzz and Lew, his voice broke as
he told them about Barry. That evening, they sat for a long
time under a full moon, talking about that damned war, about
their families and getting back safely. They slowly became tired
enough to sleep and joined Dundee in their shelter.

They stayed on a southeasterly course and headed for Mui
Gai Pass which was another pinch point in the Ho Chi Minh
trail and probably loaded with NVA going south. It was about 45
miles away. They stayed to the high ground where the streams
were smaller and there were no roads. Three more days would
be required to get them to Mui Gai. When they were within a
dozen miles of the pass, they used the binoculars to survey the
situation and spotted a bamboo grove where they could replenish
their water supply. Suddenly, the sound of automatic rifle fire
broke the silence. It was not close by so they found a spot with
a little better view and again scanned the approaches to the pass.
There were NVA training camps set up all over the area and
the rifle fire was NVA target practice. They decided to take
a detour and go around as much of the area as they could and
had to backtrack a few miles. The new route would put five or
so miles between them and the NVA camps and they would be
within shouting distance of the main road. Between the sound
of practice mortars exploding in the distance and the traffic on
the main road, they had trouble sleeping in the hours before they
were to cross the road. At 2300 hours they got up and made
their crossing in the moonlight and continued without incident
until the pass was several miles or so ahead. They made camp
and looked over the map and decided to backtrack a little more
to avoid more NVA camps in front of them. Late that night, they
eased through the pass easily by sticking to the trees until they
were right at the pinch point, then crawling through the brush
in the ditch that paralleled the road. Trucks were grinding up

the road less than 50 feet away; their inhabitants totally unaware to the three Americans struggling for life.

Somewhat south and east of Mui Gai Pass, was the Xom Hon village and they decided it was time to forage for more food, part of which they ate before they settled down for the night. They were awakened by the howling of a gibbon monkey somewhere along the route they would take the following morning. Something had disturbed its territory. The next day after an hour of steady hiking, they came across a thirty foot tall white boulder and decided to rest a while. Ray went on ahead alone looking for a high spot from which he could get a better look ahead. He saw another giant boulder on the ridge above and decided it would be a good spot from which he could survey the southern approaches to the pass. Several hours later, he returned to the first boulder. As he approached, he could hear Dundee growling. Ray froze, then ducked down and crawled through the brush to get a look. He came up behind an NVA with an AK47 and an older militiaman with an ancient bolt action rifle, that had Lew and Buzz covered from about 15 feet away. Dundee was snarling openly and straining at his lease to get at the two intruders. Ray slowly raised his hand to signal Lew that he was back. Lew then said to Buzz, "Ray's here, keep these two busy with Dundee." The militiaman was chattering about the dog as Dundee obviously made him very nervous. Ray signaled to Buzz that he was supposed to use the 22 pistol to shoot the militiaman and Ray would take the NVA.

So, Buzz then said, "When Ray goes for the NVA, I'm gonna shoot the other one. When it starts, let Dundee loose and roll back into the brush."

Lew answered, "No problem Dundee really wants to eat this slope son-of-a-bitch." Buzz had the gun in his hand behind his back and had to move his left hand back to cock it.

All of a sudden the NVA yelled, "SUNG," which meant GUN. Lew let Dundee loose and he jumped for the militiaman who fired his rifle at the dog and missed only to hit Lew in the chest knocking him over backward. The NVA swung his

AK around and fired at Dundee hitting both the dog and the militiaman multiple times. Buzz brought the 22 around and shot the NVA three times and as he fell he kept his finger on the trigger and sprayed Buzz with bullets. Ray got there just in time to kick the AK away. He could see that the militiaman was certainly dead and rushed to Lew and Buzz both of whom had died instantly. He went back to Dundee who was still alive, opened his eyes, wagged his tail, then licked Ray's hand and passed. He sat for a few minutes and let the silence overwhelm him; he was dazed. The two NVA turned out to be a father and son on leave. They had some rice and a small cooking pot along with a US made World War II trenching tool that was marked, US SPEAKER 1944. He dug graves for his three comrades next to the giant white boulder where he could find them sometime in the future to take them back home. He also buried the NVA and his father next to each other.

*(In 1988, Ray and Red traveled back to Vietnam with the National League of Families, and found the graves of their friends next to the white boulder. Their remains were taken back to be reburied in America. Lew Partridge, was interred in Arlington National Cemetery and Buzz Rakow, along with Dundee the dog, were buried in the same casket in fort McPherson National Cemetery in Nebraska. On the back side of Buzz's headstone, you will find the name, "Dundee." The remains of the two North Vietnamese were returned to their families.)*

He then realized that he should have heeded the warning of the gibbon, and felt responsible for their deaths because of his mistake. He said a prayer for his three friends, picked up his stuff, vowed to return for them and moved on. He knew the only way he could sleep was to walk until he was completely exhausted. Along the way he came out of his shock and became very tired, wrapped up in the parachute and tried to sleep. He missed his friends terribly.

He used Phong Nha Mountain as a land mark and skirted around VinVuc Ni, a large village. He came to a sizable river and had to use the parachute cord to pull himself across. It took most of the afternoon to dry out his clothes and packs of supplies. He was moving much faster now that he was alone and could see a major road ahead. Ray took up a spot in some tall grass where he could raise up and eyeball the road without being seen. An NVA troop carrier suddenly stopped abreast of his position and he felt he had been seen. About 30 troops piled out and proceeded to fan out on both sides of the road. One of the troops was walking straight at him; oddly he was not carrying a weapon. When the guy was 15 feet away he stopped and took a leak, then turned and went back to the truck as did the other troops. He was amazed the NVA didn't hear his heart beating. That night he crawled up to the road, crossed and proceeded on his way. After another lonely night, he was again moving quickly, he paralleled the road leading to Laos and eventually Cambodia. His next landmark was Len Mu Mountain and he took up a route following a river. Along the way he found apples, yams and corn and the terrain was much smoother as he burned the miles away. About 1800 hours one evening, he came upon a one lane dirt road and watched a motorbike fly by, giving him the idea to hijack one for his use.

He tied a parachute cord to a tree on one side and draped it across the road so when another motorbike came by, he could yank it up and crash the cycle, then subdue the rider and be on his way. About sunset another motorbike came by and he pulled up the cord which caused it to crash. The rider was laying face down next to the bike, and when he rolled them over he could see a very pregnant young lady. She was moaning with pain as she had a large contusion just above her right ankle. He felt it gently and could tell it was a very slight and simple break. He said to her, "Chan xuong be roi," which meant, "leg bone broken."

As she came out of her daze, she recognized Ray as probably and American and in broken English, asked, "Who you, where you come from?" He told her his name was Ray and that he would help her.

Then she let out a loud groan and said, "Going to have baby, now." He used the seat pad as a cushion for her head and braced her broken leg with duct tape. He prepared to deliver his first baby and she told him it was her first also. In between spasms they exchanged names and small talk. Her name was Phuoc Giap and she had gone to the market in Lang Mo for her mother who lived in the village several miles on down the road. When she said, "baby come now," he took off his blouse and prepared to wrap the baby in it and washed his hands as well as he could from a canteen. He splashed a little water on her head to cool her off. She let out a long groan, and the baby slid out into his hands. He washed the baby off, cut the cord and tied it off, then wrapped it in his blouse and handed it to her. The baby was squealing a little but didn't cry loudly. Ray stowed the motorbike and his packs in the ditch and prepared himself to carry her to the village. He asked her not to yell and turn him in and he would carry her to her mother's house. Her mother had married a Frenchman so she had learned both French and English when she was a girl. Phuoc had married a military man from Hanoi who was the grand nephew of General Giap, the North Vietnamese Supreme Commander. She didn't expect to see him again as he had gone south into the war months ago. She guided Ray to a small hut and as he held her and the baby, knocked on the door. When the little old lady opened the door she was awestruck and pulled them in quickly. The room was lit by a single candle and Phuoc told her Ray's name and said he had saved her life. After several minutes, Phuoc was settled on the cot and Ray turned to leave wearing only his T-shirt. The grandmother took a blanket off a small shelf and handed it to Ray and told him in French to take it with him and go quickly. Phuoc told him to take the basket of food she was bringing to her mother, and with that and a pat on the hand, he was gone. He walked as quickly as he could without running and made it back to the spot of the birth without being seen. He then realized he had left his dog tags in the pocket of his blouse; it was too dangerous to go back and he picked up the food, stowed it in his pack and left the area. If NVA discovered his dog tags, they would come after him and wouldn't give up until they had him. There was about eight days of food in the cans Phouc left behind and that should get him safely into South Vietnam.

*(In 1992, a young woman named Raylee Giap found Ray at the TelCen Corporate Headquarters in Chicago and thanked him for jeopardizing his life to save hers, and returned his dog tags. She was he baby that was born that night in 1968. Her father was killed and never returned from South Vietnam, so she and her mother immigrated to Hong Kong in the mid 1970's then to California. She was determined to find the young intrepid warrior that, in the midst of his own odyssey, stopped to help a complete stranger in her time of need; and she did. She was named after his given name Raymond Lee, and had worn his dog tags on a gold chain every day for several decades.)*

The next landmark was Len Mu Mountain; Ray figured he was about six days from the border. He kept up a blistering pace, as it was in his genes to run, stopping to eat what food he needed every four hours or so. The real food in the cans was delicious and he mixed the syrup with water to add to his energy. Early in the afternoon, he sat down to rest and looked at the map to reorient himself. There was a large river ahead and he had no choice but to cross it. About the time he could hear the sound of the rushing water he stumbled upon an old railroad bed. There was an ancient bridge across the roiling water and he sat on the edge of it looking upstream and downstream to see if anyone was around. The bridge had the rails in place, but many of the ties were missing and he would have to tight rope in places. There was no way he could cross the river by wading as the current was far too fast and deep. When there was still enough light to see, he danced across. His ankle, that had bothered him for weeks, didn't hurt a bit along the way. With the Laotian border some eight miles to the west and the DMZ (Demilitarized Zone) about three miles to the south, he slept soundly thinking he had made it.

The next landmark was Voi Mep Mountain in South Vietnam off to the southwest about 25 miles, but easily seen from his direction. He was entering a combat area without identification and was concerned about both the NVA -Viet

Cong and the Americans-Koreans-Australians. He had to carefully thread his way through areas where battles had torn up the landscape. The smell of decaying bodies hung in the air and further confirmed the horror of war; he kept his head down, stayed off the high points and avoided the sounds of battle in the distance. His map showed him there was a major river ahead and he knew in his weakened state he couldn't swim across. He found an unused road that had been overgrown and followed it toward the river hoping there was a bridge of some sort he could use to cross. After all this, the loss of three friends and his dog, the struggle and the tears, was he going to be stopped by a this final river? Finally, there it was rushing down the valley about 200 feet wide. His heart sank when he saw this last impassable obstacle. There was a large multiple span bridge that had been bombed and all four spans were in the river. Even though he could use the partially submerged spans and piers, he was going to get wet.

Using his parachute cord and a piece of jagged steel, he was able to throw across each successive span and using both the cord and the partially submerged bridge segments slowly but surely made his way across. When he got to the third span, it was completely gone and he would have no support from below. He tried repeatedly to hook something on the bank but could not. So he tied one end of the cord to his packs and threw the other end with the steel piece onto the bank and let it rest there. He emptied his canteens and put them in the pack on his back for extra floatation and jumped in swimming as hard as he could, knowing it was a life or death deal. It was only 30 feet to the bank, but the water was raging and deep. Over a hundred feet downstream, he finally snagged a hold of some bush on the bank and pulled himself ashore. Another minute and he would not have made it as he was far weaker than he thought. He was so exhausted, he couldn't stand, so he rested and thanked God for his life. After a while, he pulled his packs across, dried out, refilled his canteens and set out for Voi Mep. He planned to climb the north side and go down the south side of the mountain and avoid rivers at all cost. That one nearly killed him; he had survived by a thread. Another day went by as he was covering ground rapidly and had made it about two thirds of the way up Voi Mep when he heard the sound of F4's dropping hard bombs and napalm blasting an area to his east. As they made their turns, they would come within signal distance of him, so he grabbed his mirror and flashed them repeatedly. There were eight F4's in the battle and they each made several runs past his position. On the last run several of them rolled their wings slightly as if confirming their sighting of him, but he couldn't be sure. At this point he didn't have full control of his wits and he may have wished it to happen. Finally, all that was left was the heat and smell coming to him on the eastern breeze and he was suddenly dejected thinking they had missed him. Then out of the sun came and F4 with its landing gear down so it could fly slower. He flashed it with his mirror repeatedly and it wagged its wings back and forth in reply, it had seen him. But, he couldn't stay there because he got glimpses of the NVA spread out and following him from the north. They too had seen the F4 waggle its wings and were coming fast. Ray spent the rest of the day climbing up and over Voi Mep and finally found a good spot to make camp for the night with a good view of the south. He figured the NVA would linger on the other side of the mountain until morning and search for him there. The next morning, he consolidated his food and water into one pack and set off in the direction of Khe Sanh where he knew there was a Marine base. He was on the other side of the mountain from where he had been seen by the F4 and was concerned that the Americans may be looking for him there. He climbed a tree and used the binoculars to study the hills ahead and thought he could see American Marines moving toward him. Behind him he spotted dozens of NVA slowly working down the mountain. He spent the rest of the day moving carefully south toward the Marines. Early the following morning, he finally made contact with the platoon of Marines that had been sent to look for him. Before he saw or heard them, he could smell the smoke of cigarettes, so he knew who they were. He shouted that he was a downed American flyer and needed help, which was exactly what the VC shouted when they wanted to suck the Marines into a trap. He could hear the Marines talking to one another that, "it could be a trap." Ray decided to flank them and come up from the rear, and finally came silently up behind their Lieutenant and put the tip of Little Casino in the back of his neck. He told the Lieutenant he was the downed flyer, his name and unit, and that he was going to put his knife away and not to make any quick movements. When the Lieutenant turned and offered him a handshake, Ray told him the NVA were on his heels and to call in his men and hightail out of there. Not far away was a UH-1 Huey pickup zone and in a less than an hour he was safe at Khe Sahn. He told the Lieutenant, that when they were in the field to ban smoking as it could save their lives. Within the hour he was on another helicopter to Da Nang.

When he left the helicopter in Da Nang, he was immediately arrested as a Corporal Donahue a known deserter. He tried to tell them they had the wrong man and that his name was, Lieutenant Ray McComber, United States Air Force. But, they were having none of it and clamped him in handcuffs and leg chains. They searched him and came up empty as he had lost his identification many days ago. He was shoved into the office of a Major Wilson, who insisted that he was Corporal Donahue. Ray finally convinced the Major to call Phan Rang and ask for his unit commander, so he did and got the reply that the Seventh Squadron of the Eleventh Special Operations Wing had been disbanded some time ago. So Ray convinced the Major to let him call, and he used the classified code of his pilot Colonel Jim Flowers, and was connected immediately to Major Walther, whom he knew. Walther said he would contact General Jacobsen, who happened to be in Da Nang and he would straighten it out pronto. When the General saw Ray in chains, he was enraged and liberally chewed the rear ends off of Major Wilson and everyone in sight. The General took him to the officers club and let him shower and shave, then while

Ray was wolfing down steak, he told the whole story. How they had been forced to parachute, what they ate, how he had lost his friends and how Barry had been captured and finally how he had delivered the baby of a North Vietnamese woman. Five weeks and over 300 miles had left him with a completely different outlook on life. Ray was immediately reassigned back to San Antonio. Aboard a stretch DC-8, he found a window seat on the left side so he could say a prayer and a goodbye to his lost friends as the plane rose through the clouds, and the coast of Viet Nam slowly disappeared in the mist. It was 1968.

In a January 1973 agreement in Paris, North Vietnam and the United States signed a cease fire treaty. By March most of the U.S. installations had been turned over to the South Vietnamese Army. The agreement allowed the NVA to stay in the south and by mid 1974 they were back at full strength. President Nixon resigned; a Senator from Massachusetts pushed congress to withdraw any support for South Vietnam and the NVA restarted hostilities immediately. It was a slap in the face of over a million young Americans whose lives would forever be changed by their experiences there. Within months, the South Vietnamese Army was out of many of the supplies needed to fight. By early 1975, North Vietnam, in clear violation of the 1973 agreement in Paris, had taken control of all of South Vietnam.

# COLORADO

Eventually, Bob's four younger children all relocated to Colorado. Modern life was completely different than previous centuries. There were fast cars, computers and big houses. Concerns of the past for common personal safety, simple health care, communications and travel were taken for granted. Everyone married, most had children and some grand children. Bob passed in 1978 from a gunshot, and Fern followed in 1990. Their old house on Loofborrow Street was torn down and the giant Hackberry tree from which all the kids swung in the 1940's, was removed without a trace. So after a century of presence, the only remnants of the family remaining in Nebraska were their gray granite gravestones. Yet the wild adventures that were written by Sarah and Giles1, lost for decades, then found, read and lost again by Giles2, passed to Bob and finally to Donald, survived, and here they are.

Printed in the United States
By Bookmasters